NEVER BEEN KISSED

A Novel of
Music Hall
and
Vaudeville

Allan Prior

HARPER & ROW, PUBLISHERS

NEW YORK • HAGERSTOWN

SAN FRANCISCO • LONDON

(Continued)

NEVER BEEN KISSED. Copyright © 1978 by Allan Prior. All rights reserved. Printed in the United States of America. No part of this book may be used or reproduced in any manner whatsoever without written permission except in the case of brief quotations embodied in critical articles and reviews. For information address Harper & Row, Publishers, Inc., 10 East 53rd Street, New York, N.Y. 10022.

Designer: Eve Kirch

FIRST U.S. EDITION

Library of Congress Cataloging in Publication Data

Prior, Allan, Date
   Never been kissed.
   I. Title.
PZ4.P956Nc   1978   [PR6066.R57]   823'.9'14
ISBN 0–06–013385–6   78–2065

79 80 81 82 83 84 10 9 8 7 6 5 4 3 2 1

NEVER BEEN KISSED
is dedicated to the memory of:

My Aunt Clara,
dancer and singer of the music halls,
professionally known as Violet Grey

My Uncle Harold,
comic and singer of the music halls,
professionally known as Harold Carlisle,
The Little Man with the Big Voice

and

My Grandfather, Edward Prior,
theatrical manager and visionary

PART I

I Was a Good Little Girl

Clara sat in the Alhambra Gallery and looked down at the stage. The limelight fell on Harry Viner.

God, she thought, he's beautiful.

It's all, all *beautiful.*

The tinny pit orchestra blared a chorus, and Harry Viner—dark, thick hair, she thought, such lovely thick hair, unlike her own fine reddish mop—Harry Viner sang:

> She was a sweet little dicky bird,
> Cheep, cheep cheep, she went.
> Sweetly she sang to me
> 'Til all my money was spent.

How would those two heads look together on a pillow? Clara wondered—deep, shiny black and golden red—feeling naughty and moist and full of longing for she knew not what, shifting her legs in the long cotton drawers, down to the knee, feeling the heat of her body and the moisture, and wishing her bustle wasn't quite so large, but it was the fashion. She squirmed for comfort, and perspiring a little—it wasn't proper for a young lady to sweat—she leaned forward onto the cool brass of the safety rail and looked and listened and longed for she knew not what.

The music hall always affected her like that.

3

She was seventeen.

Harry Viner was so handsome, so manly, in the loud check jacket and the high, white, starched collar, the ever-so-slightly-blue chin dusted with powder, the harsh black line of mustache on his upper lip, and, of course, the dark eyes flashing up to the gallery.

The audience knew the song almost too well. It wasn't Harry Viner's own song, and that was a mistake, she thought. Harry Viner's hands were large and expressive, and he used them as he moved, soft-shoe, dancing across the stage, the limelight following him wherever he went, the only thing moving in the packed auditorium; everywhere else, stillness and breathing, and staring eyes, rank upon rank of them, and the scent of sweat and oranges and thick twist tobacco in a blue haze.

> Then she went off song,
> We parted on fighting terms.

Clara's eyes followed him as he danced. Ah, she thought, to dance with him, to be kissed by him, to. . . . Her imagination failed her. What would he see in me, a silly little goose from Miss Wilson's Academy?

Harry Viner waved his arms, and the whole house, even the orchestra stalls, where the men all smoked cigars and seemed to have bald heads, joined in the last two lines, heartily:

> She was one of the early birds,
> And I was one of the worms!

Harry Viner bowed, as the applause sounded out, solid and cheerful. Clara could almost feel his relief. It was a good house for Monday night. Papa, Clara's father, who owned the Alhambra, said that the Monday-night audience was the best of the week. That working people who still had money left over from the weekend, enough to afford two seats at the Alhambra, Newcastle upon Tyne, were reliable, decent, God-fearing Britons, the salt of the earth, a credit to King and Country, in this year of Grace 1904. Tall, straight-backed Edward Abbott, Clara's Papa, would say that as he sat in his study at home, counting the takings at midnight or later. He would remove the long cigar from his mouth, tap the ash from it into the silver ashtray in his study (there were none anywhere else in the house) and total the takings, long-nibbed

4

pen in hand: "Forty-five pounds, nineteen and sixpence. A good Monday-night audience, as usual."

Mostly these days there was nobody with him in his study, since Clara's mother had been dead four years, carried off with the galloping consumption—a disease Papa was ashamed of, since it was mostly confined to members of the public who paid the lower prices at the Alhambra: gallery, sixpence; upper circle, one and threepence. People in the grand circle and the orchestra stalls (half-a-crown) were not the salt of the earth. They were the cream. They came "dressed" to the theater, the men in black evening clothes, the ladies in long silk dresses. Clara could see their bare shoulders gleaming white, their necks, too—the ladies were wearing their hair piled up now—down in the orchestra stalls. Such people rarely died of the consumption.

The cream were a far cry from the salt of the earth. For one thing, the salt of the earth smelled. Honest sweat, Papa would have said, taking care not to get too near it, but Clara thought it more likely honest dirt. She pressed her lavender-scented hankie to her nose. Sometimes she had to hold her breath, high up here in the gallery, against the sweat smell.

Clara thought: I shouldn't feel like *that*. These people are the public. One day they may even be *my* public! One day I may dance on that stage, just as Harry Viner dances now. She glanced at her program. He was billed as "Harry Viner, King of Kosher Komedy." Clara thought Harry Viner in person was much superior to his billing, which he should change at once. Also, he should not be singing somebody else's song, even if he gave tribute to the owner of it, as Harry Viner had not *done*. Another mistake.

She would like to tell him about his mistakes.

She would like to tell him he was beautiful. Those hands, that black hair. . . .

Clara leaned her forehead against the brass rail. What *was* she thinking about? Far from telling Harry Viner how to run his life, she would be extremely lucky if she ever spoke to him. Backstage was a forbidden area for young ladies. What about her brother, Adam? she had demanded. Papa had removed his cigar, puffed on it again, then explained that her brother, Adam, was a man, and he was learning the business. That was very different.

"Young ladies go to school. They do not go backstage at any theater of mine." He had chewed on his cigar and pointed it at

5

her. "Let that be an official warning. The music hall is no place for a girl of tender years."

"But I'm seventeen, Papa."

"When you are married, possibly your husband will take you, if he has no more sense. Until then, out-of-bounds, my dear."

And up had gone Papa's *Times*, and down had gone Clara's face. If he knew she was here tonight. . . . Clara grimaced at the thought. That was the reason she was in the gallery. He would hardly think to look for her there. She squirmed, thinking of Papa's heavy, solemn face, his anger, and a shock of guilt and secret pleasure ran through her limbs, held encased in the long whalebone corset that stopped just under her full young breasts and sometimes made her feel she might faint, just from the sheer nagging ache of wearing it. Clara fanned her warm face with the program. No wonder I'm sweating, like the salt of the earth, she thought. A cotton chemise, a long pair of cotton drawers down to the knee, black cotton stockings up to my thighs, garters just above the knee, three petticoats of stiff linen over the awful corset and my dress of heavy red cotton over everything! Only her breasts were free, the nipples rubbing excitingly against the fabric. She had daringly turned her chemise down. Her breasts were a good shape, round and full, and she was very proud of them.

Harry Viner was telling some Abie jokes.

Clara felt a pang of envy. To be there, where he was, performing on a stage, that was her greatest desire. It was one she had kept to herself, for Papa certainly would not have approved. He approved, of course, of Clara's voice. "Not unlike the other Clara," he would boom and wink, referring to the great Dame Clara Butt, her namesake, patriotic bellower of such epic songs as "Land of Hope and Glory" and "The Lost Chord." Dame Clara sang songs that were loved by all her audience, and it was Papa's hope to get her to perform at the Alhambra.

Clara did not want to sing like Dame Clara Butt.

She wanted to sing like Marie Lloyd. Marie, with her famous buck-toothed smile and her rude little songs, sung ever so naughtily, hinting in public of private things that would have brought a maidenly blush to the cheeks of Dame Clara Butt!

Clara had persuaded Papa to allow her to go to dancing classes. It was cultural, and it did no harm for a young woman to learn to move gracefully and with poise. If Papa had seen Clara dancing à la Lloyd before her mirror, stripped down to her chemise and drawers, topped off with a shawl and one of her mother's hats, he would have stopped the dancing lessons at once. But he had not seen them; only Jean, the old housekeeper, had. She had cautioned Clara, "Now, me dear, don't let your papa see you dancing like that, will you?"

Marie Lloyd had a song that was currently on everybody's lips. The words of "A Little of What You Fancy Does You Good" seemed to Clara naughty, but . . . well . . . nice.

Clara often pirouetted before the mirror at the large house in Leazes Crescent and sang "A Little of What You Fancy . . ." or another favorite:

> Oh, Mr. Porter, what shall I do?
> I wanted to go to Birmingham and
> You've taken me on to Crewe.
> Take me back to London as quickly as you can,
> Oh, Mr. Porter, what a silly girl I am!

The way Marie Lloyd sang that song (Clara had seen her do it only last winter at this very theater) it had seemed to contain all Clara's longings: to sing and flirt to a packed house. Clara knew her voice was not a great one. She knew that she was not a first-rate dancer. But one day, when she was confident she could show Papa how much she *ached* to walk out upon a stage—a real stage!—and perform, she would put on a demonstration at the Alhambra especially for him. And he would be so impressed that he would instantly book her to appear in his own hall.

That was the dream.

Clara had told it to nobody. But she knew, she *knew,* dammit— even if it was swearing!—that she could do it, that this was what she wanted, this very thing that Harry Viner was now doing, standing out from the crowd but being part of the crowd: this urge, this want.

Harry Viner was still telling his Abie jokes.

The audience was listening tolerantly, but he was losing them. People around Clara were peeling oranges, and relighting their pipes. There was some hawking and coughing and the light drumming of feet on bare wood that Clara knew heralded outright catcalls and even the throwing of fruit, or worse. She peered through the smoke at Harry Viner; his forehead shone. He knew.

"This Jewish fella," Harry Viner said—he yelled, really, because otherwise the back of the gallery would not hear him at all, the ultimate sin. "This Jewish fella was walking down the street, and he met this other Jewish fella. He said, 'Abie, sorry to hear about your fire!' Abie said, '*Nu,* hush, that's *tomorrow!*'"

There were a few laughs. Not many. Abie jokes are wrong for this place, doesn't he know that much? Clara thought, desperate for him; there aren't any Jews in Newcastle or anyway not many, only one or two jewelers and pawnbrokers, this isn't London, what *is* he thinking about. . . !

"Abie met Morrie in the street last week, and Morrie said, 'How's business?' and Abie said, 'January's been terrible, and February's been worse; how's things with you?' And Morrie said, 'Rachel's pregnant, Bernie's in jail and the wife's just died, what could be worse than that?' And Abie said, 'March!'"

Harry Viner stopped, quite still, at the end of that joke and waited, willed the laughs to come. . . . They did, grudging and few, as he stood there, staring out at the audience. He could not see them, Clara knew. He could just hear them and feel them, and his forehead shone. The drumming of the bored feet boomed louder. Very soon now somebody would call out. Near her, a man in a black cloth cap shouted, "Bliddy Cockney! He's useless!"

Suddenly a voice cried, "Make us love you, Harry!"

It was a young voice, a clear voice, but very loud, and it carried to the man on the stage. He came out of his trancelike, defiant stare, peered and waved up at the gallery.

"Thank you, miss, always ready to *oblige* a young lady!"

That got a loud coarse laugh from the gallery, and the people around her stared at Clara. She hid behind her program. The voice from the gallery, she realized with a sudden trembling, had been *hers* . . . !

Harry Viner was leaning down to the orchestra pit. He said something to the conductor, and the band began to play a familiar tune. Around Clara, the people began to sing, long before Harry Viner's voice reached them, clear and with a growing note of confidence, that swelled even more as the house chorus thickened to join it.

> The girl I love is up in the gallery,
> The girl I love is a-looking down at me,
> There she is, can't yer see, a-waving of 'er handkerchief,
> As merry as a robin that sings in a tree.

Harry Viner gestured to the man working the limelight at the back of the gallery. He swung the arc around until it focused on Clara. The bright light of the arc blinded her, and she was unable to move or smile or do anything at all, except sit and pray. . . . Oh, God, please don't let Papa be in the wings, looking up here, don't *let* him, please, God!

"Go on, love, wave something, if it's only your drawers!" said the man in the black cloth cap.

Clara blushed and waved her large program and ducked her head behind it. The limelight swung back to the stage. Harry Viner grinned. He was safe. The audience laughed good-naturedly. The orchestra tinnily crashed out the second chorus:

> The girl I love is a-looking down at me,
> There she is, can't yer see, a-waving of 'er handkerchief,
> As merry as a robin that sings in a tree.

Harry Viner smiled and waved to the packed house.

He's safe, thank God, she thought. Get off, man, while you can!

Harry Viner took two curtain calls when one would have sufficed. Then he was gone, behind the heavy plush curtain.

Clara sat, drenched in perspiration. She felt light-headed and triumphant.

The salt of the earth smoked and ate oranges and waited in the dark for the next turn.

The girl I love is up in the gallery, she thought.

That had been good. That had been very good.

The girl I love, Clara thought, sitting there, looking at nobody.

Harry Viner stood in the wings and felt the sweat grow cold on his body, hairy and hot till now, under the long woolen underwear. The gray tweed suit, fashionably tight in crotch and leg, pulled on him uncomfortably, and the high, starched collar bit into his neck. His hair was wet under his rakish brown derby hat, and he was shaking with fright. It had been a near thing. He had all but *died* out there!

He walked past the stagehands in the wings, but they tugged on their pulley ropes to part the curtain and studiously avoided his eye. They knew how near he had been to death. They saw it every week. They probably regarded his rescue by the girl as a miracle. He did himself.

9

The girl in the gallery. She had done it for him. Harry Viner shut his dressing room door and discovered he was still shaking. God bless her, whoever she was. Harry took a half bottle of whiskey from his traveling basket, first unlocking it. You left nothing in dressing rooms that could be drunk or eaten; most performers were drinkers, and many were hungry. He swallowed, and the fiery liquid burned his empty stomach, reminding him that he had not eaten since breakfast in his lodgings.

He should never have told the Abie jokes. They didn't like them. No. Get it right. They didn't understand them.

Harry sat down and stared at his reflection in the mirror. The lamps around it flickered, and he saw, for what seemed like the millionth time in such a mirror, his own face. Tall, dark and handsome, his mother, Beckie, had always called him. Well, he *was.* But how had it helped? Men were jealous because women wanted him, and men handed the jobs out. The only way was to be so successful that the men had to respect you.

Harry Viner drank a little more whiskey, wanting confidence desperately. I need new material; I need a new act; I need some songs that aren't somebody else's songs! Harry lifted up his dancing pumps and looked at the soles. They were paper-thin. They would last maybe another two weeks. And here he was thinking about new material. Beckie's voice dinned in his head: "Harry, you dream too much. Life is not for dreaming away; it's for living!"

Still, the dream had brought him this far. He was twenty-seven, and he had been working the London halls for three years, in and out of work—all right, mostly out! But it could have been worse. He knew artistes who had it worse. Beckie had seen him only once, just before she died, at the Old Bedford in Camden Town, and in the dressing room afterward she had cried and said, "You made them laugh. You said you would, and you did!"

Tonight he had nearly got the bird, the awful shrieking death knell of the whistles. The ultimate, unforgettable disgrace! He could hear the voices on the weekend trains, people who knew him, men who disliked him, saying to their wives or girlfriends (who liked him; some of whom had slept with him): "I hear Harry Viner died the death at the Alhambra, Newcastle, on Monday." And then they would laugh when their wives and girlfriends didn't, or didn't anyway with their eyes, and they'd chew on their cigars and lean back in their seats and thank Christ it hadn't been *them.*

The girl, whoever she was, had saved him that.

10

The dressing room door opened gently. "Hello, Harry."

A tiny middle-aged man stood there. He had the thin, pale face of a street waif. The little man was dressed in a rusty evening dress suit and a white dickey shirt, and he carried in his hands a pair of long boots with enormous skilike toes. This was Little Tich, top-of-the-bill at the Alhambra that week.

"Hello, Mr. Relph," Harry said, standing up, feeling like a fool, the whiskey bottle in his hand, the sweat still cold on him.

"You got out of that very smartly," said Little Tich.

"I was a fool to tell Jewish jokes to goyim."

"Yes, you were, but you'll know better next time."

There was a silence. Harry could hear the conjuror's closing music. Tich was on next. How could he stand there, chattering? He wasn't even ready, for God's sake!

"I died at the Glasgow Empire once," Little Tich said. "They didn't like me either. That was because I was little. They needn't have bothered to tell me that. I don't like me because I'm little. I never have."

Harry laughed. "Thanks, Mr. Relph. It was nice of you to call in. I needed a kind word."

"You should try New York."

"Mr. Relph, that's your opening music!"

"Try New York, they'd like you there. London and New York, those are your towns, Harry."

A voice sang out in the corridor, "Mr. Relph, it's your music, you're on!"

Little Tich edged out of the door. "It's all right, I'm coming." He smiled at Harry. "Come and see I'm still doing it right, yes?"

Harry put down his whiskey bottle quickly, out of sight, locked his dressing room door and followed the little man along the corridor and up the steps to the backstage area. By the time he got there, by some miracle, Little Tich had his long ski boots on and was onstage, moving slowly around on the very tips of the boots, taking a cap from his pocket, setting it on his head, taking it off, coming down flat on the ski boots with a sharp slap, kicking the cap around the stage, hands in pockets, the band playing gently on. Tich paused in mid-movement and explained to the audience, "Business with cap!"

Then he turned his back insolently on them and kicked the cap again.

He doesn't *care*, Harry Viner thought with awe. He doesn't

11

care whether they love him or hate him, and because he doesn't care, they love him. It's like a woman. Harry stared out at the black pit of the audience, somewhere beyond the glare of the foots. He's playing them like I play a woman, one of the wives, or the girlfriends. He can do *that* with an audience, and I can only do it with some silly woman.

Harry walked back to his dressing room and locked the door. He sat in the rickety bentwood chair, gazed into the mirror and drank the rest of the whiskey. He listened to Little Tich's closing music and heard the loud, magical sea surge of the applause. It went on for a long time.

Slowly he wiped off his greasepaint and pulled off his suit, folding it away neatly. He took off his silk shirt and folded that just as carefully—it, too, would be on his back again tomorrow night. He inspected his collar and saw that it had begun to fray at the front.

He heard Little Tich trudge along on his way back to the number one dressing room, and he waited for the little man's knock. It didn't come. He's tired, Harry thought. Tich's act was an exhausting one, but I'd like to be tired, at that money. It was rumored Tich got a hundred pounds a week. Harry got four.

Harry stripped off his socks and the long combination underwear. He poured some cold water from the large pitcher into the washing bowl and tried to get a lather with the solid green soap provided by the management. It would hardly raise a foam, so he compromised by throwing most of the water over himself, finally standing in the basin to wash his feet. Shivering, he climbed back into his long combinations, put on his street clothes—the only non-stage suit he had, cost him far too much money, *three* pounds two years ago. He had been four whole years in the business, and he didn't own anything at all, except the stage clothes that fitted into his old skip, lying open on the floor, and the one suit he was now donning. He'd played a lot of halls, and a lot of people had said he had a future, and here he was, getting the bird, or near enough, at the Alhambra, Newcastle upon Bleeding Tyne!

Harry Viner put his brown derby on his head and patted his face with a little of the French cologne given to him by the grateful wife of the seal trainer. Harry counted up the money he had in his pocket. One pound, three shillings and fourpence, to last until the end of the week. Poverty, really. He worked like a dog six days of the week and traveled by train every Sunday to the next

12

town, what kind of life was that? But he was glad of it. This tour was his first job in three months. He grimaced at the memory of semistarvation in awful lodgings and sighed. Well, if he could not afford a new act, he could afford one thing.

A drink on the Promenade.

The Promenade was modeled on the notorious "Prom" at the Empire, Leicester Square, London, and it was not at all a bad imitation, Harry thought, as he came into it, his spirits lightening as they always did at the sight of pretty women.

Pretty, that is, until you had a good look at them.

Harry stood, a glass of champagne in hand, and watched the girls as they slowly promenaded along the thickly carpeted circular passageway that ran behind the curve of the dress circle.

Harry had heard a great deal about the Alhambra Promenade from the other artistes as they made their slow pilgrimage north from London on the train.

Anyway, the girls looked fetching in their long, overbright dresses and their large hats, decorated with imitation fruit, perched atop their carefully coiffured heads. They carried parasols, and one or two had very small Pekinese dogs in their arms, but this was merely to suggest that they were ladies. It was a device, Harry knew, to make the man feel he was picking up a clean, decent girl, while the fact was that he was picking up a tart who had probably been with somebody else an hour before. The girls circled by as he leaned against the bar, sipping his champagne, and from time to time, one would hesitate, smile, wink, raise an eyebrow, gently taunt one of the men, and the man would detach himself and take her arm. They would not complete the circle but would go on, down the back stairs and out of the theater.

" 'Allo, darlink," said a passing girl, dark and heavy, "fancy something French tonight?"

"The nearest you've been to France, love," said Harry, "is cleaning the scuppers of a Tyne coal barge."

"Cockney prick," said the girl cheerfully, in the local accent. "Haddaway, darling man, ye nearly got the bird tonight, didden ye?"

Harry said, "Poxy git," but the girl was gone, on the arm of a small, fat, bald man. Harry gazed into his drink, feeling hot and suddenly afraid. If a tart knew, who didn't?

"Good evening, Mr. Viner."

Harry looked up into two steady blue eyes. They were very

13

young and clear, and they seemed to be mocking him. Or was that his imagination? He had to be careful, not everybody knew, even if the tarts did.

"Good evening, can I get you a drink?" Harry asked.

By that time he had taken in the fine red hair and the lack of paint upon the face—indeed, the creamy skin, so rare in any girl on the game—and the cleanness of the young woman standing so squarely in front of him. Her hair was very neat, and he could see no obvious telltale signs of the tart: a rim of dirt on the edge of a blouse; dirty fingernails under the red paint; a tiny, awful smell of decay.

"I'll have a glass of champagne, please."

Harry took the glass of champagne from the barman and handed it to the girl. The barman looked past Harry and said, "Good evening, miss," to the girl, and the girl said, "Good evening, Jim." Plainly a regular, then, Harry thought, with a sense of disappointment.

"Oh, *dear!*"

The girl suddenly choked and spluttered and coughed, and Harry patted her gently on the back. He did it as quietly and unobtrusively as he could, so that she should not feel embarrassed.

"Never drink champers on an empty stomach," Harry said.

She held up her glass. "But I just have."

"So have I." A sudden feeling of generosity came over him. "Look, my belly thinks my throat's cut. What about supper somewhere?"

The red-haired girl blinked. "Supper?"

"If you have the time?"

"Yes," she said, "I have the time."

"Nothing special." Harry put his arm in hers. She didn't squeeze it or use any of the usual tart's tricks. He was surprised. "A nice hot *nosh* somewhere, first, yes?"

"First?"

Harry smiled. "Anywhere local you fancy? I don't know this town."

"Well," said the red-haired girl, "the Eldon Grill is very good."

"Then let's get a cab."

In the closed cab Harry contented himself with holding the girl's hand, which was ever so slightly moist, as if she were excited.

Suddenly she laughed to herself.

"What's the joke?"

"Nothing."

"There must be!"

"No, it's all right, we're there."

The cab clattered to a halt, and puzzled, Harry got out and paid the driver. One shilling, and a threepenny tip. He looked up at the Eldon Grill as the cab wheeled away into the brisk horse traffic of late evening. It seemed posh, hardly the kind of restaurant a girl like this would frequent. She'd probably heard the name somewhere, that was it.

"Shall we go in?" She offered her arm. Slightly embarrassed, Harry linked his arm with hers, and they went into the Eldon Grill. The fat, smiling headwaiter detached himself from his station and approached them, carrying a brace of menus.

"Good evening, miss."

"Good evening, Charles."

"Sir."

"Evenin'."

Wrong again, thought Harry. She's been here before. With somebody else. He felt vaguely annoyed and scowled at the menu as they sat at their table. The headwaiter had been discreet and put them in a corner, behind a huge potted fern. The prices on the menu jumped out at Harry. Trout, two and threepence. Steak, half-a-crown. Steak and kidney pudding, two shillings. Nothing on the menu cost less than that, and it was all à la carte. No set suppers, nothing cheap. The total bill would be ten shillings at least! The girl had seen him for a right mug and, whatever else, was plainly determined to get a good supper out of him. He felt extremely angry and said, "What will you have?" in a grating voice.

"I'm just looking." The girl smiled past him—those clear blue eyes—at the headwaiter, who stood, book open. "I think the trout, Charles. They're fresh, aren't they?"

"Swimming about, miss," said the headwaiter, indicating a large glass case filled with water, on a stand, in the middle of the room; various fish swam around in it, lazily. "You can go over and make your selection if you care to?"

The headwaiter seemed to be pointedly ignoring Harry. He felt even more annoyed. Who did he think was paying the bill for the supper, the girl? Harry said, "Pick two good ones, we leave it to you, and bring some potatoes and vegetables."

"Sir," said the headwaiter, still ignoring Harry. "And to drink?"

"We have," said the girl, "been drinking champagne."

15

"Champagne, certainly, miss," said the headwaiter, and moved away swiftly, calling out orders to his minions, one of whom instantly set about catching two trout from the glass case with the aid of a fishing net.

Harry made a rapid calculation. "This supper is going to cost me well over two pounds," he said icily. "I didn't bank on the bleedin' Ritz, did I?"

The red-haired girl smiled and asked, in a teasing tone, "Just exactly *what* do you think I am?"

"You *ain't* one!"

"No."

He blinked. "But you were on the Promenade!"

"Yes, I was."

"Well then, what the hell was you doin' on the Promenade?"

"I'd been to the show, and I walked back that way."

"Been to the show? Where had you been sitting, to walk back that way?" Harry was taking in the girl's clothes now; the cape over the dress was a good one, and although the breasts were high and plainly naked under the cotton dress—he could see the shape of her nipples—her handbag was of good leather—no, crocodile!—guineas and *guineas!* How could he have made such a mistake?

Simple. She'd approached him on the Promenade. Only one class of girl did that.

Harry felt properly outraged. "What were you doing in the gallery, with the riffraff?"

"Please, Mr. Viner, don't shout, people are looking."

Harry looked round. The headwaiter's icy gaze was upon him. The boy had fished the trout from the glass case and was disappearing with them behind a door that plainly led to the kitchen.

"Fish that swim about before you eat 'em, tarts that ain't tarts at all, but they make themselves known to you on the Promenade!" Harry stared at the smiling girl. "I give up!"

"I would if I were you, Mr. Viner."

"Oh, cut the Mr. Viner caper. My name's Harry. What's yours?"

"Clara."

"Very posh," he said dryly.

"Do you really like it?" She seemed to want to know.

"Very nice."

"I wonder how it would look in lights?"

"In lights, where?"

16

"Outside a theater."

Harry sank back in his chair. Now he understood. The girl was stagestruck.

"Been in this place before, ain'tcher?" he said.

"Yes, I have."

"With a man?"

"My father."

"Your *father?*"

"That's right."

Class as well, Harry thought. Of course! That was why the headwaiter knew her. That was why she ordered the trout without looking at the price on the menu. Her father was a local business-man, something like that. A thought struck him. "Does he know you're out tonight?"

Clara shook her head. "No."

"He thinks you're tucked up in bed, does he?"

"You made a mistake with the Abie jokes tonight."

"If anybody else tells me that, I'll smash their bleedin' face in!"

"Don't swear. It's not nice."

Harry said, now very angry indeed, "Lady, you fool me into taking you to supper at the best restaurant in the town, and then you have the gall to say to me, 'Don't swear!' I'd be a saint if I didn't swear."

"All right." Clara stood up. "I'm sorry. It's all my fault. I'll go." She rose from her seat.

"Sit down!" Harry hissed. The headwaiter's glance was on them again. "The food's ordered. It'll have to be paid for anyway."

Clara smiled and sat down promptly.

"Why do you say I shouldn't have told those Abie jokes?"

Harry, for some silly reason, wanted to know what this classy girl thought.

"Because they don't understand them here." Clara broke a bread roll with her fingers and spread butter on it, thickly, care-lessly. She's never gone short of a meal in her life, Harry thought. "Who does understand them, I wonder?"

"Cockneys, Londoners, do." He expanded. "Where I come from, Stepney, in the East End, there's thousands of us, thousands of local Cockneys as well. We all mix in, see?"

"That's right," Clara said thoughtfully. "You'll probably need to get rid of your accent if you are to succeed."

"What do you know about success on the halls?"

"I can hear what any audience thinks of an act."

"It's true I was in trouble. Some girl in the balcony. . . ."

She was smiling at him.

"*You!*"

The headwaiter arrived at that moment and placed the trout in front of them. It was garnished with almonds and looked very dead and very delicious. The wine waiter opened the champagne bottle with a flourish, and Harry, dazed, waved him to pour. When they had gone, he was still staring at her, his champagne glass untouched in his hand.

"Why did you shout out at me?"

"Well," said Clara, "I like you."

"Like me! You've only seen me tonight, and I was awful!"

"I don't mean I like your act. I mean I like you."

"For crying out loud!" Harry said.

"Drink your champagne." Clara wrinkled her nose.

"Had you," Harry asked harshly, "ever had champagne before tonight?"

Her blue eyes stared back at him.

"Tonight was the first time. But not the last, I hope."

"We'll drink to that," Harry said dazedly.

And they did.

Clara ate her trout and almonds and sipped her champagne in a dream. The clock in the Eldon Grill dining room read eleven-fifteen, but she averted her eyes from it. Papa would naturally expect her to be in bed when he arrived home from the theater, promptly at midnight, and her only problem now was to get back to the house before he did.

I don't care if I don't, Clara told herself, I don't care about anything tonight! I'm drinking champagne with a man, in a restaurant—a man, who gives his attention to me and doesn't put the *Times* in front of his face just because I'm a chit of a girl.

"Why do you sing other people's songs?" she asked.

Harry Viner closed his eyes. "I couldn't get off without a song, and since I can't afford to buy any new songs, I have to sing other people's." Harry drank his champagne, his brown eyes moody, and she thought: he *is* beautiful, and his mouth looks soft and full under his mustache, and I'm sorry he thinks I know nothing about the halls, but he's wrong there!

"How much," Clara asked, "do new songs cost?"

"Dear, they *cost!* And even if you can afford them, how do you know you've picked the right one? Say you pay a writer a fiver for a song, and it's no good. That's a week's wages gone, and more, and how do you find the fiver anyway, in the first place?"

"Five pounds?" Clara said blankly. "You haven't got five pounds?"

"Not to spare on a song that might not work!"

Clara's heart turned at the sudden harshness of his voice. She said hollowly, "How much—are they paying you?"

"You want to know, you ask, don'tcher?"

"Please, I want to help." Clara reached over and put her hand on his, which felt warm and was covered in fine black hair. He looked down at her hand, and she felt a terrible guilty urge to pull it away—but she did not.

"How can you help, dear? What do you know about it? Just stagestruck, ain'tcher?" Harry Viner covered her hand with his and held it.

At that, emotions flooded through her: longing for him to kiss her, or do something to her, something to hurt her, anything. These emotions were washed over by those of fear: somebody might see her holding hands with one of her father's employees—well, that was what he was!—in a public place, and anyway, he was a man, and no man had kissed her, never mind hurt her in that way she somehow dimly desired. . . . Clara slowly withdrew her hand, making an excuse of taking up her champagne glass. "It seems to me you'll have to get something new before tomorrow night. Unless, that is, you want the same thing to happen again?"

Harry Viner stopped eating. He almost seemed to stop breathing.

"And how am I to do that?"

"I don't know," Clara said, keeping her voice light. "We'll have to think about it, won't we?"

"*We'll* have to think about it?"

Clara was a little afraid now, of his stillness, his hostility. She had offended him, and all she had told him was the truth. Maybe men did not like hearing the truth from women? She thought: I'm doing this all wrong.

"Since when do you get in on my life, darlin'?" he was asking coldly.

Well, in for a penny, in for a pound.

19

"Since I saw you tonight. Since I liked you. Since I . . . helped you." She tried to smile, but her throat constricted. He plainly hated her for telling him the truth. "I nearly died when they started to catcall. . . . I. . . . Oh. . . . I'm *sorry*. . . !"

Tears were in her eyes, and they rolled gently down her cheeks.

The effect on Harry Viner was magical. He took his Irish linen handkerchief from his top pocket and gave it to her, glancing quickly around the restaurant as he did so. She dabbed her eyes with the handkerchief, observing through the salt tears the anxious face of Harry Viner.

"Look, I'm sorry, I didn't mean to upset you. If I was rude, it's because I was upset meself. I didn't mean anything by what I said."

Clara stopped crying. Tears, she thought, can obviously be useful with a man.

"My fault. I was trying to help. And you didn't seem to want it. And this meal must be far too expensive if you can't afford to buy a song for five pounds."

"Look," said Harry, "never mind the price of the meal! All I ask is—enjoy it!"

They ate in silence for a while. Finally, she asked, "Why do you do it?"

Harry Viner put his fork down. He was seriously considering her question. "Because I like the applause." He grinned. "If any."

"And what else?"

"I like to please them."

"Yes!" Ah, that was what she felt, what she hoped for one day. To *please* them.

Harry Viner added, "But not in the way they want to be pleased."

Clara was nonplussed for a moment. "I don't understand."

"It's easy to please an audience. All you do is pander to them. Tickle them up a bit, like a woman."

Like a *woman?* She looked at Harry's hands and looked hastily away. "I'm not sure I—"

But Harry was talking, the words tumbling out. "Most comics pander! Not the good ones, of course. They always surprise you. They say things nobody else would dream of saying, they take everything they do as far as it will go, they *dare*. . . ." He looked at her almost accusingly. "You know what I mean?"

Clara said desperately, "Like Marie Lloyd and her songs? People say she's rude, don't they, but it's—"

"Absolutely! Like Marie Lloyd! Marie goes out there and enjoys herself! Mind, she sings, and that's a help. I can't really sing."

"Oh, you can!"

"No, I can't. If I could sing, it would be easier. But I have to learn how to be funny, and that takes time. Comics age in the wood. Like champagne." He raised his glass. "And another thing dear, comics are not nice people. Keep away from them, that's my advice."

But he was smiling, and Clara smiled back.

"What do you want," she was emboldened to ask, "for yourself?"

He seemed surprised at the question. "For myself, I don't know. I suppose to be well known, have things." He shook his head. "I never had things as a kid. My mother had no money to spare. What we had went on food and clothes."

Clara felt a pull of sympathy so strong she nearly cried.

Harry, however, was smiling at the past. "I wanted to get out of that street. I can make people laugh, always could. I could turn most things into a joke. Most things *are* a joke, so it isn't really hard. The only thing is, to do really well on the halls you have to make people laugh at the things they want to laugh at." He paused. "The really great comics make them laugh at the things they *don't* want to laugh at. That's the difference. I want to be one of the really great ones."

There was a silence between them.

What a manly person he is, Clara thought, how *admirable*. I wouldn't have thought that of him! She wanted desperately to reach out and touch his hand. Now he was smiling again. "What are we doing, wasting our time on chat? We should be enjoying ourselves at these prices!"

Clara was shocked into life. She quickly fumbled in her purse and found a golden sovereign. It was all she had with her, apart from a little silver, and it was wrapped in tissue paper because it was brand-new, a present at her last, her seventeenth birthday. She reached over and pressed it into Harry Viner's hand.

"What's this?"

He looked at the coin. It winked, golden under the gaslight.

21

"A pound! I can't take that!"

"If you don't," Clara said, "I'll start crying again. I mean it!"

"No, I couldn't. I asked you to supper—"

"Next time you can pay."

He stared. "Is there going to be a next time?"

"Yes. I think so. Unless you don't want to?"

"What about the rest of tonight?"

Clara pulled her cape around her shoulders. "I have to go now."

"But it's only quarter to twelve!"

He says it, she thought, as if it's afternoon. Music hall artistes never went to bed until two or three in the morning. It sounded very exciting. It was even more exciting that Harry Viner sounded disappointed.

"Don't come with me. I'll get a cab at the door." She stood up and extended her hand. "Good night."

Harry Viner stood up, too. "You said we'd meet again?"

"Tomorrow at twelve-thirty. In Carrick's. For lunch?"

"Carrick's? Where's that?"

"Ask anybody. They'll tell you. Good night, Mr. Viner, and thank you."

Harry Viner let go of her hand—he seemed not to want to—and Clara turned and walked quietly out of the restaurant. At the door she found the headwaiter standing, smiling.

"I hope you enjoyed your supper, Miss Abbott?"

"Very much indeed, Charles, but I have to go now."

His smile was discreet. "Yes. I can understand that, miss. And naturally. . . ." He placed a white-gloved finger to his lips.

"Thank you, Charles. Good night."

"Good night, miss. The doorman will get you a cab."

Clara's cab dropped her at the corner of Leazes Crescent. Under a flaring gaslight she looked at her fob watch.

Two minutes to twelve!

Clara ran down the crescent, her feet hardly seeming to touch the ground, in at the tradesman's entrance, around the back of the dark house, and then, in a sweat and a flurry, she was at the back door, left on the latch by old Jean, and up the servants' stairs to her room.

As she quietly closed her bedroom door, she heard Papa come into the house.

Harry sat on the bed in his lodgings and puzzled about Clara whatever-her-name was. She hadn't told him her name, and that was curious.

One thing was certain. She thought she knew it all.

Not that he objected to a girl having a mind of her own. His mother, Beckie, used to have one. Beckie had always thought him to be rather like his long-forgotten father, somebody in need of care and protection. Men, she had insisted, pinning out her washing on the clothesline, washing that was white when she put it out, gray from the chimney smoke when she took it in, men need looking after, they weren't fit to be out on their own. Harry had laughed at her, and Beckie Viner had looked indignant, hands on hips. "You're no better than any of them. You're all takers. You'll be the same, till you find a woman that can handle you!"

Harry had laughed some more and helped her to pin out the washing, a row of white flags in the wind, joining bravely all the other white flags. Everybody in Stepney washed on a Monday. Beckie, clothes pegs in her mouth, said, "If you want to make people laugh, you'd better learn that half an audience is women. Nobody ever bothers to make a woman laugh, unless they want to take her to bed, God forbid you'd do such a thing, except I know you would!"

Harry pulled off his shirt and hung it carefully in the wardrobe. His trousers went into his presser. He could not afford to have baggy garments, in the street or on the stage. Harry got into bed in his long johns and lay propped on the pillows, his hands behind his head, the moonlight slanting through the lace curtains into the overstuffed room. It had a gas ring, a table and three chairs, besides the bed.

Clara had said he needed new material. She was right. She hadn't said how he would get it. The whole evening had been a waste of time and money. A man had to be realistic. He wouldn't see the girl again; there was no point in it.

The bedroom door opened, and Mae, the wife of the seal trainer, peeped in. She was forty, bottle-blond, and Harry knew she had nothing on under the tight silk kimono.

Mae whispered, "You was late tonight?"

"Went out to supper."

"Anybody I know?"

"Mae," Harry said, "one of these times your old man is going to come in here and catch us, and when he does, yer on yer own, girl."

"Not him. He's out cold. He had ten bottles of stout tonight."

Mae slipped off her kimono. She stood naked, smiling. Her breasts were very large but quite firm, and her legs plump and without veins. She still wore tights in the act and got away with it. From the front she looked thirty. Her pubic hair was black, and that always made Harry laugh.

"Doesn't bleeding matter, does it?" she had declared. "Who's going to see it but you and my old fella, and neither of you gives a damn!"

Tonight Harry did not feel like laughing with Mae.

He sighed as she slipped into bed next to him.

Mae took his arm and guided it around her neck. She liked him to seem affectionate, even if he wasn't. She didn't like to think he wanted her just for *that*. Mae snuggled up against him.

"You all right, Harry?"

"Yes, I'm fine."

"Where did you go for supper?"

"The Eldon Grill."

"Coming up in the world, aren't yer?"

Mae's husband, Jack, the seal trainer, was very tight with his money, and they mostly ate in the digs, fried trotters and black puddings and bottles of stout. Harry reckoned she resented that. Just possibly it was the reason she was in bed with him at all.

He shifted his arm from around her neck and put it back behind his head. Mae had got into the habit of coming to see him every other night. He thought it was a bit of a liberty, really. When he *asked* her, that would have been more the ticket.

"You bothered about something?"

"I'm all right."

"You seem bothered."

"No, just a bit fed up."

"Yes, I know the feeling." At least she didn't say anything about him having nearly died a death. Mae had more sense than that. She was a trouper, whatever else she was, but that wouldn't help him tomorrow night, when he faced the audience again.

Harry kissed her on the lips.

He felt nothing.

Mae's fingers touched him gently, playfully, then harder, more urgent. Nothing. Her lips moved over his whole body. Nothing.

Mae lay back in the moonlight shafting in through the windows. She said, "You don't want it tonight, do you?"

"No, love," Harry said, "I don't."

"Is it me?"

"No," Harry lied, "just me."

Mae got slowly out of bed and put on her kimono.

"You sure?"

"Positive, darlin'."

She looked sadly at him. "Was it as bad as that tonight?"

"What?"

"I heard you nearly got the bird."

Harry held in his sudden black rage.

"It was bad, love. Very bad." He even managed a smile.

"I'm sorry, Harry. I thought this might help."

Help who? Harry thought. You or me?

He said, "That's all right, darlin'. Another time, eh?"

She paused at the door.

"Not like you, is it?"

"No, it's not, is it?"

"You're usually such a sport."

"That's right."

"Night, dear. Sleep tight."

"Yes. You, too. Night, Mae."

And she was gone, and Harry lay numb and bereft. She had been wrong, of course. He was not unmanned by the memory of the audience. He was unmanned by the memory of the girl.

It was dawn before he slept.

Clara wakened with thoughts of love.

His hair, she thought, the way it curls under at the back. He really wears it too long, but it suits him. He needs new clothes, though. His cuff links had been inexpensive, large and garish, some sort of worthless stone, not like Papa's heavy gold ones. Clara got out of the bed and slipped off her nightdress. She stood in front of the long mirror and admired her body. It was plump in all the right places, and she knew that was approved of by men because both Papa and her brother, Adam, disapproved of thin women. It was not fashionable to be thin. Papa would say, "Perfectly nice woman, but a figure like a boy's."

And her brother would reply, "Yes, I like something to get hold of myself," and Papa would dart a glance toward her and frown. "No need to be coarse, Adam. A gentleman is never coarse."

"No, Father." Adam would wink at her. "But I like an hourglass figure. It's the Grecian mode. The classical style. Natural for a woman."

Again, her father's basilisk eye. "For a *lady*, Adam."

"Sorry, Pater. For a lady."

Well, woman or lady, Clara had the fashionable hourglass figure. She had measured it. Bust thirty-six inches, waist nineteen inches, hips thirty-four inches. She ran the hot water the maid had left into a large bowl and soaped herself all over with a flannel. Her mind was awhirl. She had dreamed that Harry Viner had taken her on a very long train journey and had seemed to be about to do something very naughty to her, but she had wakened before he did it—with a feeling of disappointment. She dried herself slowly, lovingly, filled with a sense of expectation.

What, though, if he did not find her attractive? Her body still damp, she ran in panic to the mirror and pirouetted. She breathed in, and her breasts swelled. She noticed the nipples were taut. She smiled wonderingly, and a snatch of a music hall song came into her head:

> I was a good little girl,
> 'Til I met you.
> You put my head in a whirl,
> My poor heart too. . . .

It was a silly song, but it expressed how she felt, exactly. She turned and turned again in front of the mirror. Surely Harry Viner would find her attractive. Please let him do that.

Clara dressed quickly (her maid had laid out a new set of underclothes and a day dress) and went downstairs to breakfast. Papa looked over his *Times*.

"Good morning, my dear."

"Good morning, Papa."

He consulted his gold half hunter. "A trifle late this morning?"

"Yes, I overslept a little."

"You are going to have to hurry."

Clara demurely helped herself to scrambled eggs from the large oak sideboard and sat down at the huge table, fresh with starched Irish linen and shining silver toast rack and tea and coffee set and Wedgwood china.

Papa put away his watch and brushed his full mustache upward with a sweep of his forefinger. He was a large and handsome man of almost fifty summers. He should marry again, Clara thought, not for the first time, but she knew better than to mention it. Papa was not the kind of man who took advice from anybody, especially a woman.

"Is Adam down yet?" Clara asked.

Papa smiled tolerantly. "Not that young man. Late abed, I imagine."

"Where was he?" Clara asked.

"No doubt playing cards or billiards with his friends." Papa dismissed the subject. "A young man must have his freedom, me dear. Especially if he is getting married on Friday!"

What about the young women? Clara wanted to ask but did not dare.

"Papa, I'm sure I should be doing something more than I am to help with the wedding?"

"Not at all." Papa folded his *Times* and consulted his watch again. "You have your studies, and I have made all the arrangements myself. All the fluttering about that you women do on these occasions, absolutely not necessary. I have issued a list of orders, marquee, catering, invitations, entertainers, from my business office at the theater. It took me two hours. If your dear mother had been alive, the house would have been in an uproar for weeks past."

"Yes," Clara said, eating her eggs, "I suppose so." She remembered her mother, a warmness and a fragrance of lavender. Her mother had used no French perfume, no lady did, but all her clothes had been laid away in wardrobes filled with lavender sprigs. Some of it was still there, faded and dry, upstairs in the vast oak and mahogany wardrobes of the empty bedroom.

"Papa, should not Marta's family be doing all this?"

Papa looked embarrassed. "As you know, Marta has no father. I am paying for the wedding because I want to. Her mother offered to provide monies, but I insisted." He changed the subject. "Is that all you are having for breakfast?"

"It is really quite sufficient, Papa."

"It doesn't look it to me. A couple of eggs is hardly enough sustenance until luncheon."

"I must not eat more or I will be late for Miss Wilson's."

"Good Lord," said Papa, "can't have that. I don't know what Miss Wilson does to you girls, but by George, she frightens me!"

27

They both laughed. That was the nice thing about having a father to herself. They could sometimes laugh together. Clara finished her coffee and got to her feet. "I'd better go, Papa."

"All right, my dear. See you tonight."

Clara hesitated. "That comic on your bill this week, Harry something . . . ?"

"Yes?" Her father looked over his *Times*. "What about him?"

"I hear. . . ." Clara faltered, but she had to know. "I hear he . . . wasn't . . . very . . . good last night?"

"Nearly got the bird, second house." Her father looked at his watch. "I can't have my acts given the bird. If they don't work, they come off Tuesday night."

Clara said, "The poor man!"

Edward Abbott looked surprised. "His own fault, my dear. He's not playing the Hoxton Empire. My house manager wanted me to sack him last night, but I believe in giving people a proper chance."

"Yes. Of course, Papa."

"If you were a boy, I'd have no worries about the Alhambra."

"There's Adam, though, isn't there, Papa?"

"There's more to running a music hall than chasing a pretty ankle."

"Marta will cure him of that, Papa."

Papa sighed. "In this business you need to be stern to survive. I know, I've survived. Of course, I had your mother; I was lucky. Maybe Adam will be lucky."

Not with Marta, Clara thought. She'll wear the trousers in that house. She did not much like her prospective sister-in-law. "Anyway, Papa, you'll be with us many years yet. Nothing will change at the Alhambra, will it?"

The Alhambra had always been there, the fount of the family's sustenance. It was as reliable a prop in all their lives as St. Nicholas's Cathedral, where they went for morning service on a Sunday, maids and all.

"My dear," Edward Abbott said, "there is only one thing you can be sure of in this life, and that is that you can be sure of nothing in this life."

Clara warmed to Papa, as she always did whenever he treated her as an equal, which was not very often. It was not that he was unkind, simply that he never really found time to do it.

Clara kissed him on the forehead. "Bye, Papa, must rush!"

"Take care, dear." The *Times* went up again, like the curtain at the Alhambra. Clara walked quickly out of the room. She closed the dining-room door behind her and walked across the hall to Papa's study. The door creaked as she entered, and a scent of tobacco and good leather assailed her nostrils. Quickly she crossed to the rolltop desk and flipped open Papa's address book. She copied down the details she needed, using her own black-lead pencil from her purse. She tucked the paper into her handbag and quietly left the house. She walked quickly but demurely to the end of the treelined crescent, where her school friend Doris Goodlaw was waiting impatiently for her. Doris, like herself, was in her last year at Miss Wilson's Academy. Doris was plain and had acne.

"You're terribly late," she greeted Clara.

"I'm not coming today."

"What!"

"I said I'm not coming today, Doris."

"Are you sick? You look all right."

"I have to see the dentist," Clara said firmly. "That's all you need to tell Miss Wilson."

"Haven't you got a note for me to take?"

"No, just say that I send my apologies, and I will be in my place tomorrow."

"You've never said anything about a toothache before," said Doris Goodlaw suspiciously. "I don't see any sign of a swelling either."

"I'm not having a tooth *out*," Clara said.

"Then why are you going to the dentist's?"

"Because I have to have a tooth stopped."

"That's new, isn't it? I only thought actresses and people like that had their teeth done like that."

"Well, I'm doing it, Doris," said Clara. She thought: I would, too, if there was anything wrong with my teeth. "So just do as I say, and I'll see you tomorrow."

"I will," said Doris, who was no fool, "if you tell me what you're actually doing today."

Clara looked at the dowdy Doris (she really *did* wear red flannel drawers!) and felt superior and reckless. "I'm going to have lunch with a man. At Carrick's. See you tell Miss Wilson about the dentist's. Bye now!"

And with that Clara walked off down the crescent, the golden autumn leaves crackling under her feet, Doris staring after her.

At the end of the crescent, well out of sight of the Abbott house, she hailed a cab. Clara settled back in the seat and took her pouch purse out of her bag. Seven golden sovereigns nestled there. They looked brand-new, as indeed they were, having been taken from the money box in her bedroom that very morning.

It should, she calculated, be enough.

Harry Viner sat in Carrick's restaurant, a cooling cup of coffee in front of him, and fretted. What was he doing here? He had intended to stay in his lodgings and try to learn a new song for tonight's show and to rehearse a few gags, culled from memory, in place of the Abie jokes. Instead, here he sat in the bustling café in his one good shirt and his second-day stiff white collar, counting the change in his pocket. How was he to face the audience that night? What was he going to *give* them? He ignored the white-capped waitress's eye. So it was lunchtime; he wasn't going to order lunch. A glance at the menu had revealed the table d'hôte lunches were three shillings each. As soon as Clara arrived, he was going to take her by the arm and sweep her out of the place. They would leave, and he would buy her a sandwich and a cup of tea somewhere. What did she think she was, a princess or something, champagne suppers and lunches at three shillings a head?

Harry sipped his coffee and said to himself: you are going to get the bird tonight, and tomorrow morning you are going to be on the first train back to London, and there's not a thing you can do about it.

"Good morning, Harry."

There she was again, bright and chirpy, new dress an' all. What right had she to be so chirpy when the end of the world began at Curtain Up, six-fifteen at the Alhambra that evening?

"I've just had a coffee," he said, rising to his feet. "We could go for a bit of a walk. I'd like some fresh air."

"We haven't time for lunch," said Clara Abbott. "I have a cab standing outside, waiting."

"A cab?" said Harry dazedly. "Why, where are we going?"

"You'll see when we get there," said Clara. "How much is the coffee?"

"I'll get that," said Harry. No woman was going to pay for him in a public place. "But why the cab and where to?"

"When we get there, all will be explained," she said.

Clara wouldn't speak in the cab either. "Just wait, don't be so impatient." But she tucked her arm in his, and Harry thought: she's borrowed somewhere for us to be alone. Or we're going to her house, nobody will be there. The idea excited him, and he put his arm around her and touched the nipple of her full breast. She removed his hand.

"Not now."

"But *where* are we going?"

"Nearly there. Don't be such a little boy."

Harry fell back in the seat and stared out. The houses were shabby; there were not too many hansom cabs in the streets; this was not a well-to-do neighborhood. He felt gloomy again.

"Here we are, Harry. Let me do the talking."

Bewildered, Harry said, "I'll pay the cabby."

"No, it's done."

They stood in the shabby street, outside the shabby house, and the hansom cab clattered away across the cobblestones. Clara rang a bell, and a young man came to the door. He was fair-haired, in his shirt sleeves, wore cheap steel spectacles and smoked a meerschaum pipe. The weskit was tight around his muscular body. His striped shirt sleeves were shortened by elastic bands, and his hair needed cutting. Not exactly poor, Harry thought, but not rich either.

The young man smiled at Clara warmly. "That was quick! Please come in. Mr. Viner, I know you by sight. I saw your act last evening at the Alhambra."

Harry said, "Don't boast about it, mate."

"I promise you I won't. My name's John Hyatt."

It was a pleasant room, and it had some books and a large green aspidistra in the window and a piano. There was no bed in the place, but there was a settee, so obviously John Hyatt ran to two rooms. Harry was mildly impressed.

"You disliked the act then?" Harry said.

"I thought you were funny. It was the audience who disliked it. As you know."

Harry looked at Clara sharply. Who was this fella to be telling him his act was bad?"

Clara said, "John is a songwriter; he's got a song for you."

"What!"

John Hyatt sat down at the piano. On the music stand lay a piece of sheet music scribbled all over with symbols and words. Clara sat on the settee and patted it. Harry sat down in a daze.

31

He found enough presence of mind to say, "I can't afford to buy any songs."

"All arranged." Clara sat straight on the settee. "Please play us your song, Mr. Hyatt, and we'll see if Mr. Viner likes it."

John Hyatt tinkled an introductory chorus and then sang, in a fair tenor voice:

> I'm the Kosher King of Komedy,
> And she's my Queen.
> She's the loveliest little doll you've ever seen.
> When I go to bed at night, I dream about my love,
> She's a little turtledove.

Harry stood up. He asked harshly, "Is there any *more* of it?"

John Hyatt blinked. "There are three more verses."

"All as good as that?" asked Harry sarcastically.

"About the same." John Hyatt fiddled with his spectacles. "I know it isn't great songwriting, but it's all I can do in one morning, and it's what you need."

"You think so?"

"Harry," John Hyatt said gently, "if you *do* sing it, instead of telling your Abie jokes, you'll get off without getting the bird." He sighed. "I'm sorry I can't promise you more than that, but I have to be honest."

"Very nice, very nice." Harry felt a burning indignation all the more intense for knowing that the young man in the spectacles was probably right. He turned to the girl. "This was all your idea, to give me this load of *drek?* You really think I'm going to go onstage tonight and throw that rubbish at them? I'd give up the game first, I would!"

Harry meant it, at that moment. He was, indeed, trembling with rage. This girl, had taken pity on him—on *him,* Harry Viner!—had thought he was so bad he had to throw out his best jokes and put in *this!*

John Hyatt said gently, "They'll like it, Harry."

John Hyatt straightened his spectacles. "Do you want to hear the rest?"

"Yes, please," said Clara. "Harry, sit down and listen."

"I will hell sit down and listen!" shouted Harry. "Who asked you to do anything for me? I don't want to listen to the rest of this poxy song. And besides," he added, "I'm a comic, not a singer.

32

If I cut my jokes out, all I do is sing. That's not what I'm booked for."

Clara said, "If you don't do better tonight than you did last night, you'll go, whether you actually get the bird or not."

"How do you know that?"

The blue eyes stared back at him. "Never mind how, I just do, that's all."

"You can't know that for sure, nobody can."

John Hyatt cut in. "*She* does."

Harry sat down, his legs suddenly weak. He waved his hand. "All right, let's hear the rest of it. It can't get any worse."

It did.

"Jesus!" said Harry Viner.

"Please don't blaspheme, Harry," said Clara firmly.

He leaned back and closed his eyes.

"I repeat, how do you know for sure I'm sacked tonight if I don't make good?"

Clara looked at the floor. Her feet and her trim ankles were pleasant to look at. She said, "It doesn't matter."

"You'd better tell him, Miss Abbott," John Hyatt said.

Harry sat up.

"Abbott! Not the owner's?"

"She's his daughter," John Hyatt said.

"No!"

Harry stared at Clara anew. She looked up, and again her blue eyes stared implacably. "Yes, but that isn't important."

"Isn't important?" Harry Viner whispered faintly. Not only the owner's daughter, but a lady, and he'd taken her out to supper and God knows who had seen them together! "If your father knew you'd been out with me, I'd be off that bill now!"

"That isn't important either."

"What's important is that I'm a music hall performer, an artiste, a nobody, a vagabond, a bohemian, darling, the lowest of the low, a bleedin' *turn!*"

"I don't care what my father thinks, I like you. And please don't keep calling me darling. It's coarse."

John Hyatt turned away, studiously, to his sheet music and made a note. Harry Viner thought he saw an expression of regret on the young man's face. She's his sort. If he fancies her, he can have her!

"Look," he said, and he could hear the snarl in his voice, "I don't want no help from you, whoever you are, or this geezer here, whoever he is! I can look after my own business!"

"You can't," said Clara. "That's why we're all here."

"What!" You tellin' me I don't know what I'm a-doin' of?"

"Well, of course I am, because you don't." The girl's voice had risen an octave, and the blue eyes were suddenly misted.

"Please don't get upset dear, I know you mean well, but—"

"It's all my fault for trying to help you in the first place. I thought we were friends." She picked up her bag in a swift, furious movement. "Good-bye, Mr. Viner!"

And she was out of the place.

Harry Viner stood in the middle of the carpet, feeling like a very considerable fool and strangely bereft.

There was a long silence. John Hyatt broke it.

"If you want to use this song, you haven't much time."

"What makes you think I want to use it?" he asked with almost, to his horror, a break in his voice.

John Hyatt got to his feet and stared out through the lace curtains. "She's got a cab, that's all right."

Harry sat down again. "How do you come into all this?"

John Hyatt said, "Miss Abbott came to see me this morning. She said you needed a song. The song, which I'm not proud of, you've just heard. She paid me five pounds. If you don't want the song, I'll give you the five pounds back."

"It isn't my five pounds," said Harry Viner. He felt cold and deflated. "How did she get your name?"

"I asked her that, and she told me who she was."

Harry started. "You don't think her father knows anything about this, do you?"

"Hardly, old man," said John Hyatt.

"What are you?" Harry Viner asked. "Your voice is funny."

"So's yours," said John Hyatt. "I'm Irish."

"What you doin'," Harry asked with genuine curiosity, "in a one-eyed place like this?"

"I had relatives up here." John Hyatt sat down at his piano. "I'm going back to London soon." It's the only place to make a mark. London or New York."

"That's funny, that is," Harry said. "Somebody said just that to me yesterday."

"Don't get downhearted," John Hyatt said. "This is the first song I've sold this month."

"But you're sure you're going to make a success of songwriting?" Harry asked.

"Of course I am, or I wouldn't be doing it, would I?" It was easily said, but it wasn't a question. Harry began to feel respect for this young man in the steel spectacles, even if he had looked at Clara Abbott's ankles a little too often. "You have to have self-confidence. You must have it yourself, or you couldn't walk on that stage in the first place, could you?"

"That's true enough." Harry brooded, trying to erase the picture of the girl and her tears from his mind. He sighed. "I should be playing Jewish weddings and not be on the halls at all if this kinda thing is a-going to happen to me every time I play outside the Smoke."

John Hyatt turned away and waited a long moment. Then he said, "I think she's very fond of you, Harry."

"She's only a schoolgirl."

"Just the same."

"And she's old Abbott's daughter."

"That's true."

"Can you see it, me an' the owner's daughter? He'd have me arrested for wenching without a license!"

John Hyatt laughed. It was a pleasant laugh, but it held a note of regret.

"Well," he asked, "what do you say? Shall we go over the song verse by verse, or will I run through it again first?"

Harry Viner stood up. Every instinct urged him to walk out of the room. He remembered the girl's face and her deep, implacable blue eyes, and he said, "Let's take it from the top, shall we?"

There was a silence, broken only by the noise of boys shouting in the street outside.

"You meant to do that all the time, am I right?" asked John Hyatt.

"You're right," Harry Viner said, "but I've surprised meself."

"Yes," said John Hyatt softly, "I'm sure you have."

As they worked, John Hyatt looked at Harry Viner with interest. What could this girl see in him? Of course, he was flashy: the suit, the spats, the hat at a rakish angle, the tight trouser legs, the long black hair gleaming with macassar oil, the thick mustache. It was all, as his mother would say, in the shopwindow. What sort of goods were in stock?

Looking at Harry Viner as he sang the song with ill-concealed distaste, John wondered. He had been seeing a lot of "theatricals" in the six months since he had left college, and he was beginning to understand that they were all two different people. Offstage they had the same doubts and anxieties about their lives that ordinary people had. Onstage they were free.

John Hyatt knew he could never be one of them.

The nearest thing would be to write songs for them. That would be his extra life, his bonus.

Nobody had understood, not even his mother.

"Why study music all those years, son," his father had asked, bewildered, "an' then go off an' write songs for the music halls? You could easy get a job as a teacher at a school. I thought that was in your mind."

"It was," said John Hyatt. "It was, Da. But I couldn't stand the life, you see?"

"It's your own life, son." His father had smiled and relit his pipe, which had gone out in shock, a thing it did but once or twice a year. "And to think I had hopes ye might come into the shop!" He laughed, but not in any hurt way. "Ah, why should a young fella want to get up at six in the mornin' and pull bags of potatoes and cabbages about when he can be lying in bed till ten, writing songs for them young actresses?"

Mr. Hyatt ran a small but successful greengrocer's shop just off the Quays. John was the first of the family to go to college. His forebears on both sides had been workingmen. If Mr. Hyatt felt in any way sorry that his son should have let him down, he did not show it.

"The thing is," Michael Hyatt had said, seeing him onto the English boat, "write some songs with a bit of lilt to them. Something a man can tap his foot to!"

For by now he was totally convinced his son was to be a great success in England. Had he not given the boy a hundred pounds to see him on his way, even if the other young men at the college, aye, and the head of the Music Department himself (a professor at that!) had advised against it? The boy was wasting himself, the professor had said, running off to England to write silly songs for whores and drunkards!

"Not the first Irishman to find himself in such company, Professor," Michael Hyatt had said, "and not the last, I warrant ye!"

"We need our young men in Ireland, not running off over the seas, Mr. Hyatt!"

The professor had seemed angry, Michael Hyatt had told his son. "Why was that, now, I wonder?"

John Hyatt knew why. The professor had expected him to write the first Irish opera, using the old songs and the old poems of the dead language. They had talked about it often enough, the professor's eyeglasses glinting, his hands moving, his long hair disarranged.

"All we have is the English past; we need to look back and dig and re-create our old songs. . . . Brian Boru. . . . The Old Kings of Ireland."

John Hyatt had not wanted to rub his life away in university libraries, poring over faded manuscripts, talking to old cottagers in the windswept villages of Galway, priming them with porter, as they sang long-forgotten songs about an Ireland that was never to return. John Hyatt did not want to re-create, he wanted to create, even if it was only silly songs like the one Harry Viner was bellowing now.

Poor devil, John thought, to have to sing this stuff or get the bird! He knew the song wasn't tasteful. Anything tasteful would perish at the Alhambra with Harry Viner singing it!

John Hyatt stopped playing and found a couple of bottles of stout in his cupboard. He poured the strong dark liquid steadily into two glasses and offered one to Harry.

"Never drink this stuff as a rule," was Harry's none-too-grateful reception of this refreshment. "But I'd drink a pint of piss, I'm dry enough!"

What can she see in him? John Hyatt wondered, sipping his treacly stout and looking at Harry over the top of his spectacles.

The girl was stagestruck. That was plainly the thing. It came off her in waves. She had stood in his room, her purse of coins in her hand, and talked about a song for an artiste, and John Hyatt had been sure that she had been asking for a song for herself. It had come as a very considerable shock to him when she had told him whom the song was for. But he had kept his face straight. John Hyatt had sold a few songs to visiting performers at the Alhambra, and he was beginning to think that he had inherited some of his father's shopcraft.

"A song, Miss Abbott? For the comic? The tall dark fella?"

37

"You've *seen* him?" Her eyes had shone, and John Hyatt had felt a pang. Why? He didn't even know this girl.

Clara Abbott had conducted their business in a brisk way, and he had been impressed by her style. Could he write a song that was sure to save Harry Viner?

John Hyatt was not an Irishman, and a Dubliner at that, for nothing.

"Of course I can, miss. Only don't expect Strauss."

Clara Abbott had smiled. It was a lovely smile, John Hyatt thought; like the finely dressed red hair, it spoke of gentle upbringing, and money. Clara, to look at, was not unlike some of the girls he had met, sisters of his friends, at Trinity College in Dublin. None of them, though, would have charged unannounced into single men's rooms. There was obviously a lot more to Clara Abbott than met the eye, and plenty met the eye: the trim ankles and small, plump hands and the creamy, smooth neck. . . . John Hyatt glanced at Harry Viner, who sat morose, drawing on his cigar. Had he touched that neck or any part of her? Was it possible that lovely girl had allowed such liberties?

John Hyatt took a deep breath. What was it to him? Nothing. This was a business arrangement, no more.

Harry Viner was trying the song again. He stopped, in mid-verse, in total agony.

"You've got nothing else?"

"No. I wrote this especially for you."

"Lordluvaduck," said Harry Viner, "is *that* what you think of me?"

John Hyatt laughed. "If you want to change the words, you can. But it will take time."

"No, thanks," Harry said. "Never tamper with genius. If it ain't right now, fiddling about with it ain't gonna make it better, only different.

The fella, John Hyatt thought, isn't such a fool as he looks. He's Cockney-sharp, street-sharp. He might make a go of it if ever he finds the right material and the right kind of audience. He has plenty of nerve, and he seems to want success. That, John Hyatt knew from his own experience, was a very great part of it. As his mother said, if you wanted a thing enough, with all your heart, God usually arranged for you to have it, sooner or later.

For himself, he expected it would be later. He sighed—the girl had disturbed him—and turned over a page of manuscript

38

so that Harry Viner could begin a new verse. There was no room in his life for girls, especially girls like Clara Abbott who needed money and houses and children and a settled life. No, he would think of girls when he could afford to, and not before.

"An Irishman an' a Cockney Yiddisher boy doing a song for a lot of Geordies?" Harry Viner said. "It do make you fair want to bleedin' cry, don't it?"

Clara sat in her usual place in the Alhambra gallery that evening. Joe, the gallery attendant, had been surprised to see her two nights running. "What's the attraction, Miss Abbott?" he'd asked, finding her a seat. "Is it Little Tich or is it Mr. Lashwood?" He smiled. There was a conspiracy among the Alhambra staff about Miss Clara and her secret visits.

George Lashwood, the best-dressed man on the halls, was closing the first half, and he was singing the song that had made him famous. He was a tall, handsome man, in top hat and evening clothes, standing quite still in the spotlight.

> In the twi-twi-twilight,
> Out in the beautiful twilight,
> They all go out for a walk walk walk,
> A nice little spoon
> And a talk talk talk. . . .

Rapt, the rows of becapped faces in the gallery sang:

> That's the time they long for, just before the night,
> And many a grand little wedding is planned,
> In the twi-twi-light!

Such ease, she thought as the big man bowed, twice, topper in hand, and the old workingwoman next to her muttered, "Isn't he a real swell?" But Clara knew (for she had heard her father say it) that George Lashwood had been working as a humble mechanic before he took to the halls. Nobody, Papa had said firmly, nobody on the halls is a gentleman. He wouldn't be on the halls if he was.

Papa had the famous ones to tea at his house (she had actually sat on Dan Leno's knee), but there was a gulf between their way of life and his own. Papa was a theater owner but he was also a Councillor of the City, a man of substance, whereas most music hall artistes, even the richest, were people of straw, rich today, poor tomorrow. Clara had heard the story from Papa's lips all too often.

The curtain closed behind George Lashwood, and Harry Viner stood on the stage alone.

Clara Abbott pressed her hands together and realized that she was praying. He's lost his nerve, she thought.

A boy in the audience called, "Say something, man, if it's only hello!"

Harry Viner smiled warily and waved his hand. "Thank you, son," he said. "But no disrespect, please. I'm old enough to be your father, and what's more, I probably am!"

That got a small, encouraging laugh.

Audiences, Clara had heard Papa say, always encouraged comics more than any other kind of act. They were always ready to laugh, ready to help. They wanted a comic to be funny. But once they decided he wasn't, the encouragement turned to dislike and, sometimes, to hatred. Jugglers and dancers and singers, unless they were very bad indeed, rarely got the bird. It was always the comics.

Clara prayed hard, her eyes tight shut, her hot forehead resting against the brass rail, as Harry Viner said, "This fella went up to the synagogue gates carrying a dead cat. The rabbi sez, 'What's this?' The fella sez, 'This cat's been a friend to me; I'd like him buried in holy ground.' The rabbi sez, 'What, a cat! Go away, please!' The fella sez, 'Sorry, no offense meant, I could pay for a resting place for him, I could go to a tenner. Do you think the Methodists up the road would be interested?' And the rabbi sez, 'You didn't say this was a *Jewish* cat!' "

Clara kept her eyes closed.

The laughter was there, but it was thin.

Surely he's learned something from last night, she thought. His next words told her he hadn't.

"This Jewish fella met Abie in the street one day. . . ."

Clara kept her eyes closed. This was going to be awful. All afternoon she had sat in Carrick's restaurant, drinking tea without thirst, eating cakes without hunger, full of conflicting emotions, hating Harry Viner for the way he had talked to her, for how horrible and ungrateful he had been, for showing her up in front of that nice polite young Mr. Hyatt. And love, the sudden physical pull she felt when she thought of his hands or his hair or his eyes.

Clara felt a tug on her arm. The woman sitting next to her, with the dark sallow complexion of the town poor, not exactly

40

dirty but not exactly clean either, peered into her face. "Are ye all right, hinny?" she asked. "Feelin' faint, are ye?"

A faint odor of fish emanated from her. Clara noted her shawl and striped petticoats, the uniform of a fishwife.

"No, thank you kindly. I'm perfectly all right," said Clara.

The fishwife stared at her, noted the accent, took in the clothes in the half-light. She said, rebukingly, "A young lady like you shouldn't be up here in the gallery, miss. It's not for such as you. It's too close up here."

Clara smiled politely. "I'm all right. Really."

"Haddaway, me dear," said the woman. "Ye're not missin' much anyroad. This comic man here couldny mek a loon laugh."

Clara turned her eyes back to the stage.

Harry Viner was still telling his Abie stories, and the attention of the audience had begun to stray. Bored feet began to drum. The fishwife proffered a slice of orange to Clara, a begrimed finger deep in the flesh of the fruit, and Clara had declined before she knew it. The fishwife nodded. She was not offended. She had not expected such as Clara to take anything from such as her.

Harry Viner was saying, "Abie met Morrie, and Morrie said to him, 'How's business?' "

He *isn't* going to do it, Clara thought dully. He's too proud to take anything from a woman, however kindly meant. He's going to stand on that stage until he gets the bird and serve him . . . in his own words. . . . Tears came to her eyes. . . . Serve him bleedin'-well-right!

The drumming of feet reached a crescendo.

A man called, "Gerroff! Yer hopeless!"

A woman screamed, "Bliddy Cockneys, ye canny tell whit they're talkin' aboot!"

Harry Viner finished his Abie story. The noise from the gallery dinned in Clara's ears. Oh, God, what's the matter with him, she almost screamed; then she *did* scream. . . .

"Sing us your song!"

Harry Viner stared up, shading his eyes, at the gallery. He stood perfectly still, as if paralyzed.

The fishwife stared at Clara as if she had gone mad.

"Hush, hinny," she said, "ye canny shout like that, not a lady like ye!"

But Clara was past all caring.

"Go on," she yelled, "sing us a song! Get on with it!"

41

"Hush, hush, hinny," cried the fishwife. "They'll think yer a street lass, they will!"

"I don't care," screamed Clara, the whole gallery turning to her now, reproachful but interested. "Harry, give us your song!"

Harry Viner seemed dazed. He didn't move.

The fishwife sighed, took a deep breath and yelled, "Come on, man, let's hear the bliddy song!" She had a voice of brass, and everybody in the theater heard it. There was a deep, rumbling laugh, and other voices joined in. Soon it was a chorus.

"Come on, canny lad, givvus the song, man!"

Harry Viner stood still, listening to the chorus.

The musical director looked up at him and said something. Harry hesitated, then nodded.

The band struck up; the houselights went down. The limelight stayed on Harry. He began to sing:

> I'm the Kosher King of Komedy,
> And she's my Queen.
> She's the loveliest little doll you've ever seen.
> When I go to bed at night I dream about my love,
> She's a little turtledove.

The fishwife said grudgingly, "He has a canny voice."

"Yes," said Clara.

"Good-looking fella, in his way."

"Yes," said Clara, tears in her eyes.

"Wouldn't be surprised if ye fancied him, miss?"

"Oh, I do!" said Clara. "I do!"

Harry Viner danced and sang in the spotlight.

> I'm the King of Kosher Komedy,
> That is my name,
> I'm always fond of love's sweet game.
> How I love my Queen to kiss me and then
> I love her to do it all over again.

Everybody in the house sang the chorus, gallery, grand circle, and stalls. The noise was deafening. Clara put her hands over her ears and wiped the tears away with the back of her hand. She never cried. Yet this man had made her cry twice in one day. Was this a portent of the future? she wondered.

I have to risk that, she said to herself, getting to her feet and going swiftly up the aisle toward the door. I have to, because I don't want the safe things like the other girls at Miss Wilson's

Academy. I want the risky, unusual things, I want . . . I want.
. . . She paused and looked down at Harry Viner taking his final
curtain bow, his face a smiling mask, the applause cheerful and
loud, the pit band playing the jaunty tune again. . . . I want Harry
Viner, she thought, I want him so badly I could die. . . . I want
Harry Viner and I want. . . .

She drank in the noise, the music, the adulation, the smell
of salt sweat and oranges and rich, heavy cigar smoke and French
perfume wafting up from the stalls. . . .

I want *this*.

And Many a Grand Little Wedding Is Planned

The wedding between Adam and Marta was arranged for Friday.

That's *today,* Clara thought with panic. Tomorrow he'll go. I'll never see Harry Viner again!

She stood in the living room and watched the workmen erecting the marquee on the large green lawn behind the house. One moment it was lying on the lawn, a tangle of red-and-white striped canvas; the next, to roars and yells from the becapped and weskited workmen, it was half-erect.

"Morning, Sis." Adam stood next to her. Her brother looked gloomy and hung-over. He wore a frogged red velvet smoking jacket, check trousers and a folded silk cravat at his neck. He had not shaved, and his breakfast, a large cup of coffee—a basin, in the French style, an artifact he had picked up in Paris—trembled in his hand.

"You don't have to cry for me, Sis."

"I'm not crying."

Clara blew her nose on her cambric handkerchief. It was, after all, Friday. He could have sent a card. After all, she had got him the song that saved him. There had been no word. None at all. Harry Viner wasn't a gentleman. It was as simple as that.

44

Clara was suddenly aware that Adam had gone back to the table, filled his coffee basin and was regarding her with concern.

It was his wedding day; she had no right to be thinking of her own affairs at such a time. She twirled around and said, "Like my hair? I've been up since half past six doing it; it took an hour!"

It was now eight o'clock in the morning. The wedding was at noon.

"Very nice. You're getting to be quite a young lady."

He was looking at her breasts. Clara felt mischievous. "How was last night?"

Adam composed his face. "It was quite good, really. We jawed a bit and drank a bit."

"And then you all went to Madame Morris's sporting house, I'll bet!"

Adam was speechless for a moment. Clara smiled at him.

"What do you know about Madame Morris? Do the girls at Miss Wilson's Academy talk about her?"

"Of course they do. Some of the girls' brothers go, and they tell the girls what happens there."

"*Do* they?"

"Is it true that they line the girls up naked and you walk up and down inspecting them, like generals?"

"No, it is not true! I don't know where you've heard such things!" Adam felt his head. It was plainly throbbing. "What is the matter with you this morning, Clara?"

Clara laughed and kissed him on the cheek. His beard scraped her face. "It's not every day my only brother gets married. *Did* you go to the sporting house?"

"Of course we did."

"And did you . . . do anything with those girls?"

"I'm not going to tell you that!"

"I'll bet you did! I know I should have if I was a man."

"Well. Two at once actually."

"You didn't!"

Adam fingered his mustache proudly. "Did."

"But you didn't love them or anything?"

"No, I didn't, you silly goose; it was only a bit of fun."

"Did they enjoy it?"

"They seemed to." He smiled. "Didn't complain."

"I sometimes wish"—Clara sighed—"that I was a man."

"Don't." Adam rubbed his bristly chin. "It looks nice and easy,

I daresay, but it ain't. You have to do a lot of damn things you don't want to do, don'tcher know?"

"Will you go to the sporting house after you're married?" she asked curiously.

"I should hope not, no," said Adam.

"But you might?" she persisted.

"How on earth do I know what I'll do?" Adam took out his gold half hunter and looked at it. "Time's getting on, I'll have to shake a leg."

"But you might? Other men do, don't they?"

"Yes, yes, yes, I might—"

"I wouldn't marry any man who'd do that!"

"Tell me when you find the fellow," her brother said, "and I'll have him framed, because he'll be an original."

"Why do *all* men do it?"

"Now look, Sis, I'm off. I have to put that damn monkey suit on for the church. And you have to dress, too, I should think."

"Do you love Marta? I mean, really?"

Adam breathed in impatiently. "Of course I do. I'm marrying the bloody woman, aren't I?"

That seemed to make him very angry, and he slammed out of the dining room. Clara could hear him bounding up the wide staircase, two at a time. Marta and Adam were to stay at Leazes Crescent for a while. She expected they would move to a house of their own when the children started to arrive.

Clara wondered about children. Did she want any? She wasn't sure.

With Harry Viner perhaps?

But he had not sent a note.

Mary, the Irish maid, came into the room.

"Time you was dressing, Miss Clara."

"Yes," Clara said. "I know."

Harry Viner was lying asleep, in the brass bedstead, with Mae, the wife of the seal trainer, when suddenly she wakened and pinched his bottom. He started awake.

"What the bleedin' *hell?*"

"It's eight o'clock, Harry."

Harry peered at the alarm clock at the side of the bed. His head ached. He had drunk a good deal of whiskey the night before.

He had been drinking a good deal of whiskey every night that week, some of it bought by Mae. It had been a bloody week, a bloody bloody bloody week, going on singing that *drekky* song every night! All he had to be grateful for was that nobody he knew from down the Smoke, none of the London bookers, had seen him do it.

Mae nudged him again. She was nude, and she was sweating, and the soft flesh of her full breasts stuck to his back.

"Harry, it's eight o'clock, dear."

Dear? Who did she think he was, her old fella?

"Right, orf you go." Harry didn't open his eyes. "Don't make a noise an' wake the whole bleedin' house, will you?"

"It's all right, he'll be flat out till I wake him, sodden old devil." Mae was referring to her husband, the seal trainer. "We haven't got all day, dear, have we?"

"I dunno, what you on about?"

Harry blearily opened one eye. Mae loomed above him. In the soft light percolating through the lace curtains she was not unattractive, for her age, which Harry guessed to be forty. He wondered how she had managed to get into bed with him again, for he could not remember. The whiskey had taken care of that. Anyway, here she was, and he wished she'd go away.

"We got this date this afternoon, don't we, dear?" Mae pushed a wisp of blond hair back from her eyes. She still had some of her stage makeup on, leaving an ocher rim around her neck. "This weddin', booked for the entertainment, ain't we?"

"What?" Still Harry did not open his other eye.

"This weddin', the whole company's invited." Mae touched him exploratively. Harry wondered if he had taken her during the night. He could not remember. His body stirred. Well, at least he was beginning to forget about the girl, he thought. The whiskey had helped there.

"What time we due at this jamboree?" he asked.

"Noon sharp." Mae's lips were busy now, and her tongue. Mae was very skilled and experienced enough not to ask a man, first thing in the morning, if he loved her.

Harry felt nothing.

Mae said, "Last night you weren't interested either."

"Sorry, Mae."

Mae didn't say anything to that. After a while she got off the

47

bed and pulled on her kimono. She stood over the bed and looked down at Harry for a long time, but although he knew she was there, he did not open his eyes.

"Have a nice little sleep, love."

Harry said nothing.

Slowly Mae let herself out.

Clara settled back in the coach and brushed the confetti from the white silk dress. She sighed. It had been a nice wedding, everybody said so. Her brother had looked so fine and manly, standing there at the altar, in cutaway coat and striped trousers and four-inch collar. He wore his fair hair longer than many of the men present. The British had, like the rest of Europe, begun to wear short back-and-sides after the German victory over the French in 1871. Papa admired the Germans, so he frowned at Adam's long hair. Her brother had looked handsome but somehow, staring down at the altar, perhaps a little sad. Marta, on the other hand, had looked very happy and, Clara supposed, womanly was the word.

Clara did not like her new sister-in-law. She did not suppose she ever would. The idea of having to live in the same house, even for a year, until Marta got pregnant, was more than she could bear to contemplate. She could not understand what Adam saw in Marta, but then Clara did not find many friends amongst her female companions at Miss Wilson's Academy for Young Ladies. The girls were silly and giggly, and Clara couldn't stand their chatter, chatter, chatter.

The coach—one of nine, it was a large wedding—rumbled through the streets of the city. People stood and waved, old women in shawls, without teeth, and men in caps and worn clothes, and children without shoes, their toes gripping the edge of the curbstones, filthy from the muddy straw lying in the gutters. A wedding as big as this one was not to be seen every day in the city, and Clara supposed she should be more excited than she was. But even the service—High Anglican, of course—had not moved her, and she had sailed through her bridesmaid's duties without emotion, even when the bride had said, "I do!" and there had been a long, low sigh from the ladies and one or two grunting, suppressed coughs from the gentlemen. Papa had blown his nose loudly on a particularly fine Irish linen handkerchief.

The coach stopped. They were back at the house.

Papa put his face in the carriage window. "Come along, young ladies!" he said. "There's a marquee on the lawn and plenty to eat and drink for everyone." He closed an eye. "Not, of course, that you young ladies would do such a naughty thing as drink a glass of champagne!"

The other bridesmaids all laughed, shifting in their watered-silk gowns. Everybody in the carriage had put her hair up, as was proper, at sixteen. Champagne, too! They were almost grown-up! Their laughter got on Clara's nerves. After all, she had drunk champagne already that week, with a man, Harry Viner, she was never to see again.

Clara wondered how she would live once the week was over and he was gone. A feeling of despair came over her. Marta would soon came back from the honeymoon, and Marta would be the senior woman of the house. Well, that was only to be expected since she was now a married woman of nineteen years of age, whereas Clara was a schoolgirl of barely seventeen.

"Come along, everyone," said Clara, "or the food will all be eaten, and there's everything!"

There was, indeed, everything.

The girls stood and stared. The marquee was crowded with people, sweating into heavy black suits and weskits and woolen underwear and stiff collars (the men) and yards and yards of watered silk and cotton and whalebone stays and flannel drawers (the women), and their faces were boiled and red (the men) and set and white (the women), and only the servants, who, Clara knew, wore nothing under their uniforms, seemed cool in the stramash of people wafting themselves with the newly fashionable Chinese rice-paper fans or, in the case of men, mopping the sweat from their faces with large white handkerchiefs.

"Not a stitch on, miss, under our uniforms," Mary, the Irish maid, had told her. "We expect to be run off our feet; we'll die unless we sweat, miss. It'll be murder there today!"

And murder it was.

Mary, the maid, popped a couple of glasses of champagne into their hands. "Here you are, ladies, drink it while yez can," she said. "I don't know when I'll get to yez again, the sweat's running down me back like the Liffey, so it is!"

There was, however, plenty to eat. Huge boiled hams, and mounds of cold beef, loins of pork, saddles of lamb, and heaps of dark beef sausage, pink potted meats, and black puddings, weighing down long trestle tables, covered in white damask. There were cold roasted chickens and ducks and geese, all cut at by chefs in white hats and aprons, especially hired for the day by Papa. To go with these meats there were many salads, tomatoes and lettuces and beetroots and cold mayonnaise potatoes. Everything was served, as was the English style, *au naturel*. Papa subscribed to the theory that only the French needed to pour sauces over food because, as he was putting it to a number of business acquaintances, "We have the best beef cattle in the world and the finest mutton on the hoof, we grow the best potatoes and the finest green vegetables—if anybody wants 'em, I don't—and I can't see the need of spoiling the taste with that muck!"

There was hearty agreement with that. The men had not yet begun to eat seriously but were simply toying with a dozen Whitstable oysters (eaten, naturally, from the shell, with red pepper and malt vinegar) or possibly chewing on a dozen Dublin Bay prawns, which had been landed at North Shields and boiled in brine, for twenty minutes and no more, only that very morning.

To drink, Edward Abbott modestly explained, there were the usual things, the champagne for those who liked the fizzy, sweetish drink. He did not. The ladies, he knew, cared for such beverages. He himself preferred a light hock, a Liebfraumilch (which he was drinking, in a large pewter tankard) with the oysters. Later, he hoped, the gentlemen would join him in a glass or two of fine claret. The gentlemen said indeed they would. There was, of course, bitter beer from the wood, if anybody was actually thirsty, and Amontillado sherry and Cockburn's vintage port, and should anybody have eccentric tastes, or be Scots or Irish, there was whiskey.

The gentlemen ran their fingers along their mustaches and craned their heads for a dizzying glimpse of a lady's ankle (should she sit down) or of her upper arms. For the ladies' breasts they had no particular eye, save an odd eccentric amongst them. Décolletage had been worn quite low for a generation, and besides, a woman's breasts were part of her divine motherhood, connected with lactation, and not strictly sexual. But an ankle or an arm, oh la la. . . .

The men laughed and fingered their mustaches and ate their oysters and cold beef and a quarter pound or so of ripe Stilton cheese. Sprawling stylishly on plaid blankets on the huge Abbott

50

lawn, they looked out of the corners of their eyes at the ladies, Clara' and her friend and bridesmaid Agnes Thorburn amongst them. The girls were aware of these masculine glances but had been taught to pretend that such things did not happen and under no circumstances to acknowledge them when they did, save to cover an offending ankle or an errant square or two of flesh on the upper arm. Now they sat and sipped their champagne and pecked at tiny sandwiches (for ladies did not have gross appetites, like the gentlemen) and felt hungry and dissatisfied.

"I'm going to eat a half of chicken," said Clara. "I'm starving!"

"Oh, no, you mustn't," protested the scandalized Agnes.

But Clara did and licked her fingers.

"Oh, my, ain't you awful!" said Agnes Thorburn.

"That Abbott gel," said the best man, twenty years old, hair drenched in macassar oil, a four-inch collar biting into his neck, "she eats like a washerwoman!"

"No mother," said an old man, staring at Agnes Thorburn's seventeen-inch waist. "No manners."

A German band in scarlet tunics frogged with gold braid, played "Soldiers of the Queen" all through the eating, which took almost two hours. The members of the band could not speak English, but they could drink beer (and did) and were generally admired for their martial bearing.

"The Germans are our cousins," Papa told his business acquaintances. "Far better than the Frenchies any day!"

There was general agreement amongst the gentlemen present that this was so.

Clara washed her chicken down with a large swallow of hock from the pint pewter mug taken from the bemused hand of her brother, the bridegroom.

"Clara," cried Adam, horrified, "you shouldn't drink hock like that, gel, you'll be squiffy!"

"Not me," said Clara, "I have a head of iron."

But the champagne and the hock and the sun's rays, which somehow seemed trapped by the surrounding elm trees, were somewhat intoxicating, it was true.

"Don't let Papa see you!" Adam snatched his pewter mug back. "He'll be very waxy."

"Oh, I don't care," said Clara. "You only get married once, you know."

"Yes." Adam fingered his mustache and looked at Agnes Thorburn, who looked away, as a lady should, while the gentleman had his fill of looking. "That's true anyway."

"When do you leave?"

"In an hour." Adam glanced at his half hunter. "I'll have to go and change soon."

"Where's Marta?" asked Clara.

"Here I am," said that lady, her eyes cold above the smile, the bridal gown sweeping around her imperially, the eyes of everybody upon her.

"My dearest, we have only an hour left," said Marta, "and we have by no means spoken to everybody yet."

"No, we must move along." Adam nodded to Clara and Agnes.

"Clara,"—Marta smiled icily—"you will see that Papa does not stay up all night, playing cards and drinking?"

"Whatever Papa wishes to do, he will do!"

Clara was not going to be held responsible for Papa. Besides, the poor dear so rarely enjoyed himself. It was the theater most of the day, and every evening, bar Sunday, the counting of pennies, the reading of contracts, the negotiating of fees and the paying of bills. Let Papa enjoy himself for once.

"I think that is very thoughtless of you, Clara."

"My dearest," said Adam, "Clara is not Papa's keeper!"

"No, I suppose not." Marta's smile was glacial. "By the same token, your papa must not overexert himself. I have lost my own dear papa, and I know one must be careful not to go to excess of spirit or exercise."

"Yes, dearest." Adam sighed and spirited her away to meet Papa's business acquaintances, who clustered around her like bees around a honeypot, Clara thought, or around a queen bee. Well, she had better enjoy her day, for soon she would be suckling children, one after the other, and the same men would pass her in the street then with but the polite doffing of a hat.

"I don't think I really like your new sister-in-law," opined Agnes Thorburn.

Tears started to Clara's eyes. "Agnes, I'm in love with a man."

"Oh, no!" Agnes Thorburn clutched at her hand, struck to the heart.

"Yes," said Clara. "He's tall and dark, and he has a black mustache, and he's on the halls!"

"Oh, Clara!"

52

Agnes Thorburn stared at her, fascinated and appalled and intrigued all at the same time. At that moment, Papa bade the German band to cease playing and instructed the bandmaster to signal that a sound of cymbal be heard, to bring silence to the gathering.

When this was effected, Papa spoke, perspiring profusely and referring to notes in his white-gloved hand.

"As you will mostly know, ladies and gentlemen, I am the proprietor of a music hall, and I thought it might be fitting to have a little entertainment from my artistes, who are appearing this week at the Alhambra." Papa looked over his glasses. "Where they may be seen at popular prices. . . ."

There was a laugh at that.

"I have persuaded them to come along to entertain us this afternoon, and they are at this very moment using the caterers' marquee to change into their . . . er . . . stage clothes. . . ." Papa closed an eye. "The ladies can rest assured that all the songs will be of the utmost delicacy. . . ."

The gentlemen all laughed, and the ladies looked prim.

"The first act for your entertainment, ladies and gentlemen, is Harry Viner." Papa stared at the paper in his hand and seemed doubtful of the next words. "King of Kosher Komedy!"

Clara's heart stopped. Or she thought it had.

"It's him," she whispered.

"Who?" asked Agnes Thorburn.

"Him!"

Clara, forgetting all her etiquette, pointed to the tall, dark figure of Harry Viner as he emerged from the caterers' marquee.

"Lor'," said Agnes Thorburn, "ain't he handsome, though!"

Harry Viner saw Clara Abbott the very same moment that she saw him. And he almost "dried." He had sat on the horse bus, moody and dull-witted, not listening to the chatter of Mae and the others. All he had taken in was that they were performing at some nob's wedding, probably for nothing because the theater manager had arranged it.

Everything happens to me, he thought. Every time I see this girl it's a tragedy! I very nearly get the bird, first off, and now here I am again, tongue-tied and useless, in front of all these nobs, and it's all gone out of my head. No music to help me, no lights, middle of the morning, a head like a stairhead, and there *she* is,

53

sitting there, as nice as ninepence, looking as if butter wouldn't melt!

They should have opened with the seal act, he thought, looking at the ladies and gentlemen spread out on the lawn or standing with glass in hand. But if they did, who would know audience from act? They looked like seals anyway, especially the men, all done up in their wedding black, with their white dickey fronts and their fat, boiled faces and their mustaches.

"The seal act won't be on," Harry Viner found himself telling them. It was true, the stage manager had decided that transporting the seals through the town in a horse bus simply wasn't practical. Mae was furious about it and was sulking in the changing tent.

"Yes," Harry Viner told the wedding crowd, "the seals are left behind, ladies and gents, because we thought if we brought them, nobody would know the difference."

The ladies and gentlemen turned and stared at each other blankly. Nobody had the slightest idea what this curious man was talking about.

Only Clara laughed.

Harry Viner raised his hat and said, "Thank you, lady! If you are a lady. Well, I can't see from here, can I? Or from there, come to that! Oh, yes, I can. My, aren't you lovely!"

Clara blushed.

"Ain't he bold!" whispered Agnes Thorburn.

Harry Viner, his head pounding from the whiskey he had drunk the previous night, eyes smarting from the full glare of the sun, his shirt sticking to him and his number nine pancake drying itchily on his face, decided to attack the audience.

"I'm Jewish myself," he said, "but I'm all for everybody living together in peace and harmony. I want Christians and Jews and Scotch and Welsh to live together as neighbors. I want them all to get together, Catholics, Episcopalians, Wesleyans, Methodists, Congregationalists and Baptists, I want them all to get together and attack the Irish!"

There was a roar of laughter from the gentlemen.

The Irish were the latest wave of immigrants and worked mainly on the canals and railways. Even the common poor looked down on them.

The ladies frowned and patted their hair. On principle, they

54

did not like fun made of religion. Like the family, religion was not a thing you made jokes about.

"Don't think I have anything against the Irish," said Harry Viner. "My best friend is an Irish coalman. Last night he was delivering seven bags of coal to a top-floor tenement. There were no lamps in the street, and the seventh bag seemed very heavy. When he got to the top, he found he had the horse by the ears!"

More laughter from the gentlemen, who were easily pleased and highly prejudiced.

Thank the Good Lord, Harry Viner thought, I've found something they'll laugh at. He told six fast Irish jokes one after the other, mostly old ones, stolen from other comics, and left the lawn to a spattering of applause. He did not sing his song for these people. He had intened to, but the moment he saw the girl, he decided against it. He would show her he could get through a gig like this without any help from her!

Back in the stifling heat of the changing tent, he found that he was shaking. Little Tich was putting on his long shoes, and he walked out as if he were going onto the street.

As soon as the wedding crowd saw him, they began to laugh. Most of them had seen him before; some of the men had seen him do exactly the same thing at least a dozen times. They did not tire of it.

"Listen to that lot." Harry pulled off his stage shirt and sat in his underwear. "Doesn't tell a single gag, and he's got them already."

"That, my dear Harry, is genius," said George Lashwood benignly. He had on his white tie and tails, and he flipped his top hat and set it at an angle on his head, craning down (he was a tall man, a six-footer) to see his reflection in the only mirror in the tent. It had been brought by Mae, and now she wasn't even to appear. Her husband sat drinking bottled beer in the corner, eyes closed, totally content.

"I wish I had a touch of genius then," Harry said.

George Lashwood looked at him. "You have talent, me boy. Be grateful. It's easier."

"You look a bit shaky, Harry," Mae said, pushing her way through the crowded tent. Two girl acrobats were dressing, down to their long stockings and undershifts, and the poodles from the dog act were being constantly fed to stop them from barking. The

55

conjuror was arranging his act in a corner. He was irritated and snappy. He did not like to prepare his act in public. Mae found her way to a chair next to Harry's. "You sounded shaky an' all when you started."

"Thanks, Mae," Harry said. "Thanks very much, darlin'!"

"No, honest." Mae looked at him curiously. "Are you all right?"

"I will be"—Harry began to wipe the stage makeup from his face—"if you stop asking me such bloody silly questions."

"Oh," said Mae, much hurt. "Thank you. Thank *you* very much!"

"Sorry, darlin'." Harry sighed. "It's just I don't seem to know how to play these audiences. I'm lost with 'em."

Mae nodded, all forgiven. "Some comics have a girl with them, don't they?"

Harry said nothing to that.

Mae said, "Gives them something else to look at, know what I mean, somebody standing there in her drawers like, it takes the curse orf of the act, I mean, it's something else on the stage besides you, innit like?" Mae stretched her leg and pulled up her long dress. "Some people think I have a good leg," she said.

"Pull your clouts down, you silly cow." Harry looked quickly at the seal trainer. His eyes were closed and he was snoring gently. "Anyway, a proper comic don't need no leg show on with him."

"Not a proper comic, no," said Mae, nettled. "But you do!"

"You think so, do yer?"

He was sick of these tarts, pushing themselves at him.

Mae leaned forward. Her fingers touched his leg.

"You've seen me. I can sing a bit and I can dance a bit and I have a few bob put by. Think about it, Harry, will you?"

Harry dropped his voice. "You'd run out on your old fella?"

"I have a hundred sovereigns in the bank," Mae whispered, her fingers moving on Harry Viner's woolen underwear. He shifted away.

"Leave off, Mae, will you?" He regarded her with respect, however. A hundred quid was a lot of money, say anything you like.

"I have a house in London as well," continued Mae implacably. "It's in my name, and the furniture's mine. It's all bought and paid for. I could do a lot for you, Harry."

"Sounds to me," said Harry Viner, "as if what you could do for me is make me your fancy man, that an' nothing else."

"Well, have you got a place to live?"

Harry shook his head. "You know I ain't."

"Have you any bookings coming along?"

"You know that as well. No."

"Have you anything saved?"

"Some hopes."

Said Mae, "I don't see what choice you have, Harry."

A very sharp retort came to Harry Viner's lips, but he choked it back. Everything that Mae said was true. When the tour was over, he would be lucky if he had a week's rent for theatrical digs in Islington or Balham. That would be about as far as his last week's money would stretch. Then it would be back to living on cups of tea and currant buns and trudging around the theatrical agencies in the hope of a job, any job, turning up, anywhere. It would mean starvation again. With Mae, there would be enough food and a warm fire. So he said, "I'll think about it, darlin'," and she patted his hand in a motherly, understanding fashion, as if she knew exactly what was going through his mind. Which she did.

With *that* staring him in the face, Harry Viner wondered, why was he thinking about this pretty little girl? But he was. His belly was full, that was why! The performers had been given beef sandwiches to eat and beer to drink, and they had all devoured them ravenously, indeed were still doing so, except for Mr. Lashwood, who could afford to eat three times a day and took only brandy and soda, the gentleman's drink.

Outside, Little Tich finished his act to loud applause, and the dog act followed (also very popular) and then the lady acrobats, who were also well liked (by the gentlemen) but not appreciated by the ladies, who considered the idea of half-clad girls dancing on a lawn at a wedding out of all conscience. In fact, the girls wore leotards—now very popular since the French acrobat, Monsieur Léotard, had become world-famous with his trapeze act. The original Man on the Flying Trapeze, Monsieur Léotard was. The girls' act was eminently respectable, but their legs *did* show, and this was a treat for the gentlemen, who never saw a woman's uncovered legs, except in the music hall.

Several of the more prim ladies left the lawn and went into the house, so that their eyes were not offended by the sight of their sisters disporting licentiously on the lawn. No gentleman left the lawn, and the lady acrobats performed their final tumble (over two beer barrels set for the purpose) to a storm of male applause and cheers. The girls came in to the tent drenched in sweat and flopped down, crying for beer.

"Bleedin' cows walked orf, some of 'em," said one, drinking deep.

"Rotten old tightarses," said her sister, doing the same.

They were twins and were said to sleep together.

Mr. Lashwood stood up, tapped his topper and left the tent to loud applause from the ladies and gentlemen. He sang the song that had made him famous, and it was one that befitted the occasion:

> . . . And many a grand little weddin' is planned,
> In the twi-twi-light. . . .

The music, the applause and the repeated choruses drifted into the changing tent. "Gawd," said Harry Viner, "there's a song for you! I wish I had a song like that."

"Who doesn't, dear?" said Mae sympathetically.

That was the moment Clara Abbott came into the tent.

The artistes, in various states of undress and disarray, stared at her. Harry, in his woolen long johns, stood up, grabbing his coat and holding it in front of him.

"Good afternoon, everyone," said Clara.

They just stared at her, like a tableau.

Harry felt cold, and then hot, and a very considerable fool.

"This is Miss Abbott," he managed, "the owner's daughter."

The tent relaxed. If she was the owner's daughter, she had a right.

"I think you were quite wonderfully good, everyone," said Clara, in her nice educated voice, and Mae said, sotto, "Oh, awfully wonderful, don'tcher know!" and Harry Viner said, "Shut up, you stupid bitch!" and Mae looked at him, startled, and then, with new eyes, at Clara Abbott.

"Hello, Harry." Clara held onto her parasol, and Harry, taking his cue, did not offer his hand. "How are you?"

"He'd feel a lot better with 'is trousers on, dear," said Mae. Clara blushed. "Oh, I'm sorry."

"I don't suppose," Mae persisted, "you ever seen a gentleman wiv 'is trousers orf, a proper-brought-up young lady like you?"

"No, I haven't, actually," Clara said, "but I expect you have."

There was a roar of male laughter in the tent, rapidly stilled

58

as Mae glared around at them all. "Yerce, that's true," she allowed, "an' I've seen a lot more than that, dear, an' let me tell you, it ain't all your imagination expects it to be, dear!"

There was another laugh from the men.

"I'll just have to wait and see, won't I?" Clara said.

Harry Viner had to admire her. She gave as good as she got.

"Not be long before you do," said Mae, "I shouldn't be surprised, dear."

"Well," said Clara, "I hope not."

The male laughter was very loud at this. Harry took the opportunity to pull on his trousers, turning his back to Clara.

"There you are, you see, dear," said Mae. "You've scared the living daylights out of him already!"

Clara smiled tolerantly. Tucking in his shirt, Harry turned around to find her eyes frankly on him. He buttoned up his front fly buttons, and said, "You shouldn't be here, miss; it ain't the place for you."

"I'm not shocked." And she didn't, Harry had to admit, look as if she were.

"Just the same, I'm sure your father—"

"Oh, Papa's enjoying himself, why shouldn't I?"

Harry nodded, slowly. He had forgotten. She was stagestruck. He sighed. They often were. Ah, well.

"Is there a glass of champagne?" Clara was asking.

"Only beer. We was promised champers, but it never come," said Mae bitterly. "As usual."

"Oh?" said Clara. "Then I'll have beer."

"You will not," said Harry. "We can't have a lady drinking beer."

"What about those girls?" Clara pointed to the twins sitting in their leotards and holding hands.

"Them ain't ladies," said Harry patiently. "Them's artistes. They'll drink anything, won't you, girls?"

The twins tittered and gazed at Clara's dress admiringly.

Papa entered the tent at that moment.

He was rather drunk or, as he would himself have put it, two sheets away. His boiled shirt was limp now, the sweat having taken the starch out of it, and his collar (the third he had put on since the wedding party began) was a soiled rag at his neck. He had drunk a pint of hock, a pint of claret and four large balloons of brandy. His third Havana cigar was in his hand, and today he

59

had married off his only son. Papa felt kindly disposed toward the world.

Nonetheless, he was surprised to see Clara there.

"Ah, me dear?"

"I'm congratulating the artistes, Papa."

"Excellent. They have done us proud, what?" Papa took a purse from his pocket. "A small consideration for your services. There's a sovereign there for each of you. And my thanks. You can leave at once if you like. The horse bus is at the door."

"But, Papa," protested Clara, "aren't the ladies and gentlemen being asked to the party?"

Her father stared at her as if she had gone mad. "Of course they ain't, nor would they expect it!" He stared blearily around the gathering, as if for help. "Would you?"

Nobody said anything.

"There you are!" Papa looked annoyed. "Now don't let me hear you talk such nonsense again."

"They were promised champagne," Clara said. "And they never got any."

"Who promised them champagne?" Her father looked around the tent. "Who promised you champagne? I didn't."

Nobody replied. Little Tich began to fold his stage garments into his prop basket. Mr. Lashwood removed his topper with a sigh. Nobody seemed surprised.

"Never heard such rubbish," said Edward Abbott, now in a thoroughly bad temper. At the tent door flap he looked back. "I think you should join the ladies, miss!"

And he was gone.

"You tried," Harry Viner said.

"Well done, miss," said the twins.

Clara Abbott had tears in her eyes. Quite blue, they were, Harry Viner thought, like the sky itself.

"Don't take it to heart, Clara!"

Before he could say more, she was gone out of the tent.

"Well," said Mae, "she's a little goer, I give her that."

The others murmured agreement.

"How you come to know *her*, Harry?" asked Mae.

Harry didn't reply.

They packed their bags in silence and carried them out with them, around the back of the house and out to the street, through the tradesmen's entrance.

"In and out the bloody tradesmen's entrance," commented Mae bitterly, "a bleedin' sovereign and bloody beer to drink!"

"No," said a clear young voice, "champers for everybody!"

Harry Viner stared. So did they all.

Sitting on top of the horse omnibus was Clara Abbott. Around her feet were several crates labeled "Moët et Chandon." She zipped open her parasol, and her ankles dangling carelessly, in full and scandalous view, she cried, "Come on everyone, *do*, let's get away!"

"Where to?" echoed Harry Viner.

"Anywhere you like. I've got champagne and a hamper of food. Anywhere you like!"

The artistes climbed onto the omnibus, and the jarvey cracked his whip. It made good speed down the crescent. Several people stopped and stared at the scene. Harry Viner thought he heard a loud, hoarse shout from behind them, but he did not look back.

Clara took his hand. She balanced precariously on the front rail of the horse bus.

"Don't let me fall!"

"Don't worry. I won't!"

"Well, what do you know, how's that for nerve, the cheeky little tart!" breathed Mae admiringly.

They all agreed, with enormous approval, that she indeed was a cheeky little tart.

Clara laughed.

Papa stood on the lawn and looked around him, well satisfied. The wedding party was a success, that was certain. The bride was well liked locally, a fine girl, a fine girl, Marta.

Papa accepted a glass of champagne from a passing maidservant and sipped it thoughtfully. His son, Adam, was to follow him in running the Alhambra, and—who knew?—he might, with his superior education (he had, after all, been to the university, which Papa had not), be able to move the family fortunes forward, not necessarily financially (he had done that himself) so much as artistically.

It would be nice to run a business one could be proud of, in itself. Legitimate theater would be nice. Actors, some of them knighted by the monarch, that would be something a man could be proud of, such people appearing in his theater. Real *plays*, not the sketches that were becoming popular in music hall. Even the great Bernhardt was not above an appearance like that, although Papa had heard that her price was very high indeed. Real plays, titled actors—ladies and gentemen—people one could be proud to know. Unlike the bohemian lot in the changing tent. Papa puffed on his cigar. The business simply wasn't respectable in the eyes of decent people. A man had to apologize for it. And that could not be right.

Why on earth, his wife had asked him, did you ever go into it in the first place?

Papa brooded. Why? He had almost forgotten his answer. It came back to him, swaying a little, on the lawn, cigar and champagne in hand. "For adventure, me dear. For adventure!"

He looked around for Clara. She was not to be seen.

"What happened to the girl?" he asked. There was no sign of her.

The stage of the Alhambra Music Hall made a very good place for a party.

Harry Viner stood in something of a daze, looking at it.

The entire bill of the Alhambra was performing. With a proviso. They were all doing, in turn, the act they would *like* to do if only the audience and the managers would let them!

Little Tich's perfect act had been to stand facing the blackened auditorium for two whole minutes, then to turn around, bend down and fart very loudly. Then to bow in a dignified fashion and walk off.

Everybody had loved that.

George Lashwood had sung a very rude song indeed to the air of "Twi-Twi-light"!

Everybody had loved that.

The conjuror had—purposely—got all his tricks wrong. Pigeons appeared from his front fly buttons; rabbits worked their way down his trousers; white rats appeared to bite him savagely on the backside.

Everybody loved that, too.

Harry Viner told a long list of extremely blue stories. He quite forgot that Clara was there.

She had laughed.

And everybody else had laughed in relief. Because she was, after all, the owner's daughter and plainly a lady. She was extremely popular with everybody and, for her own part, sang an Ella Shields song, "Burlington Bertie From Bow," in a pleasant, clear voice.

> I'm Burlington Bertie, I rise at ten-thirty,
> And saunter along like a toff.
> I stroll down the Strand with my gloves in my hand
> And I stroll back again with them off.

"Not bad," George Lashwood said. "Not dirty, but not bad."

"I'm sorry," said Clara. "My education has been neglected. I don't know any dirty songs."

"Harry," said George Lashwood, with a heavy wink, "will teach you. In fact, he'll teach you a great many things."

Harry was glad when everybody stopped laughing and started to eat and drink the rest of the food and wine. This girl, dancing around, talking to the cast, was bemusing him. Get hold of yourself, Harry Viner, he said, you're behaving like a double-barreled berk! She's only a fresh little tart—be sensible, do!

The acrobat twins were doing pratfalls and cartwheels, removing items of clothing as they did so. They were both very drunk and had taken off all their outer clothing, cotton dress, high boots and corsets. They were now down to their shifts and their hats.

"It's a good job the stage manager's at the weddin'," Harry told Mae.

"If he'd been here, what would he have done?" she asked. "Thrown the boss's daughter out on her ear?"

"That's true." Harry drank some more of his champagne. "The way she told that old stage doorkeeper off, blimey! She soon showed him who was boss, silly old codger."

The old stage doorkeeper, reading his newspaper in his cubbyhole, had been the only person in the theater. He knew Miss Clara well enough. When she had demanded he admit the company and put on the houselights, he had demurred, saying such a thing was outside his duty. So Clara had said, "Show me where they are, and I'll switch them on myself!"

And he had. And she had.

Harry said, "I haven't enjoyed meself so much in a long time."

"No," said Mae, "I can see that. She's after you, you know that, don'tcher? She done everythink bar take orf her drawers since she saw you."

Harry nodded mildly. "She's seen me before, Mae."

"When?"

"We had supper the other night."

"Oh, I see."

"I don't think you do, Mae."

"Ah, well." Mae sighed and munched on a leg of cold chicken. "You can roger her and get it over with, can't you? I don't mind, Harry."

"Mae," said Harry, "please shut your dirty mouth, will you?"

"Sorry I spoke, duck," said Mae, but she smiled. "Didden know you was such a gentleman where the ladies were concerned."

Harry walked away. He could not trust himself to reply.

Clara stood next to him.

"When you go home," said Harry soberly, "you are going to get a right royal reception, I don't think."

Clara looked rueful. "Yes, I am, so I'm just going to have to make sure it's been worth it, aren't I?"

Harry said, "I meant to write and thank you about that song."

"It's all right. I understand."

Harry shook his head. This girl had disobeyed her father, and she didn't care. She didn't feel that anything terrible could happen to her. Her eyes shone as she watched the girls tumbling on the stage (they were down to their drawers now), and she was obviously enjoying herself. She's slumming, Harry thought suddenly, that's what it is! A wave of anger coursed through him. He knew that some highborn ladies went down to Stepney in their carriages simply to look at the poor. He'd seen them himself. And he'd heard stories of highborn women who took dockers and suchlike to their beds. He looked sidewise at Clara. Was she one of those, because if she *was*. . . .

"Are they going to take everything off?" Clara asked.

"Oh, yes, I should think so," Harry said. "They're drunk, that's all."

The girls stepped out of their drawers, revealing tiny blond bushes and pirouetted around the stage, fingers on chins, thrusting out their buttocks to the beat of the music.

Everybody roared with laughter.

"Is it always like this at a stage party?"

Harry shook his head. "No, they'll be talking about this one for years."

Clara looked pleased. "Will they, will they really?"

64

"Well, of course they will. It's not every day a crowd of troupers get chicken and champagne!"

"No, I suppose not."

"You suppose right, darlin'." Harry ate his last prawn with relish.

"Please don't call me darling, unless you mean it."

Harry thought: this is no place to tell her anything, what with Mae's big eyes across the other side of the stage and the twins dancing around, silly cows, showing everything they've got, but he found himself saying the words just the same.

"I do mean it. The thing is, what can I do about it?"

Clara reached up and kissed him on the lips.

He was so surprised he didn't move.

"Hey! Not here, in front of everybody!"

"Why not? Those girls are naked!"

"I know, but that's just a joke!"

Clara laughed, but Harry could not see why. What he could see was Mae's face across the stage, her eyes fixed burningly on Clara. Women, Harry Viner thought, not for the first time, are all rivals one of another, and there's no changing that.

He did not kiss Clara back.

"Do leave off, dear," he said. "There's a time and a place for everything."

"Where's the time and place?"

"I dunno," said Harry uncomfortably. "We got to think about that, don't we?"

The twins hovered up, their little bare bottoms jigging up and down to the music being played on the pit piano by the conjuror. Harry looked at them in a detached way.

"Very nice, gels," he said. "Very tasty indeed."

Yesterday he'd have been thinking about getting them both into the same bed, he thought, and certain signals he'd had from them had made him believe this was not an outside possibility.

One of the twins said, as if on cue, "See you tonight, Harry?"

"Shouldn't wonder," said Harry, "but I'm not sure I'd have the strength, darlin'."

The twins twinkled away, finished their act, bowed to the black and empty auditorium and collapsed onto a property basket. The seal trainer gave them a blanket and a glass of champagne each and stood admiring their white and reclining forms. Mae called to him, "Here, mate, put your eyes back in, we're *on!*"

65

The seal trainer, who was now very drunk, went into his act with his favorite seal ("He loves that bloody seal a lot more than he loves me, I tell yer," Mae had reported to Harry) and succeeded in balancing a large ball on its nose only once in several attempts.

Mae called to him, "You've forgotten his bleedin' fish, you silly berk!"

"He'll do it for me," said the seal trainer, hurt, "without getting his fish."

"He wouldn't do it for Jesus Christ without getting his fish!" declared Mae.

She was right.

The seal sat down, center stage, profoundly disinterested, and barked in a melancholy way.

The seal trainer cajoled and pleaded and finally kicked the seal. The seal did not move, but sat with dignity, waiting to be fed his tidbit for work done.

"He'll do it for me because he loves me!" shouted the drunken seal trainer.

"He will hellaslike!" said Mae.

The seal trainer sat down on the stage and wept.

"I'll have a job," Mae told the company, "to get him sober for the first house."

The words acted like a chill on the entire company.

Harry brought out his cheap steel watch.

"It's ten to five," he said. "We're on in an hour."

He turned and smiled at Clara.

"It's been prime, darlin'—I mean Clara. But we have to work. The doormen will be here any minute, and we have to clear the stage an' that." He hesitated, then: "I expect your father will be down here, an' all, later on?"

"Yes," said Clara, not taking her eyes from his. "He will be. He never misses a house."

"No," said Harry. "And somebody's bound to tell him about this party."

"I wish I was in the show."

"No, you don't!"

She stared at him. Those blue eyes. "Yes, I do. It's what I've always wanted, Harry."

"But . . . with your education. . . ."

"It's what I want."

"What does your father say?"

"He doesn't know."

"Look, Clara." Harry made his voice gentle. "It's no life. You'd hate it. After the first week, you'd be crying for your mother."

"I haven't got a mother."

"No, but you know what I mean."

"I'm not just talking. I want to go on the halls."

"You're just stagestruck—"

"I'm not. I mean it, Harry."

"You can't mean it, you don't know what it's about! It's about starving, and being without, and thinking you'd do anything for a hot meal—"

"Why? Have you starved?"

Her voice was quick with sympathy, but Harry said harshly, "Look, *dear*, I don't want no pity. I took this game on because I didden know any better and I hadn't any other job." He sighed and lowered his voice. "I can stand this life because I'm used to it; even with all its faults it's a better life than I've ever had before. You'd hate it, you'd run home in a week."

"I wouldn't."

"I think you would."

"Try me."

Harry was alarmed. "Try you? How do you mean, try you?"

"Let me go on with you tonight."

Harry Viner looked at her with round eyes. "You're the second offer I've had today."

"Am I? Who else, that old Mae lady?"

"She's not old!" Harry laughed.

"She's forty!"

"Yes, well, don't let her hear you say she's old!"

Harry laughed again.

Mae, moving property baskets, called across the stage. "What's the joke?"

"This young lady was saying you only looked sixteen, Mae!"

"Wish I was," said Mae. "I'd be a rich man's darlin'."

"Don't say you didden try," Harry called.

"Nah. I married for love." She regarded the weeping seal trainer, who was now in the middle of an alcoholic crying jag, his arms around the disinterested seal. "Would you believe it?"

"I'd believe anything," Harry Viner said.

Clara whispered, "Let me try the act, just let me walk on, carrying something, let me be a sort of decoration. You need something like that in your act, Harry, honestly!"

"You're mad!"

"No, I'm not!"

Two of them had said the same thing. Harry Viner brooded. Of course, they both wanted him. But surely they couldn't both be wrong about the act? Yes, they bloody well could!

"No chance," he said. "But come back to the dressing room, and we'll think of some excuse about the party to tell your father when he turns up!"

Clara sat in Harry Viner's dressing room and listened to the Alhambra come to life. First, the doormen and cleaners arrived, calling cheerfully to each other, and the backstage staff, the sceneshifters and the lighting men, and then the orchestra, which seemed to make a lot of noise knocking over music stands and tuning up instruments. The twins were in the next dressing room, sobering up. Their cries of hysterical laughter percolated through the wall.

"Will they be all right?" Clara was sipping the last of the champagne. She felt very tipsy and very happy. She had never felt so happy in her life.

"They'll have come round by the time they get onstage." Harry was changing into his stage clothes. He went behind his screen to put on his trousers.

Clara laughed. "You're very shy."

Harry popped his head over the screen. "Got to be with you, don't I?"

He came around and sat at his dressing table. He smeared on his base and put on his eye shadow. He worked at it very intently. Clara watched with fascination.

"Can I make up my face?" she asked.

Harry looked at her through the mirror. "Why?"

"Well, just to try it?"

"Can't see the point."

"Just I'd learn how, wouldn't I?"

"I dunno." Harry shook his head. "You'd have it all to wipe off afterwards."

"I wouldn't mind."

Harry sighed and made room for her at the dressing table.

He tapped each item as he talked. "There's your base, your number nine beige. Your number nine yellow. On top of that you put eye shadow, using this grease stick, like so! You can have blue or green. In your case, blue. There, like that. You put carmine on your lips, like that. And you use the block of mascara for your eyelashes—just wet it a bit, see?—and the stick of mascara for the edges of the eyes, makes 'em bigger."

Harry was working away at her face as he talked.

"And you use the hare's foot as a makeup brush. It's as soft as Lillie Langtry's bottom, this is."

"I think it was terrible about the King and Miss Langtry."

"You know what the paper put in about them? Well, the first week they put, 'There is nothing between the Prince and Miss Lillie Langtry'—he was Prince of Wales then, see? And the second week they put, 'Not even a sheet.' "

"Oh, how terrible for her!"

"No, everybody just laughed."

"I'll bet his wife didn't laugh."

"Look, darlin'," Harry said, brushing her hair back with his fingers, "if you marry a fella that likes a bit of skirt, it's no good complaining about it later on, is it?"

"But how do you know?" Clara asked, a little depressed by the idea.

"You use your eyes, don'tcher?" Harry dusted her face with the hare foot. It was wonderfully soft. "If a fella runs around with the women before he's married, he's a-gonna do it after, it stands to reason, don't it?"

"Does it?" Clara asked. "Always?"

"Who knows about always?" Harry said. "All I know, darlin'— I mean Clara—is leopards don't change their spots, an' if you marry a leopard, you marry a leopard."

"But if they love each other?"

"It might make a difference for a bit," Harry allowed. "But forever? How could it? I reckon he loves his old missus in his way, but he's one for the women. No changing that, is there?"

"Isn't there?"

Clara had to know.

"Course there isn't. It's his nature. A lot of women get upset by that in a man, but that's stupid, because it's what he is."

"What," Clara asked, "if a woman's like that?"

"Women ain't, are they?" said Harry, standing back and admir-

69

ing his handiwork. "Women love one fella, usually for life, or anyway for a long time. Chopping and changing ain't their line. They like a bit of security, women do."

"Harry," said Clara, "are you one for the women?"

The music struck up in the theater. The twins ran out of the next dressing room, screaming at each other. Harry listened. "They're all right. They've sobered up."

He turned her head toward the mirror.

"There you are. What about that?"

Clara looked at her image in the mirror. She could hardly believe what she saw. This was not the Clara Abbott of Miss Wilson's Academy for Young Ladies, prim and proper with her hair up, under a large hat, and her face daringly whitened with rice powder—until Miss Wilson had seen and forbidden it, threatening her with a report to Papa. No, this was a quite different girl, with large blue eyes in a face of mat yellow, with thick black eyelashes coated in grease and stripes of black running along the eyelids, the lips large and red and strident.

Clara was shocked. It was the face of a whore.

"I look—"

"Like a street girl?"

"Well, yes."

"Of course you do. That's the way you have to look or your face is just a white blob from up in the gallery or the back of the stalls. You have to let them know you're a woman, see?"

Clara saw.

"Disappointed, are you?"

"No. Not really."

But she was. This face was a caricature of the things she wanted to be.

"It's like a painting in an art gallery." Harry listened for the closing music of the twin acrobats. "You mustn't get too close to it, like, or it don't make sense." He put his derby hat on his head and patted it. He was on next, and nothing, Clara thought, had really been discussed about her appearing with him. By not talking about it, she thought, he was saying no. It was his way of being kind. He really liked her, though; he had said that, hadn't he?

"Is this all?" she asked.

"How do you mean, all?"

"Well, do you intend to go away tomorrow night and never see me again?"

"Clara," Harry said, "what else can I do?" He sat and took her hand in his, but his head was cocked as he listened for his music. "I have nothing, I can't offer you nothing. Your father wouldn't have it anyway, and he'd be right. I saw your house today, remember. I saw the way you live. You'd never be any good with such as me. You wouldn't understand me, and I wouldn't understand you." He patted her hand. "All it is, you're stagestruck, and you think I'm the answer. It's very nice, and I'm very flattered, really I am, but it's no good. We're miles apart; the kind of lives we've led, it couldn't work out."

Clara stared at him, crushed.

"I wouldn't want you to marry me or anything."

Harry Viner laughed. "Darlin', I can't keep myself, never mind a wife an' kids."

"I don't want children."

"How would you stop them coming?"

"There are ways."

"What do you know about that, a girl like you?" Harry Viner looked scandalized. Clara took heart at that.

"Take me with you, Harry!"

Harry Viner looked more scandalized than ever. "Take you where? I been just this minute telling you I ain't got anywhere to go myself when I finish at Glasgow next week. Mae even offered me to go and stay with her."

Clara said, "I love you, Harry."

"God Blimey Old Riley!" said Harry. "If there's anything I can do without, it's somebody loving me!"

"But don't you like me at all?"

Tears were starting to Clara's eyes now.

Harry dabbed them with a cloth from the dressing table. "Don't! The mascara will run all over your face. Don't cry till you've got your makeup off. Even if your favorite aunt just died."

"You haven't said if you love me!"

"You know I like you." He patted her hand again, but he did not hold it, as he had before. She felt stricken. "But I can't do nothing about it." His voice brightened, as if were talking to a child. "But I'll tell you what. If I make a few quid, I'll come back North and look you up. You never know, if I get famous like Mr. Lashwood, maybe your father would think about me. Now, how's that?"

"It's all right," said Clara, "but you don't mean it."

"I do, straight," said Harry Viner.

"No," said Clara, "you don't. You're only saying that to make me feel better." There was a silence, broken only by the faint strains of the music.

When Harry spoke, his voice was bleak.

"Yes. That's right. There's no hope for us. You know it, and I know it. What you have to do is go round to his office now and make peace with your father before he discovers you're down here with me and comes in and sacks me on the spot." He sighed. "That's all I need."

Clara said, "You haven't kissed me yet."

Harry Viner stepped toward the door sharply. "No, and I ain't a-going to."

Clara stood up. "Why not?"

Harry grinned. "Because it would spoil my makeup." He opened the door, and the music quickened and came loudly into the dressing room. "Wipe that stuff off your face, and go and make your excuses to your father." He paused. "Don't be here when I come back. Give me a chance."

Then he was gone.

Clara sat, numb. Was this the end of it? Was it right, what he said, it was all a sickness for the stage, for something she was totally unsuited for, by birth and upbringing? Clara doubted that, fiercely. Yet . . . should she go and apologize to Papa, plead female weakness, a misplaced kindness of heart? If she did, she was tolerably certain of a pardon. Papa might even be proud of her later, mention it in passing to his friends. He would need some story for them, and a woman's weakness and sympathy for the lot of the traveling players, however misplaced and misguided, would be acceptable, if only just.

Clara got to her feet. She might as well go around to her father's little cubbyhole office and get it over with.

Her whorish reflection blinked back at her in the mirror.

Harry's music stopped. She could hear his voice. He was telling one of his Abie stories.

Something would have to be done about those.

Something would have to be *done!*

Clara stepped quickly out of the dressing room. She went into the twins' dressing room without knocking and found them in each other's arms on a settee. She was not shocked. It all seemed

72

in keeping with the other events of the day.

"Can I borrow a leotard?" she asked.

Two minutes later she stood at the side of the stage.

The stage manager, a bald, fussy man in shirt sleeves, wearing pince-nez, stared at her, then at his numbers sheet. "Who are you, dear?"

"Mr. MacGivenney, I'm Clara Abbott."

"Who?"

Mr. MacGivenney looked as if he might be going mad.

"It's all right," said Clara. "I'm going on now."

"You're bloody not, young woman!" shouted Mr. MacGivenney, but too late. She had avoided his clutching hand, and there she was, Clara Abbott, in full view of a music hall audience for the first time, unseen by Harry Viner, who was coming to the end of his Abie jokes, thank goodness.

Mr. MacGivenney would have torn his hair if he had any. He hissed, "Come off or I'll bring down the curtain!"

"No, you won't." Clara smiled. "Don't you dare!"

Mr. MacGivenney asked anybody who might know, like God, whether her father knew about this. Nobody was able to tell him, and he stayed his signal to the men to lower the curtain. "Surely to Jesus the boss can't know about this, can he?" he asked plaintively.

The stagehands didn't reply. They were too busy watching Clara.

"Nice pair of legs," said one professionally, through his toothpick. Nobody was allowed to smoke backstage, and unless you chewed tobacco, it could be hard. A toothpick helped. "As good as Marie Lloyd's any day!"

Clara, with all the confidence oozing out of her, stood onstage and tried to smile up at the gallery. She was blinded. She had not expected anything so bright; it was like a thousand suns. And the smoke from the men drawing on cigars and pipes out there in the auditorium floated in pure blue streams before the blaze of the footlights. And the noise, she had not expected the *noise!* The audience was humming and shuffling, like some dark, unseen monster, a low, subterranean growl like that of some starving, possibly dangerous animal.

Clara did not know what to do next. So she curtsied and staggered and almost fell over.

The audience laughed in the wrong place, and Harry Viner turned. For what seemed a hundred years he stared at her, as she staggered to her feet from the curtsy.

"You silly cow, what d'yer think yer doin'?" His whisper was low but distinct.

Clara was paralyzed. She could not answer.

The lights and the *noise*. It was all too much.

Harry bowed to her and then to the audience, ironically.

"Just stand there and smile," he hissed to Clara.

To the audience, he said, "You see how the women chase me, don'tcher, ladies and gents? It ain't for me brains, and it certainly ain't for me good looks, is it? I think it must be for the size of me. . . ." He waited for the inevitable female cackle. "You got it, lady, the size of me *wallet*, yes!"

Clara kept smiling.

"This is me little sister, though, not me dolly." Harry Viner was ad-libbing madly. "She likes to give it away, only nobody wants it. Well, she can't help it, can she, it's how yer made, innit?"

From the corner of his mouth, he hissed, "Can you sing 'Polly Perkins'?"

"Yes," shouted Clara far too loud.

The audience laughed.

"Sometimes she says yes," said Harry, "and that's worse than when she says no, know what I mean? Well, them that's been married for twenty-five years will know. The others just have to wait." He leaned over to the orchestra pit and said, in a stage voice to the musical director, who was searching frenziedly through his music for whatever it was he thought he had missed. "Maestro, can we have 'Polly Perkins,' and if we can't, we'll have her sister!"

Even the musical director laughed at that—mostly, Clara thought, with relief. He mopped his brow, stopped looking for his lost score sheet, whispered to his musicians, then rapped his music stand.

At that moment Clara saw her father standing next to Mr. MacGivenney, the stage manager. Mr. MacGivenney was talking, waving his hands, but Papa was unmoving, and his eyes were fixed on his daughter. A cold cigar was clamped in his mouth.

Clara looked steadily in front of her and kept the fixed smile on her face.

The music to "Polly Perkins" started.

74

Harry Viner stepped back, took her arm. He whispered, "Just open and close your mouth, that'll do!"

"I'll *sing!*"

"Oh, Christ!"

"And we can dance a bit?"

"No, we can't! Just sway back and forward, see? Just join in the chorus, nothing else!"

The music was all right because the pit musicians at the Alhambra could play "Polly Perkins" without music sheets.

Harry Viner began:

I'm a broken-hearted milkman, in grief I'm arrayed,
Through a-keeping of the company of a young servant maid,
Who lived on board wages, the house to keep clean,
In a gentleman's family near Paddington Green. . . .

The audience (and Clara) sang:

Oh, she was as beautiful as a butterfly
And as proud as a Queen,
Was pretty little Polly Perkins
Of Paddington Green!

Harry Viner squeezed her arm. Clara felt a sudden rush of love and confidence. Before he could begin, she sang alone:

Oh, my eyes were as black as the pips of a pear,
No rose in the garden with me could compare.
My hair hung in ring-a-lets, so beautiful and long
He thought I loved him,
But he found he was wrong!

Harry came in, laughing with relief:

Oh, in six months she married, this hard-headed girl,
But it was not a Vi-count and it was not an Earl.
It was not a Baronet, so don't make a fuss,
'Twas a bow-legged conductor of a Tuppeny Bus!

To a fair round of applause he dragged her off.

Clara was in a daze.

Harry had to pull her back to take a second curtain call.

Then her father stood before them, the cigar still cold in his mouth.

"My office," he said, "both of you, *now!*"

And he strode away, past the backstage workmen, who averted their eyes.

"Sorry, Miss Clara," said Mr. MacGivenney, who would speak often of this night. "But I had to tell him."

Clara nodded. She felt much more intoxicated than when she had drunk the champagne at the stage party. I do not care, she told herself, what happens now. I simply do not care!

Harry Viner stood, breathing hard. "What did you do *that* for?"

"Because it was the only way I could show you how I feel."

"No," said Harry. "It was done for you, not for me, that was!"

And he strode off in front of her toward her father's office.

Papa stood, the unlit cigar now in his hand. His frown was permanent, and he dealt with Harry Viner fast, as he had been dealing with recalcitrant performers, difficult or drunk, most of his life.

"Viner, you have behaved very badly in encouraging my daughter in her foolishness, but I accept, before you speak, that you did not know she would come onstage tonight. If I thought you had, I would make it my business to see that you never worked in any music hall where I had any influence—and I can assure you I have influence with many!—but in view of your obvious surprise at seeing my daughter there at all, I am simply dismissing you now, tonight, with a week's wages. I would not go on to Glasgow if I were you. I shall be writing to them, and I fear they will not want to employ you either. There are your week's wages. You may leave my theater at once."

"Thank you very much, Mr. Abbott," said Harry Viner in a low voice. But he did not leave the office.

"Papa," cried Clara, "none of this is Mr. Viner's doing!"

"I know that," said Papa, "or I would not be lenient with him, as I have been."

"Mr. Abbott," said Harry Viner, "let me explain."

"You cannot explain, sir," said Papa in a voice of thunder. It was plain to Clara that he was only just holding onto his temper. He was not looking at Clara at all, as if the sight of her offended him. "All you can do is make things worse for my daughter! Now, go, sir!"

Harry Viner looked at Papa for a long moment.

Then at Clara.

Then he picked up his four gold sovereigns.

"Sorry," he said to Clara, and left.

76

Clara felt cold. He hadn't even fought. He hadn't even spoken up. He hadn't told Papa he loved her.

He had done nothing.

Papa said, "You look like a slut, girl, a street woman! Wipe that muck from your face!" He curtly offered her his handkerchief.

She shook her head. Tears started to her eyes.

Papa looked slightly less irate at that.

He took the cold cigar out of his mouth and said, "I'm relieved anyway, young lady, that you show some shame. You run away from your dear brother's wedding reception—I had a deal of trouble explaining *that!*—and I understand you gave these people food and drink.

"Yes, I did."

"Why?"

"Because it had been promised to them, Papa."

"By whom?"

"I don't know, probably Mr. MacGivenney suggested it could happen and they took it for gospel."

Papa had his handkerchief still in his hand, and he blew his nose. He seemed to be wrestling with his temper even more. "But why," he asked in a strangled voice, "did you go on stage and disport yourself like a trollop?"

Clara said nothing.

Papa said, "The only hope is that nobody recognized you. I will see there is no gossip. I will make it my business."

"Are all women you employ trollops, Papa?"

Papa stared at her, his mouth open.

"Are they? All your artistes?"

"Some of my artistes are very respectable people. You know that!"

"Then why do you call me a trollop?"

Papa lost his temper. "Because you look like a trollop, miss! Those other people, my real artistes, have talent, miss! You have not!"

"Then you do not object to my looking like a trollop, but to my lack of talent, Papa?"

"No, I do not! You are my daughter, and I object to you being on any stage anywhere at all. I object to your association with this man Harry Viner, who is a licentious and unsuccessful artiste to boot!"

"I see," said Clara. "If he were successful and virtuous, that would make it better?"

"Nothing would make it better," said Papa. He sat down and wiped his brow. The hock and the claret and the oysters and the ham and beef and ripe Stilton and the brandy and the excitement were all too much, too much. He shouted, "You will go to your aunt's at Whitby tomorrow. You will not see this man Viner again. You will apologize to your sister-in-law by letter, and to your brother, for the intolerable bad manners of not seeing them away on their honeymoon. And you will give me your word, miss, here and now, that you will never step on a stage again."

There was a long silence, during which Papa got to his feet again.

Clara said, "I am sorry, Papa, but I cannot, nay will not, give you that promise."

"What part do you object to, miss?"

"I am determined to go on the stage. And I mean to see Mr. Viner again, Papa. I'm sorry."

For the first time in his life Papa struck her. His hand came up and hit her, open-palmed, across the cheek. Clara staggered back, but she did not cry out. She just stood there, staring at him, as her cheek burned and her eyes smarted with shame and tears.

Papa lowered his eyes. "Get out, girl! Go and get that stuff off your face. I will have my carriage at the door for you in ten minutes."

Clara said nothing. She left the room quietly.

As she did so, she heard Papa say, "Blast and bugger it all!" in a low voice, utterly unlike his usual one.

Clara went back to the dressing room and changed into her street clothes. She had thrown them into a wicker case when she left the wedding reception. Had she known it would come to this? Perhaps she had. She walked straight out of the Alhambra and took a horsecab to the Central railway station. She inquired about trains at the booking office, and the clerk, who took her for a street girl (she had not cleaned off her makeup) spoke harshly and offhandedly to her. He told her there was an express train to London that evening. It was the famous Flying Scotsman, and it would be at the station in one hour. Clara bought a single ticket to London.

It left her with one pound, nine shillings. Clara had money in her bank account, but Papa could block that, and she knew

78

he would. She sat on the platform and waited for the train.

The signals had clacked for the train's arrival when Harry Viner came onto the platform. Her heart jumped as she saw him, so handsome in his check street suit and rakish derby hat. He carried a wicker basket, and he looked despondent. Behind him came Mae, and Clara turned away quickly, but too late.

Harry strode toward her.

"What are you doing here?"

Clara said, "I'm going to London."

"Not with me you ain't!"

"I know that. I'm going anyway."

Mae's eyes were round with sympathy. "Your pa threw you out then?"

"No, he hit me, though. I'm just going."

"He hit you?" Harry Viner said through his teeth. "The big berk!"

"No, I'm all right." Clara looked away.

"You got no luggage, nothing, dear?" Mae looked quickly at Harry, who shrugged. She added, "I'm only seeing Harry off, dear, that's all."

"I'll be all right," Clara said.

"And you'll have to get that makeup off, duck; none of us goes out in the street made up," said Mae. As Clara looked at her, "Well, you are one of us now, ain'tcher?"

"Yes," said Clara, "I suppose I am."

"Well then," said Mae, comfortable and buxom in her woolen coat with the sealskin hat and collar. "You don't know where you'll be living, do you, Harry?"

Harry Viner said: "You said I could stop at your place."

"I don't think so, considering," said Mae. "Do you? I mean I'm only seeing you orf, ain't I? I won't be seein' you again, will I?"

Harry Viner looked at Mae a long moment.

"No," he said. "No, I reckon not."

The train came into the station in a roar of steam and noise. Harry Viner lifted his wicker basket. "I don't suppose," he said to Clara, "it's any good tellin' you to go home?"

"None at all."

The train stopped, and Harry Viner jumped aboard quickly. He found an empty compartment, and Mae helped Clara lift Harry's basket aboard, waving away a porter. Normally Clara would have engaged a porter and tipped him for the assistance. She felt better, not doing so.

"Come on," Harry Viner said through the window, "if you're coming!"

"She's coming," said Mae, "aren't yer, duck?"

"Yes," said Clara.

Mae put a purse in her hand.

"No, really—" Clara protested.

"Yes, *really*, dear. You'll starve else. He has four quid in the world. I was going to give this to him anyway. But don't say it's from me. Say it's yours, all right, dear?"

"But *why?*"

Clara stood in a cloud of steam and stared at Mae.

"It's you he wants, dear, not me. Even I can see that."

"But I can't take this!"

"Yes, you can. Pay me back sometime. Or give it to somebody else that needs it, when you've got it someday."

"I will! Oh, I will! Thank you! Oh, thank you!"

"Get on now, the train's going."

Clara embraced Mae and climbed onto the train. She waved to Mae as the train moved out of the station. Then she sat down beside Harry Viner. He had lit a cigar and put his feet on the seat opposite. His derby hat was on the back of his head. He put his arm around Clara's shoulders.

"Well, you done it now, ain'tcher, gel?"

"Yes," said Clara, "yes, I have, haven't I?"

The Flying Scotsman roared into the dark night, and Clara Abbott sat there, in very heaven.

If It Wasn't for the Houses
in Between

Gus Elen walked out onto the stage of the Bedford Music Hall, Camden Town, in his coster's cap and weskit. He gazed at the audience aggressively and, without preamble, sang:

> It's a great big shame and if she belonged to me
> I'd let her know who's who!
> Nagging at a fella what is six-foot-three
> An' her only four-foot-two!

Clara sat in the stalls, thrilled. Their seat was not a very good one (she had to crane to see around a pillar), but Harry had got them in on the nod of the head, so they couldn't grumble. He sat next to her, in his splendid street suit, and he smoked a good cigar, which she had insisted on buying for him. At the interval he had gone alone to the bar, without asking her, and had returned smelling pleasantly of whiskey.

Gus Elen, a tall, incredibly thin man, in a barred jersey and a cap, sang with enormous sincerity:

> They ain't been married not a month nor more
> When underneath her thumb goes Jim!
> Oh! Isn't it a pity as the likes of her
> Should put upon the likes of him?

The audience joined in, loudly. Clara looked about her, for the hundredth time. Here she was, in London, sitting in a music hall next to the man she loved. She pushed away the thought of Papa, sitting reading the letter she had written him. She wondered if he would understand.

> Dear Papa [she had written],
> I know I have been a great disappointment to you, and for that I am truly sorry. But, Papa, I must lead my own life, and I know what I want to do with it. Please do not have me looked for, or followed, or anything like that, because I am a woman now, and I must do as I must do. I will hope someday to make you proud of me, and if you wish, you may write to me Poste Restante, at Camden Town Post Office, London. Please do not worry about me, I will be all right. I am well and have money.
> Your loving daughter, Clara

Clara hoped Papa would write back and forgive her. She hoped he would, but she thought: I shall not die if he does not. She looked at Harry possessively and proudly and thought: what if Miss Wilson of Miss Wilson's Academy for Young Ladies could see me now, sitting in a music hall with a man that I shall sleep with tonight?

For they had taken a furnished room in Camden Town as soon as they had got off the train. The fat old landlady had looked at Harry slyly, and Clara had been sure she had winked, but Clara did not care about that either. Let the landlady think she was an innocent little dolly if she liked. She knew she looked it, with her makeup removed. Harry had insisted she get rid of it on the train. Clara squirmed in her seat from pure pleasure. The journey, which had taken overnight and deposited them in King's Cross Station, London, at seven o'clock in the morning, had been unalloyed bliss. Harry had not talked much but had cheered up when she showed him the purse Mae had given her. He had looked surprised.

"Hey, that's not your purse."

"No. It isn't."

"Whose is it then?"

"I said I wouldn't tell, Harry."

Harry looked knowing. "It's Mae's, isn't it?"

"Yes."

"The good old gel!" Harry smiled. "How much is in it?"

"I don't know."

Harry took the purse and looked at it, then emptied out the gold coins. "Five sovereigns!" he had said, a slow grin spreading over his features. "The good old gel!"

He had made to put the purse in his weskit pocket.

Clara spoke. "Harry, that money isn't yours. It's mine."

He had stared at her, astonished.

"What did you say, gel?"

"It's my money, not yours. Please give it to me."

Harry stared at her a long moment. Then he laughed and handed her the purse back.

"You may," said Clara, "have a sovereign for yourself if you wish, to spend on tobacco and things."

"No, I don't wish," said Harry Viner. "I have four quid of my own. That'll do for my tobacco and things."

"But we are going to have to live, are we not?" Clara had persisted. "We will have to pay for lodgings and such, will we not?"

And Harry had laughed again and put his arm around her, easily and not touching her in any deliberate way, and given her a casual hug, and said, "Yes, we will, I suppose we will," and he had kissed the tip of her nose, and she had strained, expectant, for more. But he had let his head fall onto her shoulder and gone off at once to sleep, and she had stayed in that position for four whole hours, her arms and legs going first numb, and then, as she moved them about, plagued with pins-and-needles. In this fashion, they had slept until the train had come to a noisy, grinding halt at King's Cross Station. From there Harry had taken a cab to the lodgings in Camden Town.

"I always said you needed a pretty little gel in your act, Harry duck," said Mrs. Harrington, the landlady. "What you do, gel, sing an' dance, I 'spect, pretty little thing, ain'tcher, dear?"

She did not seem to expect an answer and opened a door on the ground floor. The first thing Clara saw was a large brass bedstead covered with a patchwork quilt. There was a gas ring in one corner and an easy chair and a small table and two hard chairs. There was an old piano. A dresser stood in the window, and on it sat a china water pitcher and a bowl. A large china chamber pot rested under the bed. The floor gleamed with polished oilcloth, but there was a small fire grate, and in front of it lay a rag mat.

It was not a wonderful room, Clara thought, but it was better than nothing, and soon perhaps, they would look around for something better.

"It's me best combined room, dear." Mrs. Harrington was watching her face. To Harry, she said, "Eight an' six, seein' it's you. Do you want food?"

"No," said Harry quickly. "We'll look after ourselves like that."

"Good little cook as well, is she?" asked Mrs. Harrington. "You picked a good 'un there, Harry?"

"Yes, I did," said Harry Viner, "didden I?"

"You're a devil, you are," said Mrs. Harrington admiringly. "That'll be a week in advance, dear."

Harry had paid, and Mrs. Harrington had departed.

Harry Viner sat rather gloomily on the bed at that. "Look, it's eight o'clock now, and the post office will be open. You go along down there and write to your pa and tell him you're all right."

"Do you think I should?"

He looked irritated. "Well, of course you should! He's your old man, ain't he?"

Clara thought how very handsome he was sitting there, with his thick black hair and his large dark mustache and his lovely hands, and she said, "Yes, all right."

As she moved to the door, he added, "I might have to go out for a bit. I might not be here when you get back. Make yourself a cuppa tea. There's cups and a teapot in the cupboard. I'll be back later."

"Where are you going?" She felt suddenly afraid. He frowned. "What's that to do with you?"

"I'm sorry." Clara turned away. "Of course, you must do as you like."

He crossed the room and took her shoulders gently and turned her around to him. "I'm going to see a fella about a job, that's all. Just don't ask so many questions."

"Sorry," she sniffed.

He kissed her cheek. "Off you go. And don't say in your letter anything about being with me."

"Why not?"

"My eye! Why not? she says. Just don't, that's all!"

Clara had smiled and hummed a tune to herself, all the way down to the post office. After she had written and posted her letter-

84

card, she had shopped around at the row of shops and bought a tin of Nestle's condensed milk (which she had never tasted before, but she could not buy fresh milk since she had no jug) and a loaf of fresh, crusty white bread at the baker's, and some buns with icing on the top. She had gone into the grocer's and bought half a pound of smoked bacon and six fresh-laid eggs. In all she had spent almost four shillings. She went into a haberdashery shop and bought herself a nightgown, refusing the woman assistant's offer of a silk one and choosing a cheaper, cotton one. She also bought two pairs of cotton drawers, two pairs of woolen stockings, two cotton shifts, and was about to buy a silk scarf that had taken her eye when she felt a surge of panic at the money she was spending. She came out of the shop in a daze. I must remember, she told herself, that I do not have Papa's money now! She bought a toothbrush at the chemist's shop, and a tin of Gibb's powdered dentifrice. Her breath must be fresh. Tonight, after all, she would sleep with a man.

Clara carried the parcels back up Camden High Street and found that by the time she got to the top her legs ached.

Harry was not in the room.

Clara, disappointed, ate one of the sticky buns and drank two cups of tea. Then she took off her shoes and lay down on the bed. It was high and seemed hard, and the springs creaked. She giggled, and took off her hat and her dress (after all, it was the only one she had) and her corset, and lay down in her shift and stockings and, astonishingly, fell asleep.

When she wakened, Harry Viner was leaning over her with a cup of tea.

It was darker in the room, the afternoon shadows were lengthening.

"What time is it?"

"Five o'clock."

She stretched out a hand to him. He put the cup of tea in it. Clara said, "Harry, I wish I had a ring. Mrs. Harrington looked at me a bit oddly."

"A ring?" echoed Harry. "Why?"

"Well," said Clara, "I feel silly with nothing on my finger and living here with you."

"Easily settled!" Harry crossed to the window and took a brass ring from the curtain rod. "Try that for size!"

Clara did. It fitted her third finger snugly. "That's nice!"

"No, it ain't," said Harry, "but it's all I can afford." He indicated the cup of tea. "You drink that and then put your little ta-ta on. We're off to the Bedford Music Hall."

Clara thought; I'm lying here in my shift which has rucked up, and he can see my legs and my stockings and my drawers, and he isn't in the least bit *manly!*

Clara sipped her tea and thought about it. Harry Viner had plainly seen many girls in their underclothes, that was it. He had seen the twins naked as they were born, and he hadn't seemed surprised. She wondered about that, but it didn't help. She would have to wait and see.

So now she sat in the Bedford Music Hall, with her brass curtain ring that seemed like gold if you didn't look too closely.

Gus Elen was singing his other famous song:

> It really is a very pretty garden,
> And Chingford to the eastwards can be seen,
> Wiv a ladder and some glasses
> You could see to 'Ackney Marshes,
> *If it wasn't for the houses in between!*

The audience should like that song, Clara thought, because it was true. London was vast, there were millions of houses, rows upon rows upon rows of them, with millions of poor people trapped inside them and no way out.

Gus Elen had gone, to loud applause, and so had the great Cinquevalli, the conjuror supreme, making of his body a billiard table, with his arms and legs the four pockets. Cues whirled and ivory balls flew when Cinquevalli was on. Clara had seen him before, at the Alhambra, but she applauded heartily with the audience.

Now a thin middle-aged man in charwoman's clothes stood in front of the audience. He stared at them until he had got total silence; then he pushed his poke bonnet straight and, arms akimbo, addressed them. "The weather's so changeable," he said in an aggrieved voice, "you don't know what to pawn, do yer?"

The audience chuckled, as at a neighborly remark.

"This is Wilkie Bard," Harry told her. "What neck! Just stands there till they're quiet."

Clara realized that Harry watched every comic with an eye to how it was done. It was natural, she supposed, and she felt warm toward him. He sat and watched Wilkie Bard in silence, as he had watched Gus Elen in silence. He's learning, she thought; he's serious. He will be a good comic when he finds his way.

For herself, she liked the female performers, working-class matriarchs, lusty and certain of their audience and themselves. A plump, matronly woman with large dark eyes came on to considerable applause and sang a song that Clara had not heard before:

> Are we to part like this, Bill?
> Are we to part this way?
> Who's it to be, her or me?
> Don't be afraid to say.
> If it's all over between us,
> Don't ever pass me by,
> You and me good friends should be
> For the sake of the days gone by.

The house exploded as the matronly woman bowed simply and went off. "That was Kate Carney," said Harry. "One of the greats."

"If I had a song like that," Clara said, soberly, "I could be a real help to you in your act."

"Darlin' "—Harry shook his head—"it's not just the song, it's *how* you sing it! She knows what she's singing about, she knows that for a workingwoman her age, if her fella leaves her, that's *it*, ain't it? But if you sang it, you wouldn't sound like she does. To sing a song well, you got to have *lived* it."

Clara was desolate. "Then you don't think I could ever really sing on the halls?"

"I didn't say that. I said you could sing something that suits you. It's just finding you a song, that's all." Harry ate a mouthful of jellied eels—they were out of the Bedford Music Hall now. It was still light, and people stood around in large crowds outside the bars, which were still open, laughing and talking. It did not seem to Clara, in those first days, that the city ever slept. "You're not eating your eels."

"I don't like them." Clara found the eels gelatinous and full of bones and wondered why Harry thought them such a delicacy.

"Give them here then, gel, I'll finish them up for you."

And he did, and his laughter and fine form—he was indeed, she thought, a fine figure of a man—brought the bold eyes of the working girls around the eel stall toward him, and he returned their glances just as boldly, actually winking at a couple of them, Clara noticed with a sinking heart. He was plainly in his element in London, which he referred to as the Smoke—and smoke it did, a million chimneys pouring soot and brackish fumes into the air.

One of the bolder girls called to Harry, "Seen you on the halls, ain't I? Fella with the big . . . *wallet*, ain'tcher?"

"That's right, dear." Harry seemed pleased by the recognition of the girl, who had two bad teeth in the front of her mouth but did not seem shy about it. She burst into frequent peals of laughter and dug her friends in the ribs for no apparent reason. She was one of three girls of similar appearance, and they had linked arms, which gave them an odd look of solidarity.

"Seen you on the Bedford, ain't I?" the girl asked. "Ain't seen your wallet, though, 'ave I?" Again the peal of laughter.

"No," called Harry equably, "but you better watch out or I might show it to you!"

"Gerraway with your chat," said the bad-toothed girl. "The only one gonna see the size of your wallet's the little doll you've got wiv you, that right?"

Clara felt her cheeks grow hot, and she looked down at the ground.

"She don't have no curiosity about that," Harry said, finishing his jellied eels and licking his fingers. "She knows the size of it already."

"Yeh, I bet she do!" cried the bad-toothed girl, delighted."Bet she sees it more often than she wants to, don'tcher, gel?"

This sent them into further paroxysms of laughter, and Harry and Clara made their escape, Harry calling out, "If you meet anybody with a wallet the same size as mine, give him a chance. He'll do wonders for you."

Walking up the hill toward their lodgings, Clara put her arm through his. He did not seem to mind. Past them ran yelling children, with ragged clothes and snot-stiff jersey sleeves, their hair cut to the bone in a donkey fringe, their bare feet squashing the horse dung that lay thick in the gutters. A smell of horse urine hung like a fog in the close streets, and even now, at ten in the evening, the noise of horses' hooves and the loud catcalls of the people on the streets made a cacophony of sound loud enough to make Clara's head ache. She was glad when they found themselves back at Mrs. Harrington's house.

"Well"—Harry turned to her at the door—"how was your first night in the Smoke?"

"It was wonderful!" Clara said, lifting her face to be kissed.

But he merely inserted his key in the lock and ushered her into the house.

In the room he lit the gaslamp, and the mantle bubbled, and a pale green wash illuminated the room. Clara suddenly realized that there was nowhere to change for bed. Everything happened in the same room; you ate, slept, sat, in this one room. She thought of the ten bedrooms in Leazes Crescent but pushed the thought away. I ought to be nervous, she said to herself, everything I've ever read about the bride's first night should make me nervous, but I'm not.

It could only be because she never felt nervous with Harry Viner. She never was to feel that way with him.

Harry took off his hat and his jacket and hung them up carefully in the wardrobe. Then he sat down and removed his spats and his shoes. He stood in front of the mirror and unloosened his hard celluloid collar and his silk Macclesfield tie. His braces dangling down his back, he turned to her. "I thought you were tired?"

She smiled. "Yes, I was."

He grinned back. "All right then!"

Clara said, "I'm not shy, but there's nowhere to take my clothes off, and I'm all hot and sticky and I'd like to wash."

"There's water over there in the jug, but it'll be cold." Harry lowered his trousers and walked across to his trouser press, where he carefully laid the trousers, so that the crease would not be lost. His woolen long johns looked very funny to Clara, and she laughed. He turned around quickly, but by that time she had crossed to the dresser and poured water from the jug into the bowl. He lay on the bed in his long johns and watched her take off her hat and dress and then her lace-up boots and her petticoat and her whalebone corset and long black stockings and her shift and then, finally, her drawers. He said nothing at all, as she stood there, nude, and began to wash, using the awful carbolic soap in the dish, which was all that Mrs. Harrington provided. I must get some decent soap tomorrow, she thought; I will smell terrible with this stuff. She washed under her arms (she had heard that most ladies of the music hall shaved their armpits and most dancers their pubic hair, although the twins at the Alhambra hadn't), and she soaped her face and neck and breasts. Then she stood in the bowl and washed her feet. The water turned scummy and horrid, but at best she was clean. The soap was still in her eyes when she stepped out of the bowl, and she kept them shut and called, "Harry, a towel!"

Harry Viner did not hand her a towel.

He took her in his arms, wet as she was, and carried her across to the bed. She cried, "Harry, I'm all wet!" but he did not say anything in reply. He stretched her out on the bed and opened her legs gently and touched her and found her moist, and then he pushed into her, right away, without further preparation, and she felt a sudden searing pain so violent she tried to hold him back, but he was too strong and the soap was stinging her eyes even if they were closed, and he was thrusting into her and every thrust hurt more than the last one and she could feel an oozing of liquid from between her legs, and she cried out, "Harry, it hurts, oh, it hurts, Harry, it hurts!" and still he thrust on, and suddenly she began to relax, and a new and exquisite feeling of heat and needling sharpness began in her loins. She put her arms around him and pulled him to her and cried, "Oh, yes, I love it, I love it!" and Harry Viner thrust on, hard, filling her, and she cried and her eyes smarted and then she felt a sudden rush of feeling so intense she cried and then he pulled savagely away from her, and his seed was hot on her belly, and she knew he had retained enough control to do *that*, so that she would not be made pregnant, and she was somehow sorry that he had.

Harry looked down at her. He was sweating and smiling and he still wore his long johns.

"Well," he said softly, "you ain't a little virgin now, are you?"

"Oh, Harry!"

She had never been so happy in her life.

Harry Viner lay and watched Clara sleeping and wondered what the bloody hell he thought he was playing at. He'd done it now, and there was no undoing it! If he went on like this, the next thing he would do would be to get her in the pudden club, and then where would they be? He resolved to buy some rubber contraceptives, no matter how expensive they were and hard to obtain. And her father, what about him? There was no doubt he wouldn't leave things as they were, even if Clara had written to him. He might not notify the police, because that would make everything too public, but he would not suffer his only daughter free as air in London, that was for sure. He was a powerful man in the music hall world; all the managers stuck together. If one gave you a bad name, they all did. The consequences could be savage. He could be blacklisted. It was as simple as that.

Harry propped himself on his elbow, fumbled for a cigar and lit it. He shifted around and looked at Clara, her lovely reddish hair loose around her face. Well, Harry accused himself, she ain't much more than a child, is she? Seventeen, yes, but not seventeen like the bad-toothed girl who'd joshed him at the whelk and eel stall. That sort of gel wasn't a virgin by the time she was fourteen; some street arab had taken it away from her, probably forgotten his name by now. This one, she was different, she was a lady. Mind, she hadn't acted like a lady, had she? Ladies didn't cry out, "I love it, I love it," did they? No, they didn't.

Harry's loins stirred at the recollection. He frowned. None of that. The girl's body might be milk-white and her hair shining, and she might turn out to be, with practice, the best roger in the world. Nonetheless, he had to be sensible. He looked at the lips, slightly parted. The pearly white teeth shone through. Harry had never known a girl with teeth like that. This girl was strong and healthy, and her breasts were firm and full. He shook his head. She had a nice little voice, and she hadn't been scared on the stage of the Alhambra, and she had plenty of nerve, but how could it end, if he took her on, except in disaster?

Annoyed, he told himself he had not meant it to come to this. He had been down to see a booking agent that very morning. If the agency had been able to offer him anything, he would have been off and away. He had waited two hours to talk to the agent, who had looked up briefly when Harry walked in. The agent's name was Morrie Fine. Morrie had leaned back in his barber chair and pointed a long cigarillo at Harry. "I hear you got flung from the tour last night, that right?"

"How did you hear that already?" Harry asked, looking gloomily around Morrie's office. It was full of framed but unsigned photographs of the famous. None of them were Morrie's clients. Morrie just hoped other people did not know that.

"I got a telegram." Morrie held up a form. "It comes from the owner of the Alhambra up North there, and he says he gave you the Irishman's rise. Dunno where I can send you." He eased his starched collar with his free hand and leafed through papers

91

on his desk with the one that held the cigarillo. "The Metropolitan has a tryout on Friday?"

"I'm past tryouts, surely!" said Harry indignantly. "I've just been on a tour!"

"And sacked orf of it," Morrie reminded him.

Harry was silent.

"Let me see," said Morrie, looking. "Nothink else, mate."

"Friday night at the Met." Harry was struck down. "That's all you can tell me!"

"If they like you," Morrie said sagely, "they'll book you for next week."

"At what, four quid?"

"Who knows?" Morrie spread his hands. "Four pounds is better than no pounds, Harry. And if you go, cut out the Abie jokes, eh."

Harry shouted, "Morrie, I'm billed as the King of Kosher Komedy, what am I supposed to do?"

"Change your billing," said Morrie, and he seemed to be serious.

"Oh, sod off!" said Harry, and walked out of the office, leaving the door open.

The sound of the milkman roused him, the clang of the tin cans and the clip-clop of the horses' hooves. Then later came the postman (there were six deliveries a day, this one being the first), and the city began to come alive, a slap of feet changing to a steady march past the windows as the men and girls of the district walked to work in factory or shop or office. Everybody walked to work. Harry had walked to work at the Stepney tailor's shop, nearly an hour each way, tired first thing in the morning and dead tired at night.

He stretched out luxuriously. At least he was spared trudging to work in the rain with a piece of bread and butter in his pocket, a pie or a sausage if he was lucky.

Harry reached his arm out and touched the nude body of the sleeping girl. An urge, sharp, yet tender, that he'd never felt with any other girl or woman, came over him. It frightened him, and he drew his hand back from her hair and got out of bed in his long johns, refusing to allow his erection to grow. He padded silently across to the gas ring and put the tin kettle on and made tea, refusing to think about her. The erection subsided. There was

92

to be none of that, never no more. The girl must go home today.

When the water was boiling, he poured it on the leaves and allowed them to stand for a couple of minutes. He spooned in the condensed milk. He had grown used to milk in his tea. Beckie had always taken it correctly, with lemon and sugar, but Harry had got tired of asking for it in theatrical lodgings and railway buffets. Nobody served it, and everybody stared at him for asking. He drank it now, in the common phrase, as it came.

When he turned to Clara, she was awake, leaning on one elbow, watching him.

He sat down on the side of the bed and made sure that she could not see his excitement by pulling the coverlet across his knees.

"Are you cold?" She sipped the tea he had brought her. "Get back into bed."

"No, I'm all right." He rubbed his bristly beard. He thought: I'll shave right away. That takes ten minutes, and it'll get my mind off her. "Tea all right?"

"Yes, thank you, delicious." She reached over and kissed him on the cheek. "I love you."

Harry sat looking at his cup of tea.

After a moment he drank it down in one long, hot gulp and said, "I've been thinking, Clara, and there's no harm done, anyway nothing you need tell anybody about—"

"But there is," Clara said. "I'm not a virgin, you *said*—"

"Let me finish, woman, for crying out loud!" Harry shouted, and he had not meant to.

Clara's eyes widened at this, and her eyelashes batted fiercely, and he knew she was only just keeping back tears. He thought: Jesus, I have to say this now, or I'll never say it. He took her hand gently. "Clara, I know you love me and I love you, but we have to be sensible. Your father's going to find you sooner or later, and when he does, what can I say to him? I can say I've brought you here to my lodgings and taken you to bed, and what's going to happen then? I'll tell you. The fat's going to be in the fire. Your father is going to be very angry, and you are going to be marked damaged goods when you get home."

"Damaged goods?" Clara tried to pull away, but he held her hand tightly.

"Yes, but if you don't say anything to him about . . . about what happened between us last night. . . ." Harry saw her eyes had filled, but he averted his own eyes and looked down to where his erection pushed against the coverlet. "Look, I have no real money, nor have you, and in a couple of weeks we'll be starving. This is only a bit of an adventure to you, but your father can do me a real damage if he wants to, and if he finds you with me, I reckon he'll want to. I know I would if I was him. So"—Harry took a deep breath—"so what we're goin' to do is this. We're going to put you on the rattler going north at one o'clock today—"

"Rattler?"

"The train. You'll be home tonight, and it's all love and kisses, and I'll bet your Pa will be so glad to see you there'll be no questions asked!"

Harry Viner had run out of breath, and he sat there, miserably wishing that the bloody thing would go down!

Clara's eyes were now full of tears.

"You don't love me."

"Yes, I do," he said. "I was wrong to do what I did last night, but I—"

"Yes, what?"

"I couldn't help it, but I was still wrong." He tried again. "If you go home, you've got a good life in front of you, a lot better than anything I could give you. You'll go home sooner or later. Why not go now before more damage is done?"

"You mean you'd send me off?" To his surprise she wasn't sobbing. "Before you love me again?"

"What?" asked Harry.

"Before you love me again, like last night?"

"Yes, that's right, before I love you again. You have every reason to go, and no reason to stay, believe me. Now drink your tea, there's plenty of time. You can get the one o'clock train, and you'll be home for supper."

Harry smiled, but he did not feel like smiling. He knew what he felt like, but he wasn't going to do it, by jingo!

Clara finished her tea in silence.

"I'm not going back, Harry."

"You have to, gel!"

"It's no use talking. You can throw me out if you like, but if you do, I'll only get a room somewhere else."

"How would you live if you did that?" Harry was aghast.

"I'd get a job."

"What kind of a job would you get?"

94

"I don't know. In a shop or a factory."

"They'd laugh at you. With your voice."

"I don't care. I could work."

"You couldn't. You've no idea what it's like to work in a factory. Fourteen hours at a stretch. On your feet the whole time. You wouldn't last a day, never mind a week!"

"You're wrong. I'm stronger than I look. Anyway, I'm not going back home. I don't care what you say." Then, sliding her hand under the coverlet, she cried out, "Oh, Harry, you do talk silly! You want to love me now, don't you?"

"That's got nothink to do with it," said Harry, trying to pull away, but she held onto him *there*, the little vixen, and he gave way suddenly and pulled her to him, and threw the coverlet aside, and found that already she had learned to move with him, and with her cries of "Oh, Harry, I love it, I love it" in his ears, he came, only inside her this time, and he thought: You bloody berk, you stupid berk, what do you think you're a-doing of?

Clara smoothed his hair, and looked pleased, and whispered, "There, you couldn't help yourself that time, could you, Harry?" She kissed him and said, "You just lie there, and I'll get up and cook you bacon and eggs in bed."

And she did.

"Are you going to teach me how to sing and dance?"

He had finished his breakfast and now he was shaving, with a cutthroat razor. He stopped and looked at her through the mirror. Clara smiled back at him. It suits her, he thought, living with a fella. She might only be seventeen, but she was ready. He said, "I'm shaving, never talk to a man when he's shaving."

"No, but will you?"

"I dunno." Harry sighed. He lined up his chin for a long slow stroke. The slightest tremor, and he was cut.

"You'll never stick it, gel."

"I will. Just give me a chance."

"I don't see why you want to."

"I've always wanted to, like you've always wanted to be a comic."

"I haven't always wanted to be a comic. I'm a comic because I can do it. I can remember jokes, and I can sometimes make people laugh. I'm better than a lot of famous comics, I know I am. I don't try to play to the gallery and please the mugs. I'm talking to the smarter fella in the audience, if I can. But I dunno what will happen to me. I might get lucky and take somebody's eye if I don't die of bleedin' starvation first."

"You keep talking about starving."

"So would you. . . ." Harry's razor jagged his cheek, and a red stain appeared through the white foam. "Oh, Jesus, I've cut meself! I told you not to chatter when I was shaving!"

"I'm sorry. Let me get a towel for you!"

"No!" Harry stood in front of the dressing-table mirror, his razor poised. "Just let me finish shaving!"

Clara sat on the bed, the most comfortable seat in the combined room. She leafed through the program, price one penny, that she had bought at the Bedford the night before. She had noticed that most of the women in the acts were specialists, dancers or acrobats, or they were simply "dressing" to the acts, like the conjuror's assistant. She didn't want that.

"Could I sing a song if I came on in the act?"

Harry's razor froze in midair.

"Who said you were coming in on my act, dear?"

"Well, nobody, but I thought—"

"Then you thought wrong, darlin'."

"But when the landlady said—"

"The landlady thought you were in the act because otherwise, why would you be here with me?"

"Then you think I'm no good?"

Suffering, Harry wiped his cutthroat razor carefully and put it away in the box. "Clara, I know you're no good. How can you be? You've never had any training or anything!"

"You could give me that."

"You don't think you can walk straight on and do it, do you?"

Clara was surprised at his hostile tone. She persevered. "I want to learn, Harry, honestly I do. Please teach me."

"Darlin', I have a hell of a job to teach myself."

"Just let me come into the act and stand there."

Harry wrestled with his stiff collar and Macclesfield silk tie, bought in a good month at a cost of two and sixpence. "You can't just stand there, even if you are as pretty as a picture." Clara felt better then and kissed him. He smelled of lavender shaving soap and tobacco. "You'd either have to speak some lines or else sing. It would take time to work out what you could do, and where's your song coming from, for Gawd's sake?"

96

"Couldn't I sing a well-known one like you do?"

Harry double-tied his tie, so that the knot was fashionably large and loose. "No, you can't, not down here in the Smoke! Up north I could get away with it."

Clara was crestfallen. "You mean I'd have to find a new song?"

"And it would have to suit you, and where would you find anybody to write you one?"

"Why, aren't there plenty of people writing songs?"

"The thing is, they hope a top-of-the-bill will like their song, take it up and sing it. That makes the song famous, and everybody wants to buy a copy of the music to sing to the old piano at home. The only other people that write songs are fellas like that Irishman who wrote that song for me, what's his name?"

"John Hyatt," supplied Clara.

"Yes, and bloody awful *he* was!" Harry buttoned up his weskit and pulled on his jacket, showing plenty of starched cuff. "So there you are. No song, for a start."

Clara kissed him again. "You could teach me to dance, though, couldn't you?"

"I could." Harry kissed her back. "If you had any dancing shoes, which you ain't."

"I could buy some."

Harry detached her arms from around her neck. "Here's something to learn. Don't try to get things from me, professional things, with what you've got between your legs, darlin', because any tart can get anything by lying on her back, and if you're any good, you don't need to do it. Right?"

Clara stepped back. "If you don't want me in your act, then I'll find my own way! Thank you very much!"

Harry reached out to her. "Now, I didn't mean that, I know you're not that sort of a gel, but a woman's got power that way, and a lot of 'em use it, in fact, most of 'em do, to get started. You look back you'll always find there's a fella—a manager or an agent or somebody—started them off. Of course, they reckon they love him at the time, but really all they're doing is doing him a favor and themselves one at the same time."

"I understand perfectly." Clara stood up. "I have to go out. I'll be back later."

Clara left the lodging house, slamming the door behind her. To think that of her, that she would use *that* to her own advantage, to actually say such a thing, it was monstrous! Clara was very angry, but she tried to contain her anger. Harry Viner was not a gentleman. That was what she had to accept, or she would not be able to go on loving him. He was not like Papa or her brother, Adam; he did not stand when ladies entered the room and remain standing until they had sat down. He ate with his mouth open, and he did not use proper language. Nonetheless, he excited her. Just to be near him excited her. She loved him, and so she would have to put up with the things about him that she did not like. That was the root of it.

Meanwhile, since she could not expect help from him to get on the halls, it was plain she would have to help herself.

Clara walked around Camden Town until she saw the three brass balls that denoted a pawnshop. She walked in and was struck by an odor of dirty washing. She coughed and quietly put her cambric lavender-scented handkerchief to her nose.

"I know, lady," said the pawnbroker, a small bald man in thick, broken spectacles. "It's the sheets and blankets they bring in, they don't wash them proper, it's terrible, but what to do?" He shrugged his shoulders, pointing up at rows of brown paper parcels that reached to the ceiling. "They bring them on Monday, take them out on Friday." He assessed her rapidly. "To sell or to pawn please, lady?"

Clara put her gold fob watch on the counter.

The pawnbroker looked at it, surprised and impressed.

"We don't get many like this." He put in his eyeglass. "No, not round here, we don't get many like this." He looked at her with some sympathy. "To pawn, yes? That way you'll be coming back for it?"

"How much do I get for it?"

"To pawn? I'm a fool to myself, I give you five pounds."

"To sell?"

"To sell?" He looked at her swiftly. "It's yours, yes?" He smiled. "Of course it is. Well then, it's a lovely watch, you know the value yourself, but when you are sellin', well, that's another thing." He debated. "Maybe fifteen pounds? You see, me dear, the trouble with this watch, it's worth a lot of money, but it's engraved, it's got your name on it, and who wants a watch with somebody else's name on it?"

"Fifteen pounds will do very well."

"You sure?" He seemed sad.

"Quite sure, thank you."

"Very well, lady. Here they are, fifteen sovereigns, I count them out for you. When I'll sell it around here, I don't know, but if I don't, then I give it my daughter maybe. It's a lovely watch. Who, if I may ask, gave it to you?"

Clara collected the gold coins and slipped them into her purse.

"My father. It was a birthday present."

"Never have anything engraved, me dear," the pawnbroker said earnestly. "Never. Cuts the value to nothink."

"Thank you." Clara smiled and escaped. The pawnbroker was sadly examining the watch as she left, shaking his head at the innocence of the world.

At the Camden Town post office Clara sent a money-order telegram for ten pounds to John Hyatt. That meant he would get the money at the same time as the telegram, probably within two hours. When she paid over the coins along with the twenty-word message form, she was flushed with excitement. I must calm down, she told herself. This is my business, not Harry's. He has his own troubles. I must look to myself. She bought lamb chops at the butcher's and potatoes and peas at the greengrocer's and wondered if she would be able to cook them all on a gas ring.

Clara trudged back up the hill to the lodgings. Her spirits rose as she did so, and by the time she had let herself into the room she could not stop herself from calling out, "Harry, I love you!"

But he was not there.

There was no note.

Clara sat down on the bed, but she did not cry. She got up and peeled the potatoes.

Harry Viner approached the troupers at the corner of York Road and Stanford Street, just across Waterloo Bridge, with a jaunty air that deceived nobody. This crossroad was known to the profession as Poverty Corner. Harry was not happy to be there; it did indeed betoken real need. But there was no point in pretending. Nobody on the corner pretended. The mere fact that they were there meant that they were unemployed.

The entertainers stood in groups, mostly well dressed (the clothes were the last things to go into the popshops), and were divided by their specialty. The conjurors stood together like a covey of blackbirds. Somehow, on and offstage, they had the funereal look of professional mourners. The acrobats were in another group, powerful men bursting out of their tight suits, careful of their weight and diet, their principal topic of conversation. The animal acts were often accompanied by pets. A man there that day had a tiny marmoset that he was "breaking in" on his shoulder. It was important, Harry knew, that the animals became used to handling. Weeks and months it took, he had heard. He wondered at the patience of such people. It wasn't as if they got very much out of it. Everybody applauded the bleedin' dogs.

The comics stood apart.

There was about them an air of melancholy so great that Harry Viner almost turned tail. What was he thinking about, bothering with this crowd of no-hopers?

By that time it was too late. He had been seen and greeted, and to his annoyance but not surprise, everybody seemed to have heard that he had just been sacked up north.

Sid Jones, a Welsh comic with a squint, asked if it was true that Harry had got flung for poking the manager's wife? He seemed serious.

"If I had, I'd still be there, wouldn't I?" asked Harry. "An' top-of-the-bill at that!"

There was a reluctant laugh. It was difficult to amuse these men. They stood, mostly in silence, assessing each other's clothes and accoutrements. Harry said, "If I asked you bleedin' lot the time, not one of you buggers could tell me!"

The comics looked pained. Every one of them wore a watch chain, but there was no knowing how many still had watches attached to them.

Harry took out his steel watch. "Solid gold, that," he said, "Only it wore off."

The comics sighed. Some of them were very fat, and some were tall and thin. In the absence of this almost all of them had some kind of physical defect, like a squint or a stammer, on which they capitalized.

Harry said, "Gawdblimey, I'm the only one here who's normal!"

"Yes," said Sid, the Welsh comic, wearily, "and you've got three balls."

The other comics smiled, in pain.

Harry asked, "Anybody hear of anything going anywhere?"

Sid, the Welsh comic, said, "There's a manager in Cardiff can't get it up. His wife's looking for company. There's only one trouble, the manager's queer as well. Still, you can't have everything."

The other comics wheezed.

Harry said, "They tell me Dan Leno's on a hundred and fifty quid a week."

Several comics said they had known Dan Leno when he had nothing.

Harry pointed to a passerby. "Do you see that fella there? I knew him when he only had a horse and cart."

Sid, the Welsh comic, asked, "What's he got now?"

Harry said, "He's only got the cart."

The comics coughed and smiled politely.

"They tell me that Marie Lloyd got the bird at Sheffield," Harry Viner said.

"Did she, honest?" asked Sid, the Welsh comic.

"That's what they say." The comics sighed; Sheffield was notoriously a rough audience, a steel town, famous for its blast furnaces and its cutlery and engineering. "They gave her the bird good an' proper. They can't stand Cockney songs up North." Harry felt better being in the company of such as Marie Lloyd, Queen of the Music Halls, and besides, the story was true! "When they give her the bird, whistling fit to bust they was, Marie just stands there till they've all quieted down a bit, and then she says, "You know what *you* can do wiv your knives and forks, an' your circular saws as well!' "

The comics wheezed painfully. It was impossible to tell if they had heard the story before.

"So," Harry Viner said, "nobody knows of anything?" He hesitated. "Even anything going out on tour?"

If there was a job, he told himself, he had to take it. Even if it meant leaving the girl. Sid, the Welsh comic, said, "Fred Karno's looking for comics, but they must be prepared to actually break their necks or he won't pay them on Friday."

The comics wheezed.

Sid, the Welsh comic, said more soberly, "The Met's doing a trial turn Friday."

"I've worked the Met," Harry said.

"Who hasn't?" asked Sid. "I'm changing me act. I'm blacking up an' goin' as a member of the Wanka Tribe. Get it? Member? Of the Wanka Tribe?"

The comics wheezed, in agony.

Harry said, "Well, I've got to go and see my agent. If I can fit him in."

Harry Viner waved and retraced his steps across Waterloo Bridge. The four pounds he had left the North with was now down to three pounds, ten shillings and would soon be less than that, since the rent was due on Friday. Of course, the girl had a fiver, and that meant—what?—they were safe for about four weeks. After that, they would starve. To his astonishment, he found that he was including her in his calculations. Harry Viner, he said to himself, you are a right mug, what are you?

Nonetheless, his step was lighter as he thought of Clara.

It was a word he refused to use, but he supposed that in his own way, he loved her.

The week went by for Clara in a maze of impressions, the new way of living, hand to mouth; the fact that everything they ate had to be cooked first, with only a gas ring and a frying pan. She began to understand why working-class Londoners ate out so much as they did, at pie-and-pea stalls and oyster stalls, and why ready-to-eat foods, like black puddens and saveloys and haddocks and kippers, food that only needed warming up, not cooking, were so popular, especially in the choking heat of summer. Harry was happy with this kind of food. The lamb chops had not been a success. They filled the combined room with fumes, and the potatoes were hard.

London was a furnace. No man, however, removed his coat and weskit, unless he was a laborer. Most did not take off their woolen underwear. Harry did not, and when Clara reprimanded him, he looked at her in astonishment. "It's healthy, sweating is, you ask anybody."

"But why not get some lighter underwear?"

"Like what?"

"Well. Papa wears silk in summer."

"Papa's rich, darlin'. I have news for you. This is my only set of underwear!"

So she went out and bought him a set of cotton combinations. He did not seem pleased with them. "You sweat into these," he said, "It'll be like wearing a dishcloth. Wool now, wool absorbs, see?" He wore them for a day (while she washed his woolen ones) and discarded them.

For Clara, despite these domestic duties, the week meant the union of their bodies in the long, hot nights. She was in a dream of physical pleasure. They made love every night, often two or three times, and it seemed to her that her body was alive for the first time. Mostly, it was a thing of quickly taken pleasure because that was how Harry seemed to like it, and she did not mind that, for his seeming loss of control was the exciting thing about it—that she, Clara Abbott, could cause a man like Harry Viner to lose control in this way, that his want for her was so great that he was defenseless, although he was the aggressor, that fact alone quickened her own desire. Clara suspected, as she gladly received and held him, that there was a great deal more to *this* than the way that they were doing it, but she was content. She learned how to move with him and to pleasure him in simple ways, and she learned a little more each night. She slept deeply when she did sleep (often during the day), and she thought of home and Papa not at all. She cooked breakfast and prepared (or rather, warmed up) their food for their evening meal together. She dusted the room and made the bed. She shopped for the small amounts of food, and she moved through the week as if in a dream, a happy fleshly dream of love.

Harry was out most days, seeing agents and bookers, he said. He did not seem to have any luck, but she did not press him at all. She did not mention coming into the act again, and Harry did not mention it either. She listened for the postman all week. There were no letters. But on Friday morning (Harry was out, having left soon after breakfast) there was a tap on her door, and fat Mrs. Harrington stood there, saying, "There's a young fella out here says he wants to see you. Name of Hyatt."

He came shyly into the room, peering through his spectacles, nodding and finally offering his hand. He was in a thick tweed suit and a velour hat and looked very countrified. He carried a brown leather Gladstone bag.

"Oh, it's . . . such a surprise, Mr. Hyatt!" It *was.* "I thought you'd post it on, and when there was nothing this morning, well. . . . Do sit down please, I'll make some tea."

John Hyatt sat down, but he shook his head at the tea. He looked uncomfortable, perched on the edge of the chair. His Irish brogue seemed stronger to her ears than when she met him the first time. She found the whiskey bottle and, without asking him, poured a large measure into a cup (they had no glasses in the

103

place) and put it in his hand. He looked at it, surprised, and nodded, and drank it down in one swallow.

"Another?"

"No, thank you." He looked around. "Are you. . . . Have you left home?"

"Yes, I have."

John smiled through the glasses. He had a nice slow smile. "I saw you at the Alhambra when you went on with that Viner fellow."

"How did I do?"

"You were awful." He grinned cheerfully. "But you hadn't prepared anything, had you? I mean, Viner shouldn't have let you go on like that."

"He didn't. He didn't know I was going to do it."

"Oh, I see." John Hyatt looked around the room, and his eyes widened at the boots under the bed.

"It isn't much of a place, I'm afraid," Clara said.

"No." He did not deny it. He colored. "I'm sorry. I had no idea that you and Viner—" He stopped and fumbled open his Gladstone bag, keeping his face averted from her.

"I can tell you I was . . . surprised to get your telegram. But it made up my mind for me. I've decided to come and live down here and try my luck with my songs."

"Did you do *my* song, Mr. Hyatt?"

John Hyatt took a sheet of manuscript paper out of his bag. "Finished it last night, and I'm afraid it's only scored for piano." He recovered enough for his color to return to its usual ruddy brown, but he kept his eyes firmly on the sheet of manuscript paper. "It wasn't easy, writing a song for you, you see, because the only time I've seen you onstage is at the Alhambra, and well, as I said, you weren't very good." He coughed. This was a man who would win no hearts with flattery, Clara thought, but she was not offended. He had, after all, *written her a song!*

"Where is it, can I see it?"

He looked doubtfully over his glasses. "Can you read music?"

"Of course I can!"

He did not smile but looked around the room again. No doubt taking in Harry's extra pair of shoes in their shoe trees standing next to the fire, and Harry's stiff collar thrown, complete with tie, over the back of a chair. And the bed, which, as Clara looked at it, seemed to grow larger by the minute.

"This piano works." She opened the lid. "It's a bit out of tune, though."

"May I?" He took off his coat, hitched up his shirt sleeves and sat down on the dusty old piano stool. "I'll play it over first, and then, if you like, you can sing it." John Hyatt raised his hands to play, then stopped. "If you don't like it, naturally you get your money back.

"Well. I've written you a song called 'Naughty But Nice.' It isn't a great song, but it's tailored for you, as far as I'm able to tailor it." Clara nodded, sat down, held her hands clasped together and listened.

It was a simple melody. It didn't sound quite like anything else. Which was good.

John Hyatt sang:

> I'm one of the well-brought-up gels,
> From a family of swells,
> We eat chicken and beef every day,
> We don't go to work.
> But we never do shirk
> At the business of being quite gay!
>
> A soldier boy took me to the seashore,
> He wanted to spoon, but *I* said, 'Good Lor'.' . . .

Then they both sang the chorus:

> Naughty but Nice, Naughty but Nice,
> Never Been Kissed in the Same Place Twice!

Clara took up the next verse:

> A sailor boy took me out on the *river*,
> He had some ideas, and oh, my, I did . . . *shiver!*
> Naughty but Nice, Naughty but Nice,
> Never Been Kissed in the Same Place Twice!"

John Hyatt stopped playing and looked at Clara.

"Well?"

"It's good!"

"You really like it?"

"Yes, I do!"

"Then let's go through it tomorrow." He blinked through the spectacles. "I have to find a room to stay in."

"You can stay here; it's quite cheap. Everybody's theatrical."

"Are there rooms empty?"

"Yes, several."

He smiled. "Well. That's settled. I'll go and see the landlady."

"No," Clara said firmly, "there's no hurry for that. Let's go over the song now. All of it."

"I've just got in, I'm dirty and tired—"

"Please!"

John Hyatt looked at Clara and smiled the long, slow smile. "You usually get your own way, don't you, miss, er . . . ?"

"Clara. And yes. I do."

John Hyatt took a deep breath, adjusted his spectacles and his striped shirt sleeves with their elastic bands, pushed back his starched cuffs and began to play.

The trial turns assembled in the changing room at the Metropolitan. Harry Viner came in his best stage gear, carrying his makeup box in his hand. He sat down in the corner of the room, well away from the throng, most of whom he judged to be amateurs and prime candidates for the "hook"—a long pole wielded from the side of the stage, which pulled unpopular turns into the wings. It was only used on trial turns matinees and was the risk any beginner took. What the bleedin' hell was he doing here? Nearly got the bird in the North last week and now he was putting himself in danger of the *hook*, the awful fate of the amateurs. He closed his makeup box with a sigh. Frig it, he would leave. It wasn't worth it.

"I feel the same, boy." Sid Jones, the Welsh comic, stood there. "But you never know. A lot of bookers come along Friday nights, just for the laughs."

Harry finished making up. "What are you giving 'em?" Jones asked.

"My usual." Harry shut his makeup box. "You look after this while I'm on. I'll look after yours. Come on, let's see if we can get on early."

"Hear you got a nice little bit of skirt with you?" Sid Jones said.

"When did you hear that?"

"Don't you?"

"She's a well-brought-up young lady."

Sid Jones laughed. "Living with a comic? Is she here?"

"Somewhere," Harry said.

The stage manager knew Harry Viner and Sid Jones. He nodded and looked at his list. "I'll put you both on early." he advised, "before they get warmed up and a bit nasty with it." He meant the audience. "But I'll have to put somebody between you. I can't put two comics on following each other."

"Ta," said Harry. "That's handsome of you." He gave the stage manager a half crown, which was accepted wordlessly and disappeared into a weskit pocket.

"Excuse me, I have to do the announcements now. I'll put you on first, Harry, and Sid here on third. I'll find some other act to go between you, all right?"

"Lovely," said Harry. "Get the bloody thing over and done with and get home."

"Good luck, darling!"

He turned and saw Clara standing there. She was wearing a long blue dress, with fringes and a décolletage, and carrying a fan.

"What's all *this?*"

"Well, I wanted to look nice for you."

Harry Viner turned to Sid Jones, the comic. But Sid Jones said, "You're right, she's a lady, miracles do happen. Hello, miss, I'm Sid Jones, I wish I'd seen you first!"

Clara smiled. Harry thought she seemed nervous, but his eyes were on the stage manager, who now commanded the center of the stage, the limelight on him. He waited patiently for silence and then intoned, in a long-suffering voice: "Good evening, ladies and gentlemen. This is a trial turn night, and you all know what we allow and what we don't allow. We allow cheers and applause. Those of you who have brought fruit or vegetables to throw, please make sure your aim is good, especially those in the gallery! Anybody throwing tins or cans will be ejected from the theater! Thank you!"

The stage manager came out to the wings. "Bloody trial turns, I hate them! Good luck, son, you'll need it, they're ready to eat lions tonight!"

Harry said, "Have the band got my music?"

"The pianist has," said the stage manager. "The band have gone for a drink, and I don't blame them."

Harry decided. "Never mind the song. I'll do without it."

107

The stage manager looked surprised. "You'll never get off without a song, Harry."

"I'm supposed to be a comic," Harry Viner said, "not a singer. I'll just walk off."

The stage manager rubbed his thin face. "Not seen many do it. But it's your neck." He gave Harry a push. "You're on."

Harry Viner walked slowly out to the middle of the stage, and what he heard almost made him sick. This was no ordinary audience. There was a taunting cruel sound coming from the blackness, malevolent, teasing. He walked slowly downstage toward the footlights. He called, "I'm what they call a human sacrifice. I'm on first."

A voice called out, "Make us laugh!"

"To make *you* laugh, I'd have to break me right arm, mate, and break me left leg for an encore!"

"Do it then and see!" came the reply from the darkness.

Harry called back, "If I do, will you come out here and break yours, then we can *all* have a laugh?"

The cruel sound changed a little. Harry smiled at them.

"There you are," he said. "I knew you could behave properly. No need to come here and behave like you do at home, is there?"

The audience didn't laugh, but it was still.

Harry knew it was forbidden by unwritten rule to keep after any particular member of an audience, but he was terrified and past caring. "That fella that spoke before, you know what happened when the rent collector knocked on his door today? He said, 'I have nothing, but the missus will look after you.' The rent collector looked at his missus and said, 'No, thanks, I'd rather pay a week's rent meself!' "

The man in the audience shouted, "What do you know about the rent man? You've never *seen one!*"

"I pay my rent regularly, not like you," replied Harry. "You buy your furniture on the Kathleen Mavourneen. It may be for years and it may be for ever. Two-and-six down, and two-and-six every time the furniture man sees you first."

"We're not all Jew-boys," cried the outraged man in the audience.

"No, but can you prove that?" asked Harry. "Your mother used to hang around the Stepney Synagogue an awful lot, you know."

The dreadful malevolent audience relaxed, in a roar.

Harry said, the sweat cooling on his back, "I'll tell you about my friend Abie. He was walking down the street one day and he met his friend Morrie. 'I'm sorry to hear about the fire,' he said. . . ."

Somehow he got to the end of his act.

Then he simply bowed and walked to the wings.

No song.

He turned to the audience and closed his eyes.

Here it comes, he thought, the carrots, the tomatoes, the tin cans.

Applause. Brief and sporadic. But applause.

He bowed and walked off. The sweat broke through his makeup and blinded him. "By God," said the stage manager, "you went at them a bit hard, Harry!"

"The bastards." Harry just stood there. "The miserable, lousy bastards!"

"Jesus," said Sid Jones, the comic, "if it does that to you, I'm having second thoughts meself!"

"I had to put a singer on between you two," explained the stage manager apologetically. Harry turned, with burning eyes— his eye black was running with the sweat, and what had he achieved? Well, he'd got off, working the toughest audience in London, *without* singing a song! That was what he'd achieved! Now it remained to be seen if anybody had noticed. Apart from the other comics, who noticed everything.

"Hey," said Sid Jones, "your little lady can sing, can't she?"

Harry turned around, and there stood Clara.

He thought: this was what the new dress was for!

Clara sang:

> Naughty but Nice, Naughty but Nice,
> Never Been Kissed in the Same Place Twice!

"The cheeky little madam!" Harry breathed.

"She's not bad," said Jones, the comic, "but why doesn't she move about a bit?"

"Because she don't know any better," said Harry. "She'll get murdered if she just stands there and sings at them straight like that!" He turned to the stage manager. "Tell them to douse the foots, and just leave one spot on her!"

"It might throw her, Harry."

"Do it, for Christ's sake!"

The stage manager bawled hoarse instructions, and the stage ceased to be bathed in bright, remorseless light, and Clara stood alone in the single cup of yellow, everything else black, and if she was shaken, she did not show it.

"Green," said Jones, the comic. "Very green, but a nice little voice, Harry."

"Not bad." Harry's eyes were fixed on the single innocent figure, out there all alone. Don't let them throw things, don't let them murder her, he prayed, surprised at the depth of his feelings. It needed only one voice to catcall, and it was over. The audience was not here to be pleased. Harry began to sweat all over again. This was worse than being on there himself.

Clara sang:

> My boyfriend he takes me for rides in the park,
> I mostly say no, but sometimes I *spark!*
> It's Naughty but Nice, Naughty but Nice,
> Never Been Kissed in the Same Place Twice!

"Nice little figure she's got as well, but why the long dress?" said Jones, the comic. "She should be in bloomers with a bicycle."

"She'd be in the buff if it would help." Harry shook his head. "She's going to get murdered, Sid." For the catcalls and whistles were starting. "If only she'd *move* around the stage!" He hissed, "Move, move!"

But Clara stood still. She kept on singing, but her voice had a quake in it now. This audience, Harry knew, would hear it and go for the jugular any minute. She's frozen, he thought.

Clara sang on:

> My boyfriend he takes me out for a ride,
> I want to stand firm but sometimes . . . I slide!
> It's Naughty but Nice, Naughty but Nice,
> Never Been Kissed in the Same Place Twice!

"Not a bad little song, boy," said Sid Jones. "Catchy little tune, but she isn't selling it!"

"She couldn't sell peppermint rock in Brighton," said Harry, listening.

The whistles and catcalls were continuing, but some sections of the audience (to Harry's surprise) were resisting the whistles with bouts of applause. Clara kept singing, quite still, in the limelight.

110

A sailor boy takes me out on the *river,*
I like what he does, but it do make me *shiver!*
Naughty but Nice, Naughty but Nice,
Never Been Kissed in the Same Place Twice!

"Where did she find the song?" Sid Jones asked Harry.

"Buggered if I know," said Harry.

"Not bad. Suits her," said Sid professionally. "If she gets off alive, poor cow."

Harry thought: she's sung four verses; this has to be the last chorus. He said to the stage manager, "Put another spot on me, from the side. I'm going out there."

The stage manager said, "Why? She's all right."

"She's not," said Harry, listening. "Some berk will throw something any minute now and spoil it for her!"

The stage manager shook his head. "She's your girl, is she?" Harry nodded. "All right, good luck. Any bloody thing goes here tonight!" He bawled instructions, and Harry stepped onto the stage in a pool of light. He made sure Clara saw him do it so that she would not be surprised, and he soft-shoed gently toward her, took her arm and whispered, "Last chorus!"

"There are two more verses!"

"Never mind them. Get off now!"

The audience had quieted down, as Harry knew they would when anybody new came onstage. It was simply novelty, but it worked. The thing now was to get off while they were still interested enough to see what he was about. He tucked his arm in hers, made a windup signal to the solitary pianist in the pit (who nodded in reply) and took Clara across stage in a side step. The spot followed them. Harry sang with her:

It's Naughty but Nice, it's Naughty but Nice,
She's Never Been Kissed in the Same Place Twice!

Harry swept Clara behind the curtain. She turned to him, out of breath and furious. Her face was very badly made up. That was another thing she would have to learn. No doubt she had done it in a hurry, while he was on, in some corner, backstage.

"There were still two more verses!"

"They would have been throwing things by then, darlin'."

"How do you know? Listen to them!"

For there was a generous round of applause from the mon-

111

strous audience. Harry gripped her waist and pulled her back on-stage. "Just curtsy. Take your time."

He made a quick bow to the audience, and one to Clara, then took her off. The applause kept going, and the stage manager asked, "Want to milk it for one more?"

"Why not?" said Harry. And they did.

As they came off into the wings, the stage manager said, "Very nice. You're on now, Sid."

"Bloody hell," said Sid Jones, the Welsh comic, gloomily. "Follow *that!*"

He took a deep breath and marched onstage. He was greeted cordially with a round of boos and catcalls.

Clara was still glaring at him. "Why did you do that?"

"Do what?"

"Come onstage! I was doing very well as I was!"

"No, you weren't. They'd have started to boo any minute *and* throw things."

"No, they wouldn't!"

"Yes, they bloody would, gel! Listen to them now!"

For indeed the audience was restive. Sid, the Welsh comic, was yelling fast one-liners at them, but they weren't listening. Their patience was exhausted. They wanted blood, Harry thought. Jesus, what a business!

"Give me the hook," said the stage manager resignedly to one of his assistants.

"We can do it, guv'nor," said the stagehand.

"No," said the stage manager. "If you do it, Sid'll probably come off and clout you one. He knows me."

"You aren't going to hook him?" Harry protested.

"Listen to that audience, mate," said the stage manager, chewing on his mustache.

Harry listened. The noise was dreadful, and then there was the splatting sound of a tomato hitting the stage.

"Here it comes," said the stage manager sadly.

Clara began to move away, but Harry took her bare shoulders in his hands. "Look and learn, darlin'," he said.

Sid Jones, the Welsh comic, had, in panic, gone into a song, a parody of the Welsh hymn "Bread of Heaven," but it was availing him nothing. He was Welsh, and this was London. It was enough for this audience. Taffy was a Welshman, Taffy was a thief, as far as they were concerned. He waited for Sid to give it up, why

112

didn't he, the cabbages were beginning to fly now, great ugly things, and they were thrown with force, and they could hurt if they hit a performer. Sid, the comic, was now not only singing but making rude gestures in his fury and terror, and there was a sudden growling from the black beast of an audience. Boos, catcalls and piercing whistles filled the theater.

"Call him off!" urged Harry to the stage manager.

"He'll never hear me! It's the hook," said the stage manager. "Nothing else for it."

With the aid of the stagehands he put the long hook out onto the stage and looped it around Sid Jones's waist. Sid looked around in amazement.

"Not bloody likely!" he shouted.

But too late. He was hooked, waving his arms wildly, hauled almost off his feet, into the wings, to a roar of delight and a final shower of vegetables, tomatoes, carrots, bad apples and eggs.

The stage manager and a stagehand, a burly man in weskit and a cap, caught him by the arm. "Sorry, mate," said the stage manager. "You knew it could happen when you went out there!"

Sid Jones lunged wildly at him. The stagehand held him easily, with sympathy. His stage clothes were spattered with sour fruit and eggs.

"Jesus!" said Sid. He ceased to struggle. "The hook!" He slumped and moved away and sat on a prop chair. "Bloody suit ruined! And the hook as well!"

"Cheer up, mate," said Harry. "It could have been me."

"Sod off!" shouted the comic. Tears ran down his face.

Harry patted his shoulder and turned to Clara. "You see?"

Clara's face was set under the makeup. "Yes. Perhaps you were right."

"Where are your street clothes?"

"In the dressing room."

"Go and get them before somebody pinches them. I'll wait for you in the foyer."

"Aren't you waiting to see the other turns?"

"I'd rather go to Wandsworth and watch a hanging."

Clara nodded and ran off, cannoning into stagehands carrying scenery. She doesn't even know not to run backstage, Harry thought. But he was respectful. She hadn't done badly, not badly at all. He went out around to the stage door and stood in the alley, wiping the stage muck off his face in the mirror of his traveling makeup case. He got the thick of it off. It would have to do. He couldn't face going back to the communal dressing room along with the amateurs who had still to go on. They must be doing it in their trousers, he thought, waiting to be sacrificed to that audience. He lit a cigar and took the small whiskey flask out of his inside pocket. He was still shaking, but the alcohol helped. The shakes began to lessen. He drank again and stared out into the alley behind the theater. They had got out with their lives. That was something.

"Good evening, Mr. Viner."

Harry looked up. For a moment he did not recognize the young man in the velour hat. "Hey, aren't you—?"

John Hyatt nodded. "That's right."

"Did she—?"

John Hyatt nodded again.

"That was *your* song?"

"It was."

John Hyatt did not ask what Harry Viner thought of the song. Either he's so conceited he doesn't care, thought Harry. Or he thinks I'll be sure to hate it.

"Good little song," Harry said grudgingly. "Did you sell it to her or what?"

"It's her song. I wrote it for her."

"You wrote it for her? When?"

"This week. Is she about at all?"

"She'll be out in a minute," said Harry, dazed. "She's in the dressing room. You wrote the song in a week, you said?"

"In a night really. She sent me a telegram asking for it. I expect you knew that?"

The eyes behind the thick spectacles were shrewd.

"Oh, yes," said Harry quickly. "I knew. Of course. Oh, yes."

"I'll just wait around then." John Hyatt looked at the ground.

"It's free." Harry drew on his cigar. "It's about all that is! You living down here now, are you?"

"No point at all in stayin' up North. Nothing there."

"No, except a lot of berks," said Harry, "who don't know a joke when they hear one."

"Clara's father came round to see me." John Hyatt looked straight at Harry.

"Did he? When?"

114

"Early in the week. He was upset."

"What did you tell him?"

"There was nothing I could tell him. I didn't know where she was. Then."

"You won't tell him now, will you?" Harry asked harshly.

John Hyatt shrugged. "It's no business of mine, Mr. Viner."

"How did he get to you?"

"I don't know. Somebody must have told him I wrote your song. Did you tell anybody?"

Mae, Harry thought dismally. Of course. Mae would try not to talk, but she wouldn't be able to resist the power of such as Edward Abbott. It was only a matter of time before the ax fell. He shivered.

"You cold, Mr. Viner?"

"No, I'm all right. Where you living?"

John Hyatt looked surprised. "Same place as you. I came yesterday."

"Oh, yes, that's right, she said." Harry recovered as quickly as he could, but not quickly enough, he suspected. "Hoping to pick up some jobs then?"

"I'll have to see. It's not going to be easy."

"You written many songs?"

"For the university shows."

"University?" Harry stared at this peasant. "Which university's that?"

"Trinity, Dublin. I studied music."

"You're a varsity swell, are you?"

"I'm afraid so." Was he apologizing or being funny? Harry didn't know, but he was impressed.

"You can starve at this game, mate!"

"I hope not. But I'm prepared for it, if need be."

"Well, good luck is all I can say!"

John Hyatt took out a watch and glanced at it. It was a half hunter, and plainly eighteen-karat gold. Harry was even more impressed.

"Hello, Harry boy, wonderful little girl you've got in your act, it's nice to see a lady on the halls, even if she ain't one really— well, can't be, can she, never mind, I *liked* it!"

It was Morrie Fine, Harry's sometime agent, looking very dapper and happy in a black crombie topcoat with a fur-collar and a diamond stickpin, if it was a diamond, which Harry doubted. A

115

gray topper sat on his bald head, and he gave off an aroma of brandy.

"Glad to hear that." Harry waited. He answered none of Morrie's questions, but it did not seem to matter. The fat little man was bubbling over with joy and excitement. "I've been sitting next, well, nearly next, to Mr. Weaver, the booking manager, and he liked her as well!"

Harry said, "What about me, didn't he like me?"

"He'd seen you before," was Morrie's way of answering that. "He didn't know you had this sweet fresh little girl wiv you, and he wants to meet her."

"What a surprise," said Harry.

'He's all right." Morrie spoke quickly, without conviction. "He's going to be in the Salisbury public house in Shaftesbury Avenue for a supper snack in about an hour, and she's invited."

"Am I invited an' all?" asked Harry sourly.

Morrie put his arm around Harry's shoulder. "Well, of course you are." He puffed joyously on his cigarillo. "Nice song you got for her, who wrote it?"

"I did," said John Hyatt.

Morrie blinked. "This is John Hyatt. Morrie Fine, he's an agent," said Harry.

"Nice song, nice words. You do the words as well?"

"Yes, I did."

"Sold the song to Harry, have yer?"

"Not to Mr. Viner."

"No?" Morrie looked quickly at Harry. "Nice song."

"Don't try to steal it, Morrie," said Harry gratingly, "for another of your famous clients, if any. Clara has it tied up, that right, Mr. Hyatt?"

"It's Miss Abbott's song." John Hyatt looked awkward. "To do as she likes with."

Morrie looked quickly at John Hyatt, nodded as if to some inner music and said, "You'd better come along as well, Mr. Hyatt. You got anybody trying to sell your songs for you?"

"I've been trying to sell them myself, Mr. Fine."

"Useless," said Morrie decisively. "*You're* the goods, *you* can't praise the goods. I can. I could look after you."

"Let's talk about it," said John Hyatt.

"Good, good." Morrie puffed on his cigarillo, even happier. This peasant, thought Harry Viner, is not doing too badly for his first day in the Smoke. "When your girl turns up, Harry—Clara, is that her name?—I'll get us a cab. I can spring to that, and I should think you'll need to sit down after that lot!"

Harry said, "I only did the show for the experience."

Clara came out of the theater, carrying her stage dress in a small attaché case.

"Hello, John," Clara said.

John Hyatt smiled. His smile for Clara, Harry thought, was quite different from his usual one. He recalled that this peasant had looked as if he fancied Clara when they met in his rooms in the North. The smile made him uneasy. John Hyatt made him uneasy altogether. A varsity man, yet a peasant. *That* suit? And a *gold* watch chain?

Clara was wearing her red suit with the fur trimming. Morrie was impressed. He even raised his hat, to expose his bald head, a rare gesture, and put it smartly back on again.

"Clara, I'm Morrie, I look after Harry when he lets me. We're going for supper with somebody who might give you a job. Somebody who liked you very much, me dear!"

Clara said, "Oh, who?"

Morrie placed a finger alongside his nose, which was not small. "A very important fella, what can do us all a bit o' good, eh, Harry? You be nice to him, dear." He took John Hyatt by the arm. "John, let us find a cab while these two sort themselves out. Have you any other songs like that?"

Harry watched them go. "Clara, let me do any talking there is to be done. And why didn't you tell me about the song and this fella writing it for you?"

Clara looked stubborn. "You didn't want me going on about my doings; you said you wouldn't have me in your act. So I did these things myself, you see?"

"Yes, I think I see." Harry threw his cigar away and tucked his makeup box under his arm. "Well, we'll sort that out later. But one thing. You've paid him for the song?"

"Of course I have."

"Did you get a receipt?"

"No, why?"

"Always get one. Then there's no arguments. How much did you pay him for it?"

Clara looked affronted. "It was my money."

"I didn't say it wasn't."

"You sounded as if you were doubtful."

Harry took a deep breath. "Darlin', all you have to do this evening is smile, and whatever you do, don't tell anybody your second name or who your pa is."

Clara looked sulky. "Can't I use my own name now?"

"You want your pa down here on the next train?" If he isn't, Harry Viner thought, on his way already.

"All right," said Clara. "I'll do just as you say."

"If you always do that"—Harry Viner smiled—"you can't go wrong."

He put his arm around her. But he did not offer to carry her case.

John Hyatt and Morrie Fine waited for a cab outside the theater. John noticed that Morrie did not seem in any hurry to get one. Rather, he seemed to be regarding John Hyatt, and his clothes and manner, in a slightly puzzled fashion.

"Lovely song, that."

John Hyatt nodded. His father always said, "If you've nothing to say, don't talk." To Morrie Fine he had nothing to say, yet.

"Pity you sold the copyright," said Morrie academically.

"I wrote the song for Miss . . . er . . . for Clara." John remembered just in time that Clara's second name was a secret. "As I said, it belongs to her. I can always write another song."

"Yerce," Morrie said doubtfully. "But I can see that one catching on, see? An' if it ever gets to be popular, anything that comes in from the sheet music will be hers." Morrie puffed on his cigar and disregarded a passing cab. "And I suppose, Harry Viner's?"

"That's up to her."

Something in John Hyatt's tone seemed to alert Morrie, and he looked at John a long moment and nodded as if to his inner music. "Lovely girl, Clara," he opined.

"Yes, she is."

John Hyatt smiled to himself. He had not meant to sound quite so positive in agreeing with Morrie. He added, "She sang the song very nicely, I thought."

"Did you?" Morrie asked. "I thought Harry coming on spoiled it a bit. She would have been all right without him."

"It seems he didn't think so." Again, John Hyatt was surprised at the sharp tone of his own voice. Again, he added a quick qualification. "And maybe he was right. He's had a lot of experience."

"Experience, yerce, I grant you." Morrie sighed. "Not a lot of what you'd call success, but experience, certainly. Harry's going to be a good comic. But it's going to take time, it always does wiv a comic. And a lot can't stand it, they give up on it."

"I don't think Harry Viner will give up," John Hyatt said.

"No?" Morrie debated the point. "Maybe not. But I dunno where he's going. I don't think he does either."

"He doesn't want the soft option." John Hyatt was annoyed at having to take Harry Viner's part, even with his own agent. "He tries new things, like going off without a song tonight. That takes character."

Morrie looked at him, as if surprised. "That's true. Never thought of it like that." He threw his cigarillo into the straw-choked gutter. "What about you, got anything at all fixed up, any people interested in your songs?"

"I'm not like Harry," John Hyatt said. "I don't have any ideas about my station. I'll write any kind of songs for anybody, to start with. Later on I'll get choosy, when I can afford to get choosy."

Morrie Fine nodded in total approval of that sentiment. "You been around the stage doors, talking to people, then?"

"I've been around the stage doors," John Hyatt said, "but mostly people have not been talking to me."

It was true enough. Although he did not say so to Morrie, John had almost given up on provincial music halls. His many visits to artistes at the Alhambra and other Northern music halls had convinced him quite quickly that artistes did not take any song writer seriously unless he came to see them in London.

John glanced at Morrie Fine, who had lit a new cigarillo. He said, "I only arrived in London this week."

"I think you did the right thing, coming to the Smoke. There's no future in them Northern halls, not for anybody wiv a bit of class."

"I wouldn't say I had class," John Hyatt said. "I would say I was willing."

"Well, I say you have class," Morrie Fine said. "And I'm not letting you throw yourself away on comics. Anybody who can write a song like that, he can do himself a bit of good in no time. Of course," he added hastily, "I don't mean as how he'll be living at the Ritz tomorrow. I mean it might take a month or two." He patted John's back again and added, "Where you living now?"

"Same place as . . . er . . . Harry."

119

"I see, I see." Morrie *did* see, John Hyatt decided, and with it came the thought: if Morrie is as quick on his feet as that, perhaps he was a better agent than Harry Viner seemed to think?

"What we'll do," Morrie summed up, "we'll put our brains in steep, and we'll see what we come up wiv. One thing you ain't a-going to do from now on, as my client, is go round to any stage doors, without an appointment at least."

"Well"—John Hyatt smiled—"I can't say no to that, can I?"

"Ten percent." Morrie Fine hailed a cab at last. "Nothing's for nothing in this world, is it, son?"

The Salisbury was crowded with after-show people, many of them actors and music hall artistes. It was, Harry explained to Clara, a pro's pub, almost a club, without the need to pay a club's subscription. Ushered in by Morrie, they found Mr. Weaver, the booking manager, sitting at a large table in the back room of the place, consuming a grilled Dover sole. A bottle of Chablis was half drunk, and Mr. Weaver, who was large, white-haired, with a handsome handlebar mustache and attired in evening clothes, stood and removed the large napkin from his neck at the sight of Clara. He was fifty if a day.

"Evening, me dear." He clasped her hand in his and held it a long time. "You were magnificent. Young, innocent, dare I say . . . virginal?"

"Say anything you like, Samuel." Morrie sat down and blinked nervously at the hovering waiter.

Clara wondered how to extricate her hand from the moist clasp of Mr. Weaver.

"Thank you, Mr. Weaver." She tried to take her hand away, but Mr. Weaver held onto it.

"Samuel, what?" He looked around jovially. "We're all friends here, right, Morrie?"

"Right!" said Morrie heartily, ignoring the waiter.

"Will you join me in a Dover sole?" asked Mr. Weaver of Clara. She nodded. He still held her hand, and he drew her into the chair next to him.

Morrie cleared his throat unhappily. "Sam," he said, "can I introduce Harry Viner, Miss . . . er . . . Clara's partner, and Mr. Hyatt, who wrote the song?"

Mr. Weaver looked up at John Hyatt. "Nice song. Got any more?"

John Hyatt smiled and said nothing at all. He signaled to the waiter. "Can we all have Dover soles please?" Then he sat down.

Morrie looked at Harry and then at John Hyatt again.

"And wine, two bottles of Chablis," said John Hyatt.

Morrie tapped his ankle under the table.

"You don't need to pay, son."

"If I don't," said John Hyatt mildly, "who will?"

Clara disengaged her hand at last in a pretext to get a glass of water. Mr. Weaver poured her a large goblet of wine. As he was doing so, rather unsteadily, Harry said, "Be nice to the old buzzard. He's important."

"Nice?" Clara stared at him. "How nice?"

"Pleasant. Be sensible."

Clara wondered if being sensible included suffering Mr. Weaver's wandering hand as she ate her Dover sole. It rested on her knee and crept around her waist, but she did not betray that it was happening and hoped that Harry, on the other side of the table, could not guess. John Hyatt seemed to know, and he constantly found excuses to ask for salt and pepper or the water carafe or any table implement close to Mr. Weaver's wandering left hand. Mr. Weaver was not amused, but Clara was. John Hyatt seemed to close one eye behind the thick spectacles. There was more to him, Clara decided, than there looked to be.

When they had finished talking about the evening's show and the various antics of the sufferers of the hook, which seemed to amuse Morrie and Mr. Weaver so much they had to pause and wipe tears from their eyes, Harry suddenly said, "I believe you liked our act, Mr. Weaver?"

Morrie shot him a sharp warning glance, but Harry was not abashed.

"Easy," breathed Morrie.

Mr. Weaver was lighting a Havana cigar with a Swan Vestas match.

"I liked the little lady very much."

"I'm glad," said Harry, "to hear that."

"She needs more done on her, but I could arrange that."

"No," said Harry.

"No?" Mr. Weaver's eyebrows rose.

Morrie looked at the tablecloth as if estimating its retail value.

Harry Viner said, "We're a double act. Comic and girl."

121

Mr. Weaver pondered on this. "I'd like to hear the little lady's thoughts on that. I can offer her a job."

Clara sat quietly for a long moment; then she said, "Harry is right. We're a double now. If you take one of us, Mr. Weaver, you have to take the other, I'm afraid." She smiled, but Mr. Weaver was not deceived. He took his hand away from her thigh, drew deeply on his cigar and said, "It'll be four halls a night, you pay for your own cabs, I'll give Morrie the details, the money is a fiver for the two of you."

"A fiver?" Harry said. "I was getting four going out on my own!"

"You were a trial turn tonight." Mr. Weaver signaled for his hat and coat, which arrived at once. "It's there if you want it."

Morrie said, "They'll take it, Mr. Weaver, and thank you."

Mr. Weaver nodded and, without bidding them good-night, walked out of the place.

"He's off to Madame Fanny's in Duke Street, him. Plenty of his kinda girls there." Morrie smiled at Clara approvingly. "You got a good girl here, Harry. He left us with the bleedin' bill an' all."

"I'll pay," said John Hyatt. "Congratulations, Clara."

"Thank you, John."

Morrie drew on his cigarillo mournfully.

"Thing is, how are we going to bill you?"

There was a long pause. Harry broke it.

"Viner and Viner," he said. "What else?"

Clara did not smile, but she did not argue either.

122

Now We Live in a Top Back Room

Papa knocked on the door himself.

Clara saw him through the curtains and rushed to answer the door. Papa stood, looking around him coldly, in his splendid dark, thick woolen suit and stiff collar and tall hat, rolled umbrella in hand. Behind him was a brougham, and the driver had plainly been told to wait, for he was taking the opportunity to put a nose bag on his starved-looking horse.

Papa brushed his mustache with his lavender-gloved forefinger. To Clara's, "Oh, Papa, Papa, do come in!" he responded with a loud embarrassed cough, and he did not kiss her. Mrs. Harrington disappeared into her kitchen, and Clara ushered Papa into the combined room. He stood in the center of the carpet, staring at the large brass bedstead. He did not take off his hat. Harry's stage jacket, which she had been pressing with the flatiron, heated on the gas ring, showed that a man also lived in the room. Papa's first remarks told her that he could see that already.

"You not only sleep with this fellow, you do his washing and cleaning as well?"

Clara turned off the gas ring and took off her apron. She was wearing a button-up striped shirt and a collar and a long shirt. Her hair was piled up on her head. The style made her look older than she was. That was the aim. Papa noticed it at once.

123

"Making a woman of yourself, too, I see. . . ."

Clara still said nothing. She would wait, she decided, until he said something pleasant.

"I had the devil's own job to find you. Taken me weeks."

"I wrote to you." Clara sat down and with a hand indicated the only decent chair in the room. Papa ignored the sign.

"Nothing to say to you in a letter. Wanted to see you face to face. Only way to do it."

"Perhaps."

"You're my only daughter. Many a father would have put the police on you."

"I am above the age of consent, Papa."

"I know that, and it didn't take you long to consent, did it?"

Clara flushed. At least, she thought, he's talking to me like a woman of the world, even if he is insulting me at the same time. "I'm sorry you felt it necessary to say that, Papa."

Papa blew his nose on a fine linen handkerchief. Clara looked at him with a little awe. She had forgotten how clean and shining rich people were. Papa's boots gleamed brightly, and his watch chain gleamed, too, and so did his gold tie halter. His starched collar glistened, and the silver knob of his walking stick glinted. Clara pushed a wisp of hair back from her face. Once she had been clean and shining, too, where there was always plenty of hot water (prepared by Mary, the maid), and her shoes had shone brilliantly (Donald, the bootboy), and her clothes had been pressed daily, just as Papa's were now. She smiled. It all seemed a long time ago.

"You smile." Papa looked without enthusiasm at the chamber pot resting on the oilcloth under the massive bed. "I suppose you find me amusing?"

"Not at all, Papa. Pray forgive me." Clara thought: how differently I talk to him from the way I talk to Harry, and it's only been weeks, not months and years. It was like having to learn an old, once-known language all over again. "Will you take your hat off and sit awhile? Can I get you some tea?"

Papa shook his head to these suggestions.

Clara suggested, "Perhaps a little whiskey?"

Papa looked incredulous. "Whiskey? In the forenoon, girl!"

Clara tried not to smile. She was profoundly glad Harry had got up early for once and gone off to the pub to meet some of his friends.

"Is he likely to be in, this Viner fellow?"

"No, Papa. I fear he will be out all day."

Papa grunted. "It could be just as well. I have no desire to talk to the man."

"I wish I could think that someday you might, Papa."

Papa closed his eyes. "You are barely seventeen years of age, Clara. Leave a message for him. If it will help, I will leave some money. Come home and no questions asked." He coughed, not looking at her, as if looking at her would hurt him. "I have told everybody that you are on the Continent, at a ladies' college, learning French." He looked at his feet. "I had to tell them something."

"Poor Papa!"

"Do not pity me, girl, pity yourself! Look at what you have almost cast away! A good home, a good marriage, eventually, to some suitable person. I say almost because there is still time. Let us discuss it no more. Come home."

Clara bit her lip hard to stop the tears. "This is my home, Papa."

Papa did not raise his eyes from his shining boots. "This is nobody's home, certainly not yours. If I thought I had brought a girl into such a place, I would be ashamed."

"Harry did not bring me here. I insisted."

"You insisted?"

"Yes, I did. He has been against it all along."

Papa looked up. "He would let you go without protest?"

"I don't know. I think perhaps he would."

"Then there is some good in the fellow, after all!"

"There is a lot of good in him, Papa. But good is not what I seek in him. I love him, you see, and good or bad has nothing whatever to do with it."

Papa looked dumbfounded. "It doesn't?"

"There are many good men who would not please me. Harry is himself, and that is enough for me."

Papa shook his head. "You are saying this . . . arrangement is more your doing than it is his? I cannot believe that!"

"I'm afraid you will have to, Papa, for it is the truth."

"What you are saying is that you will not come home with me."

"What I am saying is I cannot."

Papa took out his handkerchief and ran it across his brow. It was very hot in the small room.

125

"Let me get you a glass of lemonade, Papa."

"Nothing, I thank you. . . . This fellow Viner is a comic. I could damage his prospects if they were worth damaging, which from what I hear they are not."

"He has ability, Papa. He is a man who had not had advantages. But he works hard and will make his way, of that I am sure."

"Not if I can help it, he will not!"

"I am very sorry you find it necessary to say that, Papa, because you cannot know that I am pregnant."

Papa sat down then, abruptly.

He seemed to be sunk in deep thought for a very long moment. Then he said, in a voice softer than usual, "Is whiskey all you have in the house?"

"I am afraid so, Papa."

"Then whiskey it shall have to be."

Clara gave him the whiskey in a cup. He looked at it, grimaced and swallowed the liquid. He looked at Clara in awe. "Women!" Papa said. "You have nothing to do with us. Nothing. You are with the moon."

Clara did not reply.

Papa set down the cup. "Does he mean to marry you?"

"I have not told him yet."

"When you tell him," Papa persisted, "will he marry you then?"

"He will have to decide that for himself, Papa."

Papa gripped his walking cane like a club. "The bounder! He'd better marry you!"

"Papa," said Clara mildly, "only a moment ago you were telling me to come home."

Papa shook his head. "You can't now, can you? No, I'm sorry, Clara. That would be out of the question."

"I wasn't asking!"

"Out of the question altogether." He shook his head. "I will do what I can, naturally, since things have reached this pass. I will send some money regularly so that you and the child are taken care of. I have your sister-in-law, Marta, running the household now, and I do not wish to disrupt any arrangements there. I will not tell your brother, Adam, or Marta anything of what we have discussed here today. I will simply say that you are marrying Viner and that I have given my permission."

"Papa, that is in some ways kind and generous, but I do not want your money. We will manage."

He stood up, heavily. He looks older, she thought, but I cannot blame myself for that. I have my own life to live.

"You will promise to write?"

"Yes, I will."

Clara waited for more, but there was no more.

Papa walked out of the room. After a moment or two the front door slammed and the brougham clattered away along the street.

Clara sat and listened to the horses' hooves fade away.

There was a tap on the door.

Clara called, "Come in!"

Mrs. Harrington, concerned and interested, stood there. "The gentleman that's just gone must of left this, dear. It's addressed to 'Miss Clara Abbott.' Is that you?"

"Yes," Clara said. "It was my name."

"This is yours then."

Mrs. Harrington handed her the buff envelope. The landlady said, "You all right, are yer? You look a bit pale."

Clara just nodded, in dismissal. "Thank you, Mrs. Harrington."

"You do let a body know when you don't want their company, don'tcher?" Mrs. Harrington shut the door sullenly and shuffled off down the hall.

After a long moment Clara opened the envelope. It contained two large white ten-pound banknotes. He must have prepared them before he came, in case of this, Clara thought. Oh, Papa, I love you, only I love *him* more! She wanted to call Papa back and tell him, and thought she would write tomorrow.

But she knew that she would not.

Harry seemed in good form when he returned, but he complained about the whiskey. "Hey, it's all gone. I thought I had a drop left."

"You must be mistaken, Harry."

"Ah, what do it matter?" He was sitting at the table in his shirt sleeves, eating a kipper. Clara had learned how to fry them in butter, as he liked them. Papa ate kippers only for breakfast. Harry "couldn't face them of a morning" but thought them "handsome" for tea, which meal they took at five in the afternoon, before

127

they went off on the evening's work. Clara had decided not to tell Harry about Papa's visit and had bribed Mrs. Harrington with a pint of stout. The money was at the bottom of her sewing bag, where it would remain.

Clara poured Harry a pint of thick brown tea, heavily garnished with sugar and milk. He drank appreciatively, lit one of his cigars and took her on his knee.

"You happy, are you?"

"Of course I am, why do you ask?"

"You looked a bit peaky and miserable when I came in."

"I'm all right, Harry."

"I've been thinking." Harry kissed her. "Sunday let's go to Brighton."

"Oh, I'd love that! The seaside!"

"Yes." Harry removed a kipper bone from his teeth. "Sid Jones—you remember him, got the hook?—well, he's making up a party. Only cost a few bob each."

"A party? Couldn't we go on our own?"

"We could, but it'll be a lot of laughs going with them, and anyway, I've already said we'd go." He kissed her. "We're an old couple now, that's how they look on us, don't you go telling them you'd rather go on our own, I'll never hear the last of it."

Clara kissed him. "That'll be fine." She stood up and began to clear the dishes away slowly.

"You in your monthlies or something?"

"You know I'm not."

"Aren't you due?" He looked up sharply, so she laughed. "Of course I'm not due, not till next week."

Harry creased his forehead. "We have to be careful there, duck. *That* would be all we'd need. Out of work like ninepence, we'd be."

"Would we?"

"You're joking!"

They packed their shared skip with their own items of clothing (Harry's stage suit and shirt and tap shoes) and Clara's own costume (she was wearing a satin sailor suit she'd made herself) and her own tap shoes. Clara could not really dance very well yet, but Harry had taught her enough, in the small combined room with the carpet rolled back (nobody ever complained about noise at Mrs. Harrington's or out they went!) to accompany him in the buck-and-wing that ended their turn. The dancing had been a business of bone-aching weariness, for Harry had been a hard task-master, and it had taken time for him to accept her into the act. When Morrie had told her Weaver had never wanted Harry at all, Clara had been indignant. What was the matter with Harry?

Morrie had tapped his cigarillo on an ashtray. "Don't wear drawers, does he?"

Clara had laughed, but Morrie had seemed to be serious. Even Harry had taken the line that she was only in his act because Weaver had a letch for her. What nonsense, she was there because of her song and because she had made an impression on the audience at the Metropolitan.

Their first night together, as Viner and Viner, had been near disaster. They had gone on as first turn at Collin's Music Hall, and Clara had wondered, as she stood in the wings, in her long blue dress with a parasol, how ever she would get through without losing her voice. Her throat seemed tight, and she found difficulty in swallowing.

"Nerves, dear, just take deep breaths," Harry had said, making up, and it was his offhand attitude to her nervousness (almost, she thought, as if he really wouldn't *mind* if she made a complete mess of things!) that made her the more determined to do well. They had arranged the act so that Harry went on first, told his Abie stories, and that she came on and joined him and went into her song. It wasn't really a song, she had pointed out to him, that *two* people could sing; it was really *her* song. But Harry had replied that since it was the only song they had, she must sing it, and to *him*, as he danced around her. They then went into a fast dance routine and ended with a buck-and-wing at which Clara felt foolish and out of breath, but Harry said, "If an audience sees you're working hard, you get a round no matter what."

Clara sulked at that. "I don't think of myself as a comedy lady. I think of myself—"

"As a single act?"

"I suppose I do."

"As Marie Lloyd?"

"Not yet."

"Not yet, not ever! That takes years."

And so they had gone on, at Collin's, and done it. The act *had* seemed ragged to Clara, but the whole experience had been bewildering, so it was impossible to know whether they had done well or not. John Hyatt, who had been there, had insisted they were fine; the audience liked them, especially Clara's song.

"He would say that, wouldn't he?" had been Harry's comment.

Clara packed the skip and put the makeup box in last, leaving Harry to strap it up and carry it out to the cab, which had already been ordered. It was the same cab that would take them from one music hall to the next in the course of the evening. They had been doing this for several weeks now, and they were beginning to tire. Clara could hardly drag herself out of bed in the mornings. They both slept like dead people, and their lovemaking had been much curtailed. Clara had never known what it was to be so physically exhausted. Their diet, which lacked meats and other expensive and strengthening foods, did not help. She could not get Harry to eat large meals, even if she had time and money to cook them, which she hadn't. He simply said, "When we're working like this, little and often's all we need." Clara had lost a stone in weight.

Harry got up from the table and strapped the skip. He looked at his watch. "Cab's nearly due, love."

Clara put on her red suit. It was still the only decent one she had, and she took care of it, pressing it often. When winter came, she would need a coat. When winter came, she might need many things, Clara thought, if she did not *come on* very soon! She pushed the thought away and put on her hat, having dusted her face first with rice powder.

Harry kissed her. He looked very handsome with his hat at a rakish angle. She loved him very much. She told him so. He kissed her again and said, "And I love you, too, but we have to move, there's Mr. Briggs with the cab!"

Mr. Briggs greeted them with melancholy. He was a large man with a ragged mustache. He patted his horse, Flossie, and informed them that the crowds in the West End were worse than usual. Mr. Briggs was pessimistic by nature.

"Bleedin' Jonah you are, Briggsy," said Harry, hefting the skip into the brougham. "One of these nights you'll get us there late and that'll really cheer you up!"

"Never missed getting anybody to any theater on time yet," said Mr. Briggs, flicking Flossie lightly with his whip. "Next time will be the first, mate!"

Mr. Briggs did not accord Harry and Clara the respect given to them by members of the public who saw them come out of the stage door of the music halls. He had seen them all, as he often said, come and go. His knowledge of music halls was encyclopedic, and his stories were never ones to cheer his passengers.

"Tell us," Harry said, nudging Clara, "who's having a bad time this week. Any good news, anybody got the bird or broke their leg?"

Mr. Briggs sucked on a hollow tooth, one of the few in his head.

"Marie Lloyd's asking for more money," he said.

"She's got most of it already," said Harry. "She might as well have the lot."

"Gets through it, though." Mr. Briggs cantered along with a fine disregard for other carriages. He had one speed, Harry always said, fast. "She's got all them relatives, and she do like a bet on the horses. Tell me she lost a packet at Epsom last week!"

"Well, the bookies have some of it, that's bad news," said Harry. "Anything else?"

"George Formby was taken very sick last night at Collin's, I hear."

"When George Formby isn't *on,* that's when he's bad," said Harry.

"Oh, he was *on!*" Mr. Briggs drove Flossie straight at a gentleman's carriage, whose coachman blanched at this direct challenge, gave way and cursed Mr. Briggs, who was used to it. "He was *on,*" continued Mr. Briggs, "but only just, if you know what I mean. Then," he said, swanning between a large broughan and a brewer's dray, piled with barrels, "there's one or two managers cutting salaries, I hear."

"Oh?" said Harry. "Where do you hear that?"

"From them," said Mr. Briggs, "as has had 'em cut."

"Anybody we know?" asked Harry. "Because if they cut ours, we'll be paying them for working."

Mr. Briggs kept going despite a policeman's raised glove. The policeman saw it was Mr. Briggs and simply smiled and waved him on. "They know me, the cozzers," explained Mr. Briggs. "They know I has no time to stop or there'd be no music halls." He navigated them through the choked horse jams of the Tottenham Court Road, through Holborn and the Strand, and set them down with time to spare outside the Tivoli.

"You're on a soft spot," he told them, "compared to some. The Immobile Comedian, don't reckon you'd know him, funny fella, used to stand there, never move, you'd swear he was dead, you would, well, he once did nine turns at nine different halls in the one night. I know he did it, becos I took him to all nine of them. He died after he done that." Mr. Briggs watched Harry as he manhandled the skip onto the pavement. "I'll be here a-waiting for you at half past." And he jogged away, into the thick stream of cabs and carts, looking neither to the right nor to the left.

"One of these days he'll smile, and it'll stay on his face forever!" Harry picked up the skip and they walked past the curious eyes of shopgirls and street arabs, around to the stage door.

The stage doorkeeper, in the tradition an old music hall turn himself, greeted them with a wave of his blackened pipe, from his cubbyhole. "Evening, both!" Clara was always thrilled to be hailed in this way. Her pulse quickened, and she thought: this is wonderful, all right, I'm tired, bone-weary, in fact, but I wanted this, and now I have it I'm not going to complain about any of it, even the sore feet!

They dressed quickly, since they were the first turn on, and applied their makeup. Their dressing room was shared with another double act who appeared later on the bill, and they saw little of one another. Clara had learned to paint her face now and was no longer shocked by the whorish appearance it always gave her. She was concerned that her skin, even in this short time, had begun to take on a yellowish tinge and a tendency to spots, but Harry had explained it was usual. "You can't sweat, see, under the grease, and it goes inward, so you get a poxy skin. Everybody does. Price you pay, dear. Nobody asked you to go on the halls!"

Clara had always been proud of her milk-white skin, considered by all men a prize. Only a laboring woman, in the fields, had a brown skin, and this was a sure sign of poverty. Clara loosened her hair and let it fall over the satin sailor-boy suit, which tonight she would wear for the first time. "I can't dance a buck-and-wing in that dress," she'd told Harry, "so I'd better make myself something I *can* dance in." The blouse was cut low, with a sailor collar, and the trousers were tight to the knee ("Give them a treat!" said Harry without a smile) and full-bottomed, like a sailor's. Clara hoped it would be all right with the song. She was by no means sure of it. Somehow it seemed to be against the sentiments of the song. But as Harry said, they were a double act. They had to compromise.

"Next on, Mr. Viner!" sounded out, and Harry yelled, "Right!"

132

and then they were rushing along the passage and backstage.

Harry walked onstage. "Abie got a job as a railway porter. I know it's unlikely but he did. A fella points to a compartment full of Japanese. He sez to Abie, 'They're the cleverest people on earth, the Japs. One day they're going to take over the world.' 'Where are they going to now?' asks Abie. 'They're on their way to Birmingham,' says the fella. The train pulls out of the station, and Abie sez, 'They can't be all that clever, that train's going to Cardiff!' "

The band began to play "Naughty But Nice," and Clara skipped onstage. Harry had told her, "Don't try to be too smart, too professional. It don't matter if you seem young and silly. They'll like that, the innocent thing. They see plenty of hard old tarts. You'll make a nice change."

Clara was blinded, as usual, by the spots and frightened as ever, by the noise, but less so than before. She was getting used to it, able to smile at the monster even. Clara smiled, stalls, balcony, gallery, as Harry had taught her. One, two, three. Stalls, balcony, gallery. Four. Stalls again. Five. Turn to me. Smile at me. Let them see you smile at me. Bend you knee, just like that, let them see the shape of your leg, that's what they've paid for. Put a finger on your lips. Pout. Stick your bottom out, darlin', that's right, let them see you've got one. Then blow me a kiss. A big kiss. The song is all about kissing. Right! So you pirouette round me, blowing kisses. Then you stand still. And you sing as the band starts, let them play the opening bars, always tell an audience a song is coming, don't throw it at them suddenly, they'll think it's a gag, and they'll laugh. Nice and easy. Look sincere. One, two, three. Stalls, gallery, balcony. Four, stalls again. *Now!*

Clara sang:

> My young man takes me out for a dip,
> But once in the sea I feel I might . . . . *slip!*
> Naughty but Nice, It's Naughty but Nice,
> Never Been Kissed in the Same Place Twice!

During the verse Harry made comic swimming motions and winked at the audience.

Clara sang:

> My young man takes me to a military tattoo,
> But when he kissed me, I felt I might . . . *ooooo!*

133

Harry danced around, saluting and coming to attention and pratfalling as if his rifle and pack were too heavy. The audience laughed, and once again Clara wondered if they were doing the right thing with the song. It seemed wrong somehow to laugh *not* at her words but at Harry's actions. They got off to a round of applause, after their breathtaking buck-and-wing.

Clara ran all the way back to the dressing room. Harry had already packed the skip and had thrown a light coat over his stage clothes. Clara pulled a cloak over hers, and together, without a word, they ran out into the street.

Mr. Briggs was waiting with Flossie. He had her moving almost before Harry had thrown the skip into the brougham, and Clara had collapsed onto the leather seat. "Lot of traffic tonight," he said, ignoring the snarl of a foppish young man driving a hansom. The young man had a broad Cockney accent and no fare inside, and he pursued Mr. Briggs along the Strand at a spanking pace until Mr. Briggs cut across him abruptly and forced him to pull fiercely on his reins. His horse slipped on the cobbles and fell, "Take a dozen strong men to get him on his feet again," Mr. Briggs said mournfully. "Some of these young cabbies shouldn't be in charge of a decent animal, never mind driving people about."

The brougham careered under the flickering gaslamps toward Trafalgar Square, where Mr. Briggs outdrove the fastest gigs, and up St. Martin's Lane toward the Pavilion. Clara and Harry simply lay back, their eyes closed, hanging onto their seats.

At the Pavilion they ran into the stage door, avoiding the first of the Johnnies, who would congregate in large numbers at the end of the show. They were sending in cards and great colorful bunches of flowers, roses, carnations, already.

"Any for me?" Clara asked the stage doorman as a joke.

"Yerce, I 'ave!" He produced a large bunch of violets.

"Blimey," said Harry, "you've got an admirer."

"Not you?"

"Look, dear, even violets cost money!"

Clara took the bunch of violets and sniffed. "They're lovely!"

"Hurry up, or we'll be off!"

They ran into the dressing room. Eugene Stratton was headlining, the top blackface comic and singer in the country. They could hear the haunting sound of his famous song, drifting in from the stage:

> She's my lady love, she is my Queen, my baby love.
> She's no girl for sitting down to dream,
> She's the only Queen Laguna knows.

"Viner and Viner. You're on!"

"Coming," Harry called breathlessly. "Ready, darlin'?"

"Ready!"

She kissed him, on impulse.

They ran backstage and just made it.

Eugene Stratton was dancing his last magical chorus, his shoes moving in the sand, a single spot playing on him from the gallery.

> I know she likes me,
> I know she likes me,
> Because she sez so,
> She is my Lily of Laguna,
> She is my Lily and my Rose.

He came off to tumultuous applause. "God," he said, "I'm pig-sick of singing that song."

Harry ran onstage. He clutched his heart. "I've just made it from the Tivoli, where they eat Jewish comics alive. I'm told *you* boil them first. . . ?"

There was a laugh.

"I was going to dance for you," Harry said, "but I promised Eugene Stratton I wouldn't show him up."

Stratton said, "I like your fella. Plenty of neck. He'd do well in the States."

"People say that."

Stratton said, "I was born there. But I've been lucky here, so why go back?"

Clara could only nod. Stratton was the top, the best. If he said something good about Harry, Harry had to be right about himself.

Clara took her cue, went on, sang, danced, came off and to-gether they ran back to the dressing room, packed the skip, threw on their coats and cloaks and ran out of the theater. Mr. Briggs waited, whip raised. "You been a long time there," he informed them sadly. "Dunno if we gonna make the next one!"

Harry gasping, fell back in his seat. "Mate, I don't care, I just want to put my feet up for ten minutes."

Clara massaged her calf tenderly. "God, I hurt!"

135

"Don't put so much into it then." Harry's eyes were closed, and his stage clothes were clinging to his body, under the topcoat thrown over his shoulders.

"I can't help it." Clara was in a sweat, too, but she hugged her long cloak around her. "What do we do in winter, running about like this?"

"Die of pneumonia." Harry's mouth was open, taking in drafts of air.

"I seen turns collapse in my time," said Mr. Briggs. "I see a professional strong man collapse once, the Great Pardo, that was 'im. Got outa me cab an' just sank down onto the pavement, he did, the Great Pardo." Mr. Briggs cut up a thrusting four-in-hand. "Dunno what happened to him. They took him orf to hospital, and I never see him agen."

Harry said, "I don't care where the bed is, I'll sleep in it. I could sleep in this thing with you driving."

Mr. Briggs took that as a compliment and swerved Flossie across a delivery wagon, pulled by a gray. For a moment the horses jostled, but Flossie was larger and stronger and her teeth showed and the gray gave way.

"Some of these delivery men," said Mr. Briggs, "I wouldn't trust them to post a letter, never mind put them in charge of a decent animal."

They arrived at the old Middlesex Music Hall in Drury Lane, ran in, ran on, did their turn and ran out, hardly knowing whether they had been applauded or not. Mr. Briggs was waiting, as ever. "Last one," he said, "til tomorrow night."

Clara collapsed on the brougham's seat. Every day she thought she would get used to this, and every evening she wondered if she ever would. She said nothing of this to Harry. They did not speak at all but lay back, fighting for breath and nerve, as the brougham racketed through the carriage-choked streets, toward their final hall. Clara looked sidewise at Harry. His eyes were closed, and she knew he was even more exhausted than she was. He had to go out and face the audience first each time. All she did was come out and sing and dance. Clara reached out and pressed his hand. "Love you!"

"Love you, too, darlin'," said Harry, not opening his eyes, "only I couldn't even if I wanted to!" He took a pull at his whiskey flask. It was something he only did, she knew, when he was exhausted. Lately he had been doing it between each hall. Suddenly

136

the brougham swerved around. Flossie, in the middle of a maze of horse-drawn traffic, began to walk around in a circle.

"What the hell's happening?" yelled Harry.

"It's that bleedin' Sally Army band!" Mr. Briggs hauled on the reins to no avail. A Salvation Army band was playing lustily down a side street. Their notes sounded sweet and clear above the noise of horses' hooves and wheels and whips. "Every time she hears a band Flossie goes round in a circle," explained Mr. Briggs.

"Why?" demanded Harry.

"Used to be with George Sanger's Circus, didn't she?"

"You mean she used to be a *circus* horse?"

But Mr. Briggs was too busy avoiding the whips of outraged drivers as the big horse turned contentedly in the road, blocking it to all comers.

"In the middle of the Charing Cross Road!" shouted Harry. Both he and Clara began to laugh hysterically, but Mr. Briggs was not amused. He sweated and pulled and yelled, but Flossie plodded around and around, and the huge buildup of horse carriages and carts and drays went on, with a policeman now gaping wonderingly at the sight.

"I thought I'd broke her of the habit!" said Mr. Briggs. "Jeesus, I ain't, though."

The Salvation Army band stopped playing, with a flourish.

Mr. Briggs whipped up Flossie, and before the policeman could exact retribution, they were on their way, at a spanking pace, all of Charing Cross Road open before them, since nothing had passed them once Flossie began her circling to the music.

"Even the bloody horse can do a turn!" Harry gasped. "We should put it in the act; then we'd have everything!"

They were still laughing as Harry ran onto the stage, back at the Tivoli for the second house, and somehow the audience caught their good spirits and they received the best round of applause of the evening. When they got back to the dressing room, they looked at each other and burst out laughing. Harry offered her his whiskey flask, and Clara took a mouthful. She did not like the taste, but it burned and seemed to give her strength. She took another, a longer one.

"Hey, hey!" Harry took the flask away from her. "Easy does it."

"I like the taste of that."

"That's a bad sign." Harry shook his head. "All the boozers in this game say that."

"Do you like the taste of it?" she asked.

"No, I just need it." He didn't seem to be joking.

They stopped laughing then and sat in total exhaustion for ten minutes. Harry took another long pull at his flask and then started to whip off his stage clothes. There was no sink in the dressing room, but there was some water in a jug. They used it to wash when they had cleaned off their greasepaint. There was no possibility of a bath, and Clara missed that, but she was resigned to it. She folded Harry's show clothes away. He had let them fall to the floor as he took them off, which only showed how tired he was, poor dear. They pulled on their street clothes in silence, wearily, like two sleepwalkers. Clara could not remember when she had felt so tired.

Harry combed his hair and stood back from the mirror.

"What about a supper? It's Saturday night."

All Clara wanted to do was sleep, but she said, "Do you want to?"

"It's sleep an' work and nothing else, if we don't," said Harry, kissing her. "Come on, we can afford it, and come on, if we can't!"

They couldn't, Clara thought, but they did. To an Italian café along the Strand. "We can't afford Romano's yet, that's for the cream," said Harry. They drank a bottle of Chianti and ate steak and mashed. Their eyelids drooped over Harry's cigar and Clara's coffee, but they came out feeling better, Clara especially. They had sent their skip back to Mrs. Harrington's with Mr. Briggs and Flossie. "All I need from old Briggsy is a Thought for Today," said Harry. "Cheer me up for the night, that would. Death Is Nigh, that's his motto." Now they walked down the Strand, drifting with the midnight crowds. "The naughtiest street in London, the Strand is," said Harry.

Clara looked around at the milling crowds. There did seem to be rather a lot of men and some unaccompanied women.

"This is the nobs' street and the tarts' street," said Harry.

A very young child with a painted face peered up at them. "Watch your language, mister. You're in with the nobs."

Harry stopped and regarded the urchin. Clara stared at her in horror. "How old are you?" she asked.

"Twelve, I am." The eyes in the child's face were very old. "Why, you fancy me, lady, do yer? Well, I ain't particular, am I?

Take the two of you on, only I ain't got a place, have I? You got one, have yer?"

"Bugger off," said Harry, "before I call a copper!"

The child laughed. "Call one, mate. They all know me. Some of 'em too bleedin' well." She waved her tiny hand and walked off up the street, in her children's overall and dirty lace-up boots.

"Is *she* . . . ? That *child?*"

Harry shook his head. "Dozens of 'em around, boys as well. You go up the side streets you'll see a lot worse than that, dear. Nothing you can't buy along the Strand, of an evening."

Clara fell silent. "What must you live like to do that?"

"You just got to be hungry enough, that's all," Harry said.

They walked along in silence.

Clara said, "All the girls can't be starving?"

"No, they like the life. It's lazy, and most of them drink anyway." Harry pointed out girls to prove his point. They teetered, young and old alike, under gaslamp standards, calling to the passing men in a phrase or two of French, as was the fashion.

Clara began to see London with new eyes. The thin boys in doorways accosted by the fleshy middle-aged men in long opera cloaks and top hats, the cab that halted and an uncovered ankle extended, the door invitingly open, the young man in evening dress rapidly getting inside. "Where are they going?" Clara asked.

"Nowhere," Harry said. "They'll have it off inside the cab. It's quick, and it's cheaper."

"I think it's horrible." Clara was truly shocked.

Harry kissed her on the cheek. A passing street arab shouted, "Gimme one for me sister, mister!" and Harry said, "Clara, life ain't all love and kisses, darlin'."

"No," said Clara. "I see that."

They got back to Mrs. Harrington's in a carriage, which cost them another two shillings. It had been an expensive evening, but Clara felt better for the food and the wine, which had made her feel fuzzy and soft and more cheerful. In the combined room, her tiredness returned. This is nobody's home, Papa had said, but he was wrong. Home was where you laid your head. She laid her head here.

Harry kissed her on the lips. He seemed excited suddenly. Clara began to take off her clothes. Harry took off his suit and shoes and shirt, turned down the gaslamp and lay on the bed in his long johns.

Clara went behind the Chinese screen she had bought at the secondhand shop in Camden Town. It had cost ten shillings, and Harry had been annoyed at the expense. "Gone all modest all of a sudden, ain'tcher?" but she thought he was pleased, really, by something in his voice and manner. She undressed quickly and soaped herself with a flannel. The cold water was refreshing, and she felt a ting of sexual anticipation. It would be nice, she thought, he hasn't done it to me for days, I love him, oh, I love him! She patted eau de cologne over her breasts and under her arms, and as an afterthought a dab between her legs, and walked out from behind the screen, shy but ready for Harry's eyes.

Harry was sound asleep on the bed.

Clara did not wake him. She collected the clothes that had fallen to the floor, folded them and put them away. Then she turned out the gas jet, pulled the covers over them both and lay in the bed, waiting. Harry did not waken. After a while he began to breathe very deeply.

Clara wondered who had sent her the violets.

She wondered if she was going to *come on*.

Then sleep came, like a hammerblow.

On the Sunday morning Harry got up early. Clara, exhausted from the rush of the night before, lay quiet.

"Come on, love. It's today for Brighton sands and sea breezes," said Harry. He had shaved and was already in his good suit.

"Harry"—Clara held her head—"I feel a bit, you know?"

Harry looked disappointed. "Don't you want to go?"

"It's not that." She tried to look disappointed. "I just, well. . . . It's the time of the month. You go on your own."

"You sure?" Harry tried to keep the eagerness out of his voice. She felt a pang. He wants to go, she thought, he really does. With me or without me, he'll enjoy himself just the same.

"Sorry about last night. I fell asleep!"

"So did I," lied Clara.

"Too late now," said Harry, smiling. "Missed the bus."

"Never mind. There's a lifetime." Clara kissed him back. "You look very smart. Bring me a bar of rock."

"I will," promised Harry, consulting his watch. "I'll get off then. Just nice time, I'm meeting them at the railway station."

"Don't drink too much," called Clara.

"What, on my money?" said Harry, and was gone.

The door slammed, and she heard him whistling cheerfully up the street. Then she got up and washed and put on clean underclothes and took from her handbag the address that Mrs. Harrington had given her. She had no watch to consult now that she had sold the fob watch but London's chiming church clocks told her it was ten o'clock. Mrs. Harrington had said she would be expected at ten-thirty. Clara ate no breakfast. Mrs. Harrington said not to.

Clara hoped Mrs. Harrington would keep her mouth closed. She felt she would, on a matter like this.

The cab that Clara picked up took her to the address in Chalk Farm. It was a solid, respectable-looking house, and the cabby let her off as directed, at the corner of the crescent. It all rather reminded Clara of Leazes Crescent. What would the girls of Miss Wilson's Academy for Young Ladies think if they saw her now?

Clara went around to the back of the house, as Mrs. Harrington had told her she must, and not to the front door, in case the doctor's wife answered and actually saw her. Plainly she would be considered unclean. She tapped at the half-glass door facing the garden, as she had been directed to, and it opened at once. The doctor was an elderly man in a none-too-clean frock coat. He wore sidewhiskers in the old style and a wing collar. He did not say good-morning to her, or anything else. Even when she told him the name she had given, which was Abbott, he did not seem to actually wish to look at her at all.

The doctor simply turned away and said, "Money?" and gestured to a small desk. Clara put five pounds, in golden sovereigns, on the desk. The doctor swept them into his weskit pocket. A scent of alcohol and peppermint came from him with the movement. "Take off your clothes." He dried his hands and turned as Clara struggled with her bodice. He looked pained. "Only the lower garments."

"Do you not have anyone in attendance?"

The doctor looked at her over his pince-nez. "Who would you want here, madam?"

Clara shook her head.

The doctor pointed toward a couch. "Lie down and put this between your teeth." He offered her a tube of rubber. "Don't want you screaming the place down."

Clara took the rubber. "Will it hurt?"

"Yes, but you said no chloroform?" The doctor was testy.

141

"I don't know. If it's a lot of pain?"

"Let us see, shall we?"

Again he pointed to the couch.

Clara lay down and closed her eyes.

If I die, she thought, how will Harry live?

Harry came back whistling, from the last train home from Brighton. He walked home to Mrs. Harrington's house from Victoria Station, which took him over an hour. It was almost two o'clock when he put his key in the lock of Mrs. Harrington's lodging house. He was surprised to see a light on in the window of the combined room he shared with Clara. She had waited up for him. She was a good girl. Harry smiled to himself. He loved her. Pity she hadn't come to Brighton. It had been a good day, just lying on the sands, hat tilted over his face, broiling in his shirt sleeves with the other comics and music hall artistes. There had been a lot of laughing and some eating and a fair bit of drinking. Some of the girls there had ogled Harry, but he had not taken too much notice, except to josh and fun with them. Clara was his girl. He was very lucky, he reflected; she even stayed awake and kept a light burning in the window for him.

He opened the door and found John Hyatt facing him, with a solemn expression on his face and his finger to his lips.

"What the *devil*. . . ?"

"Shush!" John Hyatt gestured to the stairs. "I want to talk to you, Harry."

"What's happening?" Harry looked at the door of the combined room. It was slightly ajar, and a soft light percolated into the hall. "Is she all right? Is Clara all right?"

"She's sleeping now. Come upstairs a moment, will you, Harry?"

Harry moved toward the door of the combined room, but John Hyatt caught his arm. His grip was very strong. Harry jerked his arm free. "I want to see her."

"Keep your voice down." John Hyatt spoke low but sharply. "The doctor said let her sleep."

"Doctor? What doctor?"

"The one from the end of the street. Not that other butcher, whoever he was!"

Now he understood. "Oh, no!"

John Hyatt gazed at him a little more sympathetically. But

he kept his grip on Harry's arm. "Come upstairs to my room. We can talk there."

Numb, Harry nodded, and they went upstairs. In his room John Hyatt produced a bottle of Irish and poured Harry a large one. Harry sat, feeling very weak, on the best chair.

John Hyatt said, "Drink that down fast, and have the next one slow."

Harry did as he was told. When he looked up, John Hyatt asked, "You knew nothing about all this?"

"Not a thing. She just said she wasn't feeling well enough to go to the coast. So I went on my own." He was conscious that there was a fine sand on the uppers of his boots and that his face was burned by the sun and that a bar of Brighton rock stuck out of his pocket. He felt like a bloody fool. He said, "I suppose she decided she'd do it her own way. The women do. I don't know how they go on. I'm not a woman, am I?" Harry thought: why am I defending myself to this peasant? He said, "How is she, did the doctor say?"

"He demanded the name of the person that did the . . . operation. Clara wouldn't tell him. He says she's lost a lot of blood, but she'll be all right, probably. She has to stay in bed for a while. He's coming again in the morning. He's a decent stick. I don't think he'll take the matter of the operation any further."

Harry stood up in horror. "Is she hurt? I mean badly?"

"You can talk to him yourself in the morning."

Harry put his head in his hands. "I never knew any of this was on the cards, I swear it!"

"Yes, well, the thing is to see it doesn't happen again."

Jesus, Harry thought, he's talking like her brother now.

"That's something between me and her," he said.

"It would be if she was your wife, but she isn't, is she?" John Hyatt spoke in a mild tone of voice, but he was looking at Harry very directly. "So you've got to be twice as careful, haven't you?"

"Keep your lectures to yourself." Harry put his glass down. "Thanks for the drink and what you did. Did anybody pay the doctor?"

John Hyatt made a gesture. "I did; it doesn't matter."

"How much do I owe you?" Harry put his hand in his pocket. It encountered two two-shilling pieces, all that was left. The day out had cost more than he expected; these things always did.

"It's all right," John Hyatt said. "We can sort it out later."

143

Harry nodded, avoiding his eyes. "I'd better go down and have a look at her."

"Mrs. Harrington's sitting with her now; the doctor gave her a sleeping draft. You can borrow my couch if you like."

Harry shook his head, dazed by it all. "Can't do that. I'd better go down there."

John Hyatt sighed. "Just as you like."

Mrs. Harrington sat at the bedside, and her manner was not as solicitous as John Hyatt's had been. "Back, are yer? About time, isn't it?" She did not seem to expect an answer. She sniffed. "Poor gel, I only hope she's a-goin' to get better. Bloody men, bloody pigs more like!"

"Steady on, mother," said Harry. "I didn't know nothing about any of this lot, y'know."

"No, you only caused it."

"Well, takes two." Harry felt that had to be said; he was getting sick of criticism.

"Hah!" Mrs. Harrington moved, and Harry could see Clara's face, pale as the white sheets, her red hair loose on the pillows. She looked waxen and strange, and her eyes were closed.

"Oh, sweet Jesus!"

"Yes, I see you still know how to blaspheme!"

"I wonder," said Harry, looking at Mrs. Harrington, "how she got the name of anybody what would do this."

"I dunno." Mrs. Harrington looked indignant and gripped her woolen shawl more tightly around her black bombazine dress. A scent of snuff emanated from her. "Dr. MacKenzie stopped the bleeding. Mr. Hyatt ran for the doctor. Got him out right away, on a Sunday at that. Said if he didn't come, she'd bleed to death." Mrs. Harrington warmed to the subject. "Poor dear. She would have. The *blood.*"

Harry felt sick. "Look, missus, I'm very grateful for what you've done. I'll sit with her now. You go off and get some sleep." Harry took the four shillings out of his pocket.

Mrs. Harrington looked at them with contempt. "I'd do this for anybody. And anyway, Mr. Hyatt give me a drink to keep me company." So saying, she picked up a pint bottle of stout, almost empty, and made her way stiffly out of the room.

Harry sat at the side of the bed. He took off his boots and brushed the sand off his stockinged feet. He took off his collar and tie and his jacket. He sat there, just looking at Clara's waxen face, thinking how much he loved her and wondering, with panic and desolation, what he would do if she died. He had not thought of that before. He had lost his mother, Beckie, but she had been old, well, sixty was old really, and worn out with a lifetime of hard work and scraping to make ends meet. Beckie had brought him up. And now she was gone. He had held her hand in a room a lot worse than this only three years ago. That had broken his heart. Surely it was not going to happen again? Harry Viner vowed if it did, he would not give his heart to any other woman, ever. All that happened was that you got hurt. If he were to survive, to do all the things he wanted to do with his life, to become a great comic, to have his name on the billboards with the greats like Leno and Formby and Albert Chevalier, then he could not allow himself to be fettered to women and their feminine needs and weaknesses. He had been a fool to take the girl on. It was all his fault. He should have sent her back to the North. He should have telegraphed her father and told him where she was. He should have taken care that he did not make her pregnant! It was all his fault, all of it, but what could a man do when a girl as lovely as this was offering herself to him? What was he supposed to do, kick her out of bed? The things he should have done were all easy to list, after the event. Harry shook his head, marveling at his stupidity and the mystery of it all.

How was he to carry on with the act? He had forgotten all about that! Well, he would have to talk them into letting him go on as a single act, that was all. If they refused, he didn't know what he would do.

Harry sat there, holding Clara's moist white hand, until the dawn filtered through the lace curtains. "I love you, don't die, darlin'," he whispered. Then his head sagged, and he laid it on the bed, just for a moment, it felt so heavy, and then he slept.

Dr. MacKenzie made Clara his first house call. He was an elderly Scot, dour and to the point. Harry was still asleep when he arrived at eight o'clock. He wakened and stood up, feeling something of a fool, without his boots and collar and tie and desperately needing a shave.

"Has she been asleep all night?"

Harry nodded guiltily.

"You're the husband, are you?"

Harry gave a small nod. The doctor looked stern. "A very

serious business, young man." He took Clara's wrist and massaged it gently. Her eyes fluttered open. Harry had to turn away to prevent the doctor from seeing the tears coming into his eyes.

"I see you pretend to be fond of her," the doctor said.

Harry choked. "I am fond of her. I love her."

"You allowed a butcher to get at her!"

"I did not! I knew nothing of it!"

"Don't shout!" The doctor patted Clara's cheeks. She tried to smile. It tore Harry apart to see it. He felt sick and sorry, the way he had felt when Beckie was dying.

"How are we this morning?" the doctor asked in a surprisingly soft voice. "Slept all right?"

"Yes, thank you." Clara's voice seemed faraway, and Harry stood helplessly, listening.

"I'm going to keep you sleeping because I don't want you to move about. Any pain?"

"Not now."

"How old are you, my dear?"

"Seventeen, doctor."

"Aye, well. Rest now."

Dr. MacKenzie got up from the bedside and gestured Harry into the hall. Still not wearing his boots, Harry followed him. The doctor looked stern. "She's going to need a nurse in attendance for a week. I could get her in hospital, but I'd rather not move her. Can you afford a nurse? It will cost two pounds, I'm afraid, for a proper one."

Two pounds, Harry thought. He said, "Get her, please!"

The doctor looked slightly mollified. "She will be here before noon. She will need to be paid in advance. You will also need a night nurse. The same conditions will apply. Two pounds, in advance. Is that possible?"

"Yes," Harry siad. "Anything at all that's needed, we must do it!"

The doctor looked at him hard and then seemed to make a decision. He put his hand on Harry's arm. "She's been a foolish young woman, and you've been a foolish young man, but we'll pull her through, never fear. I'll be back this evening, but if she bleeds or is in pain, send for me at my surgery at once. Good morning." And he was gone.

Harry took his handkerchief from his trouser pocket and blew his nose. He looked up to see John Hyatt standing on the stair.

"What did he say?"

What the devil, Harry thought, is it to do with you, mate?

"He's left her another sleeping draft, but she needs a nurse, day and night, for a week, he reckons."

"How are you for money?"

Harry said, "I'm all right."

"How much will it take?"

Harry sighed. "Four quid. And his own fees."

John Hyatt put his hand in his pocket and took out four sovereigns. "I'll leave these with Mrs. Harrington."

"Oh, no, you won't!"

"Will you be here this evening?"

"No," Harry said. "I hope not anyway. I'll be working."

"You'll have to tell them, I suppose?"

"Yes." Harry rubbed his bristly chin. "They ain't gonna like it."

"Will they let you go on alone?"

"If they don't, we're on the floor, mate. I'd best get a wash and shave then."

"I'm glad she's a bit better," John Hyatt said. "Last night I wouldn't have given a lot for her chances. I'll give Mrs. Harrington the money."

Harry said nothing. He went back into the bedroom and shut the door. Very quietly, keeping his eyes on the sleeping girl, he shaved and changed his shirt. It was difficult shaving in the soft light of the bedroom, and he cut himself. He cursed and waited for the blood to congeal. He rubbed macassar oil on his hair, combed his mustache, put on a clean collar and his best tie and brushed the sand from his shoes with a rag. He looked at Clara's sleeping face, and tears came to his eyes. "I'm no good for you, darlin'," he whispered.

Vi, Mrs. Harrington's help, a sniffy, thin girl, tapped on the door. Harry let her in.

"How is she, Mr. Viner? I'm going to sit with her."

"Oh. Look, Vi, let me give you something for doing this."

"It's all right, Mr. Hyatt's already given me a shillin'."

"He would have!"

"Sorry?"

"It's all right, duck. You just keep your eyes on her, and if she stirs, you go for the doctor." Harry paused and sighed. "Or rather, get Mr. Hyatt to go for him."

147

Vi nodded. "Right you are, Mr. Viner."

She sat in the chair. "Looks peaceful, don't she?"

Harry swallowed and took his hat and went out into the street. He was blinded by tears. "No good," he said to himself. "No bloody good at all!"

Passersby stared, but nobody spoke to him.

Mr. Weaver kept Harry waiting for two hours, even though he had sent in a written note to say what had happened. The secretary, a prim, fussy young man in a dark suit, had suggested it, looking at Harry admiringly.

"Nice idea, son," Harry said. "With your brains and my looks we'd both be rich."

"Or very, very happy," said the secretary, whose name, Harry discovered, was Colin. He dealt with a succession of callers, mostly agents and out-of-town bookers, with courtesy and skill, putting them at their ease in the plush and gilt office. Mr. Weaver's voice could be heard booming from the inner sanctum.

"Not very often we get ordinary turns in here." Colin wrote swiftly, looking up and smiling. "Only the top-of-the-bills. Mr. Weaver has to see them."

Harry nodded. He knew how Colin regarded him in the scheme of things, very low on the list. "Sorry," said Colin. "Might take awhile yet."

He looked up as a large, pleasant-faced woman, hair piled up, big hat, prominent front teeth, came into the office. She was expensively dressed and carried a parasol. Harry knew at once who this was. Marie Lloyd's face was as well known in London as her songs. In a Cockney voice she challenged Colin, who was already on his feet. "Any chance of seeing your boss? I'll only keep him a minute." She added, noticing Harry, "Are you waiting?"

"That's all right, Miss Lloyd," said Colin swiftly, "I'm sure—"

"No, it isn't all right," said Marie Lloyd. "Unless it's all right with this gentleman here? You're an artiste, aren't you?"

"Yes." Harry stood up. "Harry Viner. Please go in. I'll wait."

"Shan't be long, duck, that's a promise," said Marie Lloyd. She went into the office—Mr. Weaver came to open the door and greet her himself—and Harry could hear very little after that, but the atmosphere certainly heightened. Colin lost a little of his cool manner and ran in and out at Mr. Weaver's call with longhand-

148

written contracts and came back and amended them and ran in with them again. Marie Lloyd was a top-of-the-bill. If you were top-of-the-bill, that's how people treated you. Lucky Marie Lloyd. Would it ever happen to him? Harry sat gloomily, deep in his private sorrow, hearing only Mr. Weaver's voice, low and accommodating, and Marie Lloyd's sharper one, and gusts of laughter from Miss Lloyd. Mr. Weaver did not laugh at all. If he laughed, that berk, Harry thought, he'd get a rupture. After almost an hour Miss Lloyd came out. She said, "You been waiting all that time?"

Harry nodded. "It's all right, Miss Lloyd."

"No, it ain't, it's all wrong! I made you wait, didden I?"

"No, really—"

"No, really nothing. I'm going to Romano's for lunch. I call it luncheon now I'm posh. Come and be my guest. A lot of pros there, you'll enjoy yourself, I promise you."

Harry said, "I couldn't—"

"Why not, got to eat your dinner, don'tcher?"

Harry smiled. "It's very nice of you but—"

"No buts! Go and get your business over with Mr. Weaver, I'll wait. I got a carriage outside. We'll go down in style! Colin, fix this young man up with your boss, I'm starving hungry, there's a love!"

Colin looked at them both, then smiled and went into Mr. Weaver's office. He spoke in a low voice, and Mr. Weaver's voice rose in protest, but Colin persisted and then came to the door, smiling.

"Please go in, Mr. Viner."

Harry went into Mr. Weaver's office, hat in hand. Colin closed the door behind him.

Mr. Weaver was sitting behind his desk. He looked as Harry remembered him, except that he was in a brown suit and had a large pearl stickpin in his tie. He did not seem in a good mood. He looked at Harry's note.

"It says here your wife is ill?"

"Yes, she is."

"When will she be better?"

"In . . . in a week or two. I don't know. The doctor—"

"What's wrong with her?"

"Er . . . a woman's complaint, if you see, Mr. Weaver."

"No, I don't see. Is she drinking?"

"No, she's not that sort."

149

"Can't stand the four turns a night, too much for her, that it?"

"No, no, not at all, sir."

Mr. Weaver put down the letter. "I need an act, Viner."

Harry sweated, standing there. He hadn't been asked to sit down. "Sir, I've done a lot of gigs on my own. Clara, she's a new part of the act."

"No good on your own, were you, Viner?"

Harry swallowed and said nothing.

"Tour cut short in the North, I hear?"

There were no secrets in the profession.

Mr. Weaver consulted his watch. "You're lucky, Viner. I have to go to lunch. Two weeks on your own. Three pounds instead of five. If your missus, or whatever she is, isn't sober by then and fit to carry on, that's your funeral."

"Thank you, sir." Harry swallowed it; he had to. "But she *is* ill."

"No interest in her plumbing." Mr. Weaver looked sour. "I believe you're going to lunch with Miss Lloyd? Lucky fellow. Better not keep her waiting."

"No, sir. Thank you."

Mr. Weaver nodded. "She likes to eat with her own sort, Miss Lloyd."

He hasn't been asked himself, thought Harry. He backed out of the office. Colin stood sympathetically.

Harry said, "It's all right for two weeks."

Colin nodded. "You wouldn't have got two days if you hadn't been lunching with Miss Lloyd."

"You told him? Thanks."

"Anytime. I think you're wasted."

Harry shook his head and laughed and squeezed Colin's arm (well, he deserved *something*, after all!) and took the stairs two at a time.

Marie Lloyd sat in her carriage like royalty. She had one of her sisters with her and two other lady friends. She patted a seat, and Harry sat next to her.

"Mr. Weaver give you a job, did he?"

"I had one, Miss Lloyd. But my partner fell ill, and I'm having to go on on my own."

"Comic, aren't yer, dear?"

Harry nodded. People were staring at Marie Lloyd as they

150

made their way along the Strand, busy and respectable in daylight. She acknowledged the occasional call from passersby with a wave of her gloved arm. The plump upper flesh of her arm was bare, a rare and daring mode. She smiled at Harry. "The lady being taken care of, is she? It *is* a lady?"

"Yes," Harry said. "She's all right. There's a nurse."

"Then you enjoy your lunch, give you strength for your show! Where you working?"

"Well, I'm doing turns. Four halls a night."

Marie Lloyd exploded. "Bloody nerve, what they giving you for it?"

"It was five. He's knocked it down to three. I couldn't argue."

"Love, none of us can argue," Marie Lloyd said. "Fill the halls, that's what you have to do. You do that, they'll pay you. I've made a fortune for other people, bringing them easy money, and they won't bring their wives and children to see me 'cos I'm too vulgar!"

The friends laughed and reassured Marie Lloyd, but she said, "If I sing 'I sits among the cabbages and peas' at them, I suppose they'd pee themselves out of plain embarrassment, dear." The carriage stopped outside Romano's restaurant, and a doorman opened the carriage door and pulled out the footstep.

Marie Lloyd did not ask Harry if he had been to Romano's before, which Harry thought kind of her. He was seated at a long reserved table, at which several people were already eating. He recognized some of them as famous faces of the halls. I ought not to be here, he thought guiltily. I ought to be back at the lodgings, seeing if there is anything I can do. But how did you refuse an invitation to lunch from Marie Lloyd?

Marie Lloyd sat at the end of the table and said to the others, "Darlings, this is Harry Viner, just met him in Weaver's office, wonderful comedy man."

Harry felt a rush of warm emotion that almost brought tears to his eyes. He sat down and found himself gazing at an immense menu in French. Marie Lloyd called down to him, "I'm having roast beef and then crêpes Suzette, right?"

"Right!" said Harry thankfully. "I went to the high school, on the hill. They only taught three languages: English, Yiddish and rubbish."

The famous faces smiled kindly at him.

Marie Lloyd said, "I've just signed a contract, so it's all on me. Anybody know a good horse running today?"

Harry sat back, closed his eyes and tried to take it all in.

Romano's! He looked around the discreet room, long tables glinting with glassware and silver, soft net curtains at the windows so the vulgar could not look in, gentle lighting, as if they were under water, the traffic of hoof and whip and wheel subdued. This was the way the rich lived.

Harry opened his eyes and smiled vaguely around the table. The great comedy actor Albert Chevalier was talking to an impassive little man with a droll face. He said, "Dan, all acting is merely simulating."

"Your words are too long for me, Albert, I can't understand them by day, I only went to night school." The droll man winked at Harry. With a shock he recognized him without his makeup. Dan Leno, no less.

Albert Chevalier said, "I believe that the actor must feel his part—"

"Feel his parts? I'm surprised at you," said Dan Leno with another wink at Harry. "I thought you were a clean act."

"An actor must have his emotions under control," continued Albert Chevalier urbanely, "because only then can he get those emotions across to an audience. By simulating. By pretending. It's the root of all acting."

"I think," said Leno, "you and me are in a different business. Did you know," he continued mournfully, "that Moss has found a Russian giant? Call him Machno. He's nine feet nine inches tall. They're putting him on with the boxing kangaroo."

Marie Lloyd laughed. "That ain't true, Dan!"

"Wish it wasn't," said Leno. He did not laugh.

Albert Chevalier said, "American audiences don't understand my Cockney, but they understand the emotion. That's the thing."

Dan Leno said, to nobody, "Did you know 'Ta-ra-ra-boom-de-a!' was a brothel song? American at that. American brothel song. Lottie Collins made it respectable. Wish I'd seen it done in a sporting house."

"You've never been in one, Dan!" assisted Chevalier.

"I was, and what's more, they gave me my money back," declared Leno.

The roast beef was delicious. The wine was strong and red and lay on Harry's stomach like warm toast. The pancakes, when they came, made at the table flambé with Cointreau and brandy and served hot, were delicious. This, he concluded, was indeed living.

Albert Chevalier said to Leno, "Dan, you pretend you don't *act*, but you do."

Dan Leno said, "I hear they're putting Hackenschmidt, the wrestler, top-of-the-bill at the Palace next month! The week after that it's Sandow, the strong man. He's lifting a horse with two hands. Or is it three?"

Harry told the story of Flossie, the circus horse. Everybody listened politely and laughed.

"Barnum said," went on Dan Leno, "the average man likes to look respectable in public. He also said no man ever went broke underestimating the taste of the great American public. I hear," he added, "they have a monkey who can walk a tightrope coming to the Pavilion week after next."

The brandies arrived then, and Harry drank his and smoked a cigar and listened to the stories. "I started as a public-house dancer," said Leno, "and I've been going downhill ever since," and Harry laughed and was happy just to be there, as of right, amongst the greats. Then suddenly Marie Lloyd called for the bill, and there was a lot of noise about who would pay, and Harry thanked Marie Lloyd, and everybody said, "Good luck!" to him and "Hope your missus is soon well again," and suddenly Harry was alone in the Strand, faintly tipsy, a cold cigar in his hand. He signaled a cab with it. All right, it would cost half a crown, but he couldn't take the bus home after lunch with Marie Lloyd.

As he sat in the cab, jogging through the sunny afternoon streets, he thought, they could have done something for me, one of those famous people around the table, and then he thought: no, they couldn't, they had no real power, only their power over audiences. It was the bookers, the Mr. Weavers of the world, who had the power. Harry had collected himself by the time he got back to the lodging house. The new nurse sat starchily with Clara, and there was a scent of disinfectant in the room. She reported frostily that Clara was resting peacefully, after her latest sleeping draft. Harry looked at Clara, so still and pale, and a feeling of great tenderness flooded over him. But there was nothing he could do. He tiptoed out of the room and up to John Hyatt's room, having nowhere else to go, save Mrs. Harrington in the kitchen and he couldn't face her, sour old bag.

John Hyatt was writing away at a manuscript paper on the table. He was, as usual, in shirt sleeves. He took off his spectacles and polished them, but he had apparently noticed the cold cigar in Harry's hand. "Been out to lunch then?"

"I had lunch with Marie Lloyd."

"That must have been nice."

"It was free anyway."

John Hyatt put his spectacles on again. "Clara's slept all day. That's good, I think."

"Yes." Harry sat down. He felt very tired. "I saw Weaver. I'm going on, on my own."

John Hyatt looked surprised. "He agreed?"

Harry was annoyed. "Yes, he did!" He said nothing about the reduction in money. He said nothing about money at all.

"That's fine." John Hyatt looked at his manuscript on the table. "I'm working, but if you want to use my couch, please do."

"I'm not drunk!" Harry protested.

"Didn't say you were. But you've only got two hours before you go out. You'd better be fresh."

Harry saw the sense of that. He'd have it all to do on his own tonight. He should really have come home and worked out an act, polished up some gags, a song, worked out a running order. But it wasn't every day you had lunch with Marie Lloyd. He took off his jacket and boots.

"You got any work, or is it all on spec?" he asked John Hyatt.

"Two songs ordered. After that it's on spec. I'm writing them for special artistes, something I think suits them. I go to a hall, see an artiste, write a song for him or her, go round back and see them, try to sell it."

"You go to a lot of halls?" Harry lay down on the couch and closed his eyes. Waves of tiredness flooded over him.

"Yes. Morrie makes appointments for me these days."

"Fond of violets, are yer?" Harry asked, not even bothering to open his eyes. John Hyatt made no reply, and Harry grunted to himself, smiled and fell asleep at once.

John Hyatt sat and looked at the sleeping Harry for a long time. He had tried to hate this man, but he found that he could not do it. Dislike, yes. Hate, no. Harry behaved badly, or so it seemed to him, where Clara was concerned. No decent man would get the girl into the club and not offer to marry her, a girl like

154

Clara anyway, a lady. But Clara would not blame Harry Viner. She loved him. Man, man, John Hyatt said to himself, it's their business. Neither of them even sees you.

John Hyatt opened his manuscript case, and the song sheets spilled out. He did not feel like working, but he forced himself to start, turning away from the sleeping Harry Viner.

Morrie Fine, the agent, had been as good as his word. He had badgered artistes to see John Hyatt, but not a lot of good had come of it yet. Nonetheless, these people (halfway down the bill, most of them, Morrie had few connections with the topliners) had been polite to John, as he sat, hat on knee, in their dressing rooms, and talked songs to them.

"What about Mr. Weaver?" he had asked Morrie.

Morrie had looked cautious. "I dunno, he's a funny bugger."

"Look, I'm fed up with queueing up at stage doors for people who've never heard of me! If I can get a couple of songs into one of Mr. Weaver's shows, I can go in with a bit of confidence! I've been to six halls this week, seen thirty artistes and made one sale!"

And so Morrie, greatly daring, had sent him along to see Mr. Weaver, with a letter.

The great man had been friendly. John's clothes were still good, and his watch was of gold. Mr. Weaver had been interested to learn that John Hyatt had attended Trinity College, Dublin. He had been even more interested, remembering "Naughty But Nice," in more songs of the same kind from John. If he commissioned any such songs, he would, of course, expect to own all copyrights. John Hyatt had been warned by Morrie not to agree to such conditions but he had thought: beggars can't be choosers, and agreed.

There was, as his father said, nothing in nothing.

If Mr. Weaver commissioned a song, Mr. Weaver risked money.

A man who risked money expected a decent profit.

"Done!" said John Hyatt, and shook Mr. Weaver's hand. Mr. Weaver had been impressed by that. He had not yet mentioned a price, but now he did and found himself offering ten pounds a song in advance, against thirty pounds if he used it in the Christmas pantomime he would be staging. This was exactly twice what he had intended to pay. This puzzled Mr. Weaver a little. It was to puzzle many people who would, in the future, do business with John Hyatt.

Clara lay in the combined room for a week, hardly moving. On the eighth day, sometime in the evening, she wakened enough to look around. She felt better, the fever seemed to have gone, her body did not burn, her hair was no longer soaked with sweat, her nightclothes and the sheets did not stick to her, as they had all the long, drifting days of danger. Vi called out to John Hyatt, who brought the doctor from his supper (his napkin was still around his neck), and Dr. MacKenzie pronounced her free of the fever and much recovered. He examined her at length, clearing the room to do so, and then sat and took her hand.

"My dear young lady," he said, "you've been very ill, but you're young and you'll recover. I think you know that you have been fortunate and you must never do such a thing again." He coughed. "In future, your husband must control himself. Not just for a few weeks till you are well, but after that. Do you understand me?"

Clara nodded tiredly. "Doctor, is there nothing you can suggest? We are performers. I must not get. . . . I must not find myself in that position again."

"Just what I say. And I have nothing to suggest. You and your husband must not confuse joy with duty. His duty is to be abstinent if you cannot afford or do not want children."

"We cannot, we must not have them!" said Clara faintly. "Our work. . . ."

"Work, aye, work," said Dr. MacKenzie. "That must be out of the question for several weeks, mebbe longer."

Clara said, "But, Doctor—"

"No buts." He still held her hand. "You have to rest, my dear. Plenty of beef tea, boiled fish, coddled eggs. We must strengthen you and get you well."

Clara closed her eyes. "Thank you, Doctor. Where is . . . Harry?"

"I understand at work. The music hall, is it not?"

So Harry was working, the dear soul. A flood of longing and warmth spread over her. God was good. Harry was working. There was hope. "May I see him when he comes in?"

Dr. MacKenzie looked at the frosty nurse, who imperceptibly shook her head.

"We'll see. He may be late. Drink your warm milk the nurse gives you."

"Thank you, Doctor."

156

"Thank me by getting well." At the door he paused. "Is there anybody else should know of your illness? Father? Mother?"

"No," Clara said. "Nobody."

Dr. MacKenzie looked at her a long moment, nodded his head and went out of the room.

She heard him talking in low tones in the hall. The answering voice was that of John Hyatt. There was a chink of coins. Clara closed her eyes.

John Hyatt came into the room softly. He raised his eyebrows to the frosty nurse, who actually smiled at him. "Just a few moments, Mr. Hyatt," she said, and left quietly.

John Hyatt sat at the bedside. He looked serious.

"You nearly died on us!"

"I'm sorry."

"Can you remember anything?"

"No. It's all like a bad dream."

"Then let it be one. Forget it."

"You helped, John. I know that. Thank you."

"Forget that as well."

"I will not. Ever."

John Hyatt smiled sadly. "I hope you will. Now the thing is to get better."

Clara asked, "Is Harry all right?"

"He's working. I don't know for how long. But don't worry. We have enough money."

"We?"

"All of us. Me."

"I have some," Clara said, remembering. "Papa's money in the workbasket."

"Keep it," said John Hyatt. "Chances are you'll need it."

"It isn't much," Clara said, "but the doctor—"

"All paid," said John Hyatt. "And not a word to Harry."

"Oh, John." Clara squeezed his hand. "You are good."

"Not good." He sighed. "Not good at all. I love you."

"What?"

Clara was not sure she had heard aright.

"Nothing at all, I just . . . love to help you. That's all I said. I'll go now and let you sleep. Good night."

He went quietly out of the room.

But Clara had heard what he had said.

How very sweet, she thought drowsily.

157

Harry came off at Wilton's that very night to find Morrie waiting in the dressing room. He looked sad and regarded his cigarillo gloomily. Harry knew what was coming before he said it.

"It's the sack, isn't it?"

"Mr. Weaver booked Viner and Viner, Harry. He gave you the two weeks, and now they're up."

Harry sat down. "I've been working well. They like me!"

"He was in last night himself, he told me." Morrie sighed. "He says your jokes won't get laughs out of London, and he wants to know why you've started going off without a song."

Harry stared in the dressing-room mirror. It was cracked and, like everything else in the artistes' changing rooms, old and worn. "I go off without a song because I ain't a singer, I'm a comic. Why should I suddenly burst into a song, just so a lot of silly berks will give me a round? It's begging for it, that is, they're clapping the song, not you! I can stand up there and tell them a lot of old gags they've heard before, beg them for a round, go off with a rotten old song, take off the hat and bow, Jesus!"

"They nearly all do it, Harry."

"I know, I know, but I've been getting a hand when I went off, you saw tonight?"

"Harry! They was too surprised to clap, most of them! One minute you're telling them gags; next minute you're offstage. You don't prepare them. To do what you're doing *and* get a big hand, you'd have to be a genius!"

"I don't reckon I'm that," Harry said, "but I know to the right audience, I can work as well as anybody."

Morrie said, in a neutral voice, "The little lady? Is she fit to work?"

"No, she ain't," said Harry. "Not for weeks."

Morrie breathed in sadly. "Well, anything comes up, I'll be in touch, Harry. Sorry, son!"

"Yes, I know," Harry said. "Thanks, Morrie."

He changed, packed the skip and carried it, walking, home to Camden Town. It was a time for economies.

Clara was awake when he got in and seemed much better. His heart jumped when he saw her smile, and even the frosty nurse was impressed enough to leave them alone. Harry sat, holding her hands. "How are you?"

"I'll be all right. My poor dear. How are *you?*"

"Oh, I'm fine, fine. You look better, not so sweaty and hot."

"No, the doctor says I'll be all right. I think . . . in a couple of weeks, I could go back to the act?"

"No," Harry said. "Not till you're well enough."

She looked anxious at his tone.

"Is everything all right, Harry?"

"Of course it is, couldn't be better. I've been going off without a song, getting a hand, too!"

"Oh, that's marvelous! I wish I'd seen you!"

"Yes, well, it come to an end. Tonight."

He had to tell her. She would know soon enough anyway. "Morrie's looking for something for me."

"Oh, Harry, what a shame!"

She looked so concerned for him, he could have wept. "It'll be all right. I'll get jobs. All you have to do is lie there and get well."

Clara was silent a long moment. Then she said, "Pass me my workbasket, Harry. It's on the dresser."

He did so, and she rummaged in it and brought out the ten-pound notes. Harry stared at them in disbelief.

"Where did they come from?"

"Papa came to see me. He left these."

Harry slumped. "Didn't he order you to go back with him?"

"No."

"Why not?"

"I told him I was expecting a child, your child. Which I was."

"Clara, *why* didn't you tell me?"

"If I had, what would you have done, Harry?"

He clutched her hand. "I dunno. Something."

"You wouldn't, you couldn't have, there was nothing you could do. It was all my fault." Clara looked pale but determined. "It isn't going to happen again, not till we want it to."

"I feel a swine," Harry said. He did.

"No. Please don't. Take this money. We'll live on it till I'm better. Then we'll look for work again, the two of us."

"You won't be fit for weeks."

"We'll see."

Clara said, "Pay John Hyatt ten pounds. Keep the rest."

Harry shook his head. "You're a pal."

"I love you."

He kissed her softly. "And I love you. Now don't worry about

159

anything," Harry said. "Everything's going to be all right. Just sleep now."

"Yes, I will. Good night, my love."

"Good night."

She closed her eyes, and Harry tiptoed out of the room.

John Hyatt refused point-blank to take the ten-pound note.

"Put it back in your pocket, Harry. Pay me when you can afford it. You're going to need every penny you have until she's well again, you know that."

"Yes," Harry temporized. "I know, but she said to pay you."

"Tell her you have. I'll say nothing."

Harry thought: he mustn't be short of a few bob if he can afford gestures like that. He said, "You got some money of your own, right?"

"I had a hundred pounds left to me." John Hyatt lit his meerschaum pipe, the white bowl gleaming. It was thought to be very masculine, as everything German was in Europe since the German victory over the French thirty-odd years before. "If I find I can't make a go of the songs before my money runs out, then I'll go home and get a job in a bank."

Harry put the note back in his pocket. "I'll pay you back when I can."

"That's what I said."

"I will!"

"I know you will, Harry. You're a good comic, it'll work out for you."

Harry was impressed. "You think so?"

"Yes, I do, but I don't know when. For either of us. It could take time, and we might even have to go to the States for it."

"The States?"

"Well, you're Jewish and I'm Irish, and there's thousands of our own people over there."

"Little Tich said that about me."

John Hyatt poured them a measure of Irish whiskey each. "Still, I'm selling a few songs here. Slainte!"

"Cheers, mate," said Harry. "Here's to me last job, tomorrow night. Thanks again." He coughed; the Irish was strong, or he was affected by the other man's decency, he didn't know which. "And that song you wrote Clara. It's good, any of the top-of-the-bills would have bought it off you."

"Perhaps," said John Hyatt, "but Clara bought it, and I'm glad of that. Another?"

Harry had another. He sat drinking his Irish, looking at John Hyatt curiously. This man loved Clara, and he didn't want or expect anything. He behaved generously, without any expectation of profit or return. Different animals, Harry thought, him and me, different animals altogether.

Clara got better slowly.

Harry tramped around the agencies and the bookers' offices, but he did not go to any more trial turn matinees, though Morrie offered him some. He had seen the hook and knew that he would not survive such an experience. Sid Jones, the Welsh comic, had begun to drink since he had been hooked off at the Met. He had stopped washing and shaving and was to be seen in bars at all hours of the day and night. Harry avoided Sid Jones. He sallied out into the chilly streets of London—the leaves were brown in the parks now—and knocked on doors and joked and asked and joked and almost pleaded and joked and actually did plead once or twice. His feet began to hurt from the walking, and his throat got hoarse from the talking and the fannying up he felt he had to do, and the leaves fell, and it began to blow ice-cold in the London streets, and in the words of Sid Jones, the only people who weren't wearing overcoats were "those what hasn't got 'em!"

Harry had no overcoat.

It had gone into pawn the winter before, and he, foolishly, had not redeemed it. Now it would have to wait on better times. He walked more and more and faster and faster and laughed more and told more jokes.

Nothing.

He cut out eating at a bar, where for tuppence he could drink a half pint of beer and eat cheese and biscuits free. His own money was gone, and all they had was Clara's few pounds, now almost gone. Harry offered himself for Smokers, Masonics, public houses that had singing licenses.

Nothing.

Clara slowly got stronger. While Harry was out walking the streets, she lay in bed, recovering, watched over by Dr. MacKenzie, who seemed to have taken a liking to her, though his manner toward Harry was still distant.

Harry bought half a bottle of whiskey, his first for weeks. He

161

kept it in his pocket and took a nip when the cold got to his bones. It was cheaper than an overcoat. He got into the habit of always carrying the bottle in his pocket. He pawned his silver flask. It bought another half bottle. He developed a cough, and it did not seem to go. He got to nipping a little more of the whiskey before calls on agents and bookers. It gave him confidence. "It doesn't help the cough," he said, "but it certainly helps me!" Everybody laughed at that. Even bookers.

But . . . nothing.

Clara was a good patient. She did not get up until Dr. MacKenzie said she could, and then she only sat in a chair for the time he advised. She walked when he said walk. She ate what he recommended. Homemade milk puddings and custards and beef tea and steamed fish, with warm milk to drink. But her eyes were anxious.

John Hyatt looked in to see if she was all right most afternoons, and the thought did not so much make Harry jealous as frustrated. He knew that Clara would rather have half an hour of his company than a week of John Hyatt's. Harry put on a smile whenever he went into the combined room. "Hello there, gel. How's my love today?" He kissed her, but Clara held onto his hands, which were ice-cold. "You're freezing, Harry!"

"As one brass monkey said to the other."

"Be serious. That cough of yours, it gets worse. You'll be the one in bed next."

"No, I won't, you sit there, I'll get you something to eat."

Clara held onto his hands. "You won't! Sit down! I'll make some tea."

"You shouldn't, love—"

"Harry, sit in front of the fire, and let me do something for you! I feel so useless."

Harry recognized the need in her voice and sat before the grate. He did not stir the coal because if you did it burned quicker, and they were down to their last few shovelfuls. Soon there would be none. When that happened, he did not know what he would do. He supposed he would borrow from John Hyatt again. He now owed John twenty pounds. How would he ever repay it? The fella might be a peasant, Harry thought, but he was a decent peasant. Still, he would ask him no more.

Now, it seemed, Clara knew the situation, too. "You've been borrowing from John Hyatt. My money went a long time ago, didn't it?"

"Yes, but there's a chance of a gig—"

"No, there isn't, and where's your overcoat?"

"I never wear one, darlin'."

"You do, and it's in pawn. I found the ticket. In your skip."

Harry got up and looked out the window. "You'd better pack your own skip and go back home."

"Do you want that?"

"What does it matter what I want?"

She put her arms around his neck. "Because what you want is the only thing that matters."

Harry shook his head. "I want a gig, any gig for Christmas, anything at all. That's all I want. And I'm not going to get it. I've tried, but the word's about that I'm unreliable. I get thrown off tours. Nobody wants to hear my name, Weaver, Morrie, even. I'm bad news."

"If the word's about that you're unreliable, then it's because of me!"

"Maybe it is, but I don't care about *that!*"

Clara was crying. "But I do. I'm the one who got you into trouble with my father, lost your job! You were going along very nicely till I came into your life!"

"No, I wasn't." He kissed her. "I was getting the bird, remember?"

He held her as she struggled to free herself.

"The money's all gone, there's no grub left hardly and very little coal, and we owe three weeks' rent. I've pawned my watch." He lifted his useless mock-silver Albert out of his weskit pocket. "I'm just like all the other comics now. Anyway, why should I want to know the time? If I don't know it's dinnertime I won't get hungry."

Clara was a pace away, staring embattled into his eyes. "I can't go back home. Papa was quite definite on that subject."

"You're his daughter. He'd do something."

"Get me a job as a governess, out of everybody's sight."

At that he put his arms around her and kissed her and said bitterly, "What am I thinking about, rabbiting on, and you ill—"

"I'm not ill. I'm going to make your tea to prove it."

Harry sat and watched her as he shivered and coughed before the small fire. She fried a kipper and cut him some bread and margarine and made him a pot of tea.

"Harry, my love, are *you* all right?"

163

"Yes, don't worry, I'll be fine. Good night's sleep, I'll be right as rain." He grimaced. "So long as it *don't* rain; me shoes are worn out." She looked; the soles were paper-thin.

"Harry, I can't, I won't go home!"

"Darlin', you've no choice! I won't be here."

"It's all right, I don't mind going without—"

"But I mind you going without!"

Clara looked at Harry's white, angry face and said no more. She borrowed some honey from Mrs. Harrington and thinned it with hot water, and Harry sipped it through the long night. He coughed a good deal, but he still went out in the morning, on a breakfast of tea, margarine and bread. He dressed as carefully as ever in a clean starched collar and his best tie. Clara had pressed his suit.

"Anyway, it ain't raining." He coughed. "See you later, love. Don't do too much now. Take care."

Clara watched him walk jauntily up the road, coatless. Her heart pulled at her. She went back into the combined room and sat before the tiny fire for an hour before she knew what she must do. She got to her feet, took off her apron and skirt and blouse and corset and put on a set of clean underthings, bodice, shift, petticoat and drawers and short black stockings with a garter. She washed her face and hands and brushed her hair and patted the last of her eau de cologne on her wrists and neck. She dabbed her face lightly with rice powder. Then she put on her good blouse and the red suit and her boots and, finally, her large hat. It seemed strange to be wearing her best clothes again.

She took off the curtain ring and left it on the dresser.

Then she went out of the house.

Mr. Weaver was surprised to see her. He told Colin, the male secretary, that he did not wish to be disturbed, and Colin, with the same raised eyebrow with which he had greeted Clara's name ("Viner, oh, yes, I know *that* name, don't I?"), replied, "Very well, sir," and closed the door quietly.

Mr. Weaver said, "Sit down on the couch, me dear. Take your hat off."

"You've no idea," said Clara, "the trouble I had to get it on!"

"You ladies and your hats," said Mr. Weaver, looking at his watch, which was of gold. "Still, they look nice." He frowned. "I have people waiting, as you see. I saw you at once because you said it was important." He selected a Havana cigar from his cedar-wood box and lit it. "Who is it important to, me or you?"

"Both of us, perhaps?" Clara sat on the couch and did something she had never done before. She raised her skirts a couple of inches and crossed her ankles. Mr. Weaver stared at them as if hypnotized, coughed out a large amount of smoke. His cigar suddenly seemed not to be drawing for him, and he lit it again. How odd, Clara thought, he's seen me on and offstage, wearing very little. I cross my ankles, and because I'm fully dressed, it makes him very manly.

"Did you remember me?" she said.

"Of course I did." Mr. Weaver was still looking at her ankles. "I heard you'd been sick?"

"Nothing very much, I'm glad to say. I'm well now, as you can see." Clara moved an ankle, and Mr. Weaver ran a forefinger around the inside of his wing collar.

"You look in splendid form," he said hoarsely.

He's talking about me as if I'm a filly, Clara thought, amused. It probably is how he thinks about me. She adjusted the cleavage of her blouse, but Mr. Weaver was not interested. His eyes were fixed on her three-inch exposure of black boots and ankles and an inch of white frilly petticoat. Clara thought: how much power I have! It made her feel quite giddy at the idea.

"I think I'm ready to go back to work again, Mr. Weaver."

Mr. Weaver looked unhappy. "I don't know about that. You see, things are pretty tight just now. There's pantomimes every Christmas, of course, but that's weeks away yet."

"Well, I'd like a panto, but I'd need something to last till then."

Mr. Weaver shook his head. His eyes moved from Clara's ankles to his desk. He picked up a paper and looked at it. He said, "I don't know how I can help. You worked turns and then you fell ill. Turns are bad, but it's all I've had."

"No tours going out at all?" Clara asked quickly. Adding, "It's warm in here, may I take off my coat?"

"Only one." Mr. Weaver breathed heavily. "Six dates in the Midlands and the North. Yes, do take your coat off, me dear. It is warm."

Clara took off her jacket and left on her hat. The blouse she wore was sleeveless, and Mr. Weaver gasped as her upper arms came into view. He said, choking on a large gulp of cigar smoke, "Forgotten yer arms. Lovely arms."

Clara said, "Thank you. Is the tour going to Newcastle?"

"What?" asked Mr. Weaver foggily. "Oh?" He looked at the paper on his desk. "No. It ain't."

Clara breathed a sigh. "That would be all right. Unless you're made up?"

"We ain't made up, not altogether."

"What about me?" Clara said. "Is it a long tour?"

"Only six weeks." Mr. Weaver gazed at her in obvious hunger.

"Would you think I'd suit?" Clara recrossed her ankles.

Mr. Weaver was having difficulty with his cigar again.

"Excellently," he managed. "I'd say excellently. What was that song you sang again?"

" 'Naughty But Nice.' "

Mr. Weaver closed his eyes. "I fancy that song. Like you. Fancied you from the first. You're not a tart, I reckon you're wellborn. Fed up with tarts. Dirty. Don't wash. You. . . . You're. . . ." Mr. Weaver's eyes were still closed. "Virginal. Like a little girl. You'd look prime dressed like a little girl, in a bodice, hair in ringlets, an innocent virgin, never been kissed ever. . . ."

"Were you thinking of me like that for the panto, Mr. Weaver?" Clara asked.

"No," said Mr. Weaver, "not for the panto, no."

"Would you think of giving me the tour?"

"It'll take you away from London. It starts tomorrow morning. I'd have to put you on as an extra turn."

"I don't mind."

Mr. Weaver groaned. "I will."

Clara laughed. Mr. Weaver got up and came around the other side of the desk. He sat next to Clara on the couch. His hands ran up and down her arms. Clara felt nothing. She was determined not to. Smile, she told herself, just smile.

"You know I want to roger you, don't you?"

"Oh, the things you say to a girl!"

"Can't say them to my wife, can I?" Mr. Weaver sighed and took his arm away to consult his watch. Outside, one of London's hundreds of church clocks struck the hour. "Twelve o'clock! I'm expecting Vesta Tilley any minute! Oh, Jesus wept!"

Clara said, "Miss Tilley? Isn't she wonderful? Is it true she's had an operation *there*?" Clara touched her own breasts. Vesta Tilley was a famous male impersonator, and the rumor was that

166

she had had her breasts removed to give her a more masculine outline.

"I don't know, dear, never asked." Mr. Weaver touched Clara's breasts and found the nipple, but Clara felt nothing.

She said, "Will the tour be all right, Mr. Weaver?"

Mr. Weaver's eyes were closed, but he said, "Yes." He took Clara's hand and put it between his legs.

Clara moved her fingers. The *power,* she thought . . . Clara said, "And the panto?"

Mr. Weaver said, "Yes, the panto as well."

Clara said, "Same money as before?" and Mr. Weaver said, "Yes, same as before." And Clara said, "Oh, thank you, Mr. Weaver," and offered her lips to be kissed in genuine gratitude, but Mr. Weaver just said, "Ohhh," in a strange voice and turned away from her, with a low, soft sigh. Clara quickly put on her coat.

After a few moments Mr. Weaver turned to her and said, in another voice, "Talk to Colin about the contracts. He'll give you the details. I'll see you when you get back from the tour." He relit his cigar. Colin tapped on the door softly. Mr. Weaver called angrily, "In a minute!" and in a softer voice added, "Ask Miss Tilley to wait just one moment!" and pinched Clara's cheek.

"Like champagne?"

"Yes, of course," said Clara.

"It'll be weeks, but I can wait."

Clara smiled as best she could. Mr. Weaver opened the door. Clara said, "Naturally, it's Harry and me. I can't go without him, can I?"

Mr. Weaver's brow darkened.

"Cause trouble," Clara said, and then, inspired, "Cause talk?"

Mr. Weaver smiled. "Clever girl, Clara. Little girl." He breathed in. "In a pinafore. Just a pinafore, I think. Not a bodice, just a pinny. Prime!"

Clara smiled and passed into the outer office.

Vesta Tilley rose from her seat. My, she was beautiful! How very feminine she looked. And yet, dressed in top hat and tails and singing her famous "Burlington Bertie," how swell she looked! Clara stood aside, and Miss Tilley swept into Mr. Weaver's office. Mr. Weaver did not close the door when he talked to Miss Tilley, and his voice was different again. How many voices, Clara thought, do men *have?*

Mr. Weaver called Colin into his office, and when he came back, Colin was smiling. "I see you convinced Mr. Weaver," he said, finding two long handwritten contracts and taking pen in hand.

Clara said nothing, but her cheeks burned. Fortunately it didn't show under the rice powder.

"It's the tour *and* the panto, isn't it?" said Colin. "My, weren't we persuasive this morning!" His pen raced across the paper. "Let's see, it's Viner and Viner, isn't it, dear? More successful than Mr. Viner was when he called in, weren't we?"

Clara said nothing. She was beginning to tremble. She felt weak. She had not eaten that day.

Colin offered his pen. "You can sign, can't you, don't want to hold it up, the contract I mean, do we? Train call is at Euston Station tomorrow morning, that's Sunday. There's the sheet. You're doing the Argyle, Liverpool, the Hippodrome, Glasgow, the Theatre Royal, Birmingham and the Empire, Cardiff, aren't you lucky?"

"Yes," said Clara, in a low voice. "I think we are."

"There's your signing-on fee, four guineas," said Colin. He handed her the four sovereigns and four separate shillings. "You pay your digs, provide your own band parts, first band rehearsal, ten-thirty Monday morning, you know how it goes. Oh, and there's the complete bill." He handed her a sheet of paper, and Clara thanked him and got to her feet.

"Don't thank *me*," said Colin. "*I* didn't do anything."

Out in the street, Clara felt so weak she almost fainted. She stood for a long moment in a doorway. When her head had cleared, she thought: I'll have to look after my health. She raised her arm and summoned a cab. The coins were still clutched in her hand; she hadn't even put them in her purse. They were in her hand all the way back to the lodgings. It had started to rain.

Harry was sitting in the chair in front of the tiny coal fire when she went into the combined room. He looked up at her stonily. His jacket hung over a chair, steaming; his shoes were sodden hunks of wafer-thin leather and lay, stuffed with newspaper, in the hearth. Harry's stockinged feet were dark with water. A cup of whiskey nestled in his hand.

"Where the hell have you been?"

"I went to see Mr. Weaver about a job, Harry."

"Oh, yes, and did you get one?"

"As a matter of fact, I did."

168

"And as another matter of fact," Harry said in a grating voice, "what did you have to do for it?"

"Nothing."

"I don't believe you!"

"Then don't believe me." Clara sat down. She felt very weak.

Harry said, "Why did you leave this behind?" He held up the brass curtain ring. "You haven't had it off your finger since you put it on first day you was here!"

Clara looked at the floor. Oh, Lord, it's all going wrong, she thought. It rained and he came home early and it's all going wrong. "I couldn't wear it, could I, going to see him? I had to look good, didn't I?"

"You never took it off before!"

"Well, I did this time. But I won't ever again."

Clara closed her eyes. She felt so tired. All she wanted to do was crawl into the huge bed and sleep.

"You all right?" Harry peered at her.

"Yes. I told Mr. Weaver I was fit to work again, that the act was all right again."

"What did you *do* for it?"

"Nothing, nothing, nothing!"

Harry stared implacably at her. "I know Weaver. I know what he's like."

Clara said, smiling with an enormous effort, "I can't help what he thinks I'll do for him, can I?"

Harry stared at her a long moment. Then he roared with laughter. "You did it! You fooled him!"

"I don't know. He'll be angry later. But I got a tour, starts tomorrow, four weeks out, then a panto. There's the contracts, look for yourself." Clara put the coins on the table. "There's the money, first week in advance."

"Never, I don't believe it!" Harry read the contract swiftly and looked at the coins in a daze. "You didn't put it through Morrie? Well, never mind, what did he ever do for me?" His brow knitted. "But look, love, you didn't get these on promises, did you?"

Clara said, "I think I'm going to faint."

And she did.

When she came to, she was lying propped on pillows on the bed, and Harry was bending solicitously over her, a cup of water in his hand.

"Are you all right, girl?"

Clara smiled. "Yes. Sorry. I don't know what happened."

But she did.

I made myself faint, she thought.

"You're not angry, are you?" she asked.

Harry shook his head. "No. How can I be? I have a job, and I have you."

"You don't believe I did anything wrong, do you?"

Harry shook his head. "You couldn't."

Clara leaned back and smiled. The things, she reflected, I've learned today.

The troupers waited at Euston Station. "The word," said Harry to Clara, "comes from the old word 'troubador,' traveling musician, see?" He was cheerful and looked, Clara thought, very handsome indeed in his dark blue melton overcoat that had come out of pawn. She had insisted he buy a new pair of stout leather shoes to go with it. They had come to Euston Station in a cab, which Harry said made it seem they were not scratching for money but doing well enough.

The troupers had greeted her cheerfully, for she was pretty, despite her pallor. The men all smiled and raised their hats and touched their mustaches at her, and the women smiled in a friendly way, for she had a man with her and would therefore not be a danger to them.

The station was full of smoke from the engines, and there were black specks in the air everywhere. A pea-souper had descended on London, the smoke from a million chimneys held down by low cloud. They boarded the train in good spirits, the gentlemen in their traveling cloaks and ulsters, the women in heavy plaid costumes with capes attached. Everyone wore gloves and scarves, and the gentlemen wore black or brown boots or, if they wore shoes, button-up spats to keep their ankles warm. The compartment was heated, to the relief of all, and the gentlemen distributed cigars (asking no permission of the ladies first, which Clara thought poor manners) and drinks from flasks.

Clara sat in a corner seat and opened the handbill that Colin had given her. It was two feet long and contained the names of all the artistes appearing in the company. There was a strong man. He sat in a corner and grunted and twisted a very fine waxed mustache. He was a foreigner, German probably by the sound of his voice. The others were an acrobat and his girl assistant, a ven-

triloquist and a conjuror, who obviously knew each other and were
already playing cards, along with a specialty dancer and a man,
who, Harry told her, tore up packs of cards. He tore them better
than he played, for he cussed, always with apology, at almost every
hand he was dealt.

The top-of-the-bills were not in the carriage. One was Tom
Costello, singer of sentimental songs.

In the next weeks they were to stand at the side and listen
to Costello sing his famous songs.

> She told me her age was five and twenty,
> Cash in the bank she said she'd plenty!
> I like a fool believed it all.
> I was an M.U.G!

The audience joining in:

> At Trinity Church I met me doom,
> Now we live in a top back room,
> Up to me eyes in debt for renty,
> That's what she's done for me!

Harry was to shake his head and say, "If only I had a song
like that!"

But Harry was happy, Clara knew, as they traveled on from
theatrical boardinghouse to theatrical boardinghouse, the land-
ladies all looking the same, often old music hall performers themselves, obliging enough to shop for the food the women cooked
on the gas rings in their rooms.

Clara was back to wearing her long white dress and a parasol
for the number, and she had managed to talk Harry out of a buck-
and-wing finish, arguing that the song was good enough to end
on, and besides, she hardly felt strong enough to dance.

Harry said morosely, "I'm the fella that says a comic shouldn't
end on a song, and here I am ending on a bloody duet!"

Still, he it was who adapted their song to fit the town they
were performing in.

For Birmingham, Harry had worked on the song, coming south
from Scotland on the train. He had found the chatter in the compartment too noisy for composition and had sat on a case in the
drafty corridor. He had come back into the compartment complaining of a chill, and by the time they got to their lodgings in Birmingham he was shivering violently. His cough was still very bad the

171

next day, but despite Clara's pleas, he wrapped himself in his new coat and a woolen scarf and braved the raw winds that blew across the Bull Ring. In the dressing room he was worse and had utterly lost his voice. The stage manager was in no doubt, overrode his objections and sent him back to his lodgings in a cab.

"I'll be all right, mate," Harry croaked.

"No, you won't," said the stage manager, a large man with a belly and a watch chain. "You'm fit for nothing, you'm aren't, stay in bed till termorrer night, an' us'll see then!"

Harry turned to Clara. "Can you manage on your own?"

"Course she can," said the stage manager. "Now, get home!"

So Harry went back to the digs, and Clara sat in the dressing room and waited for her call. By the time the band had played Harry's opening music she was at the side of the stage. "Nervous, darlink?" asked the German strong man, with a smile.

"Course she ain't!" said his girl partner. "She's a-gonna be a sensation, ain't you, Clara?"

"I'll be satisfied to get off alive," Clara said modestly.

She did not mean it. This, she told herself, is my chance. To-night, all on my own, I'll prove to myself that I know how to do it, alone.

"You're on, lass!" said the stage manager. "I haven't announced you or anything. Just go on and sing your song. Nothin' to it."

Clara nodded, took a deep breath and walked onstage.

The music floated about her, the band playing softly, the musical director smiling encouragingly, the limelight following her across the stage.

Clara, on impulse said, "I'm all alone in Birmingham tonight. I wonder if some gentleman would like to . . . look after me?" She unfurled her sunshade and twirled it prettily and kept moving, as Harry had taught her to. She looked at them. Stalls. Balcony. Gallery. Stalls. *Now!*

Clara sang:

> On Sundays you'll see me around the Bull Ring,
> I'm game for a flirt, boys, I'm game for a *fling!*

There was a low cheer from the gallery, cheerful whistles and cheers.

A sudden feeling of power surged through Clara. I have them, she thought, they're mine. She relaxed, and her voice lost the shrill

172

quality that she had always felt it to have until now. It became rich and round and naughty like the song itself. She walked the stage, up and down; she smiled at the musical director; she lifted her skirt higher than usual (but oh, so innocently).

It's Naughty but Nice, Naughty but Nice,
Never Been Kissed in the Same Place Twice!

The gallery had obviously taken her to their hearts, and she had to sing the chorus twice more before they would let her off. So much for Harry's insistence that they needed to "illustrate" the song with his comic pieces!

"Get back on, dear," hissed the stage manager. "Give them somethin' else."

"I can't," wailed Clara. "It's the only song I have."

"Then sing it again!"

So she did. And milked it, holding the musical director up once and, amazed at her own nerve, telling the audience one of Harry's Abie stories, imitating his Cockney accent, the one about the cat. They laughed at that. The musical director looked quizzical. "Pushing yer luck, ain'tcher, dear?" he inquired with a weary smile as he signaled the band to play the last chorus.

Totally happy, utterly in control of herself and her audience, Clara sang and, when she had finished, bowed, offering her face to them, and her neck and breasts and all of her. The sound came back. They loved her. They did not want her to go. They loved her.

Clara took four curtain calls.

"Lass, you ran two minutes longer than you do with your fella," said the stage manager. "But you're better on your own."

"No," Clara said, her head spinning, "that's not true."

"Have it your own way, love."

Clara moved aside to allow the strong man and his girl assistant on stage. The strong man was looking at her in a warm and curious way that was not sexual. The girl squeezed her hand. "You was lovely. They loved you!"

Yes, Clara thought, they *did*. I can do it, I can do it!

She was not as surprised as she should have been. It was as if she had always known it.

Harry returned to the act the next day. She said nothing to him of her triumph of the previous evening, and if anybody else did, he did not allude to it.

173

Three weeks before Christmas they were back in London.

They were very tired, and they had three pounds, four shillings in the world.

At Mrs. Harrington's lodging house John Hyatt received them with a glass of Irish each and the news that he had sold two songs to the pantomime. Mr. Weaver had paid him promptly, and he was promised two other songs and had found active interest in his songs from Gertie Gitana, Clarice Mayne and other famous lady artistes. He stood in the middle of the combined room, in his shirt sleeves as usual, and said, "I think it's going to work out for me, Harry, I do believe it is. I think I'm going to sell a lot of songs."

"Good luck, mate," said Harry dryly, sitting on the bed. He had thrown his new overcoat down in a chair and his hat to follow it. The skip stood in the middle of the room. Clara would unpack it later. "I wish I could pay you back the money we owe you," said Harry, "but we're stony-broke till we start at the panto. We have three pounds in the world. You don't get rich on tour!"

John Hyatt poured them another Irish apiece. "Here's to your homecoming!" he said. "It's going to be a grand Christmas, with me writing the songs for the panto and you two singing them!"

He's toasting us both, Harry thought, but it's Clara he's looking at. A thought came into his head. From nowhere. Or it had been there a long time without his knowing it. Harry said, "We're getting married on Saturday morning."

John Hyatt was a long time answering. He took off his spectacles, which seemed to have misted, and polished them with his tie. Then he put them on again and smiled uncertainly at Clara.

Clara said, "This is the first I've heard of it!"

"Camden Town Registry Office, eleven o'clock," said Harry.

"Congratulations to you both," said John Hyatt.

"Thanks, John," said Harry Viner.

Clara walked slowly across the room to Harry.

"You might ask me first, Mr. Viner?"

"All right," Harry said. "I'm asking you."

"The answer's yes."

"I thought it would be."

She kissed him. Slowly John Hyatt let himself out of the room. They did not seem to notice him go.

174

On the Friday morning Harry and Clara reported to the panto-mime theater for a band call, as instructed. Clara seemed to Harry very nervous and tired, but he put it down to the excitement of their wedding the next day. "Hey," said Harry, looking at the list, "we have a dressing room to ourselves!" Harry excused himself and went around front to talk to the musical director.

"It only had *Miss* Viner on it," said the stage doorkeeper to Clara, holding back the dressing-room key.

"There's some mistake. It's Viner and Viner."

"Only got Miss Viner here. That you?"

"Yes, it is."

"Then here's the key, dear. Number six, right at the end." He winked. Clara stared at him and went off down the corridor. All around was the noise of a big new show in preparation. Carpenters were hammering; the designer was shouting instructions they could not hear; the musical director was trying to sort out his running order; the acts were beginning to arrive. This, Clara thought, is why I'm here, it's a chance for me—and for both of us, to be seen in a London panto! A feeling of richness came over her. This was why she had run away; this was what she had come here for. A big show, a good part, with luck her own song spot, and Harry at her side!

Clara opened the dressing-room door, and her heart died in her.

Mr. Weaver sat in the only chair. He had a bottle of brandy in front of him, and he was smoking a cigar. He said, "Close the door, darlin'. We're in no hurry this time."

Clara said dully, "Harry's in the theater."

"Not for long. My stage manager will tell him it's just you working this panto."

"No!"

"But, yes! You had him on tour. I have one comic in this panto. I don't need him." Mr. Weaver got to his feet unsteadily. "A bargain is a bargain, darlin'. Now it's your turn to pay."

He reached for her.

Clara stood as still as stone.

"Sorry, Harry," the stage manager was saying. "No need for another comic. That's what I was told. Your missus—Clara, is it?" He consulted his acts sheet. "She gets two songs. The same money as for the two of you." As Harry just stared at him, he added,

"Here, we're drinking this morning, dead against house rules, have a beer, have mine, Sorry! Sorry!" He clapped his hands and moved away. "Hey, musical director, we start rehearsals in an hour!"

"A week," said the musical director, "would be more likely!"

Harry walked down the stairs backstage to the dressing room. He felt numb. The beer glass was still in his hand as he opened Clara's dressing-room door.

Clara was standing there, and Mr. Weaver was just putting his hand to her breasts.

Harry pulled him away, threw the glass of beer in his face and hit him very hard with his right fist. Mr. Weaver's nose burst, and blood flew across the room as he fell back heavily against the dressing table and then slid to the floor. He lay there, making choking noises, as Harry looked down at him. The stage manager looked in and gasped. "Harry, you've done it now. . . . You'd better get out before he calls the police. Take her with you."

Harry pushed the stage manager hard against the wall and took Clara by the arm. He propelled her out of the theater, Weaver's voice screaming after them. "You're finished, you bloody maniac! Nobody will give you a job now anywhere!"

Harry called a cab at the door of the theater, and they went home in silence.

Clara said, at last, "Nothing happened."

"If I thought there did," said Harry, "I wouldn't be marrying you tomorrow. And you know what Tom Costello sings about marriage? 'At Trinity Church I met me doom, Now we live in a top back room'." He put his arm around her. "No top back room for us, dear. We'll live in style in the best hotels before we've done."

For the first time in their knowing each other, Clara cried unashamedly, and Harry held her close to him. They made love that night for the first time in many weeks, and Clara used her new douche, after Harry had turned over to sleep. The pale, wan girl who was with the acrobat had told her about it. "It ain't as safe as not doing it, dear," she had said, "but it's a hell of a lot safer than doing nothing."

They were married at the Camden Town Registry Office the following morning. Somehow word had got about, and present were Little Tich and Tom Costello and the German strong man, and the acrobat and his wan girlfriend, and George Lashwood and Eugene Stratton and Mae and her husband, the seal trainer, and two or three dozen other artistes, all of whom had heard about

Harry's fight with Mr. Weaver. Nobody mentioned it. Marie Lloyd came, not for the ceremony, but for the reception at the private room upstairs in the Rising Sun public house, on Haverstock Hill.

The best man was John Hyatt.

There were no speeches and only beef sandwiches to eat and beer to drink.

Clara refused to have a cheap new ring and wore her brass curtain ring at the ceremony.

The artistes had a private collection for the couple, and it came to over fifty pounds. Gene Stratton gave it to Harry and added a word of advice. "I know about your little trouble, and I don't think you're going to work here for a while, till all this has quieted down."

Marie Lloyd shouted to them, "If we had a union, we could help. As it is we're as useless as a bishop's balls!"

"She's right." Gene Stratton looked sorry and like a stranger without his makeup. "Have you thought about the States for a year or two, till all this has blown over?" He dropped another ten-pound note into Harry's hat. "That makes sixty, and I've written you some references, and so has Marie and Little Tich."

He passed Harry an envelope.

Clara had been standing with her back to them. She turned. "I heard that, Harry, and I think Mr. Stratton and Miss Lloyd are both right."

They sailed for New York on the SS Baltic a week later. John Hyatt saw them off, and his white-gloved hand was the last thing Clara saw as they sailed out into Southampton Water.

Harry said, "Well, I really buggered it all up for us, didn't I? I knew my way about London, I thought, and I made a mess of it."

"London?" said Clara. "I've never been there."

"Nor I," said Harry. "You never been in music hall?"

"Never!"

"Nor have I," said Harry. "It must have been two other people!"

They both laughed.

Clara stared down over the rail at the wake of brown water and white foam.

Viner and Viner.

She hugged his arm. He smiled, and she was happy.

PART II

East Side, West Side,
All Around the Town

"Is 'fuck' a rude word in New York?" Harry Viner asked.

The burlesque audience on Forty-second Street woke up. Nobody laughed.

Harry shouted, in total despair, "Is 'fuck' a rude word in New York?"

Clara held her hand across her bosom. She was wearing long white cotton stockings and a silver whalebone top with a deep décolletage. Her face, Harry knew, was probably paler than either.

"I said—" he shouted. He was beginning to enjoy himself. He had gone too far, and there was a certain relief in that.

"I know what you *said!*" Clara gasped. "Of course, it's a rude word in New York!"

Harry dropped his voice. "That's funny. It's a rude word in London as well."

This time he got a loud yak. The men (no women in this audience) stretched their legs and grinned and pulled on their sidewhiskers and mustaches. Harry took a deep breath of the stale, beery air. It was his seventh show of the day, and certain, he knew, to be his last.

181

At least he had got their attention, which was more than any other comic had done that week.

The musical director had recovered. "Harry, for Chrissake! Keep it clean!" Some director, thought Harry; he doubled on the violin, and there were only three in the orchestra.

"Don't worry, Manny." Harry Viner smiled beneath his makeup. "You can only commit suicide once. Give us a music cue."

Manny did that. He sighed. He had always laughed at Harry Viner's jokes. Behind him, the audience had brightened up. Dirty jokes were rare in burlesque these days; it was going to the dogs since the cleanup people started spoiling everybody's fun. Sober family men, who worked hard for a living, moved uncomfortably in their serge suits and fingered their stiff white collars. It was a very hot night, and the little auditorium reeked of sweat and tobacco. A fan turned slowly in the ceiling, but none of the moving air reached the stage. Harry Viner had never been so hot in his life. He told the story about the cemetery cat.

They laughed, this time a shade disappointed. Plainly, this comic was not going to be properly dirty. It was a pity, who was nowadays? They sighed for the old afterpieces, those who could remember them, when you could be as blue as you liked and nobody cared. Now here was a fella saying "fuck," and he would get thrown out for it. Or so he said.

For Harry was telling them so, the sweat gathering on his back at the enormity of what he had done. "Gentlemen, I'm standing on this catwalk, and they tell me that means I'm not breaking any laws if I'm dirty. I only hope they're right because if they're wrong, I'm on my way to the Tombs!"

He did not dare look at Clara. He knew that she had frozen, that her smile was fixed on her face. She was waiting for him to sing. Manny, the musical director, was waiting for him to sing. He was buggered if he was going to sing; he was a comic, if he was going to be kicked out tonight, he'd go fighting. "Twenty dollars a week, friends, seven shows a day, a man should pay to lose this job. . . ." Harry found he was talking aloud. "Like the girl said, who do you have to sleep with to get out of this show?"

Manny, the musical director, closed his eyes. He also closed Harry's well-thumbed band book with an air of finality and folded his arms.

"Even the musical director is waiting to see what I'll do next," Harry told the audience, who by now were well and truly awake.

182

"I might do the splits, but I have years ahead of me, and who'd take care of my little girl here"—he indicated Clara—"if I did meself an injury?" He held up his hand. "The queue forms outside the stage door at the end of tonight's performance. No Irish, Jewish, Italian, German or Dutch need apply."

He refused to acknowledge Clara's whispered "Harry, *please.*"

They had told him Hammerstein was in the house.

If he was ever going to get out of burlesque, this was his chance. He shouted desperately, "Fellas, listen, I'll confess, I'm Jewish, but the little lady isn't; she's Catholic." The audience stirred. Half of them, Harry knew, were Catholic, half Jewish. "It's a good arrangement. We have so many holidays between us, we never work. The trouble is, we ain't got no money. So we have to sing for our supper. . . ." He stepped back. "Sing, little lady. . . . Music, Manny, if you please."

Manny, astonished, flipped open his music and cued his musicians with a tap on the music stand with his baton. They went into "Naughty But Nice."

Clara whispered, "I can't. I've dried."

Harry shouted, "She says she's dried. It's because she's still in shock, hearing me say *that* word. Shall I say it again, while we're waiting?"

The audience, delighted, shouted, "Yes!"

So Harry said it again.

They laughed loudly.

Manny closed his eyes in pain, signaled hastily, and the musicians went into the chorus. Harry smiled at Clara and this time, falteringly, she began to sing:

> I went for a walk down Broadway today,
> The fellas all eye me, and to me they say. . . .
> "Who is this nice girl who yet looks quite . . . gay?"
> And one bold spark, just for a lark, asked me,
> "Miss, are you going my way?"

Clara hated to sell the song in such a brief costume, Harry knew. She said it took the mystery away, and of course, she was right. But this was burlesque. Clara was wearing more clothes than any other girl in the show.

Harry gestured to her to step out onto the catwalk with him, and she did. It was unrehearsed. Usually she stayed on stage. Below them, the mustached faces stared up. It was, Harry thought, like performing in a brothel. Well, from tonight they weren't even performing here.

Clara sang:

> This boy he took me across on the ferry,
> I know that I shouldn't . . . but he made me feel
> . . . *very* . . . *umm* . . . *you* know!"

The audience stirred again, staring at Clara's legs. Harry wasn't sure if they listened to the words at all. With a comic they had to, or else eat pretzels or break wind or talk to their neighbor. Most comics worked through a hubbub. They could not be heard at the back of the hall. Well, he thought, they heard me tonight.

> Naughty but Nice, Naughty but Nice,
> Never Been Kissed in the Same Place Twice!

The audience applauded. Harry joined in a reprise of the last chorus and hissed to Clara, "Stay on, we'll dance a last chorus, a buck-and-wing. Manny, now!"

They threw themselves into a frantic buck-and-wing to a last, fast chorus, ably conducted by Manny, who had now given up any hope of following his music sheets. As they danced, Harry called, "No iron cleats! No bells in the heels! You're hearing the real thing, fellas. . . ."

And indeed, they were, Harry's shoes slapping the stage, hard and loud.

Clara's dancing was not as good as his, but she could move, and she had learned a lot in six months. If Hammerstein *was* out front, then he would get the whole repertoire, jokes, songs, taps, the lot.

Manny hissed, agonized, "Wind up and curtain, Harry, be *nice!*"

They both whirled into the last mad steps and took a quick bow to cheerful applause. Harry could feel Clara droop, and he dreaded the scene that was to come in the dressing room. As they exited behind the curtain, Harry left his foot there, in full view of the audience.

He did not know why he did it. He just did it.

Clara said, "Thank God that's over."

"It isn't, you know," said Harry, and walked back onstage. Alone.

"Just before I go . . ." Harry said.

A drunk called, "Gerroff, English. We paid to see the girls, not youse."

"Prejudice, you see?" said Harry, tapping his straw cady. "My friend is Irish. I've nothing against the Irish. Some of my best friends are Irish. One of them was marooned by a mad doctor on a Pacific Island. The mad doctor put a monkey on the Island with him. He gave the Irishman an envelope and the monkey an envelope. The monkey opened his and read: 'Take calculations of tides, high, low and meridian, calculate differences in meters and inches. Use sextant to plot exact nautical lines of latitude and longitude of island and make detailed notes of flora and fauna on the island, using Latin names. . . .' The Irishman opened his envelope, and it read: 'Feed monkey.' "

"I'm not Irish," called the irate drunk. "I'm Dutch."

"My friend, you have my sympathy."

Harry raised his straw cady to catcalls mixed with laughter and left the stage.

The manager stood there, his face red above a boiled shirt and a bow tie. His hair was plastered over his forehead in a cowlick. "Viner . . ." he began.

Harry said, "I give notice. If Mr. Hammerstein comes looking for me, I'm in my dressing room. Tell him he can't miss it, just follow his nose, it's next to the john."

"Hammerstein?" asked the manager. "Is he in? Nobody told me he was in?"

Harry felt cold. He did not look at Clara.

He ad-libbed fast. "He told me he'd call by. He has us in mind for vaudeville."

"With that act?" said the manager.

"Changed a bit." Harry tried to smile.

"Oscar Hammerstein would never let you say 'damn,' never mind 'fuck.' Who told you he was in?"

"The girls," Harry said.

"You've been taken, Harry." The manager took out his large white handkerchief and rubbed it across his face. "I heard you say the word myself, and I still can't believe it. If the cleanup people stop by and talk to you, you never said it, hear?"

Clara said, "Oh, thank you! Thank you, Mr. Richter."

"What you thanking me for, lady? I didden do anything but fire you."

"Oh. . . ." Clara faltered. "You didn't say we were fired."

185

"Did I have to?" The manager waved his unlit stogie. "A comic uses language like that, he has to go. Sorry, lady. I like you. But this fellow you got here, I wouldn't wish him on my wife for a husband. Good luck with Hammerstein, Viner. You are gonna need it." The manager put ten dollars into Clara's hand. "You look after this guy, lady, y'hear? He's either gonna be very, very big or he's gonna be very, very dead. Good luck to you both, and good luck to me also."

Clara sat in the tiny dressing room and stared at herself in the mirror. She was still shaking, and the ten dollar bills were clutched tight in her hand.

I will not say anything, she told herself. He was trying too hard, that's all. I understand. I have to understand.

She put the money down on the dressing table. Slowly she peeled off the white stockings and the whalebone top. She wore nothing under the top—it was far too hot—and looking at herself naked in the mirror, she was pleased with her firm breasts and flat stomach. She had lost her puppy fat in the last six months and a lot else besides. But she was more mature, she thought, really much more attractive, *that* way.

Clara turned around from the mirror, quite deliberately, so that Harry could see her.

He was staring at the floor.

"Harry?"

"What?"

He didn't look up. The sweat had soaked through his cotton shirt and his new beige linen suit. It had cost seventeen dollars they could use right now.

Clara covered herself hastily with a towel.

"Was Hammerstein in the house?"

"What do you think?"

It was astonishing how they had both begun to pick up Americanisms. Somehow it did not seem possible to live and work in the city without using them. With everybody being foreign, Clara supposed there had to be a new, easy language everybody could speak.

"You joke with the girls too much, Harry, and it's cost you."

"Yes, I know. They said they're sorry. That helps a lot."

"They didn't expect you to say that word," Clara admonished him. "So why? You knew it would lose us the job."

186

Harry took off his straw cady and wiped the sweatband so that it would not discolor. "It's a rotten job."

"We *are* eating," she reminded him.

"We're eating and what else are we doing?"

"Two weeks ago, just to eat would have been enough." Clara closed her eyes. She had said it. And after she had told herself not to. Whatever happened, it did no good to criticize Harry. She should have learned that much by now.

To her surprise, he did not shout or fly into a rage.

"You're right," he said slowly. "I was a bloody fool. I don't know what came over me."

Clara, still wearing only the towel, kissed him on the forehead. His arm went around her. "I'm sorry, darlin', I always seem to cock things up, don't I?"

"When you said that word, I nearly died."

"When I said that word, *I* nearly died." Harry buried his face in the towel, and she held him to her. His hands explored her body. That, at least, had not changed between them. She detached herself and began to put on her street clothes, beginning with her drawers.

But Harry was aroused by now, and he pushed a chair against the door and took her, standing up, against the dressing-room table. It was all over in moments, and then they were shaking and laughing, and she said, "Harry, the door, somebody might come in!"

"Not tonight, darlin', we're outcasts tonight."

Clara tried to cling to him, but he had cooled now, and so she just kissed him gently and disengaged herself and put on her street clothes slowly, packing her costume into the skip.

Harry sat down again, after kicking the chair away from the door. He took his flask from his pocket and swallowed. He did not offer her a drink. Harry disapproved of women drinking. Clara liked the taste of the stuff, and if anybody else offered her a drink, she took it. If Harry was not around, that was.

"How much money do we have?" he asked.

Clara silently indicated the ten dollars on the dressing table. "Is that all?"

Clara said, "It's all that's there."

She was becoming a very good liar. In her purse lining there was a twenty-dollar bill, saved for a rainy day. The rainy day was here.

"Ten dollars!"

"We were lucky Mr. Richter gave us anything. He didn't have to."

Harry said, "Sacked, paid up and a long way from home."

Clara pulled on her long black stockings and her diamanté garters. She held out her leg and admired it. She had always wanted a pair of garters like that. Now she had them. Harry had bought them for her, in a cheap little store on Broadway. They had cost two dollars they did not have.

"Never mind. Something will turn up," she said. "If this is bad, remember Brooklyn."

"Don't remind me." Harry shivered.

Clara buttoned her blouse and put on her hat. She found it difficult to thread the hatpin through it.

"I'm still shaking. Look."

"Here. Let me." Harry pushed the pin into the hat, through the black straw and her closely piled hair, and out again. All women wore hats in the street. No woman would wear a hat in a theater. The notices said, "Will Ladies Please Remove Their Headgear," even in this awful place, where no ladies were ever seen.

"I'm starving," she said, turning and kissing him. "Why don't we go eat?"

"Go eat? Why not? Hey, I'd better change."

"Wipe your makeup off, and come as you are."

Harry did just that, and ten minutes later they were in the street. They left their skip with the stage doorman, to be collected later. He was Irish and clucked sympathetically. "I liked the one about the Irishman and the monkey, Harry. That word was a mistake, though."

"So everybody tells me, Pat."

"You'll learn our ways yet, Harry."

"Well, I'd better, Pat. Or I'll starve."

"Youse will, for sure."

In the restaurant Harry ordered plank steaks.

"Not for me," said Clara. "I'll just have a salad."

"Salad is a side dish here. Eat your steak and enjoy it. It might be the last one in a long time."

The plank steaks came on a wooden platter and were very large indeed. They cost a dollar each, plus tip. They could not afford it, but it was useless telling Harry that. The only thing to do, she had learned, was to go along with him. It was that or leave.

188

And she still loved him beyond anything in the world.

Clara glanced across at Harry as he ate his steak. It was a magnificent steak, and he enjoyed it, making noises of appreciation and stabbing cheerfully at the gherkins and tomatoes and lettuce and onions that came as side dishes. Harry liked American food. Clara missed the old English cooking, the suet puddens and gravies and fresh green vegetables. New York was not like London, though, where there was rich and poor and not much in between. Here, if you had a few dollars, you ate well.

Harry looked better when he had finished his steak and drunk a stein of lager beer. He lit a stogie and exhaled the smoke. She pressed his hand. "Feel better?"

"Ready to take on the world, darlin'."

Harry leaned back and smiled expansively. Clara was, as always, thrilled by his masculinity, his air of confidence in this strange, alien city. He suited the place, although nothing really good had happened to them since they arrived. Quite the reverse. None of it had shaken Harry's certainty that it was only a matter of time, not even the fact that they had actually run out of money three weeks before and Harry had gone out into the street and got a job selling fruit from a pushcart. He would never have done that in London. "Here," he explained to her, coming back to the room with bread and cheese and fruit (naturally!) and beer, "nobody cares what you do or who you are. All that class stuff is over. The only thing that matters in this city is the dollar."

It was true. And where did he think the rent was coming from this week, spending two dollars on one meal? Clara smiled. Nothing seemed to get him down for long. He smelled success in the very air. Some of the restlessness of the place had got into his bones, or he would not have risked the job, as he had that night. What on earth had he done it for? Vaudeville had been cleaned up for a long time, even Tony Pastor's famous old vaudeville house at Fourteenth Street had been "clean family fun" for years. So why Harry should think saying *that* word would help them get a job with Hammerstein she could not imagine. So she asked him.

"Well, darlin'," said Harry, "what a man will laugh at himself is one thing. What he thinks other people will laugh at is another. I was hoping Hammerstein would see I could do both things. Amuse him and amuse the audience."

"How do you know a blue act would amuse him?"

"A blue act amuses everybody. If they're on their own. It's being in company that spoils it. Hammerstein wasn't there, so I made a mistake. Let's try to forget it." Harry picked his teeth with an ivory toothpick. This, too, was a new habit. No gentleman, in London, ever picked his teeth in public. "Anyway, it's better than Brooklyn, like you said."

They could laugh about Brooklyn now. They had not laughed at the time. The trouble had been that their introductory letters were *too* good.

They had gone to see the agent with the letters of introduction as soon as they had got off the boat. That had been an error. They had booked into a hotel, recommended to them by Gene Stratton—the Knickerbocker on West Forty-sixth. Twelve dollars a week with kitchenette and private bath. They had stood, gasping in the steam heat, unable to take in such luxury. At five dollars to the pound, it had seemed cheap to Harry, expensive to Clara.

"We have to have a decent address, darlin'. The first thing they'll ask us is where are we living." Harry had thrown off his topcoat—the streets were arctic; Clara could not remember when she had been so *cold*—and taken her in his arms. "Don't you like this place?"

"Of course I do. It's fairyland."

They stood at the window and looked at the lights of the magic city. They walked the streets in total wonder that first night. Above Broadway blazed the lights; along the vast canyons every little shop was still open at a late hour; despite the bitter cold, the streets were full of people, laughing and shouting to each other, in every possible language. Unless people had money and dressed American, they seemed to be clad in the style of their native country, whatever it was. Irish tweed and large peaked cap, German half coat, belted at the back and buttoned high, an occasional fur hat, bowlers and derbies a-plenty, men in long gaiters or shining city boots. They had walked and walked until they could walk no more, the huge buildings looming over them, down Broadway, on one side, and up again on the other.

When they got back to their hotel, it was two o'clock in the morning, and the city was still alive with noise and light. Clara could not sleep for it all, so Harry got the bell captain up to the room (he was sixty, Irish and wizened) and asked him how they kept out the light and the noise.

"Put chewing gum in your ears," said the bell captain, "and

190

I'll put you some shutters over the windows to keep out the light."

"Where do we get chewing gum," Harry asked, "at this time of night?"

"Here," said the bell captain, and produced some from his pocket. He put up the wooden shutters across the large windows and stood back. "There you are, mister."

"Thanks," said Harry.

"No tip?" asked the bell captain.

Harry reached in his pocket. "What would be right?"

"Two bits would be fine, mister."

"I must ask the manager for a scale of tips," Harry mused.

"Make that a dime, buddy," said the bell captain.

They slept in each other's arms like babies that first night. Then they ate at the coffee shop across the street (boiled eggs and coffee and toast for fifteen cents) and made their way across town by streetcar to see Max Rober, the agent.

They were as astonished at the city by day as they had been bemused by night. It had snowed during the night sometime, not heavily, and the buildings looked like fairy cakes. Harry tucked Clara's hand into his topcoat pocket. "The bad times are over, darlin'. With our introduction, we must get a chance."

Max Rober's office was next to Hammerstein's Victoria at Forty-second and Broadway, the most famous vaudeville house in the city. Harry stood outside the vast building and looked with wide eyes at the billboards: Eva Tanguay, the American Comedienne, in an Original Repertoire of Songs; Will R. Rogers, Expert Lariat Thrower, headed the bill.

"The only one I've heard of is Eva Tanguay," he said. "Who are all the others?"

Clara shook her head. Few acts made the Atlantic crossing. It occurred to Clara that if they didn't know anybody else on that bill, hadn't even *heard* of anybody else, then it was absolutely certain that the agent, Max Rober, would not have heard of them.

Nor had he.

But he was very polite and saw them almost at once. His office impressed Clara. It was large and furnished in heavy dark woods and real leather, and it was warmed by large radiators with the stunning steam heat that all offices seemed to have. There was, apparently, not an open fireplace to be found in New York. Well, so long as they were warm, they could get used to the heavy, moist air.

191

Max Rober offered Harry a cigar, not one of the kind New Yorkers called stogies, but a genuine Havana from a cedarwood box. Harry took one and choked on it. Clara knew he was unused to Havanas, but Harry would always try anything once. She had learned that much about him. Max Rober did not smoke a cigar. He smoked—in a tortoiseshell holder—something Clara had not seen before, a long brownish paper tube with a dark-looking tobacco inside. He saw her glance. "Turkish, not everybody appreciates them. Do you find the smoke troublesome, Mrs. Viner?"

Clara smiled and said that she did not. She liked gentlemen to smoke. It was, she thought, a manly thing to do.

"If you will allow me a moment to glance through your letters?" asked Max Rober politely.

"Of course." Harry waved his cigar, settled back in his chair. Clara thought: Let him be lucky, let us both be lucky. He deserves it; he's worked for it. She had the same feelings of hope herself as she glanced around the warm, well-appointed office. The thick carpets and mahogany desk and Max Rober's splendid suit spoke of prosperity, of the fact that good livings could be made from the business of vaudeville. Framed and signed photographs of the great names (which she did not yet know) stared back at Clara from the walls. Many were in blackface, which made it even more difficult. She recognized George M. Cohan because all the world knew George M. Cohan. That apart, the faces were all fresh to her.

Yet she felt an expectation. This was not London, but it was a city as big (well, almost) and as important (well, not quite, but nearly), and at least she would not have to hide away from her own relatives or the embarrassment of her father. If she was to prove to the world and herself that she had talent, this was the place to prove it, surely, where nobody knew who she was, or cared.

Clara sat and thought: I'm in New York, and I'm married to that handsome man smoking the cigar, and I'm going to succeed in this city, we both are. She smiled at Harry, but he was not looking in her direction. His eyes were on Max Rober, who read the letters of introduction very thoroughly and finally nodded his head and looked first at Harry and then at her, and said, "You come very well recommended, Mr. and Mrs. Viner."

Harry puffed on his cigar and smiled.

Clara said, "We are new over here, Mr. Rober, but we are willing to learn."

Harry frowned and broke in swiftly with: "Not that we don't know our business, Mr. Rober. We do."

"Of course, of course." Max Rober smiled at Clara. "We see quite a few English acts in this office. There is quite a lot of traffic. It is not often two-way, I'm sorry to say, from the point of view of my American clients. It seems that our audiences will accept European acts, but your audiences do not care for ours." He smiled again. He was, Clara thought, a very nice man. "Something to do with our accents, I suppose, the way we speak. We are expected to understand Harry Lauder, who talks in a broad Scottish accent, but our rube comics would never do in London."

Clara was not sure what a rube comic was—had she misheard him, did he say *rude?*—but Harry was talking again.

"Well, I suppose it's a bit different over here."

Max Rober smiled and yet he didn't, quite. "It's very different, Mr. Viner, but you would expect that."

"Yes." Harry waved his cigar. "Of course. Certainly."

Ask him, Clara almost shouted, *ask* the man in what way it's different. We don't know, and it's no use pretending we do. But Harry did not ask. He contemplated his cigar and waited for Max Rober to say more. After a long silence, Max Rober did.

"We don't have the same tight little system here that you're used to in London, but we do have an enormous lot of vaudeville houses." He drew on his Turkish cigarette, the smoke of which was scented and to Clara very agreeable. "There are two types of vaudeville tour and house. One is Big Time—that's the top places, countrywide. The other is Little Time." Max Rober paused. "There's nothing the matter with Little Time, it's nothing to be ashamed of. The trouble is, once you get stuck on the Little Time circuit, you don't get out of it all that often. Little Time means playing Peoria and places like that. Some of the Little Time circuits are known as the Death Trail."

Harry said, "That sounds the end."

Max Rober smiled and said, "The Orpheum Circuit—that's Big Time—is the one to be on. That is a tour, starting in this city, going up through New York State, across Canada, down through Washington State, all the way to San Francisco, Los Angeles and back again by the Middle West. That is known as going the Route."

193

Harry said, "That would be for us."

Max Rober shuffled the letters. "We'll have to see, won't we, Mr. Viner? The thing is to arrange something where the bookers can see you, isn't it?"

Clara said, "That sounds wonderful, Mr. Rober."

Harry said, "We've done the best English halls. We aren't afraid of bookers or audiences. Throw us in at the deep end. We'll swim." He smiled. "And if we don't, we'll drown, won't we?"

"Yes, well, let us hope that won't happen." Max Rober lit another Turkish cigarette, inquired where they were living and, when told, nodded. "I know it, nice little place, do till you find somewhere better, eh, Mr. Viner?" and laughed tolerantly.

Clara, who had never known such luxury as the Knickerbocker since she had left home, smiled. Harry said, "Yes, Mr. Rober, we hope to move to the Astor soon. I hear it's a top place."

"The Astor on Times Square? Yes, sure. It's fine." Max Rober looked over his gold-rimmed glasses. "Will it be convenient if you wait a few moments?"

"Yes, of course," said Harry largely. "By all means."

When Max Rober had gone out, Harry looked around the office: the large desk, the leather easy chairs in which they sat. "I think we're in," he said.

"Do you think we're ready? I mean, do we know enough? It must be a different kind of audience here."

"They speak English, don't they?"

"Well, yes, but—"

Harry held up his hand. "No buts. If we get offered anything we take it. We'll learn on our feet, darlin'."

So Clara said no more.

The Brooklyn Academy of Music had been the offer. Max Rober had come back into his office beaming, and asked them if they felt ready to try out at the All Star matinee on the following Sunday. Slipped in—he apologized charmingly with a slight bow towards Clara—as an extra act.

"Yes, *sir!*" said Harry promptly. His ear was good, and already he was sounding American.

Max Rober looked surprised, then smiled and extended his hand. "You come very well recommended, Mr. Viner, and I don't think there is very much I need say, except it will be a family audience, many of them Irish, of course. . . ." He smiled. "Well, I don't have to tell you your business, do I?"

194

Yes, you do, Clara wanted to cry out, please do tell us our business, because we certainly don't know it yet, over here, even if we did in London, and I'm not sure about that. But there was Harry, already on his feet, smiling and confident, shaking Max Rober's hand and thanking him and never mentioning money or anything else except the time they were expected at the theater on the Sunday. Then they were outside, and Harry was waving his hat, euphoric with joy.

"I told you! What did I say, darlin'? We've got a booking already."

Clara stood stubborn in the freezing wind. "It isn't a booking, Harry. It's a tryout. To an audience we don't know. What will they expect from us? Shouldn't we have asked Mr. Rober a little more?"

Harry's face changed. "What sort of a mug would I look if I asked him a lot of questions like that? He'd have thought I was a real idiot. We got good letters of recommendation, dear, from top-of-the-bills—headliners—Eugene Stratton, people like that. Mr. Rober knows we'll be good."

"Harry, they wrote those letters because they were sorry for us."

Harry crammed the letters into his topcoat, crushed his hat on his head and turned away from her. He walked off down the street. Clara stared after him. "Harry!" she called. "Please! Harry!"

Harry did not turn around. He simply walked into the crowds of people on the sidewalk, bent into the wind and the sleet that had just started to fall and disappeared in the trudging throng.

Clara did nothing for a few moments. She waited. She told herself that he would not just walk away and leave her like that in a strange city.

When ten minutes went by and he did not come back, she knew that he had. She stood there for fifteen minutes until her hands were numb and the feeling had almost gone from her feet, and then she stopped a man in a mackinaw coat and asked him how she got to West Forty-sixth Street.

"You walk, lady. It's only four blocks." He jerked his thumb and walked on. He did not touch his hat or break his stride or even look to notice the twin tears forming in her eyes. He spoke to her as he would have spoken to another man. Clara tightened her fur collar around her throat and plunged her freezing hand back into her muff. Very well, she would act like a man. She walked

195

across the street, avoiding the horse traffic as best she could. She was splashed, just the same.

Clara walked the blocks, thinking hard, refusing to cry or give way. Plainly, the honeymoon was over. It had been a glorious one, coming across on the SS *Baltic*. It had been everything a honeymoon should be. Different, romantic, full of tender love and sexual fire. She tried to smile. It had certainly had *that*. It seemed to her that they had done very little else but eat, sleep and make love. Of course, there had been ship's dances and deck games (not for steerage, though), and the ship's officers had smiled at her and nodded enviously to Harry. Clara had been blissfully happy. It had been something she had never expected, a real honeymoon. It was as if they were suspended between two worlds, which of course they were, the Old and the New. Clara trudged through the snow (the sleet had thickened, and her muff and collar were turning white) and thought how near to heaven the voyage had been. They had traveled second class (first was too posh, and only the really poor went steerage), and Harry had, on demand, given a turn in the concert in the first-class saloon. He had returned tipsy and happier than Clara had ever seen him before.

"I felt right amongst those fellows," he had said, waving a large Havana somebody had given him. "Absolutely at home. One of them."

"But you aren't, are you?" Clara had said. Fortunately Harry had not heard her but had fallen asleep across his bunk, fully clothed. Clara had kissed him as he lay there and thought how much she loved him and how lucky she was.

On the ship Harry had divided his time between telling her how much he loved her and talking about the act. They had rehearsed gags and sometimes (when the ship wasn't moving too much) routines, and Clara had been entirely, blissfully happy. Even at Immigration, where the poor steerage people were put through what they heard was an awful time, things were made easy for the first- and second-class passengers. The Purser had taken a liking to Harry ("Some of his *jokes,* madam!" and he had shaken his head at Clara) and whisked them through with little formality.

It had all been perfect.

It had been a time out of life.

Now she had to start the hard business of living again, in this cold and suddenly unfriendly city.

One thing she must resolve to begin to do that day. She must not criticize or in any way censure Harry. All he had was his confidence in himself, and if she damaged that, he was nothing. He might start to hate her. He might even leave her. Clara stopped in the street, and the snowflakes fell soft and heavy upon her dark coat.

Leave her, what nonsense!

But was it nonsense?

He had just left her in the street, had he not?

Thoughtfully and much shaken, she had made her way toward the Knickerbocker, feeling lost and lonely.

"Clara?" Harry stood in the doorway of the hotel, peering into the snow.

Clara ran into his arms. He kissed her. The snow got into her eyes, but she didn't care. She was never so pleased to see anybody in her life.

"Oh, my darling, oh, Harry."

"I'm sorry, I'm sorry."

"Don't ever leave me again!"

"No, I won't, ever."

"Promise?"

"I promise."

In the hotel room Harry prepared hot chocolate on the Sterno stove, while Clara took off her wet boots and coat and hat.

"How did you get back?"

"I walked."

Harry was solicitous. "I don't know what came over me, I just felt you didn't understand how I felt. . . . I think we have a real chance, we mustn't lose our nerve. If we're afraid of that audience in Brooklyn—wherever *that* is!—we're *dead.*"

Clara sat on the bed, sipping the chocolate, and felt supremely happy. Harry was right. Here they were, in a new city only two days, and already they had a real chance opening up before them. It was only four days to the show, there was no point in fearing failure and anyway, what could they learn in four days that would stave off disaster, if it were to come?

For, looking back on it later, Clara had felt disaster to be on the way. That evening in the hotel bedroom she pushed the possibility to the back of her mind. She swallowed the last of the hot chocolate and reached out her arms to him.

"Come to bed, Harry."

He looked startled; he was in the full flow of explaining to

197

her again—apologizing really—that she must trust him about the business decisions they made, that he had some experience, that he knew best, not just because he was a man, and she was a chit of a girl. . . .

Harry smiled and put out his cigar. He was in striped shirt sleeves held up by elastic bands, his vest open and his long knitted tie awry from his hard white collar, exposing his brass collar stud. His hair was slightly disarranged, and Clara thought he looked dashing and romantic and very handsome.

"Come to bed," she said again, more urgently.

It was the way all their quarrels ended.

Brooklyn started well enough. The American artistes were very kind, even the headliners, and nobody seemed to be making anything of the fact that they were foreigners, coming over to steal the bread out of everybody's mouth.

The matinee was crowded and cheerful, and it felt, as Harry said, very odd to be working on a Sunday. They had a decent, warm dressing room to themselves, and it was strange to see the old wicker skip lying in the middle of the floor. Clara had talked Harry into letting her wear a blue sailor top with the white cotton tights and a parasol. He had also agreed to cut out the dance that most people seemed to think was a surefire way of ending their act. Harry was doubtful about ending with their song—he still harbored his old feeling that a comic should just *walk offstage*—but Clara convinced him, mostly in earnest late-night discussions in bed, that if it was risky to do that in London, how much more risky was it to do it in New York?

Harry finally agreed. "All right, let's play it safe then."

That was how he regarded it, she knew. Part of Harry's talent lay in his feeling for risk, for pushing everything as far as it would go. It was one of the things that attracted her to him and at the same time made her fear for him.

Max Rober came backstage to see them. He was wearing a different but equally splendid suit, and his topcoat had a fur collar. He seemed quietly cheerful and said how much he was looking forward to seeing their act.

"This is a nice audience," he said, looking at them both and smiling. "But if it goes very quiet, then is the time to worry." Max Rober paused.

Harry was looking at him through the dressing-table mirror,

applying his makeup. "It won't go quiet, Mr. Rober. We've done this act with great success on the London halls."

"Yes, I know that." Max Rober shone the silver top of his cane with his glove. "It's simply that this is not a sophisticated audience, and you might find they take to you a bit slowly. Give them time."

Harry said nothing. Max Rober smiled. "But if we understood exactly what audiences would go for, Mr. Viner, we wouldn't be agents and actors, we'd simply be rich." He touched his hat, which he had not taken off, and added, "I'll come round afterwards. Good luck to you both," smiled once more and left quietly.

Clara glanced at herself in the mirror. She was beginning to get butterflies in her stomach, but she knew she would not be sick because she had not eaten all day. She would eat later, when the show was over, like everybody else. Almost everybody did his act on an empty stomach. Empty, anyway, of food. Harry took a quick gulp at his hip flask and got to his feet. "I'm going out to look at the other acts. Want to come?"

Clara shook her head. "I'll stay here. I get too nervous, waiting out there." She looked at the bill, pinned up in the dressing room. Like the artistes on show at Hammerstein's Victoria on Forty-second Street, the names were mostly new to her. Presently, she became impatient and walked out of the dressing room, past the backstage workers, who nodded to her face and looked at her legs once she had passed.

Clara did not mind, quite the reverse. Her legs were good, plump and showed no light between them, as was the fashion. She heard a stagehand say to another, "You couldn't get a knife between those pins."

"I know what I could get between them," said the other, loud enough for her to hear.

Clara turned and looked him in the eye.

"Nothing I'd notice, I don't suppose," she said.

The men grinned at each other, and she moved to the side of the stage to watch the acts. Later the senior stagehand moved next to her. He was a gnarled man in his fifties, the only one of the stagehands in a collar and tie and braces. A billycock hat crowned his attire. "Me name's Clancy," he said. "And don't take no notice o' these bums of mine, Clara. If they didn't like you, they wouldn't talk to you."

Clara nodded. "I know. It's all right."

Clancy chewed on his mouthful of tobacco. "People been to mass today, feeling good and holy. I dunno what your husband usually gives them, but a little old Irish song always goes down well here."

Clara said, "Thanks. I'll tell him."

"My pleasure, lady," said Clancy, whose face seemed to have been gashed by a hundred bloodless razors. "Next on, aren't yez?" Clancy turned to his minions. "Stand ready, boys, now, for the change."

Clara stood, thrilled at the very newness of what she saw. There was no doubt about the popularity of anything Irish. Bessie and Nellie McCoy were onstage, two pretty young girls playing old Irishwomen, in bonnet and shawl and baskets, singing:

> Now we must be leavin'
> The kids will be grievin'
> To tarry too long is not right.
> The children will be cryin'
> The meat should be fryin'
> For supper on Saturday night!

"Gawdalive," said Harry, an unlit stogie in his mouth. "They go off to a waltz, and a clog dance, after *that!*" He made way for the two young girls, faces shining, to go back and take their bows. The applause was very loud, and even Clancy nodded to the girls approvingly as they scampered off to their dressing room.

"Two lovely girls," said Clancy. "Everybody loves them, indade they do."

"I can bloody believe it, mate," muttered Harry bleakly. "How do we follow that sort of act? It's like following Lauder at the Glasgow Empire."

Clara said. "It's an Irish audience, easy on the Irish jokes, Harry."

"Jesus she's telling me how to run the act now." Harry put his derby on his head, gave it a sharp tap, took her hand and squeezed it. "You just do like I've told you, and you'll be all right."

Clara nodded. The butterflies were back in her stomach. She felt cold all over. The music for "Naughty But Nice" started, then stopped, and Harry walked out onto the stage.

"Your husband's not short on nerve," said Clancy, "is he?"

Clara shook her head.

"Believes in going on cold. Well, you got to admire anybody

200

goes on cold. It's doing it the hard way, right, lady?"

Clara nodded. Everything Harry did, he did the hard way. He wanted no favors from anybody, and that included audiences. Clara waited with some trepidation for him to begin.

Harry opened by standing and staring at the audience in total silence for a very long time. Then he took off his derby hat and said, "The worst song I ever sang was sold to me by an Irishman. He'll be famous one day, I'm sure of it. Not as a songwriter, though. As the man who made the English language unnecessary. There's another Irish song, though, and I know you all know it. I'll give you a verse, so you can get the hang of it, shall I? Mr. Musical Director."

Harry waved to the musical director, who nodded, tapped his baton. A catchy little tune, Clara thought, but what *is* it? She had never heard it before. But here was Harry singing it.

> Now if they'd let me be, I'd set Ireland free;
> On the railroad you'd never pay fare.
> I'd have the United States under my thumb,
> And sleep in the President's chair.

The whole house rocked to the chorus:

> Is that Mr. Riley, can anyone tell?
> Is that Mr. Riley, that keeps the hotel?
> Is that Mr. Riley they speak of so highly?
> Upon me soul, Riley, you're doin' *quite* well!

"Jasus," said Clancy, at Clara's side, "if I hadn't been at your husband's bar mitzvah, I'd swear he was a Cork man, so I would." He shook his head. "Oh, he's the bhoy, he knows what to give them here, yez home and dried, missus, home an' dried."

Harry, riding the applause, was into the second verse of the song. Where had he learned it? How? Did it matter?

Harry sang, in an Irish voice, thumbs in armpits, half dancing a jig:

> I'd have nothing but Irishmen on the police.
> Patrick's day would be Fourth of July.
> I'd get me a thousand infernal machines
> To teach the Chinese how to die.
> Help the workingman's cause, manufacture the laws,
> New York would be swimming in wine.
> A hundred a day would be very small pay,
> If the White House and Capitol were mine!

Harry took several bows to thunderous applause.

Clara waited for her cue to go onstage. It was to be the opening bars of "Naughty But Nice." The stage manager, officious in dark vest and pince-nez, appeared at her side, looking at his large pocket watch. "I see your husband has used some new material, Mrs. Viner. That's all right, but he must not overrun his time."

Clara shook her head. "I'm sure he won't."

"He'd better not." The stage manager put his watch away. "He has only three minutes left. How long does your song usually take?"

Clara was going to tell him, with an awful foreboding, that it took five minutes exactly when the stage manager took off his pince-nez, polished them on his sleeve and clipped them back on his nose. "Can you tell me," he asked Clara, "exactly what he thinks he's doing, lady?"

"No," faltered Clara. "No. I can't."

For Harry had ushered the house into silence and was regarding them with a smile. Not a particularly pleasant one, as far as Clara could make out, and she was an expert on Harry Viner's smiles. Harry was angry; she could hear it in his voice. But *why?*

"My dear people," Harry was saying, "I have just demonstrated to you, and to any agent, booker or manager who happens to be present, how easy it is to *please* you. All I had to do was sing an old favorite of the great Pat Rooney's, and you were content. Am I right?"

A voice from the pit cried, "Stop your blathering, man, and sing us another."

"I could do that, friend," conceded Harry, "but I'd only be doing a fake. Like I did a fake when I sang Pat Rooney's song. You deserve better than that because anybody could do that. I just wanted to see if you were still alive, really."

"Oh, rahlly?" called the Irish voice. Not so nicely this time.

"Is your man drink-taken at all, at all?" asked Clancy, at Clara's elbow.

"No. No, he isn't," said Clara.

"Ah," said Clancy, "then it's a pity, it is so."

Harry told the joke about the Irishman and the monkey.

The audience went absolutely silent.

Clancy cackled. "I loike that one. But I think your fella is taking his own life out there, and I shouldn't even *say* a thing the loike o' that."

Harry told the joke about the Irish coalman carrying the horse by the ears.

Even more silence.

"Jasus," said Clancy, "the very neck of the man, sure yez have to admire it. Is he looking for work, did ye say, or was it a wake?"

Harry asked the audience, "Did you hear about the boss who asked how many bricklayers were up the ladder? And a voice calls down, 'Three.' He shouts up, 'Come down, half of yez!' An' to another fella he says, 'Murphy, what are yez doing over there?' And Murphy says, 'I'm oiling the wheelbarrow.' 'Let it alone,' sez the boss, 'what the hell do you know about machinery?' "

This time there were a few laughs.

Harry held up his hand. "You liked that one, didn't you, ladies and gentlemen? Shall I tell you why you laughed? You laughed because it was *old;* you laughed because you'd heard it before." He leaned forward over the footlights. Clara watched him, trembling with anger and fright. What did he think he was doing?

Harry said, "Well, I'm different, aren't I, anyway?"

The Irish voice shouted, "No, you're just English!"

"Wrong, my friend, I'm Jewish, like what you are."

There was a more general laugh at that.

Clancy said, chewing judicially, "If he sez no more, he might just get off before they lynch him."

Clara brushed past him and onto the stage.

Harry just stared at her.

She curtsied to the audience.

"This is the wife," Harry shouted into the silence. "She comes from a very good Irish family. I've been trying to give her back to them for years. Her father is quite a nob. He has a lovely blue suit with gray trousers and a brown vest . . . in England I say weskit. . . . Yes, he has a suit for every day of the week and he tries it on on Sundays to see if it still fits. . . . Closing music, maestro, if you please. . . ."

The musical director looked quickly at his sheet, tapped his stand.

They both sang the "Naughty But Nice" chorus and got off.

The applause was only moderate, but as Clancy said, pushing them out to take a second bow, they were lucky indeed that they got off without being taken downtown to Tammany Hall for public trial. "Is that right, now," he asked Clara, "that you're Irish?"

Back in the dressing room Clara confronted Harry.

"What the hell was all that about?"

He sat on one of the two bentwood chairs, exhausted and wet with sweat, smiling at her. "That showed them."

"Showed who what?" Clara was so angry that she could hardly trust herself to speak. He was sitting there, looking so pleased with himself. Didn't he realize what he had just done? "What about that song?"

Harry took a slug from his hip flask. "I learned that song this morning from one of the musicians. I wasn't going to use it unless I had to. I told the musical director to keep it handy, just in case I needed it." He shook his head. "That audience. I thought I'd played to some hometown audiences in England, but this one. . . ." He shook his head, laughing.

He's enjoying all this, Clara thought. Her anger boiled over. "You made fools of the audience, Harry, and it's one thing you should never do, I don't care where you are!"

"What?" He looked surprised at her tone.

"You offended that audience, and you offended me. You didn't think I was important enough to tell me you might make a song switch in the act—"

"I didn't think I'd need to, I just told you."

"And when I get on, what do you do? You steal my only song—"

"I had to do that, it made sense!"

"Yes, but you had to have the lines, didn't you? I felt an absolute fool, coming on like that."

"Why did you come on then?"

Well, he had asked for it. "I came on because if I hadn't, you would have gone too far; you were on the very edge, and there was no chance you were going to get off without being booed off. If you think I felt happy walking on like that, you've got a bigger head than I think you have, and that isn't possible. You never gave me a thought; you only considered yourself, what sort of impression you were making. I felt an absolute idiot, standing there in the wings, waiting for my music cue. I'd be standing there now, if it had been left to you." Clara thought, to hell with it— her language, really, what would Papa say if he heard it?—I'll go the whole hog. "You're selfish, Harry Viner; you think of nobody but yourself."

Harry sat there looking at her, silently, for a long moment.

He had opened his mouth to speak—and she could see how angry he was, and she didn't care—when there was a tap on the door and Max Rober came in. He stood there, looking from one to the other. Clara turned away to the mirror and began to remove her makeup. She did not trust herself to speak.

Harry got to his feet quickly, putting the hip flask away, but not quickly enough, Clara thought, for Max Rober not to have noticed it.

"Sit down, Mr. Rober." Harry offered his chair.

"Thank you. Only for a moment." Max Rober removed his hat, and a fragrance of expensive lavender oil from his hair dressing filled the room. There was no doubt, Clara thought, that the rich smelled differently. Expensive cigars and Yardley's lavender hair oil, good creamy soap and fresh linen every day, say what you liked, it made a difference. Clara looked at Max Rober through the mirror. He was not the slightest bit like Papa, but somewhere, there was a resemblance.

She supposed it was money.

"Well, tell us the worst, Mr. Rober?" Harry was saying, a small, half-apologetic smile on his face.

"Why," Max Rober asked, "did you do what you did?"

Harry shrugged. "I dunno. It just seemed right somehow. I mean, how could I follow that Irish act, except by doing what I did?"

"You decided at the last moment?" Max Rober sounded genuinely surprised and curious.

Harry nodded, emboldened. "I had it handy, just in case. Even Clara here didn't know; she's just this minute been having a go at me about not telling her."

"So I should hope, eh, Mrs. Viner?" Max Rober nodded in her direction, and Clara smiled back through the mirror, feeling a little less foolish. "I thought," continued Max Rober, "that your wife looked very good. Of course, she wasn't on long enough to form any opinion of what she can really do."

Harry looked at his feet. "No. That was a pity. She's got a nice little voice, Clara has."

Not so much, Clara thought indignantly, of the "little."

"Just as well you arranged for her to come on when she did." Max Rober was looking directly at Harry. "Or you might have had trouble with that audience."

"Yes, I know." Harry wasn't using the tone of voice to Max Rober that he had been using to her earlier. "But I had to do something, Mr. Rober. I had to try something new. There wasn't much point in dying a death without putting up some kind of fight, was there?"

There was a long silence.

Then Max Rober said, "I see your point, believe me, Mr. Viner. The trouble is, the two people I brought here to look at you . . . one from the Albee Circuit, the Big Time—"

"What did he say?" Harry asked eagerly.

Max Rober polished the silver top of his cane with his yellow kid glove.

"He said, he couldn't see you in the Big Time."

"Hooray for him," said Harry bleakly.

Max Rober went on quickly, "But he only said that, I'm sure, because he didn't know your usual act and presumed what you were doing at this performance would be"—he coughed—"your usual form on all occasions."

"He calls himself a booker," Harry said, "and he thinks that?"

"The trouble is, Mr. Viner, that you broke the house rules that govern the Big Time. Your act was full of jokes about one minority—in this case Irish—and you directly addressed individual members of the audience." Max Rober sighed. "I daresay that is perfectly all right in some London halls. But vaudeville is only recently respectable in this country. Not long ago no man would take his wife into a vaudeville house. There are pretty firm rules, and talking directly to members of the audience is one of them. How was he to know—how was I to know?—it wasn't part of your act?"

"It isn't," said Harry coldly, "unless some berk in the audience tries to take me on."

"Well, I'm sorry, Mr. Viner, but I don't think I can hold out any hope of the Big Time." He hesitated. "On the other hand, I think I could, if I had your permission, get you some Little Time. One Little Time booker was in, at my invitation, and he liked your style. Yonkers has been mentioned. There, it's all right to talk back to the audience. It's altogether more. . . ."

"Common?" said Harry. "Low-life?"

"Well, in a way I suppose so." Max Rober looked uncomfortable, glanced at his pocket watch and got to his feet. "Think it over, and let me know."

Clara said, "Thank you. We will—"

Harry ignored her. He looked straight at Max Rober. "The

206

other day you said if we got into Little Time, we'd never get out of it."

Max Rober looked apprehensive. "Yes. But as it is all that is being offered, I felt I had to tell you that." He moved to the door. "Do think it over. There's no hurry. The money would not be a lot, but I think you would find it enough."

Clara looked at Harry, willing him.

Harry said, "I didn't come all the way from England to play what we call number two halls, Mr. Rober. I think we are good enough to play at the best vaudeville houses."

Max Rober looked at Clara directly. "Don't make your mind up now. You've just come offstage. You aren't thinking as . . . well, as straight as you will be tomorrow."

Clara said, "I think that's true. Harry—"

Again Harry ignored her. "You know where we are, Mr. Rober. If you can book us on the Big Time, you know where we're staying."

Clara exclaimed, "Harry, no!"

He silenced her with a look.

Max Rober stood in the doorway for a moment. Then he said, "If you should change your mind, please be in touch. Good night to you both."

Then he was gone.

Harry sat down abruptly.

Clara closed her eyes. Don't say anything, she told herself. Nothing. He could be right. He could just be right. And what is done is done.

"Little Time!" Harry ground out the phrase through his teeth. "I haven't come here to play to a lot of swede bashers out in the bloody fields!"

Clara turned around, to say a thousand things, but then she saw his face, white, set and utterly miserable. Her heart melted.

"Oh, my love," she said. "Oh, my love."

That had been six months ago.

Now, watching Harry drink his beer and relax in the soft, warmed-over air from the overhead fan, Clara wondered how he had come through those months without total despair. He had told her, "Don't expect anybody to do you any favors in this game. Nobody's your friend, agents, managers, audience, nobody. They're all ships that pass in the night. Don't take no notice if anybody praises you, and don't take no notice if they say you're bloody awful. None of that matters. What matters is gettin' up there and doing it your way and nobody else's. If Max Rober thinks we're Little Time, he's entitled to his opinion, but I don't have to bleedin' share it, do I? We'll pick up something, you'll see."

What they had picked up was burlesque.

They had been glad of it.

Slowly their money had gone down and down, although they had continued to stay at the same hotel. "If we go into rooms, dear," Harry had reasoned, "we'll be finished. While we still live at the hotel, nobody knows what we've got or what we haven't got."

Clara had supposed he was right. She only wished that she had some of the toughness and confidence that he had. For herself, she needed people to say that they had *liked* her; otherwise, why was she standing up there singing at all? Even the applause of the beery customers in the burlesque theatre had been welcome. Harry did not agree. "Don't get hooked on them loving you," he said. "It gets to be a drug, that does. After a bit, you'll do anything to please them. It's ruination, that is."

Clara did not argue. She tried hard not to argue with Harry. He was her husband now, and it was bad wifely business (she had always been taught) to hold contrary views from those of your husband. Just the same, there was something wrong with Harry's reasoning. If he was right, there was no enjoyment to be had out of performing, and that could not be so. She enjoyed it all. Even in the burlesque house her blood ran quick, and her eyes shone, and her heart felt as if it would burst out of the skimpy whalebone top. She supposed the business of being a comic was different. The only act that impressed Harry was down the bill, second after the intermission, at Hammerstein's Victoria. He was billed as an "Expert Lariat Thrower," and his name was Will Rogers. "All I know, folks," Rogers told his audience, "is what I read in the papers. But it does seem this fella got caught riding this doggie in the rodeo with his hands tied to the cow's horns, and when he was accused of tryin' to win the hundred dollars' prize by foul means, this ole boy just says, fellas, I look at it this way"—and Will Rogers spun his lariat and chewed on his tobacco—"If you ain't cheatin', you ain't tryin'!"

Harry had liked that. He had gone off, sometimes with Clara, often alone, to many of the other vaudeville houses in the city.

Clara had been mesmerized by Eva Tanguay. She was an electric performer, a comedienne who could actually sing. She attacked her audience at Hammerstein's Victoria. She threw sex at them and shrieked songs at them, deafened them and delighted them.

> I don't care, I don't care if you don't like my song,
> I don't care, I don't care, I just keep jogging along,
> My voice may sound funny,
> But it's getting me the money,
> *So I don't care!*

After the show, Clara said to Harry, "I wish I could do *that.*"

Harry looked surprised. "No chance, darlin'. That's legalized assault and battery. 'Naughty But Nice,' that's your number, darlin'."

Clara did not argue. Harry obviously admired Eva Tanguay but did not remark on her beauty, and Clara had to be content with that. She had suggested, after a month had gone by, that they approach Max Rober again and see if he had changed his mind about them. Harry said no, he would wait. Max Rober knew where they were. They rehearsed their act endlessly, in their hotel room, on sharp walks around the frozen city, while they ate frankfurters in cheap coffee shops, getting up, going to bed, sleeping and waking, or so it seemed to Clara. She was learning a lot, and she was blissfully happy. Harry was still trying to get Americanisms into the act, picked up on the street, in bars, at the ball park. "Baseball, it's like bleedin' rounders," he reported, astonished, after a visit to the Polo Grounds.

Still, as the bitter winter finally receded, and spring caught them unawares, in thick coats and scarves, one suddenly warm day in Central Park, Harry made his decision. "It's no use going out on the road in Little Time, they don't call it the Death Trail for nothing—I'm going to try these burlesque halls. I've been looking at them. Money's nothing probably but it would be experience, working these sort of audiences. And we'd still be in New York, close to the action."

It had been experience indeed.

Clara had never seen so many girls with so little on. They were all around, all the time, but Harry did not seem to notice them. "A lot of brasses, dear, good-hearted tarts the lot of 'em," was his sole comment, but he seemed to get on well enough with them and knew most of them by their first names. Often he made small rude jokes to amuse them.

209

Burlesque was not vaudeville. It was a strip show playing to men, and the comics were only there to give the girls time to change costumes, if any. Vaudeville was where they should be, it was where they deserved to be, Big or Little Time or whatever they could get, playing to mixed audiences, amongst real talent.

After they got the job, on a week's trial, which had turned, as Harry said, into an "indefinite run," Clara breathed again. The money, carefully spread out, was about enough to live on. They couldn't save anything. Apart from the twenty dollars she had in the lining of her purse, they had nothing. But the burlesque experience had taught Clara one thing. She was not afraid to take off her clothes in front of an audience. Of course, she did not strip down to a G-string, the way the bumps-and-grinds girls did, some of them laconically chewing gum as they did so and making rude gestures with their fingers to men shouting, "Take it off!" Yet she felt that if she had to, she could. The idea rather thrilled her, in a secret way. It was quite a discovery about herself, but she did not mention it to Harry. She knew what his reaction would be—probably to leave the job.

Well, he had managed to do that all on his own without any help from her.

So, here they were, out of work and broke, all over again.

Harry blew out silvery cigar smoke and gazed through the window of the restaurant at the crowds outside.

Clara said, "We're down to our last few dollars, Harry."

He nodded. "I know that, love."

"But what are we going to do when they're gone?"

"How about starve?"

Clara blinked back tears. "It's easy to say that with a plank steak inside you. It'll be a different thing if we do get to that point. And we will unless we do something."

"No, we won't." He patted her hand. "Something will turn up."

With that Clara had to be content.

The next two weeks passed miserably. It was unbearably hot even in the hotel room, and Harry lay about in his underclothes, reading *Billboard* and the *Morning Telegraph*. She had finally got him into cotton, but he complained about its clinging to his skin. He did not seem to be doing anything about another date in burlesque, and whenever she suggested it to him, he spoke to her

210

sharply, so she stopped it. They ate frugally, which did not matter, since it was too hot to eat anyway. Fortunately the room had an overhead fan. Without it Clara felt she would have died. She did not share Harry's wild enthusiasm for the city. To her it seemed full of people in strange clothes, speaking strange languages, and she could recognize no reassuring social order. Even the policemen, who were mostly Irish, looked different and were not overpolite if asked the way. They did not touch their caps in salute to a lady. Nobody said "Please" or "Thank you" in a café or on the streetcar. It was all very odd; it was as if "good manners" had been left behind in Europe with all the bad things that most people seemed to have run away from: poverty and pogroms and starvation.

It was lively, she had to admit that. Even the workingmen ate well. Drank well too. If anything, they drank more beer than the English did. They ate hugely, too, many of them, of sausage meats on bar counters. The wealthy ate steaks and chops for breakfast. Most successful men had what in England was called a corporation—huge bellies ballooning out in front of them by the time they were thirty years of age. Only the poor were thin.

Soon, unless they did something, they would be thin, too.

Yet Harry lay on the bed reading *Billboard* and called out the news that Hammerstein was headlining boxers like James J. Corbett and escapologists like Houdini. "But where are the *comics?*"

"I could telegraph home to Papa," said Clara, greatly daring, "and ask him to send us our passage home. I'm sure he would do that."

"If you do any such thing"—Harry turned a page of *Billboard* without looking up—"you go home on your own."

Clara turned away from him. She was stripped down to her skin in the bed. Her face, in the mirror, was flushed.

"But, Harry, what do we do?"

Harry put down *Billboard* and reached over to her.

On this first occasion in their time together, Clara did not come to a sexual climax in Harry's embrace. He did not seem to notice but fell into a light sleep, his dark hair tousled, his member small and wrinkled and somehow pathetic.

Clara lay naked, her head resting on her arm, and looked at him for a long, long time, as the noise of the city, horses, streetcars, the roar of the odd automobile engine, wafted into the room from the streets below.

Something would have to be done.

The next day Clara went to see Max Rober at his office on Fourteenth Street. She was wearing a velvet dress with a deep lace collar and spotless white linen gloves to the elbow, and her hat was heavy with wax fruit. No, she did not object to waiting, she told Mr. Rober's lady secretary, and wait she did, all the way to lunch, which in New York seemed to be midday, not one o'clock, as in London. She supposed it was because people started work earlier. Most men were at their office desks at eight o'clock in the morning.

Max Rober was charming and apologetic. "I'm very sorry, my dear, but I was in an important conference. As you saw, I had Mr. Hammerstein with me."

"Was that Mr. Hammerstein who just went out?" Clara remembered a thickset figure in a frock coat and top hat. "Really him, I mean?"

Max Rober looked amused. "Of course it was. And if you want to see more of him, why, we can do that at lunch. I'm afraid it's the only time I have free today. If you will accept, of course?"

"Well," Clara said, remembering Mr. Weaver.

Max Rober seemed to read her mind. "I will have to leave you, I'm afraid, on the very stroke of one o'clock. I must be at Proctor's Theater on Twenty-third at one-fifteen promptly."

"Then," said Clara, "I would be delighted to have lunch."

Max Rober smiled, and they drove to lunch in his Duesenberg. It was the first time Clara had ever been in a motorcar, and she was terrified and yet elated. The car had an open top and made a great deal of noise. Nobody seemed to mind. She sat there, trying to look as if this were everyday, and hoped nobody noticed the trembling of her knees. There was a chauffeur in splendid beige livery and a shiny peak cap. She sat in the back with Max Rober.

"This is wonderful. It's a miracle." She smiled at him.

He put his hand on hers. "Nervous?"

"Not with you. . . ." She corrected herself. "Not with a gentleman with me."

Max Rober nodded. He seemed to be pleased. He let her hand go, for which she was grateful (she really only liked Harry to do that) and to the chauffeur's query answered, "Delmonico's."

The famous restaurant was crowded, and even Clara, who hardly knew the local scene, recognized many faces in the place, including Mr. Hammerstein's, as Max Rober had predicted. It was, of course, very warm, but no gentleman removed his tie or jacket or in any way showed that the heat was intolerable. Everybody ate a good deal of hot food. This was a restaurant with an excellent cuisine, and plank steaks were not a feature of their carte. Clara felt entirely at home and pleased the headwaiter by her use of schoolgirl French.

Max Rober suggested they eat cold lobster. Clara agreed. She had not eaten such rich food for a very long time. The cuisine was indeed European. Their wine was a German hock. "My father always says, French for red, German for white."

"Your father sounds wise." Max Rober was looking at her, smiling at her evident enjoyment. "What does he do?"

Clara had said, "As a matter of fact, he owns a music hall," before she knew it.

Max Rober looked surprised. "Do I know him?"

"I doubt it. It is in the North of England, the Alhambra."

"His name is. . . ?"

"Abbott."

He frowned. "I seem to have heard of it. It is a good music hall?"

"He books the best acts in England. I met Harry there."

"I see." Max Rober was silent a long moment, sipping his wine. "You must be the only daughter of an owner on the boards."

"I think I probably am." Clara laughed.

"I need not ask if he approved?" Max Rober tilted his head.

"Don't ask!" said Clara. "Mr. Rober—"

"Let us eat this very good lobster and talk afterwards."

Clara smiled ruefully. "Of course. I'm sorry. I seem to have forgotten my manners. They are almost the first thing to go, I find, once you are poor."

Max Rober put his hand briefly on hers again.

"Please don't apologize. Eat your lobster. Besides, I know what you are going to talk to me about. I'll be thinking while we eat." He looked around the room. "Meanwhile, I'll tell you who all these very important people are."

Clara was wide-eyed as Max Rober pointed out the famous ones. Eddie Foy, a small, sharp-eyed man, sat at a large table, surrounded by his friends. "A headliner for twenty years and likely

213

to be as long as there's a vaudeville house," said Max Rober. George M. Cohan, gray-haired already, small but imperious. "A hard businessman but very fair," said Max Rober, shaking his head and smiling, "and big enough to walk out on Albee." There were many others (all famous in the city, or they would not have been eating at Delmonico's), but Clara lost their faces and names in a welter of impressions, the most final of which was: they lived like this every day of the year.

Clara ate fruit after her lobster and found Max Rober watching her as she peeled and quartered her pear with the small silver knife. He seemed to approve her expertise. There was one thing that Miss Wilson's Academy for Young Ladies taught a young woman, and that was how to behave at table. No husband would wish a wife whose table manners were not of the most impeccable taste, Miss Wilson had averred. She was, of course, wrong in some instances. Harry Viner did not seem to notice how she ate, and truth to tell, her fastidiousness had declined in consequence. Looking around the large and select room, at the gleaming silver and white napery, Clara felt suddenly (perhaps it was the wine?) quite at home.

Max Rober consulted his pocket watch and sighed. "I will have to make my excuses in ten more minutes, my dear. Business calls. I take it you wish me to find you and Mr. Viner some Little Time bookings as soon as possible?"

"Yes. If you would find . . . that agreeable to do . . . after we have seemed so very ungrateful."

Max Rober looked even more pleased. "It will be no trouble, I'm sure. I will make inquiries and write to you in a day or so. Are you still at the same hotel?" Clara nodded. "Then rest assured I will do everything I can."

"How did you know why I came?"

Max Rober's eyes twinkled. "What other reason can there be?"

Clara blushed. "There's just one other small thing, Mr. Rober. My husband doesn't know I'm here. If you could write to him, as if it is. . . ." She faltered.

"As if it is my own idea, certainly." Max Rober nodded. "A man has his dignity. And I would say your husband has more than most."

"Indeed he has," Clara said fervently. "But he is a very good comic."

"Yes, he is." Max Rober drew on his Turkish cigarette. "Nonetheless, he is not the only one in your act. You are there, too. And from what little I saw of you, I felt you had a quality. A nice voice, yes. But a quality, too."

"What . . . kind of quality?"

Clara knew it was unladylike to ask, but she had to know.

"You have good looks and a talented voice. The quality I'm speaking of is something extra. How can I put it?" He leaned forward and looked into her eyes. "Most vaudeville ladies look as if the world has treated them badly. You don't."

Clara was disappointed. "You mean I look like a lady?"

"I think you are a lady."

"That's what Harry says."

He smiled. "You don't want to look like a lady?"

She pouted. "Of course not. Anybody can look like a lady."

"Not on a stage. Don't underestimate it." He leaned back and sipped his wine.

"I think you are going to be late for your appointment. I should hate you to blame it on me."

"I have a moment. Just to ask you this. When I try to obtain bookings for you in Little Time, I may have to say what you have been doing since you arrived in New York."

"We have been in burlesque, I'm afraid."

"Yes, I had heard something of the sort." Max Rober smiled.

Pray God, Clara thought, Max Rober had heard nothing about Harry uttering that awful word. If he had, he did not show it but merely signed the check and escorted her out to his car, offering to drop her wherever was convenient. Clara said, "Times Square. I love Times Square. But not as much perhaps as Harry does."

"Are you capable," Max Rober asked, "of answering any question without referring to your husband?"

"No, I don't think I am," Clara said wonderingly. It was all too painfully true. No, that thought was disloyal. "We are only recently married, you know, Mr. Rober."

Max Rober tapped his chauffeur on the shoulder. "The lady will get out here."

Clara enjoyed the stares of loungers and passersby as the chauffeur stopped the gleaming silver and blue monster and opened the door for her to alight. In doing so she inadvertently showed a sliver of ankle, and the loungers, cheered by the sight, looked at each other and muttered approval. Clara smiled at them all and waved to Max Rober, who raised his hat several inches from

215

his head and put it on again. She watched until the car was lost in the melee of horses and carts and clanging trolley cars.

All the way back to the hotel she wondered about Max Rober's remarks on her looks and talent. He was an important man and a grave and serious one, despite his ready smile. He would not say anything he did not think to be true. She decided she would report no part of the conversation to Harry. He had quite enough to worry him, poor love, without a disloyal wife added to it all.

The letter from Max Rober arrived four days later.

It was as well that it did. Clara had four dollars left in her purse—enough, she knew (for she had inquired) to send a cablegram to Papa, asking for assistance. She took the letter to Harry, who was still lying on the bed, in his underclothes, reading *Billboard.*

He opened the letter without curiosity, read it and passed it to her without comment. It was to offer them a booking for the rest of the summer at Atlantic City. An act had fallen out. They were to start on the following Monday. The fee offered was seventy-five dollars a week and was not negotiable. Max Rober regretted that it was so low but felt that he should make them aware of the opportunity.

"We have to take it, Harry." Clara found that she was trembling. "It's a good date. All right, we're down the bill, but it's a place we'll get seen. We have to take it!"

"Of course we have to." Harry returned to *Billboard.* He did not seem surprised at the letter or its contents. Clara felt the truth bursting to be told.

"Did you expect this?" she demanded.

He looked at her but said nothing.

"You knew I'd seen Mr. Rober, didn't you?"

"I guessed that you had, yes."

"Then why didn't you say something about it?"

Clara felt so angry that all she wanted to do was strike him. "You knew I'd gone. You knew I would go, didn't you? All you cared about was that you didn't go; all you cared about was your dignity. So I went and did the dirty work."

"I don't call Delmonico's dirty work." He was smiling, rather crookedly.

"You followed me there! You have the nerve—"

"You brought one of their cards home. I saw it in your purse."

216

"You went through my purse?" She hated him now. She wanted to jump at him, to scratch him, to hurt him, anything.

"No, I didn't go through your purse. I looked in for small change when the boy brought up some ice."

"But you *knew* I'd go to Max Rober. That's why you didn't worry. That's why you just sat around and read that bloody *Billboard* and let me worry. You planned it like that." Clara found herself yelling, a thing she had never done in her life before. "You did, didn't you, you rotter! Well, what else should I expect?"

There. It was out. She had called him a rotter.

A rotter was not a gentleman.

What had she done now?

Too much, apparently. For Harry had got up and gone into the bathroom. He washed noisily, and she heard him shaving. He came out of the bathroom, tight-lipped, and put on a clean shirt and his beige linen suit. Then he brushed his hair with the cheap hairbrushes she had vowed to replace with silver ones (like Papa's) as soon as they were in the money and went out. Just like that. Without speaking.

Clara sat down, but she did not weep.

It was no use weeping. The important thing was to say no more hurtful, upsetting things to her husband and to get him to write and accept the job in Atlantic City. She tidied the little room, remade the bed, drank iced water and had a cold bath. She ate nothing; to eat would have choked her. At midnight she went to bed, naked. The heat was intolerable, was her excuse to herself. For normally she wore a thin nightgown, anyway to begin with.

It was almost two o'clock when Harry came back.

She had put out the light and feigned sleep.

Harry took off his clothes quietly and got into bed. Still, she pretended to be asleep. He lit a small cigar and lay with his hands behind his head, inhaling steadily. From him emanated an aroma of whiskey and tobacco and a flowery scent that could have been a woman's perfume—or was she being fanciful?

Clara kept her eyes closed and buried her face in the pillow. She was being fanciful. She had to be.

Atlantic City was a whole lot cooler than New York.

In many ways it could have been an English seaside resort, like Brighton or Margate. There were crowds, the men with open

217

collars and sunburned faces, and women with parasols to keep their skins the desired white of gentility. There were deck chairs in striped rows along the promenade and silver cruets in the windows of the rooming houses and guesthouses where most people stayed. The breeze from the sea was fresh along the famous boardwalk and the Steel Pier on which they were to perform. The manager seemed honest and fair.

Most of the other acts were not of any real quality, Harry decided. The most popular by far was an oldish nut juggler called Sparrow, who confessed he had worked a great deal in burlesque. Harry sat through his act in stupefied wonder. Sparrow began by throwing a ripe melon into the air and taking it full in his face. It burst, and ripe fruit splattered his shirtfront (which was of rubber). He attempted to juggle a goldfish bowl, which soaked him in fish and water. Eggs splattered down his dress suit (which was of oilcloth). On a fork held in his mouth he attempted to catch soft fruit thrown by the audience. Most of it hit him in the face. Everybody enjoyed his act. He had to go on last. It took almost an hour to clean the stage when he had finished.

"If that man ever stops playing, there'll be a fruit glut."

Harry turned around to look at a paunchy man in a dark tramp getup, with ragged top hat and an eyepatch. He seemed neither young nor old and spoke in a raspy monotone. He said his name was Bill Fields, and he commiserated with Harry upon his booking at the Pier. "Of course," he said, "you should have my luck. I'm billed as the Greatest Juggler on Earth, and I have to be on the same bill with that man, who *is* the greatest juggler on earth."

"He doesn't juggle; he misses everything," Harry protested.

"That is why," Bill Fields said, "he is the greatest juggler on earth." Fields looked speculatively at Clara. "I see you do not lead the life of a monk, my friend." Harry admitted that he did not. "Do you take a drink?" Fields asked. Harry said he had been known to. "Do you happen to have any of the liquid upon your person?" Harry gave him his hip flask. Fields mellowed. "A man after my own pocketbook," he said. "This is a fairly good grade of whiskey, sir. Do not think of this demonstration of thirst as evidence that I am a constant toper. On the contrary, I never drank anything stronger than beer until I was twelve years old." He drank all the liquor in the flask. He did not buy Harry a drink all that long, hot summer. He did not buy anybody a drink all that long, hot summer. Sparrow said that he opened a bank account instead.

Sparrow did not seem to be joking. He said Bill Fields was the closest man with a dollar he had ever met, and he had met a few. Harry liked Bill Fields, despite his grouchiness. He was a genuine comic and did more things with twenty cigar boxes on end than anybody would have thought possible. "Learned with cigar boxes, my friend," boomed Bill Fields in his monotone, "because it was all there was. That was in my hometown Philadelphia, the greatest cemetery in the world." He used his hometown in his act a good deal. "Don't anybody in this theater go out and tell anybody else I'm working the Pier in Atlantic City. This kind of thing could get back to Philadelphia and ruin me socially."

He was successful and was demanding a weekly rise of ten dollars from the manager and (Sparrow glumly reported) getting it. Bill Fields had a few words of advice for Harry as they sat, beer (bought by Harry) in hand, and surveyed the people queueing up for the evening performance. "My generous friend, I have a word of advice, which as a foreigner you should accept gladly. Steer clear of Washington, Kansas City and St. Louis. They are the igloos of the theater world."

"I'm damn lucky to be in work, I reckon," said Harry. "I can't afford to choose where."

"Then let me give you this further note. In all big cities in the States, there is a nearby place that is funny to the audience. In Boston, it's Nahant. In Chicago, it's Winnetka. In Portland, it's Kennebunkport. In Detroit, it's Hamtramck." Bill Fields rubbed his large nose. "And Bismarck, North Dakota, is funny anywhere."

"What about here, for this audience?" Harry pointed his stogie at the line of people in their striped blazers and white trousers and boater hats with colored ribbons around them. "What place is funny to them?"

Bill Fields looked at his empty glass. Harry refilled it from the jug of iced lager at his elbow. "Most of these people are from New York City," opined Fields. "Try Canarsie." He drank deeply. "Though what an Englishman is doing in Canarsie in the first place is a mystery known only to his Maker."

Harry found the audience easy. They were away from home and prepared to laugh at almost anything. The company of the fruit-nut Sparrow and the general air of relaxation about the place made the whole episode bearable. If performers like Sparrow and Bill Fields could bear this, then so could he. Clara was popular and sang:

219

Yesterday I strolled along the boardwalk,
A young man he asked me out for a . . . talk."

Clara broke her song, leaned forward confidentially, and whispered, "We strolled under the pier and he really could . . . well—
He was ever so manly. . . ."

Naughty but Nice, Naughty but Nice,
Never Been Kissed in the Same Place Twice!

They roomed at a guesthouse on the seafront. Most of the people from the show stayed there. The food was plain, home-cooked, and there was fresh-baked bread every day. Harry ate hugely and felt better for it, although he put on no weight. He would never *look* a success, Clara said; he wasn't the build for it. Everywhere they went in the resort they were recognized. They dressed accordingly and took coffee and cream cakes in the fashionable and crowded cafés, where they could be seen and Harry's dashing suits admired. He had bought a new white duck three-piece with vest, as soon as they had confirmed the booking. He wore a white panama hat with a yellow and blue ribbon around it and basked in the admiring glances of the summer people. It was a good time, composed of long and hard hours (three shows a day) and lots of fresh air—it was impossible to avoid it working on the Pier—and plenty of good food. They both slept heavily and well, in the deep feather bed of the guesthouse, lying most nights with only a cotton sheet for covering. They made love often, usually in the mornings. They were too tired at night, after a day of work.

Harry found that his resentment of Clara had left him, and he responded to her eager loving. "Turning into a proper little hot drawers, ain'tcher, darlin'?" he would ask in the Cockney he was trying so hard to lose in his act.

She pouted and said, "I thought you wanted it." And he kissed her, laughing, and she still pouted and said, "I only want to please you, Harry. Teach me how to please you. I don't want to be one of those wives I hear you men talking about, who just lie there like logs. I don't want you to be like all the other men who go away to those loose women who do all the naughty things. I want you to do the naughty things with me."

So he did. But he wondered if he was being wise in teaching Clara such things. Somehow it was a risk because once a woman got a taste for it, so the masculine myths went, you had created

220

a monster, and if it wasn't you, it was going to have to be somebody else. It was especially wrong, and in some way disloyal to the masculine code, to subvert a woman, especially a wife, in this way. Harry found that he did not laugh at jokes about frigid wives, nagging wives, sexless and waspish and dried-up wives any longer. His wife did not comply to the usual pattern, and while he was pleasured by it, he was not proud of it and felt a sense of guilt about it. Dammit all, Clara was his wife, not what the Americans called a chippy. Her innocent passion, though, ignited his own, and their nights passed in deep sleeps and hot, sexual bliss.

Harry felt happier than ever before in his life.

The act he made broader and included more songs, many of them American favorites like "In the Good Old Summertime" and "In the Shade of the Old Apple Tree," both of which suited Clara's voice and to which he could harmonize. He told old jokes that got laughs and older jokes that got more laughs and some of his newer jokes that didn't get any laughs at all. He did a sketch with Bill Fields in which he played a barman and Fields said to him, "Those were the days back in Philadelphia. Do you remember when I knocked Waterfront Nell down?"

Harry, dressed as a barman, in a long apron, replied, "You didn't knock her down. I did."

"Well," said Fields, "I started kicking her first."

The Concert Party (as Harry insisted on calling the Pier show, after the English tradition) mixed in well together. The older performers—the monologists and animal acts—talked of long and awful train rides across the continent to places of which Harry had never heard, like Scranton, Pennsylvania (well known to Fields, who shuddered at the mention of it), and Ogdensburg and Chattanooga. They had played these places, been marooned in them by bilking managers, had played in the bars for "throw money" to get them the railroad fare home, wherever that was. Harry listened and sympathized, but one thing he became determined upon in that long, hot, idyllic summer in Atlantic City.

They would have to get into the Big Time.

His determination grew when Bill Fields left before the season ended. He was going to bill in Providence, Rhode Island, as a headliner. "I regard the name of the town as an omen, my English friend," he told Harry as he made his farewells, which were only alcoholic because other members of the troupe had put up the money to buy beer and whiskey. "I wish you joy in these United

States." Then he was gone. Said Sparrow, the fruit-nut comic, "If he opens a bank account in Providence, I hope he forgets about it."

Harry sprang to his friend's defense. "He sends his mother ten dollars every week, no matter what."

"If she's anything like him, she banks it," said Sparrow gloomily.

Clara bloomed and grew a little plumper that summer. Harry approved of that. A woman should have a figure. No thin girl was thought to be attractive to men. The girls were urged by their mothers to eat until they burst, and a plump young woman queened it over all. Clara sang, on and offstage, and Harry was proud of her gentility and good manners, in café and dining room. She ate with a knife *and* fork, a thing that caused stares everywhere. She received a number of letters from Papa. She had felt it proper to write to him saying that she was married and now living in the United States. He wrote to her care of the hotel, and the letters were forwarded on. Harry suffered Clara to read out sections that did not allude to him. Plainly some did and probably not in flattering terms. Let her be happy, Harry thought, gazing across their breakfast table at her flushed young face, eyes shining as she read the long copperplate writing. Let her be happy; she's a good sort, and she deserves it.

From time to time, usually during or before the sexual act, he told her that he loved her.

He was not sure, either, if this was wise.

John Hyatt stepped off the boat with what he stood up in and a hundred pounds exactly. At five to a pound sterling, that was five hundred dollars. A man, his father had told him, at the Cork boat, should not go to a new country without the means of coming back if he felt like it. The brass band played "Come Back to Erin" as it had played to a whole generation of exiles, and many people were crying or drunk or both. They were mostly young men going steerage with their worldly goods in a pack upon their backs, and most of them knew they would never see Ireland again. Nor, from what they were to tell John on the journey across the Atlantic, did they wish to. It was starvation, they said, the ould country, the eldest son got what bit of land there was, and the younger one had nothing to look forward to but working for the stranger, if he was lucky enough to find a stranger to work for—

usually an Englishman at that, for sure, didn't they own the land itself? These were a new generation of immigrants, fired by letters from uncles and cousins singing them the songs of America.

"Just why are ye going, son?" his father had asked at the Cork boat. "The truth now."

"To chance my luck, Da."

His father said no more. John waved good-bye to the diminishing figure in a pot hat, waving a sad pipe, to the fading strains of the band:

> Come back to Erin, mavourneen, mavourneen.
> Come back again, to the land of thy birth. . . .

To chance his luck? That was a joke. He was waving good-bye to his father just as Clara Abbott had waved good-bye to himself at Southampton two years before, and with her going, something had gone from his life and, he suspected, his work.

He had written nothing as good as "Naughty But Nice" since then and wondered if he ever would. He had buried himself in his work. Once she had gone, he had burned the lamp oil far into the night, mostly writing things to order, like the music for the pantomime. Dan Leno had not sung his song, another comic much less well known had, and he had altered it, too (improved, he called it) to suit his own act (so he said), and there was nothing John could do about it. Morrie, the agent, had encouraged him, waited anxiously upon him whenever there was a singer who needed an extra number, sat in on discussions with the singer (who usually would have written the song himself if only he or she had the time) and in the end all those discussions in dressing rooms at the Gaiety or the Metropolitan mostly came to nothing.

John Hyatt discovered that he was going through the motions of composing songs but not really feeling them. And once you had the technique (and that took a long time, and he still had a lot to learn) the feeling was all that mattered. Truth to tell, he had felt very little for a long time after that day at Southampton, when the SS *Baltic* had disappeared into the fogs of the English Channel. He sat, some nights, at his chenille-covered table in his rooms in Bloomsbury (he had moved out of Mrs. Harrington's) and just stared at the lines of manuscript paper. All he saw was that girl's face. Even in the night it came to him. He would wake in a sweat, eyes staring. He felt he must be going mad.

He worked harder and longer hours and grew thin and pale,

223

so much so that even Morrie noticed and pleaded with him to take a holiday. "Go home, get some decent grub inside you for a couple of weeks, old love," advised Morrie. "Give the folks a treat, get some fresh air in your lungs and sleep round the clock a few times. Work wonders, that will."

"I think I might try the States, Morrie."

"My life!" said Morrie.

So here he was.

John Hyatt had a letter of introduction to an uncle, one of his mother's nine brothers, four of them working in this great stewpot of a city. Every Irishman of this generation had a letter of introduction. His Uncle Matt, a large, farmerish man, looking like an older version of himself, sat in an office that did not look like an office, in a derby hat and vest and shirt sleeves, and toasted John Hyatt's arrival with a glass of the craythar from a bottle in his desk. After two jiggers of the stuff John had a distinct sense of unreality. He refused a third libation, and his Uncle Matt said, "Ah, you're one of them sort, are ye?" and John hastily added, "Well, just the once more if it's in the bottle there." His Uncle Matt poured him another jigger and spat his cigar expertly into a brass spittoon. "Now then, your Da says you're a songwriting fella." John Hyatt said that was so, and he did have a couple of letters of introduction to New York music publishers. "You think you'll be all right then?" asked his Uncle Matt.

"Oh, I think so, Uncle Matt. I just called here first because Mother said I should, since I haven't any lodgings or anything arranged."

"Well, neither ye would, would ye, just off the boat now. Now, the thing is to get you settled with a nice Irish family."

"I thought of a rooming house," Johh Hyatt said hastily. "Somewhere where they don't mind a bit of noise."

"I thought you weren't a drinking man yourself."

"It's the piano, you see?" John Hyatt explained. "I'll have to buy one and find a place to put it. I really need a room of my own, where nobody cares about the noise."

Uncle Matt did not seem unduly surprised by the request. John had a feeling that he was a man who was surprised by nothing. "Well now," he said, "let me have a wee bit of thought about that while you an' me have a crack about what's happening at home. Is your Da still puffing on that ould pipe o' his and keepin' his thumb on the scales when he's weighing out the spuds?"

John told all the news, good and bad, of births and deaths, and his Uncle Matt listened gravely. From time to time they were interrupted. A woman in a shawl, who might have stepped out of the Four Quays, asked for a few minutes of the big fella's time, apologizing in a courtly way to the gentleman (John Hyatt) whose drinking and crack she was interrupting (she noticed the bottle at once), but it was the boots that had been promised the childer. Uncle Matt dealt gravely with this, took no notes, heard the old woman out with great courtesy and walked her to the door, making reassuring noises. His voice changed when he returned to the outer office (which again, did not seem like an office and was full of large men reading newspapers), and there was a small consultation, and several of the men seemed to leave at once, as far as John Hyatt could see through the half-open door. Uncle Matt came back in and sighed. "John, you wouldn't want to come to work for me, would yez? I could do with a fella with his wits about him, so I could."

John shook his head, smiling.

Uncle Matt nodded, unsurprised again. "I think the place for you would be Mooney's."

"Mooney's?"

"It's a bar, but Mooney has rooms above. It's not a noisy bar, but it's not as quiet as the grave either. Now, I know Mooney has an ear for music, and I also know he has a pi-anner. I'll have Paddy out there take ye round. Come an' see me again if there's anything ye need. An' come to your Sunday dinner every week ye can, after mass, twelve o'clock prompt. Just come, don't bother to let us know, Brigit will skin me if you miss this first Sunday. Don't forget now. Paddy will show ye where we live. Ye pass it on the way to Mooney's."

At the stoop, Uncle Matt paused and regarded the crowded street. It was full of children, some ragged and thin, but none, as Uncle Matt pointed out, without boots. "Not a one on the street, and that's a fact." The children skipped rope, the boys in knicker-bockers and caps and the girls in pinafores, and sang:

> East side, west side, all around the town,
> We all sang Rosie O'Grady,
> Brooklyn Bridge is falling down.

"Do you write songs of that class?" asked Uncle Matt.

"I try." John Hyatt smiled.

"If ye has trouble at all gettin' started, tell me. I know one or two people that knows one or two people in this town."

John Hyatt smiled again. He could not imagine Uncle Matt in the presence of music publishers and itinerant comics. "I have my letters. I just want to get the feel of things first, Uncle Matt."

Uncle Matt hummed the tune the children sang:

> We tripped the light fantastic,
> On the sidewalks of New York.

He called along the street, "Sunday at twelve prompt, mind!"

John Hyatt was in an alcoholic daze, but he did not need to do anything but walk through the crowded narrow streets and alleys, which could, at a pinch, have been in Dublin had they been a story or two smaller. Paddy, his uncle's assistant, trotted at his side, carrying his large leather case as if it were a shopping basket. He was a small man with a black eye, but John Hyatt felt it would be indelicate to refer to it. They skirted the moving crowds at the doors of bars and the children skipping and the Italian with the monkey and the piano organ playing "Sweet Rosie O'Grady" with a fine sense of time and place.

Paddy was a mine of misinformation delivered in a strong Dublin brogue. "Ah, sure, it's a foine country, so it is. Course I've never taken to the Broadways an' that. I went up once, when I first come over, but a man's happiest amongst his own, am I right now?" He pointed to a tall brownstone house. "That's your Uncle Matt's place, a foine house, all his own, no rooms let or anything the like o' that. Oh, sure, he's a foine man, your Uncle Matt, a foine man, so he is." Paddy saluted a policeman in a tall helmet, who stood on a corner, a cigar in his palm, behind his back.

"I see yez ran into a door again, Paddy," said the policeman.

"I'm gettin' careless, so I am, Joseph." Paddy indicated John Hyatt. "The big fella's nephew from the ould country."

"Ah, so," said the policeman. "Good luck to ye, young man."

John Hyatt smiled and nodded. Paddy ducked down a cobbled alley, and the tenements loomed above them. There was a smell of drains and cooking, and the air was hot and steamy. Paddy entered a door, after knocking twice sharply.

A small, dirty man with a squint, wearing a long starched and spotless white apron, stood there. "Ah, it's yourself, Paddy." This, John Hyatt gathered, was Mooney. Indeed, he confessed, he did have a room. More like a stable, except it was at the very

226

top of the house. Paddy told him John Hyatt was a writer of songs, Irish songs. Mooney, on hearing this, shook his head and called for drink to be brought. They sat in the long cool bar and drank whiskey of great strength with beer chasers. Mooney sang a song he had heard in his youth in Ireland, "She Walks Through the Fair." He sang it without embarrassment, naturally and well. John Hyatt, now fuddled with alcohol, congratulated him. "I had a voice, oh, aye," said Mooney modestly. "I had a voice. Come now, I'll show you your rooms."

The stable, as Mooney insisted on calling it, was huge and contained no other furniture but an iron bedstead.

"It's very hot this weather, top of the house, y'see? It gets the heat. But it's clean, no bugs." Mooney looked earnestly at John Hyatt as if he might not be believed. "I wouldn't put the big fella's kin in any room that had the bugs in it."

Paddy attested to the truth of this. "A foine room, it is indade," said he.

"It's three dollars a week to you," said Mooney. "Mrs. Mooney will do your laundry with our own, and she'll get some sheets fixed up for tonight. You can eat with us in the kitchen downstairs anytime you loike. You can arrange that with Mrs. Mooney."

John Hyatt nodded his thanks, and the two men left, laughing and cheerful, after shaking hands again. He sat down on the bed and took off his jacket and boots. I'll just have a lie-down, he thought, and then I'll go out and look around the town. He lay down on the straw mattress and stretched out. I feel at home, he thought, I feel absolutely at home. He slept for fourteen hours.

Tin Pan Alley, at the railroad flats at Twenty-eighth and Broadway was easily found. John Hyatt could hear the noise a block away. He had taken a streetcar and then walked, and he was wet with sweat. The brilliantine from his hair was beginning to run down his forehead from under his velour hat, and his shirt stuck moistly to his back. He had put on his lightest suit, but it was still too thick for a New York summer. The letter of introduction he held in his hand was to a Mr. Will Rossiter of the music company of that name and had been given him by the musical director of the pantomime. He wondered how well the man knew Mr. Rossiter. He had not read the letter. It had never occurred to him to do so.

Rossiter's office was in the middle of the block surrounded

227

by rooms on all levels, with the windows wide open against the heat. Piano music blasted out from each window. The pianos were mostly being played loudly and badly, John Hyatt noticed. Men ran in and out of the doors, carrying bundles of sheet music. It sounded like a musical madhouse.

Mr. Rossiter did not seem to notice the noise. John thought he probably had cloth ears. Mr. Rossiter was middle-aged, well dressed in a thin dark suit with white piping on his vest, and he wore his hair parted stylishly in the middle. He read the letter of introduction and asked, "Right, where's your material?"

John was disconcerted. "I'm sorry?"

"Your songs? You've got some songs?"

"Not really. Everything I wrote in London I sold."

"You did? You play piano?"

Mr. Rossiter indicated an upright in the corner of his small office, topped with bundles of sheet music, the most prominent title of which was "Meet Me Tonight in Dreamland." "Give me one of your best tunes."

John Hyatt mopped his sticky fingers and his brow, sat at the piano and played, on impulse, "Naughty But Nice." Mr. Rossiter looked interested. "Nice tune. I like it. You got words, never mind, I got a fella who can give it words." He got to his feet and called out, "Hey, Jimmy, come in here, willya?" A young man with carrot hair, wearing a loud striped shirt and suspenders over high-waisted trousers and a straw hat, came in.

"Play it," said Mr. Rossiter.

John Hyatt played it.

"Well?" Mr. Rossiter inquired of Jimmy.

"Nice toon," said Jimmy. "Yours?"

"Not exactly, no." John looked apologetic.

"We don't pirate, sorry," said Mr. Rossiter sharply.

"I sold it to an artiste in London."

"London's a long ways off," said Jimmy.

"It is," agreed Mr. Rossiter thoughtfully, looking out of the window.

"The artiste is in the United States," John Hyatt added hollowly. "For all I know, singing it."

Mr Rossiter looked pensive. "So it's no?"

"I sold it," John said, despairing.

"Contract? Lawyers? All legal?" asked Jimmy.

John Hyatt shook his head. "As good as."

"Nothing," said Jimmy, "is as good as. Either it is or it isn't."

"In that case it is," John Hyatt said firmly.

There was a silence, or the nearest thing to a silence possible in the street. Finally, Mr. Rossiter said regretfully, "Come back when you have something new. That was nice." He shook hands with John, picking up a copy of "Meet Me Tonight in Dreamland" and putting it in Jimmy's hand. "Little old lady wrote this song, Miss Beth Slater Whitson. This little lady is just like a beautiful flower filled with goodness, and it is her mission on this earth to give out good thoughts to others. . . . Right, Jimmy?"

"Right, Mr. Rossiter," said Jimmy, without change of expression.

"It is going," said Mr. Rossiter, "to sell a million."

There was another silence.

"Miss Beth lives in a pretty little farmhouse in Tennessee."

There seemed to be no more to say to that, so John Hyatt took his portfolio of songs (which he had never opened) and went out into the street. The noise and heat were worse out there than inside. In Mr. Rossiter's premises at least you could hear only three or four pianos. Now he could hear at least a dozen.

"Hey, buddy, you got a minute?"

It was Jimmy, struggling into a coat, following him.

John stopped. "Yes. Why?"

"Wanta beer?"

They went into a bar on Broadway. It was cool and dark inside. They drank a beer each before Jimmy said anything more, but his eyes were on John Hyatt's thick suit and his red face above the starched collar.

"Just off the boat, huh?"

"Yesterday."

"Jesus, you didn't let any grass grow, did you?"

John shook his head. "I want to do some good here. Might as well get myself started."

Jimmy ordered two more beers. "That's a nice toon. You got words for it?"

"Yes, but they aren't mine."

"You got a title?"

" 'Naughty But Nice.' "

"That's good, y'know." Jimmy snapped his fingers. "If we could get some headliner to sing it, we'd be on Easy Street."

"Not mine to sell."

"Could be mine. In my name. No problem."

"I may be just off the boat." John sipped his beer. "I may be Irish. But I'm not that green."

Jimmy looked hurt. "Only trying to help you, buddy."

"I'm sure," said John Hyatt. "Have another beer."

Jimmy had another beer. "You're new to Tin Pan Alley. Let me advise you. Get another suit. Get a new set of duds altogether. As my old father didn't used to say, people take you for what you look." He snapped his suspenders. "Like the shoes?"

His shoes were of tan and white leather.

"Cost twenty bucks. The suit a hundred. The hat, thirty. You have to dress kinda snappy round the Alley, y'know, or you're just a rube." He looked at John Hyatt speculatively. "You don't have a contract on that song, do you? You could sell it to Mr. Rossiter now, right?"

"I could, yes. But I won't."

"A doll, is it?"

John Hyatt flushed. "None of anybody's business but mine."

"Sorry. I know how it is with women. Make it a golden rule: give them money, but don't give them songs. I done that myself once. I can't remember the doll, but I can remember the song."

John said, "I'll write another one."

"Sure, sure, sure. We all will." Jimmy drank his beer. "A ballad that hits the spot around here can start at half a million copies. At twenty cents a copy that ain't hay." John Hyatt shook his head disbelievingly. "Look, headliners singing songs, that helps. But here we got a music industry. We sell songs. Plenty do a million. There's a new one. 'I Wonder Who's Kissing Her Now.' That'll do a million. It's a good song, but it don't sound a whole lot better than your song that you just played to me." Jimmy shook his head. He sang:

> I wonder who's buying the wine,
> For lips that I used to call mine?
> I wonder if she ever tells him of me. . . .

His voice trailed away. "Shit, it's a good song, but so is yours. I write words, and I can't find songs."

"My words aren't all that good," said John Hyatt.

They both drank in silence. Jimmy gave him a cigar.

They smoked in silence.

"When I have a tune," John Hyatt said thoughtfully, "sometimes I get stuck for words."

"I never get stuck for words." Jimmy shook his head. "Right now, any song about dreams is fine. Write me a dreamtime song, nice and slow, waltz time, I'll find you some words. Right?" He extended his hand across the table.

John Hyatt hesitated; then he took it.

First day in New York and I have a partner, he thought.

"What's your name?"

"Cohen, but I changed it to Cowley. There are sixteen Cohens in the Alley as it is. My name ain't Jimmy either, but who can say Isidore, right? You eat dinner?"

"What, now?"

"No, later. Seven o'clock. Meet me here, I'll take you to a few places, meet a coupla dolls, you got anything against that?"

John shook his head.

"Where you living?"

John told him.

Jimmy Cowley looked incredulous. "Over a bar. In that suit. Unbelievable. But you wrote that song. Right?"

"Right."

"Tell you what. If you're buying some new clothes, why not do it now? We go out with the dolls tonight we wanta look good, right?"

"Well, I don't know. . . ."

"I do." Jimmy looked at his pocket watch, which he wore on a strap from his button hole into his top breast pocket. "I just got time. We go to a store I know, fix you up so you look like Diamond Jim Brady." He stared at John. "Come to think of it, you are like Jim Brady. Come on, I have to hustle, I'm due back at the sweatshop already."

In the store, John Hyatt put himself in Jimmy's hands. Indeed, he had no choice. He found himself wearing a striped shirt, a blue cotton blazer and a pair of sponge-bag trousers, with a straw boater, in no time at all. He paid seventy-eight dollars for the lot (Mooney had changed his English money for him) and remarked that it seemed cheap, by British standards.

"It may never go through the books, that's why it's cheap," said Jimmy. "What you gonna do with that old suit?"

"I don't know."

"My advice is leave it right here. You look like a rube in it. And no rube ever sold a song in the Alley."

So, profoundly against his upbringing, John Hyatt left a per-

231

fectly good suit in the store. The store clerk (who seemed to be a close friend, if not a relation, of Jimmy's) said it was worthless. "Who'd wear it?" he asked. "It's old country."

John Hyatt walked around the Alley, listening to the tunes that were being played, for the rest of the afternoon. He heard nothing (and he listened hard) that seemed to him of any real value. He sat in a coffee shop and tried to take "Meet Me Tonight in Dreamland" to pieces. He did it, but it told him nothing. The song was simply good, that was all. So were the words. Anybody could hum the tune. Anybody could remember the words. A million seller, Jimmy had said. It was possible.

Sitting in the coffee-shop window, looking out onto Broadway with the traffic rushing by, automobiles mingling with the horse traffic, pedestrians dodging across as how and best they could, cool and odd-feeling in his bright new clothes, John Hyatt thought that anything was possible in this strange new country.

Jimmy Cowley brought the girls along himself. They were called Patsy and Mamie. Patsy was Irish and looked like a lot of girls John Hyatt had seen in Dublin. Mamie was Jewish and dressed in a bright red-striped blouse with the lowest décolletage John had seen in public. She seemed oblivious to it and talked brightly, in an accent later identified by Jimmy as Brooklyn. Patsy wore a blue polka-dot dress with a turned-down white collar. She had blue eyes and a nice smile. Her teeth, John saw, were good. She looked like a country girl, but she worked at Rossiter's as a typist. Mamie the same, except that Mamie had ambitions to be the first woman song plugger in the business. "Why not? Just 'cos I'm a woman? Why not?" she demanded of John Hyatt. He didn't know what to say, but Mamie didn't need an answer. John was astonished to be sitting in a public bar talking to two respectable young ladies. He presumed they were respectable. They certainly looked it. They had a militancy about them that was new to John. They talked up without waiting to see what the men had to say. That was new. He didn't know whether he liked it or not. Clara was independent but not in quite this way. The girls drank beer. It was explained by Jimmy that they were in a special saloon bar and it was just about all right, here on the Alley, to buy a girl a drink in public. Elsewhere they would be regarded as ladies of the town. "Which we ain't," said Mamie. "Just in case anybody gets any wrong ideas." She looked sternly at Jimmy Cowley, but he smiled serenely and stared right back at her.

"Jimmy tells me you're just over," Patsy Keenan said.

"That's right, I'm a Dublin man." In Ireland a man always declared where he came from. It was expected of him.

"My mother and father came over from Galway. I was born here. Where are you living?"

John told her. She laughed but seemed pleased. "You're staying with your own anyway, not in some hotel."

"Where do you live?" he asked.

"At home, sure, where else would I live?"

"No offense, I was only asking."

Mamie leaned over. "We've come for a nice pleasant evening out, Irish. That's all."

"She means it," said Jimmy Cowley, boater on the back of his head. "She always says it, and she always means it."

"You bet I do." Mamie drank her beer. "Are we going to sit here all night, or what?"

"Some girl," said Jimmy Cowley. He seemed admiring of her forcefulness. Plainly, there was a lot to learn here in the States, and one of the things he had to learn about was the women.

Out in the Alley a lot of perspiring song pluggers were standing on trucks with open backs and hard tires, singing to crowds of people going home from work. Jimmy Cowley regarded them with pity. "Listen to it," he told John Hyatt. "What do we have to beat?"

The song pluggers were singing, in harmony:

> Meet me in Dreamland,
> Sweet Dreamy Dreamland,
> Where all my Dreams come true.

"See the fat boy," Jimmy asked John Hyatt, "in the front? Only thirteen, best voice on the Lower East Side. They go around the synagogues, looking for singers. I'm glad all I do is write the stuff."

"And that for no dollars a week," said Mamie.

"I am on the staff," said Jimmy Cowley with dignity.

"That's no way to make any real money," said Mamie, taking his arm possessivley nonetheless. She waved to the song pluggers. "You need a lady to help you out?"

The fat boy said, "Go home where you belong."

Mamie grabbed a pile of sheet music from his arms and shouted, " 'Meet Me Tonight in Dreamland'—it's the only place you will! Come buy! Fifteen cents a copy. The next million seller!"

."Hey, Isidore," called the fat boy, "get those copies back from her."

"The name," said Jimmy, "is Jimmy; don't let me have to tell you again, Fatty."

The fat boy looked near to tears at the taunt. "Aw, give him the sheets," said Jimmy.

But Mamie had already sold a dozen copies, to admiring men in cloth caps or greasy derby hats. She threw the coins into the truck. "Have a drink on me, *shmucks!*"

The men on the truck shouted angrily after them, but the encounter seemed to have cheered the ebullient Mamie. "She's terrible, isn't she, though?" asked Patsy of John Hyatt. He nodded. It was true. He was glad he had not drawn Mamie in the raffle. Patsy was more his style. She slipped her arm softly through his, and he breathed out, in some pride. Here he was, barely off the boat, and he had friends and a girl on his arm.

They went to the Colonial and saw Professor Lambertini's comedy act. The professor crossed his eyes and kicked his long legs sideways while playing the xylophone. His lady assistant removed most of her clothes during the act. Mamie thought it "terrific," a new word to John Hyatt, but Patsy said, "How terrible, taking off all your clothes in public," and squeezed his hand.

John did not squeeze back. No sense in going too fast. He was in the States to write songs, not flirt with girls. They sat in the orchestra. Mamie declared she hated heights and would not go into the balconies. Jimmy just sighed, and the men split the costs. They bought the girls bags of peanuts to eat. Most of the audience seemed to be eating or smoking or both.

John Hyatt sat and analyzed the songs. There were few of any real quality, but wasn't that always the case? The bill was full of specialty acts, like the cartoonist Will Ferry, the Frog Man, who sat on a huge plinth with a frog's head of papier-mâché, dressed in an opera cloak and hat. The girls were full of wonder at him and at Julian Eltinge, the female impersonator, so real in his bridal dress they could not believe he was a man. "I'll take the dress," said Mamie, "you can keep the fella."

But Patsy squeezed John Hyatt's hand again and whispered, "Isn't she terrible? She says she's never going to get married. Ever." Her breath caught at the scandal of such an idea.

"What about Jimmy?" he whispered back.

"Jimmy's not the marrying kind, is he now? Just look at him!"

234

Jimmy Cowley had his feet up on the seat in front and was slouched down, eyes closed. He was asleep or near enough. "It's all that work he does," said Patsy. "Sure, he works half the night at his songs. I'm certain you don't do that."

"Sometimes," John Hyatt said crisply. Patsy Keenan was a nice girl, but she was a lot friendlier than any Irish girl would have been on first acquaintance. He was here to watch and learn. The headliner was Nora Bayes, and it was she they had come to see. Jimmy woke up. "Her husband's Jack Norworth. Look at your programs." John Hyatt looked. It read: "Nora Bayes, the Single Greatest Woman Singing Comedienne in the World, Assisted and Admired by Jack Norworth."

"Not only that," said Jimmy Cowley, "she has her own railroad car. Travels everywhere in it."

Nora Bayes, a dark, splendid-looking woman in a long-fringed dress and a peacock-feather hat, with the head of the dead bird protruding at the front, was a riot of song and dance. Jimmy Cowley was informative, eating after-show pizzas at an Italian restaurant, on the subject of Jack Norworth. "He's written 'Shine On, Harvest Moon' and 'Take Me Out to the Ball Game' already! With two songs like those under our belts, John, we would be taking out a coupla Ziegfeld girls, not these two."

Patsy merely smiled, but Mamie took offense. "You're lucky you should have two decent girls to go out with you. If my mother saw the way you're dressed, she'd lock me in my room for a year for being seen on the street with you!"

Jimmy Cowley was especially tender where his dress was concerned.

"What's the matter with the duds?" he asked, hurt. "What have I got on that would offend your mother?"

"Everything," answered Mamie promptly, chewing into her pizza. "Your taste in clothes is *drekky;* you look like some kind of cheapskate."

John Hyatt was shocked. No Irish girl (or English one for that matter) would be so aggressive to a young man taking her out for the evening, unless she hoped never to see him again. Jimmy Cowley simply beamed and said. "Whadda girl. And can she eat? More than a boa constrictor she can eat."

"A what?" asked Mamie suspiciously, her mouth full.

"A snake that eats rabbits whole," said Jimmy Cowley.

"In that case, if you're a rabbit, fine."

Jimmy Cowley paid for more coffee. "Maybe you should go into vaudeville," he told Mamie.

"A short life," said Mamie, "and not a merry one either."

"The headliners come into our place looking for songs," explained Patsy. "Furs and jewels they've got, an' big fancy fellas."

"To sleep with them," Mamie supplied.

"I wasn't going to say that, Mamie," protested Patsy.

"I know you weren't, doll. But it's true, they've all got fancy men they pay to do it. They're rich and famous, see; no ordinary fella wants them."

"I might apply for the job," said Jimmy Cowley.

"You haven't got what it takes," said Mamie.

"How do you know?"

"I got imagination, ain't I?"

"Yeah, and that's all." Jimmy Cowley looked at his pocket watch. "I sometimes get to take her home, y'know? That's one hour. Each way. And what do I get for that? I tellya what I get. I get a kiss. On the end of the nose. I don't go in and have coffee. With her mother, I'm not allowed to be seen already. The Princess of Brooklyn she is."

"Right," said Mamie. "And we gotta go now, the both of us, right, Patsy?"

"Well?" Patsy looked silently at John Hyatt, waiting.

He said nothing. This was not lost on Mamie.

"Come on, Patsy. Let's us workin' girls get on our way."

"Don't we see you to the subway?"

Mamie debated. "Well, that far then."

Patsy slid her hand into John Hyatt's. "Will you be coming into the office at all?"

"Course he will," cut in Jimmy. "When he's written a new tune and I've written the words for him. When we make a thousand dollars, you will be standing in line asking us to take you to our secret dens of vice."

"John's living above a bar," said Patsy. "It's not much of place to be living. But I'm sure it's not a den of vice, is it, John?"

John Hyatt laughed. "A den of boozers maybe."

Jimmy Cowley said, "Let's have a look at this place of yours," after they had waved the girls good-night.

"It isn't much." John Hyatt looked after Patsy Keenan's plump figure and felt a pang. She had been very forward for a good Catholic girl. Perhaps it hadn't meant anything, though. He sighed.

236

"She likes you, y'know, fella," said Jimmy Cowley.

John Hyatt coughed. "She doesn't know me."

"She's looking for a husband. Be warned."

"You tell me we are going out to see some broads, and we take two nice girls to a theater and eat pizza, and they go home. I could have done the like o' that in Dublin."

"If you want to," said Jimmy Cowley seriously, "I know a good sporting house. It's only three dollars, and they don't rush you."

"No, thanks," said John Hyatt. "I never enjoy it in those places."

Jimmy Cowley nodded. "Me neither. But what else is there? I can't afford to marry anybody, and nice girls don't. Or if they do, it's all hunky-dory for a while, and then kazam, you're on the way to being a father." He shuddered. "That Mamie. The things I want to do to her. And she knows it." He blinked at the lights. "It's early, only eleven, so what do we do?"

The city was still alive and moving, and John Hyatt wondered at it, the vitality and the crowds of cheerful people of all nationalities and styles of dress, sprinkled with the ones who had gone American, as he had that day.

"If you want, you can come and see my room," said John Hyatt on impulse. "We could look at my songs. I have a portfolio here." He tapped the leather case under his arm.

"I wondered what was in there,"—Jimmy Cowley grinned— "besides the gold from the Chase Manhattan Bank. Let's go and see this Irish bower, right?"

Mooney had put in a piano.

He stood, duster in hand, wiping it over proudly.

"It's not the finest instrument in the world, but I've only got it standing doin' nothing in the back bar there, collecting dust. Ye might as well have it yourself, seeing as you're the big fella's nephew, it's no trouble at all."

"The big fella, who's he?" whispered Jimmy Cowley. He gazed around the cavernous loft with surprise.

"My uncle," said John Hyatt. To Mooney, he added, "How can I repay you? Will you take a drink with me?"

"No, I will not," said Mr. Mooney. "I'm glad to help out the nephew of himself." At the door he added, "Tell him I put it in for you if you like."

"I will, I will," said John Hyatt. "Will it be all right to play it now?"

"Why would I be puttin' it up here at all if I minded ye playin' it?" asked Mooney. "Sure, we won't hear a note of it downstairs." He nodded to Jimmy Cowley, whose clothes he seemed to have forgiven. "Not a Protestant, are ye?" he asked.

"No," replied Jimmy Cowley, "no, I'm not."

"Ah, well then, that's all right now," said Mooney, who had plainly carried all his prejudices across the Atlantic. "I've left a bottle of Irish under the bed there. The missus has put you a few blankets and sheets on the bed itself. I'll say good-night to ye both then."

And he was gone.

Jimmy Cowley sat on the bed. "Hard but clean." He looked around. "If you tried, you could make this place something. Look at the *room* you have. In this town men live in smaller rooms than this, them and their whole families. I live in a box with three other guys, y'know."

John Hyatt shook his head. "I'm not used to it all yet." He opened his portfolio and passed some manuscript sheets to Jimmy Cowley. "Here, these are some things I've done. I'll play them over."

He played. Jimmy Cowley listened intently. At the end (and it had taken an hour) he just nodded and said, "Talent. I thought you had it. You do. I don't like any of your words much, though."

"Nor do I," said John Hyatt.

"I have some words." Jimmy Cowley fumbled in his pocket. He did it as if casually, but John Hyatt knew somehow that he had been leading up to it all evening. "Here, take a look."

John Hyatt took a look. He read aloud:

> I dream of summer when I dream of you,
> Yes, I do, the whole night through.
> I dream of summer when I dream of you,
> The lovely sun of summer.

"Shakespeare it ain't," said Jimmy Cowley, "but it's the kind of thing we might sell. Try the next verse."

John Hyatt continued:

> I dream of spring when I dream of you,
> Yes, I do, the whole night through.
> I dream of spring when I dream of you.
> The lovely green of springtime.

John Hyatt said, "All the seasons?"

"That's right. "Dream of Summer," though, that's the title, yes?" Jimmy Cowley leaned forward. "What do you think?"

"Nice simple words." John Hyatt strummed on the piano. Jimmy Cowley poured them another glass of Irish. They worked until dawn and did not notice it come up until the bright sun was beginning to make their eyes water. They had finished the song and the bottle.

Jimmy Cowley stretched out on the bed. "Not bad, partner, not bad at all." Outside, the city started to come to life. "I sleep for one hour, then back to work."

"I'll copy it out and bring it down to the office later," John Hyatt said guiltily, but Jimmy Cowley was already snoring. His face looked thin and gray suddenly, and his suspenders hung down and there was a hole in his sock. John Hyatt felt a sharp touch of sympathy. Jimmy Cowley was a good sort, a man who kept the others cheerful, even when he had nothing to be cheerful about himself. One of the good people, who don't look it, John Hyatt decided, who would hate you ever to say it.

He closed his eyes. One day in the city, and he had a girlfriend, a partner, and he'd written a song.

Anything could happen here. Anything.

Meet Me Tonight in Dreamland

Harry and Clara worked Atlantic City three straight summers. They were popular with management and public alike. They changed their act a little each season. Harry made his gags more topical, and they rang the changes on their songs. They still made "Naughty But Nice" the last song of their piece. Harry had given up any possibility of going off cold. They both felt well during the summers, sitting on the ironwork seats of the Pier or occasionally bathing in the sea, Clara covered neck to knees in a dark bathing suit, with a mobcap over her hair. Harry had a red hooped bathing suit, with legs down to his knees and arms down to his elbows. They ate well, and Clara put on weight, and they both basked in the applause of the crowds. For good attendance, as Harry ironically put it, they now went on next to intermission, the second-best spot on the bill. The best spot was next-to-closing, and they never got that, principally, said Harry, because they were English.

"Can't expect it, can we? We're an odd act as far as they're concerned, that's all. They like us, but they're on vacation, and they would probably like La Peptomane."

"Who *is* La Peptomane?" asked Clara.

"The French fella that farts to music," said Harry, sitting cleaning off his makeup in the tiny dressing room. "He's wonderful, they tell me. He can carry a tune with his backside. Packed houses everywhere in France. Course, he never appeared in England. They barred him, like they barred Wilkie Bard—that's how he came by his name. Bard, see?" Harry removed his crepe side-whiskers. "You show me any comic that's any good, and I'll tell you one thing for certain. Somebody will want him barred."

Clara said, "Fancy people paying money to see a man break wind? It sounds disgusting."

"So is nearly everything that's any good."

"I wish we could save some money." Clara did not mention Harry's poker sessions with the other acts and the musicians, from which he always returned a loser. "Atlantic City's a good spot, one of the best. If we saved money, we could pick and choose our dates in the winter. We seem to spend all we make."

"Darlin', the whole world spends all it makes."

Clara said no more. They were through another winter, that was the important thing. The winters in the city were getting harder to bear. Not just the bitter cold, they had almost got used to that. They had even got used to the steam heat in their new rooms at the Madison on Thirty-sixth and Madison, where the tariff was a dollar fifty a day. It was cheaper than the Knickerbocker. Every dollar counted in these last awful winters, and any booking at all got to be welcome. Slowly they worked up a connection on the Little Time. They played split weeks in theaters all over the city, humping their skip in cabs and often by hand, and they discovered which managers were picklepusses and which were not, where it was possible to be naughty in the act and where it wasn't. They learned which audiences were German and which Jewish and which Irish and which a combination of all three. They had songs and jokes to fit each minority's tastes, and although it went against the grain for Harry to do it, they shamelessly played down to the prejudices of the neighborhood. They got used (in the winter) to the tryout system whereby a manager would engage more acts than he could possibly use, then pay off (or rather *not* pay) the least popular as "unsuitable." They ate in beaneries and tried to save money and never succeeded.

They worked as much as possible in the city. Max Rober got them all the town bookings he could but they had often to make thrice-weekly jumps by train, in the freezing midwinters of New England. Their shoes began to take in water, and they wore protective rubbers far into the spring seasons; their makeup boxes fell empty and were only tardily replenished. They bought no new clothes for the act or the street after the first season at Atlantic City. Clara refashioned their old costumes to look like new (they deceived nobody), sewing and ironing far into the night when they had no work, which was often. In these times Harry went down to the local pool hall where a few performers gathered and played pool or poker. Clara never made any complaint to Harry about his losses. A man was entitled to his masculine pleasures. He would not be a man if he did not gamble or drink or both. Or even twirl his mustache at a passing skirt.

Clara accepted that. Harry Viner was not a plaster saint, but he loved her. The certainty of his love made everything worthwhile, the backaching journeys and the false gaieties and the need to put on a smile and sing when her monthlies were unusually crippling.

Clara was happy, and she hoped Harry was. Things would improve as they got better known, she was certain of it. She told Harry so, but all he replied was, "Darlin', things aren't improving; they're going from worse to terrible. We just about lasted the winter this time, and that's all. Next winter we need new underwear and new topcoats, and where do they come from, you tell me?"

Just the same, he bought her a cake with candles for her birthday and daffodils at Easter and a bottle of French perfume at Christmas. They enjoyed many laughs and many cheap meals with other performers. They loved the freemasonry of the profession and felt part of something useful and good. Clara was proud of Harry, he looked so handsome and dark and intense. She was jealous when girls in the troupe ogled him, as they did, often. They made love regularly but without quite the same hunger as before. However, Clara expected that was usual. They took great precautions to see that Clara did not get pregnant, or rather Clara saw that they did. Left to himself, Harry would not have taken any precautions at all, save that of withdrawal, the most practiced of all birth-control methods of the time, but highly risky, as the countless pregnancies all around them testified. The new rubber contraceptives were on restricted sale, but Harry seldom bothered to find them.

All told, she was happy in those three years, despite the hardships and privations. The summers were good and sometimes seemed as if they would go on forever. She was acclaimed in the act and knew that men in the audience and on the street found her attractive. Her voice deepened and improved, and the responsibility for keeping them afloat (Harry handed over the money to her, after deducting what he felt was his due, usually twenty dollars of the seventy-five or eighty dollars for a full week, if they had one) gave her an assurance and calm that she recognized as a quality of Papa's. Clara was also aware of the improving quality of her act. She was getting a different kind of applause, solid, more appreciative. She wanted success as much as Harry did, but she could wait for it if she had to. They were in a new country. They could not expect miracles.

The miracle was that they still loved each other, Clara thought, in the arctic nights and the burning suns of the city. That was the miracle.

Harry found the last of their three summers in Atlantic City the worst because he knew that there would not be a fourth. The manager had changed, and the new man had his own preferences, and they did not include acts that had done well under his predecessor. Harry said nothing of this to Clara. He could not see how it would help for her to know, and he did not want to spoil her happiness. He had come to use the word "love" in connection with her now and not just during the sexual act. She seemed to him to be a good wife by any standards at all, and he began to consider himself very lucky to have her. The trouble was that however happy they were (during the summers; the winters were mere survival) they were getting nowhere with the act. It still remained implacably English, and while that had a certain novelty value, it could not go on forever. Harry laughed and clowned and told his joke about the coalman (sometimes he was a Swede, sometimes he was a Pole) and tried to find other jokes that had a common denominator for the audiences of Little Time.

Slowly he came to the conclusion that he had been right in the first place.

They were too good for Little Time. It was as simple as that.

If they could only get a chance at the Big Time, Harry said, they might well go good. In the Big Time theaters people of wit (to appreciate him) and some education (to appreciate her) were to be found. In Little Time everybody was a rough or a rube. When George M. Cohan sang "Forty-five Minutes from Broadway"

243

he told the God's truth. The people who slammed down the aisles at the Little Time theaters, banging the seats noisily, ignoring the opening tap-dancing act plaintively giving their all, were the very ones who slouched into the dozens of nickelodeon arcades to stare at the canned melodramas that would never, surely, amount to anything. There were said to be ten thousand of these arcades in the United States, but they were plainly a passing fancy, a fad. The patrons were warned not to stamp their feet, in case the floors of the arcades gave way under the strain. Yet vaudeville was also booming, *Variety* reported. There were two thousand houses across the nation, playing capacity most nights. Money was going up, Harry read with a bitter envy, for the headliners. Fifteen hundred dollars a week was getting to be usual for a next-to-closing act. Plenty of acts were earning over two hundred and fifty dollars a week. That was where they should be—at least amongst the standard acts (the reliable ones), not down with the fill-ins. Harry determined that no matter what, he would have it out with Max Rober when the last season at Atlantic City ended.

Max Rober was sympathetic. He regarded Harry, dressed in his best winter suit but wearing the now slightly threadbare topcoat (he had not been asked to take it off), and sighed. "You've had a long hard haul out there in Little Time. I think people have forgotten your . . . er . . . indiscretions of a couple of years ago. How's your charming wife, by the way?"

"She's fine." Harry was losing any pretensions he had ever had to gentility. The city did that to him. He asked, more sharply than he intended, "Look, Mr. Rober, I know we're a small act, but we could be a good one. Get us a chance somewhere big, and we'll surprise you."

Max Rober lit one of his Turkish cigarettes. "If I have your word you won't do anything foolish and disgrace me?"

"Mr. Rober," said Harry, hating himself, "I've learned my lesson."

Max Rober considered him for a long moment. "We'll have to see," he said. "I'll be in touch soon. Tell my secretary where you live now. You moved, didn't you?"

Harry nodded. One day, he thought, I'll tell this ponce and every other bloody manager and booker and agent to get stuffed. Till then I bite on the bullet.

"Thank you, Mr. Rober," he managed. "Thank you very much."

Clara was shopping at the butcher's when she ran into Mr. Richter from the burlesque house. She was buying a very cheap cut of meat, and this was not lost on Mr. Richter. He raised his hat and touched his mustache in ritual appreciation of her sexuality.

"How are you, Mrs. Viner? Long time. Working?"

"We've been at Atlantic City three summers."

"Nice and cool there," said Mr. Richter, replacing his hat on his oiled quiff, his fat, round face innocent. "A lot of work coming up for the winter?"

"Some," said Clara, smiling. "We always get a few winter dates in New York City."

"Harry hasn't broken into the Big Time yet then?"

He wasn't smiling, but Clara felt he was, inside.

"He'll get there."

Mr. Richter touched his mustache again. He seemed to be looking over Clara's figure as if he had not seen it before. Or as if he were trying to remember what it looked like. Clara was used to men's eyes now and no longer felt embarrassed when they looked at her with sexual desire. It was a compliment, after all, to make a man feel like that. Mr. Richter, however, seemed to have more than simple sex on his mind.

"Had you ever thought," he asked, "of posing *plastique?*"

Clara said, "I'm not sure what it is."

"Just what it says. Posing."

"Where?"

"At a sort of club. A gentleman's club. But I don't know if you'd be interested in the proposition."

Interested, Clara thought, one hand clutching the string shopping bag with the cheap cuts of meat and the other her purse with exactly twelve dollars in it, all they had in the world, I'd be interested in almost any proposition, this side of going to bed with you, Mr. Richter. She said, "It sounds very interesting."

"Can I buy you coffee and tell you about it? At the Biltmore? I have an appointment there in a half hour."

Clara said, "I'll look very strange in the Biltmore Hotel, carrying my shopping."

"You'd look good anywhere, Mrs. Viner."

Clara bowed to the compliment. "Thank you." They took a cab, and on the way Clara tried to think what posing *plastique* was. She seemed to have heard of it, and what she heard was compounded of male sniggers and laughs behind the hand. Ah, to hell! She smiled sweetly at Mr. Richter and thought: Harry will wonder where I am, gone for such a long time. No, he won't, he'll go out and play poker down at that pool hall. It was what he did now most afternoons when they weren't working. He had been depressed since he had pocketed his pride and gone to plead with Max Rober. Clara's heart went out to him. He had never had anything easy. He did not know how to let people help him. So few of them had ever done it.

Twelve dollars, she thought, sitting beside Mr. Richter, who was silent, occasionally brushing his mustache with the back of his hand. I hope, Clara thought, he's not taking me to the hotel for an assignation. She shot a glance at him. He seemed to be brooding rather than amorous. His mind was evidently on business. Let it stay that way.

The Biltmore reassured her. It was full of potted palms, and the clerk at the desk spoke four languages, English, French, German and Spanish. A flurry of important people entered and left, in fur coats (both men and women) and gray top hats, the men. Some of the women were carrying the very popular Pekinese dogs. There was a scent of Havana smoke and French perfume and success.

They sat in the coffee lounge and were attended to at once. Mr. Richter was plainly a good tipper and well known here. He allowed her to serve the coffee, which she did graciously, and this seemed to make him nervous.

"You're too much of a lady, Mrs. Viner, for this stuff." He mopped his brow. "I shouldn't have suggested it. Let's forget, huh?"

"No, really," said Clara. "Do you have sugar?"

"Two spoons," said Mr. Richter. "This is not for you. I was wrong."

"I don't even know," said Clara, "what posing *plastique* is." She handed him his coffee. "Will you tell me?"

Mr. Richter debated. "Well. It's . . . something a lady I know asked about. She runs a gentleman's club, know what I mean?"

"Yes," said Clara, smiling encouragingly. She didn't.

"Well, every Friday and Saturday nights she puts on a kinda *art* show. Fridays and Saturdays are the busy nights, see?" Clara nodded. She didn't. "And she sometimes has girls in, as guests, somebody lovely, not the kinda girl generally gets in such a place, know what I mean, Mrs. Viner?"

246

"Of course," nodded Clara, totally mystified.

Mr. Richter looked relieved. He even drank some of his coffee. "The thing is, this lady likes her gentlemen to see a refined act now and then, and she asks me if I can send somebody along, one of the girls from the burlesque. But they ain't all that refined, and you are." He coughed. "I mean, compared to the other girls, the ones that're usually there."

Clara nodded. She still didn't follow too well.

Mr. Richter leaned forward. "Look, it ain't dirty or anything, Mrs. Viner, or I wouldn't suggest it. It's just standing there, in these poses."

Clara said, "What kind of poses?"

"Oh, I dunno. But you keep still. You have to. That's what makes it artistic."

Clara began to understand. "What would I be wearing, Mr. Richter, while I was posing?"

Mr. Richter drank some coffee, and it went down the wrong way. He coughed for a while, recovered and mopped his face. "Well. Just the muslin. That's why they call it *plastique*. I suppose you're shocked? Sorry. I shoulda never said nothing."

Clara did not see the connection, but she began to gather what Mr. Richter was talking about. She was not shocked. It vaguely excited her. "What kind of money will there be in it?" she asked.

It was Mr. Richter's turn to look shocked. "You'll do it?"

"If the money is worthwhile."

Mr. Richter sighed, like a man whose dreams are often shattered. "They pay a flat rate. Fifty dollars."

Clara waited. Papa had always told her never talk too soon when money is mentioned.

Mr. Richter sighed again and said, "Per show."

"Any commission or anything like that?"

"Nothing to me," said Mr. Richter. "They take care of me."

"Then," said Clara, "I'll do it."

Mr. Richter nodded, but he looked sad. "It would have to be tomorrow night."

Clara nodded yes. "Not a word," she said, "to my husband, should you see him, Mr. Richter."

Mr. Richter nodded again. "He don't know how lucky he is."

Clara said nothing to Harry of her meeting with Mr. Richter, other than that she had run into him while shopping.

"Your shopping," said Harry, "takes longer than living. What did you buy?"

"What you're eating." Clara kissed his cheek. "The veal."

He nodded. "It's good. And you bought fruit and cheese." He looked inquiringly at her. "I thought the money was running low?"

Clara felt cold. "It is, but I found I had a little more than I thought I had."

"That's the best news I've heard this week." Harry turned a page of *Variety*, propped up against the coffeepot.

"All I read in here is that Anna Held is now one of the top-paid acts and she's going to marry Ziegfeld. Maybe you should do something like that, dear?"

Maybe, Clara thought, maybe.

"Even to sleep with somebody important would help," he said, deadpan.

He's so sure of me. Oh, God, if he ever finds out. She put the thought from her mind.

"Anna Held is a great act," she said.

"Well, Chicot doesn't think so."

"Who's he?"

"Only the top vaudeville critic in the country."

"Is he the one who didn't like Marie Lloyd?"

"Yes."

"Then he doesn't like anybody, critics never do, anybody the audiences really like. It's their good time, knocking the headliners."

"That's right, it is." Harry smiled. "The girl's got brains as well as beauty." He peeled an orange with two fingers and ate it in quarter segments. He had never, she supposed, heard of a fruit knife, never mind used one. "I wish I was big enough for him to knock me, I'd be happy." Harry sighed. "I don't think we're ever going to hear from Max Rober. I think he's died."

"We'll hear," Clara said loyally. "You'll see."

"Yes, but meantime?"

"We'll manage."

"You're a darlin'," Harry said. "Have half my orange; it's all I have to offer, I'm skint."

"You can have five dollars if you like."

"What?"

Harry looked so surprised she quickly added, "Well, one dollar. To go and play poker."

"Can't go with less than two."

"All right, two. Here." She gave them to him.

He hesitated, then put them in his pocket. "If I'm lucky, I might play it up into ten, you never know."

They ate the orange, and he got up and put on his coat.

She said, offhand, "Oh, Harry, I saw Maisie Bailey." Maisie was a burlesque girl they both knew. "She has some costumes she wants to give away. I thought I'd go and see them tonight."

So easily done.

Harry nodded. "All right." He put on his derby hat and tapped it. He was cheerful because he was going out, away from her. Oh, well, what harm can a game of poker do? He enjoys it so.

"I may be late, that's all, she lives over in Brooklyn."

"See you when I see you." He kissed her.

"I may even stay over if I get very late."

"Stay over?" He looked surprised.

"Well, you know, these costumes, dresses and so on, she says they need some work done on them, and it'll take both of us to do the fittings and alterations. I can't do it alone."

Harry pondered. Plainly, it sounded like woman's business to him. "Sure. Whatever. Just don't do anything I wouldn't do."

Clara felt a pang. I tell him I might be out all night (she didn't know how late she might be, in truth), and he just says, don't do anything I wouldn't do. She said, "Win some money for us."

"With my luck?" And she heard his step in the corridor, light and cheerful and thought: he sits in this room most days and waits, and nothing happens except that we get one day nearer being totally broke. Let him enjoy himself; he had a lot to put up with.

Clara bathed and powdered herself, surveying her figure. It was nice to be admired; really Mr. Richter could have chosen anybody. She dressed in her best hobble skirt and black straw hat, and checked the address that Mr. Richter had given to her.

When she told the cabdriver where she wanted to go, he looked at her incredulously. "You sure you wanta go there, miss?"

"Yes, I am. And I'm late. So please get there as quickly as you can."

"Right you are, lady." But he still looked puzzled.

The club was not a club. It was a sporting house. Clara knew it the moment she saw the men in evening dress and white scarves going into the house with the big windows—lights shining outside onto a lawn. There was a drive, and several cabs and one or two expensive motorcars were parked in it. She hesitated at the door, a massive white one with a brass knocker in the shape of—she saw to her astonishment—a penis.

The cabdriver was at her side.

"You still want it, lady? If not, I'll take you back where I found you, no extra charge."

"It's all right. I'm expected."

"Don't do it, is what I say," said the cabby, departing. "But who listens to me, my own daughter don't listen to me!"

Clara swallowed, took hold of the penislike knocker and slammed it down. The door opened at once. A black maid in a uniform, wearing the shortest skirt Clara had ever seen, stood there. "Yes?" she asked, not opening the door completely. Clara noted that the bosom of her dress was so low that her breasts could be seen, almost down to the nipple.

"I'm here to see Nevada." It was what she had been told to say. "She's expecting me." The girl still stared at her. A noisy motorcar roared up the drive, and four men got out laughing and plainly drunk. Oh, God, Clara thought, what am I doing? "I'm to pose," she said. *"Plastique."*

The girl smiled, showing beautiful teeth. "Sure, honey, go around the side door to the right. Evening, gentlemen."

For the men had passed Clara and walked into the house. One of them squeezed the black girl's breast as he passed in. She smiled and took their coats.

"Boy," said one, "do I feel like my oats tonight."

The black girl peered at Clara. "Around the *back*, honey," she said in a softer voice. The door closed.

Clara hesitated a long moment. If I don't go in, she thought, we starve. She looked at the lighted house and felt a tremor of excitement. Then she went around the side of the house.

Nevada was a large hennaed lady who talked like a man. Her face was irregular and exuded strength. She wore a red sequined dress and carried a fringed silk purse full of dollars. She gave Clara her fifty at once. "Here you are, honey. Thought you weren't comin'. Let me get you fixed up, all right?" Clara nodded. She could not have spoken if she had wanted to. All around her were girls, white, and Clara saw to her surprise, Chinese and black, too, some in kimonos, some in full dress, two or three naked, all sitting around in a huge carpeted room full of moquette sofas and

250

stools. Some were arranging their hair at mirrors; others were filing their nails; one or two had their eyes closed and seemed to be sleeping. They all looked up as Clara and Nevada came in, then went back to what they were doing. Now and then a black maid entered, whispered to one of the girls, and the girl went out.

Nevada said, "It's all right, honey, none of the girls knows who you are, and they don't care. I never use names to anybody ever. If I told all I know, there would be no government!" She laughed, a deep, masculine boom, and Clara smiled politely.

"Come and look at the podium." Nevada took Clara through the room, along a dark passage and opened a velvet curtain a few inches. Clara looked in, wide-eyed, to an even more surprising sight. Girls, some quite naked, others in filmy wraps, sat on the laps of fully clothed men, who smoked cigars and drank from balloon brandy glasses. Cut-glass decanters stood on low mahogany tables, and there were long mirrors around the room, to give it size. The walls were decorated in a deep red paper, and all the heavy-brocaded lampshades were pink. Some of the men were talking animatedly to each other, the while balancing a nude girl upon their knees. There was a busy hum of voices, and somewhere a violin played softly.

It all seemed strangely domestic.

The podium was directly in front of the curtain. It was raised three feet from the floor and seemed about twelve feet square. A soft white light fell on it from a concealed spot somewhere in the ceiling.

"When you go on, I put all the houselights out." Nevada had taken Clara's arm. "The violinist plays something nice, and you pose. You can pose, can't you, I mean, you know what I mean, pose?"

"Yes, of course," Clara said quickly.

"Your room's here." Nevada found a formidable bunch of keys beneath her skirt. She saw Clara looking and pulled the skirt up to her waist. She was naked under the dress and her pubic hair was thick and red. Around her leg a derringer pistol, in a leather holster, was strapped. "You never know when you got to defend your honor in this business, honey." Nevada roared with laughter and opened the door to a small room, decorated with a dressing table and a chair. She came in with Clara and, as Clara hesitated, looked at her fob watch and said, "Honey, I just hate to rush you, but all you are is an appetizer, and every minute we lose costs me money." Clara smiled, weakly, and began to take off her clothes. Nevada did not offer to go out of the room. Cheeks burning, Clara took off her skirt and blouse and made to take off her hat.

"Leave the hat till last," Nevada said.

Clara took off everything except the hat.

Nevada sat and looked at her.

"Honey, you're lovely. You sure all you want to do is pose?"

Clara could hardly speak. If Papa could see her now! If Harry could! If anybody could! "Just . . . that . . . that's all."

"You could make ten thousand dollars in a year, turning tricks. Retire then if you wanted to. I could show you everything."

"No, thank you. But I'll need some help with the poses."

"You will? You surprise me." Nevada sighed, got to her feet, opened a drawer and took out some sheets of cotton cheesecloth. She draped them around Clara's body skillfully, and poured water over it from a jug on the dressing table. Its impact chilled Clara, and she shivered. "Sorry, honey, but this ain't the real *plastique*. That's got specially made stuff, real close to the body. With the time we've got, this should do."

Nevada stood back and looked, critically. "No rehearsal needed, Richter said. I 'spect he thought you'd run away. Do you want to run away?"

Clara shook her head.

"You can, you know. You're trembling."

"I always am, before."

"Before what?" Nevada roared and seemed pleased. "The thing to do is just pose. I'll show you. Unlatch me, honey."

Clara did. Nevada stepped out of her dress, and her body was huge, white and unwrinkled, her breasts enormous and firm. She saw Clara's gaze. "Some of the most famous heads in New York City rested on these, baby."

Clara said, "Do you—?"

"Sure, honey, but I don't like guys, not anymore. Seen too many. Been on the game since I was twelve, a big house down in my hometown, Dallas. I only do it for special clients these days. They like to go around saying they've done me. It's like saying they shook hands with Jim Corbett or Jack Johnson. It don't mean nothin'."

Clara said, "You'd better show me the poses."

Nevada did.

Clara sat entranced at the subtlety of the huge woman. At the end, she said, "That was . . . lovely."

"Get out there, and do just that, and you'll be all right." Nevada pulled on her dress, winked an enormous kohled eye and left the room.

Clara wet the cheesecloth again, wrapped it around her body and sat waiting to be called. She was numb with excitement or nerves, she didn't know which.

The black maid in the short skirt came in and said, "You're on, honey. Nevada says to tell you there'll be a blackout between each pose, right?" Clara nodded. The girl said, "Gee, you're lovely, ain't you, though, honey?" They all called each other honey, Clara thought. It was a house for men, but the women acted as if they were not there. The black girl squeezed her shoulder and said, "Good luck, English, make it nice and spicy for the poor things."

Clara went out, parted the curtains as Nevada had told her to and stood there, motionless in the white spotlight.

The black room was suddenly silent.

Clara stayed in the first pose, motionless. Each pose lasted a minute, but it seemed like an hour. The spotlight went out.

A round of applause and a hubbub of male voices followed it.

She adopted another pose, her hands away from her body this time. The cheesecloth clung to her limbs.

More applause.

She turned her back to the darkness and arched her arms and bent slightly forward. There was a hiss of appreciation and the largest roar of applause yet.

In the next tableau she let the cheesecloth fall from her breasts.

The response was ecstatic.

Nevada had told her that she could please herself what she did for the last pose.

Clara stripped off the cheesecloth altogether and stood, legs slightly apart, her arms locked behind her head, and swayed backward. Then froze. She could not have said why she did it; she just did it.

The applause was deafening.

She smiled gratefully into the darkness.

Back in the little room Nevada was smiling. "Honey, that was great. You did just right."

Clara took a glass of champagne and drank it at a gulp. She

was sitting, nude and un-selfconscious now. Nevada poured her another glass from the bottle she had brought into the room. Clara felt pleased, and relaxed, as she did after any successful performance.

Nevada said, "I hear you have a husband."

"Yes, that's right. Was it really good?"

"You love him?"

"Oh, yes. Very much."

Nevada sighed and stood up. "I got to go and talk to the clients. See you tomorrow, same time. Oh, and I'm booking you for the next four weeks, same money."

"If I'm free, I'll be here," Clara said.

Nevada turned at the door. "You change your mind about turning tricks, don't forget where I live."

"No," said Clara uncomprehendingly, "I won't."

The black maid came in and helped her to dress.

"You done real good. The clients loved you. You could get a hundred dollars a trick, if you was interested, Miz Nevada tell you that?"

"Well, something like that."

The black maid helped Clara into her skirt. "You want any of that hundred-dollar action?"

"Is it for me to go to bed with them? They want that?"

"Sure it is, and sure they do."

"Oh, no, I couldn't."

The black maid laughed long and loud.

"Honey, that's what we all said!"

Going home in a cab, Clara discovered it wasn't very late after all, only midnight. She paid the cab off and walked a block home. She felt strangely light-headed.

Harry was asleep in bed. She woke him up and made love to him, not allowing him to do anything at all. He moaned and groaned, half asleep under her tongue and breasts and her wetness, and they came together in an explosion of flesh and juice.

"Hey," Harry said, "you ought to go out to Brooklyn more often if it does this to you."

Clara said nothing. She closed her eyes and slept. It had been a long evening.

John Hyatt and Jimmy Cowley sold "Dream of Summer" and made themselves some money. "If this is success, I like it," said

John, over a bottle in the loft above Mooney's bar.

Jimmy Cowley said, "This isn't success; this is just a song we got published and had a few dollars for. The million seller, that's what we need."

John looked around the vast stable, now littered with music manuscripts and empty beer bottles. Mrs. Mooney had made up some velvet curtains for them, and they had a large Axminster carpet on the floor, and a partner desk with a leather chair both sides, picked up in a street market. Mooney had brought in a carpenter, who had partitioned off the bed, and they now slept in a cubicle that looked like a bedroom. They still shared the same bed. Nobody thought that anything but normal. A single bed for a single man was an unheard-of luxury. There was only one drawback. Jimmy Cowley snored, and when he didn't snore, he ground his teeth.

One of the great surprises of Jimmy Cowley's life had been the instant sale of "Dream of Summer." Mr. Rossiter had made no offer. "I like that song, boys," had been his reaction, eyes closed, smiling behind his desk as John thumped the piano. "I've always liked that song."

Jimmy Cowley had been cast down. So had John Hyatt. So much so that he had mentioned it to Uncle Matt, at the ritual Sunday dinner (prompt at noon) after mass. Jimmy Cowley always turned up to eat and was made welcome. "Sure," said Uncle Matt, "the fella tells a good joke, so he does, he livens up the party."

On the subject of the song Uncle Matt was ruminative. Pulling on his stogie a long minute, he poured more Irish for everybody in sight and, returning to his place at the head of the vast table (they sat seventeen to dinner, a vast, unvarying meal of roast lamb or beef and potatoes done in their jackets), pondered. Then he said, "I'll talk to one or two people."

The next day Paddy came to the loft with a message for John Hyatt and nobody else. "The big fella says take the song to Mr. O'Donnell. He'll be expecting you."

Mr. O'Donnell was expecting them. He was a large man with a splendid beer belly and a baritone voice. He had yellow spats and a flowery cravat. He stood at the piano and sang "Dream of Summer" himself, seeming, to John Hyatt, surprised and relieved. "Hey! That's not at all a bad wee song, young fella."

"I only wrote the music." John Hyatt indicated Jimmy Cowley, who was ready to go into a sales pitch and had dressed in his newest and brightest clothes for the purpose.

"Ah, yes, the words are foine, too," said Mr. O'Donnell. He looked out over Tin Pan Alley. The firm was his own, he told them, although another name was on the door. "Sure, what's in a name, as the Bard said." He puffed smoke. "I'll buy the wee song. Give you an advance of three hundred dollars against royalties, at the usual rate. We'll get a contract prepared and signed right now. Is that in order?"

Jimmy Cowley said, "No possibility of five hundred dollars advance?"

Mr. O'Donnell sighed. "Four hundred I can go to."

Jimmy Cowley shook his hand. "It's a deal."

Mr. O'Donnell went out and told his secretary to draw up the contract, and Jimmy Cowley went with him to look over the details. John Hyatt had no knowledge of such things, and Jimmy was an expert. Mr. O'Donnell came back in and sat down behind his desk. He gave John a cigar and they smoked a moment.

"Your partner's a good businessman."

"Is four hundred too much?"

Mr. O'Donnell shook his head. "It's a nice song. We'll get it back. We'll try to find a headliner to sing it." He adjusted the flowered cravat. "And it's a start for you, just over from the ould country."

"I can't say how pleased I am that you like it."

Mr. O'Donnell held up a hand and looked to see that the door was closed. It was. "Give my very best to your Uncle Matt."

"I will," said John Hyatt.

"The Irish," said Mr. O'Donnell, "have got to look after the Irish, or who will, you tell me that now?" He poured three fingers of whiskey from a bottle in his drawer. John thought: the Irish, if a pleasure isn't hidden, what's the pleasure in it at all? "Slainte," said Mr. O'Donnell. They drank, Mr. O'Donnell in one gulp.

"That," he said, "is the real stuff, John."

John Hyatt agreed that it was indeed.

Jimmy Cowley came back in.

"Do you take a glass of Irish, young fella?" asked Mr. O'Donnell.

"I didn't use to," said Jimmy Cowley, "but when you live over Mooney's bar, do you have a choice?"

Mr. O'Donnell smiled and poured.

Jimmy Cowley drank. He had a head, John Hyatt knew, of iron.

Mr. O'Donnell poured again.

John Hyatt refused, but Jimmy Cowley accepted.

It happened three more times.

"Bejasus," said Mr. O'Donnell, "here's a fella that can carry his liquor and himself not an Irishman, at that."

"Who knows," said Jimmy Cowley, "you go back far enough, who knows what anybody is?"

"Begod," said Mr. O'Donnell, "isn't that the truth, though?"

They drank a final swallow to a United Ireland and made their way out of Mr. O'Donnell's office. He saw them out himself.

"That partner of yours," he said to John, "he's a grand wee fella. You wouldn't do better if you were tied up with an Irishman, indade you would not."

In the street, John Hyatt said, his head spinning, "It's not the music that's the hard work; it's the drinking."

They took the girls to Coney that Sunday in celebration.

Even Mamie was impressed by their success. She did not show it too much, though, and was not at all impressed by the boomers who were plugging songs. "They can sing, but they can't sell!" she insisted, gazing at the close-harmony groups shouting hoarsely in the arcades. Four of the songs they heard, she pointed out, were about dreams. Who, she asked, needed another song about dreams?"

"We sold it, didden we?" demanded Jimmy Cowley. "And you're eating on the advance, so be polite."

Patsy Keenan said very little but clung onto John Hyatt's arm and looked admiringly into his eyes. They drank beer and ate ice cream and hot dogs, and the men threw wooden balls at coconuts. They went on the rides and sat on the beach and got sunburned. John Hyatt bought Patsy a little silver ring, and Jimmy Cowley said that had been a mistake. He said buy a woman anything you like but not a ring. A woman took a ring serious. "You aren't serious, are you, fella?"

"No," said John. "It just seemed a nice thing to do, and she admired the ring."

"Sure, she admired the ring, but watch which finger it's on next time you see her. Don't say I didn't tell you so."

The next time they met, to go to see Pat Rooney, Jr., sing their song, the ring was on Patsy Keenan's third finger of her left hand. Pat Rooney, Jr., sang only one verse and a chorus of "Dream of Summer," but it enabled Mr. O'Donnell to put "As sung by the Great Pat Rooney, Jr." on the sheet music, and they were grateful. "And they say," said Jimmy Cowley, "that the Jews look after their own."

To all who knew him he declared, "I'm the only Irish Jewish honorary Catholic in captivity. And I tell you what, it ain't bad."

"Dream of Summer" sold a respectable number of copies those hot months and the bitter winter that followed. John and Jimmy wrote song after song, following the fashion of the day for ballads about mothers ("The Irish," said Jimmy, "have even more mothers than the Jews, and that is some kinda record, right?") and long-lost sons who return home to save the family's fortunes. They wrote songs of the American hinterland, which neither of them had ever seen, about hayrides and horses. They wrote novelty songs about women who rode bicycles in bloomers. They followed fashion and sold enough songs to eat. They went to the "Parlors for Professionals," where the headliners of vaudeville sat, bored, as the song demonstrators yelled at them in chorus. They failed to interest anybody big in their new songs, but Mr. O'Donnell declared himself content with their efforts. He had, however, a word of advice for them. "Give me a tune," he said, "an Irish tune. But one for everybody, right?"

Jimmy Cowley groaned, and they set to work.

They ate and drank and slept sometimes and bought new clothes for summer and winter and took the girls to Central Park to skate and even to the ball game, and winter followed summer, and they did not count the days or months because they were so busy. The sheet-music business was cutthroat, Jimmy Cowley said. Some stores were selling copies for two cents each.

They did not get rich, but they were happy.

John Hyatt found that he rarely thought of Clara these days. She had faded from his memory, and he was glad of it. The hectic night sweats of London had gone, and he was grateful for the quiet, tender company of Patsy Keenan. They went around together, in a foursome mostly, with Jimmy and Mamie, but now and then Patsy would meet him on her own. They would walk the parks and streets, her arm tucked in his, and he would tell her of Ireland, where she had never been. It was quiet, and it was restful. He did not think he loved her, but he knew that she loved him. She took him home to meet her parents, and they

258

approved of him. "I hear," said Mr. Keenan, "that you're the big fella's nephew?" Mr. Keenan was in New York's Finest, a sergeant at that. He was a man who gave life the hard look and a suitor for his daughter a harder one. John Hyatt took Patsy home to Brooklyn very promptly, and even when she pleaded to "just take a peep at where you live, what's the harm in that?," he refused her. He was not ready for attachments, and he finally told her so. "Sure I can wait till you are," said Patsy Keenan, not easily put off something she really wanted. "I'm in no great hurry at all, at all."

Jimmy Cowley said, "She's got her hooks in you, fella. Take care."

"What about you and Mamie?" asked John Hyatt.

"If you get Patsy pregnant, her father will kill you," said Jimmy Cowley. "If I get Mamie pregnant, *she'll* kill me."

"You mean you and she *are* . . . ?" asked John Hyatt, scandalized.

"No chance," said Jimmy Cowley. "Sometimes I ache for an hour after those clinches with the girls, don't you?"

John Hyatt said he didn't, but he did.

Said Jimmy Cowley, "If only Mamie came across and Patsy came across and we didden have to worry about having to marry them or think about chasing after ten-dollar whores instead, wouldn't that be somethin'?"

John Hyatt agreed that it would.

"Not," said Jimmy Cowley, getting into bed, "that such a thing is ever goin' to happen to such as us."

"It would be against nature anyway," said John Hyatt.

"I have to agree," said Jimmy Cowley. "I'll think about the ten-dollar whores."

He slept and snored.

John Hyatt lay thinking of Patsy Keenan. He liked her, but he did not think he loved her. If he loved anybody, he loved Clara Abbott.

On that thought, he too slept.

Three months later they finished "Sullivan's Daughter Ruth," and John Hyatt did not like it. Jimmy Cowley said it was one for the market. The boomers would like it, he prophesied, because it had comedy and not a bad lilt to it. Mr. O'Donnell would like it because it would sell a bit. Mr. O'Donnell did like it, and he lined up Fanny Brice to hear it, even sending a limousine to bring her from the theater. "The problem, boys," he told John and Jimmy, "is, who sells it to her?"

"Why not Mamie?" said Jimmy Cowley.

"Mamie who?"

"Selznick."

"Is she vaudeville? I don't know any Mamie Selznick," said Mr. O'Donnell, bewildered.

"She's got a personality a bit like Brice's. Give her a try, huh, Mr. O'Donnell?"

Mamie was sent for, showed no nerves and sang the song:

> I'm Sullivan's daughter Ruth,
> I tellya nothing but the truth.
> At our house we have Sunday twice,
> I wouldn't live anyplace else at any price.

Mr. O'Donnell said she was a hell of a girl—not, of course, to her face. That would be indelicate. Mamie sang the song at the performers' parlor, and Miss Brice, a dark, formidable lady, surrounded by agents and managers, said, "Not a bad little song. I'll think about it, I really will," and disappeared back to Hammerstein's Victoria for the second house.

"Did she mean it?" asked Jimmy Cowley, depressed.

"Miss Brice is a big lady," retorted Mr. O'Donnell. "Sure she means it."

John Hyatt and Jimmy Cowley went to the Victoria to talk Fanny Brice into using the song. First of all, they had to see her act, which was new to John but not to Jimmy Cowley. John was captivated by Fanny Brice. She closed, to loud applause. Said Jimmy Cowley, "If she sings our song, we're made."

Miss Brice never sang the song, but another vaudevillian, Sarah Winter, did, and it sold a respectable number of copies. When John and Jimmy received their royalty checks, they took the girls to supper and celebrated.

"Five hundred dollars each," said Jimmy Cowley incredulously, after they saw the girls, inevitably, to the subway. "We're rich."

"Not rich, " said John Hyatt, "but we aren't starving anyway."

They stood at the corner of Broadway and Forty-seventh, and Jimmy Cowley said, "I know a place, but the whores are fifty dollars. I reckon we can afford it. What say?"

John Hyatt sighed. The evening did seem to have fallen flat, and the idea of going back to the stable, even in its improved condition, did not seem attractive.

"Is it far?" he asked.

Jimmy Cowley whistled for a cab.

Clara kept her secret but with difficulty.

Harry asked, from time to time, what money they had. She always answered that she was selling some of Maisie Bailey's reconditioned costumes for a few dollars each. This excused her visits to the club and explained the fact that there was enough to eat and a dollar or two to spare. She had to resist spending too much on food or anything else in case Harry became suspicious. However, he showed no particular curiosity, and Clara was grateful for that. She had been appearing at the club twice weekly for three weeks, and that was three hundred and fifty dollars earned. This was to be her last evening. A new attraction, two savages from Borneo, man and wife, or what passed for it in Borneo, posing in the nude, so Nevada had told her, adding, "We need something new pretty regular. It's getting now most of my clients have seen you at least twice, honey. Mostly they come every week or two weeks. A man uses a sporting house at all, he uses it regular."

Clara had lost her nervousness about posing. She could not see the customers sitting out there in the darkness, the girls on their knees. She enjoyed it really, almost as much as if she were giving a regular performance. Nevada watched her with resignation. "You're wasted, honey, chasing around them vaude circuits with all them hoofers and jugglers."

"If only we were chasing around the circuits," Clara said.

"Nothing coming in for your fella?"

"Our agent said he was trying, but nothing seems to be happening."

For there was no news at all from Max Rober. Harry fell silent for longer and longer periods, and went out more and more to play poker down at the pool hall.

"So money still matters, honey?" asked Nevada.

"Yes, it does, I'm afraid."

Nevada shook her head. "It's what I've always said: happiness will never take the place of money."

As Clara was beginning to dampen the muslin to wrap around herself, Nevada suddenly said, "Hey, would an extra fifty dollars come in useful, since this is your last throw of the dice?"

Clara said, "Would it!"

She was becoming quite American, she thought proudly.

Nevada said, "We just have time." She opened a cabinet and took out a costume. "Try it on, honey."

Clara did. It was a French cancan outfit, with décolleté top and long white drawers to just above the knee and black stockings. She looked at herself in the mirror. "Do I pose in this? They wouldn't be very excited if I did."

Nevada smiled. "Take off the drawers."

Mystified, Clara did so. Nevada began to unpick the threads in the seat of the drawers. "They'll open wide if you do a split or a try at a split. Can you do a split?"

"I can try."

"Put these on, and try then."

Clara did. Nevada stood watching her. "Legs wider when you go down. That gives them a nice view."

"But what's so special about it? They see me naked doing *plastique?*"

"Honey, I don't think you'll ever understand men."

"No," said Clara, "I don't think I ever will."

"Here, let me show you the steps. The girls at the Folies in Paree do this; they're what the French call *poules.* I had one here for a while, and she told me about it. This was her costume."

Clara said, "Where did she go?"

"A rich fella's keeping her. It's easier work, till they get tired of you. She'll be back." Nevada smiled. "Now, let's see you cancan like they do in Paree."

"Show me first," said Clara, thinking: why am I so very cool about all this? So long as I'm in front of an audience it doesn't seem to matter what I do. Is this what they call being a good trouper? She smiled to herself.

"Pay attention, honey. I ain't doing the splits more than once." Nevada hitched up the skirt of her dress and stretched her magnificent legs. She kicked half a dozen times and then went down in a split. She held the position. "That's all there is to it. Now you try it."

Clara did, several times. She had danced a lot, and she could kick, and she could—just—throw herself forward in the splits. "Three times, six kicks each time and three splits, one to your right, one left, one center. That should do it. I've told Joe on the violin; he'll be watching you and keeping time." Nevada looked at the long, innocent-looking drawers. "That'll give them the shock of their lives. Nice finale, huh, honey?"

Clara smiled. She felt a sudden surge of doubt. The *plastique* was rude, but it was artistic. This was cunning deliberate provocation of the customers' manly instincts. She sighed. What difference did it make, and anyway, who would know her in the light she worked in?

It was all right. It was fifty dollars extra.

It had to be all right.

Jimmy Cowley had never been to the house before, despite his big talk, John Hyatt decided. Outside the place, with its blazing red-curtained windows brazening its purpose to the world, he hesitated. "I'm not sure I want this, Jimmy. Let's go home. The last house I went to it was awful."

Jimmy Cowley slammed the penis knocker down. "Hell, are we men or are we boys?" The door opened, and Jimmy Cowley saw, close up, the nude breasts of the black maid. "We're boys," he said.

"Come in then, boys," said the black maid. "If you gotta dollar and a desire, you're welcome."

They went inside. John Hyatt was impressed, against his will, by the splendor of the place, the expensive dress of the men and the youth and comparative nudity of the girls, but mostly by the gentle good manners of it all. Cigar smoke hung in the air, and a violinist played, somewhere out of sight. The maid sat them down and raised an eyebrow inquiringly to a large hennaed woman in a fringed green dress, who came over to them at once.

"Hello, boys. You two hell raisers or just nice quiet fellas?"

Her voice was throaty. John Hyatt did not find her attractive. Menacing, more likely. Jimmy Cowley was not abashed. "It's Nevada, am I right?"

"To my friends."

"How do I get to be your friend, Nevada?"

"You get to be my friend by paying me five hundred dollars if you want a naughty with me." Nevada smiled, but her eyes didn't. "A little strong for you?"

"Got to admit it is," said Jimmy Cowley, "but if you don't ask, you don't get, do you?"

Nevada studied him. "Don't take anybody else upstairs, kiddo.

263

Who knows, I might just change my mind." She paused. "You boys know there's no cheap cuts of meat here, don't you?"

"Sure we do," said Jimmy Cowley indignantly. "We aren't cheapskates; we have the necessary." He grinned. "In every department."

Nevada smiled politely and moved away. At a sign from her, two young girls, one black, came across the room and sat on the settee. They both wore kimonos of thin material, and their breasts were exposed. The maid brought cigars and glasses of brandy, and John and Jimmy lit up and drank. John Hyatt's hand was outspread on the sofa, and the black girl sat on it. She squirmed. She wore no drawers. John withdrew his hand as if she were red hot, and she laughed, a merry child's laugh.

"Jesus," said Jimmy Cowley, as his partner sat on his knee. "Do these kids know some tricks."

"You two boys are ready to go upstairs right now, I betcha! Two big manly gennelmen like you?" said the white girl.

"Can't go up till the show's over, Mais," said the black one, who John Hyatt realized, couldn't have been more than fifteen. Gloomily he drank his brandy. The black girl's fingers explored his crotch tentatively. He moved away, shocked. She laughed again. "You not used to a Nigra girl where you come from, honey?" John Hyatt smiled politely, but in truth he was not. He had seen a few Blacks on the streets of New York but not very many. They were an absolute rarity in London and never ever seen in Dublin.

"It's not that," he said.

"No? Then what?"

He coughed, desperate. "What's this show?"

"Oh, just a girl. Nevada thinks it gives the house class. I say, how can you give a whorehouse class? All I know is it costs me money. You know I ain't cheap, don'tcher, honey, you know the prices?"

Before John Hyatt could reply, the lights were turned down by the maids, all over the large room. John Hyatt was grateful for that. He had been in such a place before, in London, but he had not sat in public with a nude girl on his knee. He found it difficult, also, to avoid the bored eyes of the other men, wealthier and older, in the room. He felt as if he were in the wrong place in the wrong clothes.

Jimmy Cowley had no such reservations.

"Class," he whispered to John. "Really high class."

264

For a curtain had opened, showing, in a spotlight, a girl in cancan dress. This was greeted with muted applause and some excitement. French meant spicy as far as this audience was concerned, Gay Paree and black stockings and ta-ra-ra-boom-de-ay!

But there was no brass orchestra to help, only a violin. Yet the girl danced, lightly, kicking her legs, turning her back on them and flouncing her dress up above her bottom, in a naughty, provocative way. The spotlight did not fall upon her face but on her body, her firm young breasts, boldly exposed, and her lovely bare arms. John Hyatt stirred and stared. There was something familiar about the girl. He could not think how that might be.

The girl, still dancing lightly, kicked again half a dozen times and then executed a very high kick and a split. Her drawers parted at the front, and a tangle of hair showed, just for a moment, so quickly it might not have happened. But every man in the place knew that it had. There was an appreciative stir rising to applause and open delight when she did it twice more.

"I told you, John." Jimmy Cowley's eyes were wide. "Real class."

The girl threw herself into the final split, with the final tantalizing glimpse of hair, and this time she stayed down in the split. The applause was loud. The girl lifted her head and smiled. For the first time the audience saw her face.

John Hyatt stared. He suddenly felt cold.

He stared and stared. Surely there was a mistake?

There was no mistake.

"Hey, honey, whatsamatta, you sick or somethin'?" asked the black girl.

But John Hyatt was on his feet in the darkness and stumbling to the door, shaking off Jimmy Cowley's restraining hand. "You stay, I'll be all right, I just don't feel like it."

Then he was in the cool night air. He walked down the driveway slowly, numbed by what he had seen, his thoughts tumbled and tormented. He found a saloon and drank a great deal of raw, cheap whiskey. He went back to the sporting house and waited for an hour until Clara came out. She looked quite different in her street clothes, demure and decent. But he knew better.

"Clara!"

She stared at him, a shadow in the darkness. "John? Is it John?"

"Yes."

She was quite still a long moment. "Have you been in there?"

265

He nodded.

She said nothing, just looked steadily at him.

"Can we talk? I can get a cab?" he asked.

"Well, I should get home." Her voice was even. The shame of the girl, John Hyatt thought, or the lack of it.

He felt curiously light-headed; none of this was real. "I live not too far away. Come and have some coffee, tell me the news."

"You still want to talk to me? After *that?*"

"Of course I do," he said. He meant it. "More than ever." He meant that, too.

Women, he thought, the things they *do*.

"You don't think it was awful of me, to do that, to pose like that?"

"No," he lied. "Why should it be awful?"

"Money," she said. "I did it for money."

John caught something in her voice, an inflexion that told him she wasn't entirely telling the truth. He controlled his voice as best he could. "Only a few minutes. You can tell me all about it, yes?"

Clara nodded. He thought she looked relieved. Women, he thought, women. He whistled a cab.

Clara was impressed by the stable. John had smuggled her upstairs the back way, out of Mooney's view. She walked around the room, touching his manuscript papers. She paused at the piano and smiled. "You remember how you played and I sang 'Naughty But Nice' in Mrs. Harrington's in Camden Town?"

"I'll never forget it." He tried not to look too hard at her body moving under the street clothes. I was staring at you in the nude an hour ago, he thought, and now you stand here as if nothing has happened. He said, "Do you still use the song?" He poured himself a glass of whiskey (Clara refused one) and noticed his hands were trembling.

Clara struck a note on the piano. "Every performance. Trouble is we're out of work. Otherwise—"

"Of course," John Hyatt reassured her. "You must have hated doing that, naked in front of all those men." I've lain in bed lusting for you, he thought, I've run to America after you, I've wanted you and idealized you, and you take your drawers off for people you've never seen before in your life. A slow anger mixed with his sharp desire. "You must have hated every moment of it."

"Well." Clara shrugged. "Not really. Sometimes I quite like

266

it. I enjoy the applause. It's like being onstage."

John Hyatt stared at her uncomprehendingly. Did it mean as little as that to her?

"Does Harry know you've been doing it?"

"No, of course not." She sat down on the bed and smiled at him. "Can you imagine his face if he found out?"

So she hadn't even told her husband. Then it wasn't entirely for the money, John Hyatt reasoned. The deceit of women; it passed understanding. He poured himself another slug of whiskey. His hand still trembled. There's danger in this, he thought, but I have to do it, and why not, she isn't what I thought she was at all. He swallowed the whiskey and sat down on the bed next to her. His arm went around her, and he pulled her to him. At first she did not resist (was she surprised, surely she wasn't shamed, how could she be, doing what she had just done?) but simply cried out, "John, please don't, John!" His hand found her breast and covered it, and still, she did not wriggle away as any decent girl would, not her. Her lips were open, and he kissed them and felt no love, only lust, raw and blind (the picture in his head was of her legs in the splits and of the tangle of hair), and his other hand swept under her long skirt and bore it upward, and his fingers slid above her garter to the soft flesh between her garter and her drawers, and then she bit him.

"Jesus Christ!" He let her go and put his handkerchief to his mouth. Blood flowed. The pain was sharp. "What was that for?"

"What do you think I am, a whore?" Clara's blue eyes blazed at him.

"Why not?" He was dismayed. Christ, this had all gone wrong. He was suddenly cold, bleak sober but still angry. "I saw you in a whorehouse an hour ago, bare-assed!"

She stood up, suddenly deathly pale.

"Did you think that? Did you see me like that?"

"Of course I did, and so did every man there. I expect you're at least a hundred dollars a trick, aren't you?"

He did not know why he said that. The moment he said it he wished he hadn't. She was lovely in her anger, and he wanted her, he thought miserably. Even if she was a whore now, he wanted her.

"If that's what you think of me, I'm sorry."

"So am I." He surveyed his bloodied handkerchief.

"I have never slept with any man but Harry. Ever."

"And the band played 'Believe It if You Like.'" John Hyatt didn't know why he said that either.

Clara walked to the door. She turned and said quietly, "I can see why you felt how you did, John. It was my fault. I shouldn't have come here. I'm sorry. Good-bye."

And she was gone.

John Hyatt wanted to run after her and apologize and tell her he loved her whatever she was, but he did not. What would have been the good? She still loved Harry Viner; it was as simple, and as complicated, as that.

John Hyatt sat on the bed in the attic for an hour, finishing the bottle of whiskey, trying to make sense of it all. "I'm sorry, Clara, I'm sorry," he called, before he fell back and slept. Nobody heard him.

A month later he married Patsy Keenan at St. Patrick's on Fifth Avenue. It was a big wedding, an Irish wedding, and everybody was pleased at the union, especially Uncle Matt. Jimmy Cowley was best man, and everybody was agreed no Irishman could have performed the office better.

They went to Niagara Falls for the honeymoon.

Harry met Belle Alvin in Central Park.

He had got into the habit of walking there most afternoons for an hour or so. It reminded him of London, not that his memories of London were all that pleasant. Simply, this was a green place, and he was on his own, away from Clara's reproachful eye. She did not need to tell him that she thought he should have seen Max Rober long before this. Well, now he'd done it, and he hoped she was bloody satisfied. He'd eaten dirt, and he didn't like the feeling. Beckie had once said to him, "Harry, you're too touchy for your own good. It's no use being touchy in this world. People don't care how you feel, just how you look. So look good and smile, and you'll do all right. People don't want to know about touchy."

It was hard to smile when you'd worked three full seasons at a top resort, to good houses and applause, and nobody had even heard of you, and now you were down to your last few dollars again. It was hard to smile when you knew how good you were and nobody cared a damn. It was possible, Harry brooded, sitting there in the chilly winter sun, that he would do better as a single comic, without Clara with him. He had never intended to work with a partner; comics who worked with partners were just making it easier for themselves, they talked to the partner instead of directly to the audience, they copped out.

Had he copped out by having Clara as a partner? She always came on and got him offstage with her bloody song. Did he need her that much? Harry brooded, in his warm but aging topcoat, and gazed at, but did not see, the nannies with their prams and children walking around the park. *Did* he need Clara that much? People liked her, even Max Rober went on about her all the time; was it possible that they liked her better than they liked him? Harry shook his head. Beckie was right; he was too touchy for his own good. But he had started out to be a solo standup comic, and what was he now?

Now he was a man in a double act with a beautiful wife everybody loved. Now he was out of work and broke. Now he was a man who had just gone along and crawled to his agent—again—for any kind of work at all. How had all this come about?

It had come about because of Clara.

No doubt of it.

"I'm sorry, did you say something?"

Harry looked up in surprise. A dark-haired young woman in leather button-up boots and a sealskin coat and matching hat was regarding him with curiosity, from her seat farther along the bench.

"You spoke, something about 'no doubt of it?'"

Harry laughed. "Talking to myself. It's a habit I've picked up since I came to New York."

"You're British, aren't you?" The girl was pretty, Harry thought. Not as pretty as Clara, but she had large dark eyes and a good mouth.

"Guilty as charged, ma'am," Harry said. "I speak three languages, English, Yiddish and rubbish. You look worried about something."

"It's just I feel I know you, seen you somewhere. But I can't think where."

"Do you go to burlesque houses?"

The girl laughed. It was a nice quiet laugh. "No, but I mean it. I do know you. From somewhere."

"Hey." Harry laughed. "That should be my line, not yours."

"What do you do for a living?" the girl persisted. She did not seem at all put out at talking to a strange man in Central Park.

269

Harry was surprised at her persistence, but he answered, "I work in vaudeville."

"Atlantic City?"

He stared at her.

"I saw you in Atlantic City. This summer? Right?"

Harry nodded, even more surprised. "Right."

The dark eyes sparkled. "I thought you were very good."

Harry was gratified. At least somebody had seen him working, somewhere. "That's nice. The trouble is, not too many people share your opinion."

"Is that so?"

"Very much so . . . er. . . . Do you have a name?"

"Belle Alvin."

Harry thought a moment. "That's familiar. Should I know it at all?"

"I work for the *Trib*. I do shows sometimes."

"Knew I'd seen it somewhere." Harry felt better. The girl worked for a newspaper; her word meant something. She wasn't just a punter, somebody who liked the act but had no pull at all. On the other hand, most newspaper writers copied the influential critics. What Chicot of the *Telegraph* said, they all said, sooner or later, usually sooner.

"You didn't write anything about the act, did you?"

"I was in Atlantic City on vacation. With my mother. She likes it there."

"Don't you?"

"It's all right. I'd rather go to Europe."

"Don't bother, I've been."

She laughed. "I really liked your act. You may be British but the audience liked it, too."

"Tell that to the bookers, as the man said."

"You're too good for Little Time, you know."

"Lady, I know, you know, the world knows I'm too good for Little Time. The bookers think Little Time's too good for me."

"It's as bad as that?" Her voice was sympathetic.

Much to his surprise, Harry found himself telling Belle Alvin exactly how things stood, exactly how he felt about the act and about life. It was a none-too-brief but wry catalogue of events since he and Clara had landed in New York City, and it took half an hour. He did not mention Clara by name in the account.

Belle Alvin listened, and she laughed, often. At the end she said, "You don't seem to have had the best of luck, Mr. Viner."

"Harry, please."

Belle Alvin glanced at her fob watch. "Gosh, I'm late. I have to rush." She fumbled in her purse and took out a card. "That's my office number. If you get a New York date, ring me there, and I'll try to cover it if I can. I can't promise, of course. But I do think you are a good comic, and I don't know how many I can say that about. . . . There are one or two things you might improve. . . ."

Harry said, "What?" He wanted to know; this girl spoke with authority, she worked for an influential newspaper, she might be able to tell him things nobody else could or would.

But Belle Alvin was on her feet and making her apologies. "I can't talk now. I really must go."

"Can I walk you to the streetcar or whatever?"

"No, I've got to run." She put out a gloved hand. "Don't lose heart, Harry. You're too good to go under." She smiled. "I'm not sure you know how good."

Then she walked off very quickly, not looking back. Harry stood with his velour hat in one hand and Belle Alvin's pasteboard card in the other (he had never known a *woman* to have a business card) and stared regretfully after the sealskin coat, until it disappeared in the throng of nannies and strollers in the wintry sunshine.

Max Rober wrote to them at last.

"Not before time," Clara said. The money from her performances at Nevada's place had all but run out. She had ten dollars left the day Harry opened the letter.

He stared at it, his suspenders dangling, his collarless shirt open, and even he seemed impressed.

"We have a tryout matinee at the Jefferson, certain, and Max Rober is going to get Eddie Darling to come and see us. If Darling likes us, he'll recommend us to the Orpheum Circuit, and they could book us for a tour across the country." He stared at the letter. "That's an awful lot of ifs, but I still don't believe it, Clara."

"Oh, my love!" Clara kissed him. "Oh, my love."

Max Rober, in his office next day, was pleasant but emphatic about the way they must present the act. He had had some opposition, he reported. Harry's habit of changing his material in mid-act was known about and would never do here. Whatever he played at the tryout matinee, he must stick to, religiously, all the tour.

271

They would be allowed ten minutes exactly, and there must be nothing blue, no mention of anything doubtful of any sort, no blatantly upsetting remarks about one or other of the city's ethnic groups. The tour, if it materialized, was going out to the sticks, and New York humor simply didn't move them. A good song, the one they had, suitably arranged, though never rude, for each town, that they could retain. Harry should not tell a great spiel of one-line or shortish jokes, which Max Rober knew was his natural style. Rather, he should look around for a good monologue. Or write one himself. Under no circumstances should he go off without a song. They should end with "Naughty But Nice."

Harry said, "Nobody's going to love us, Mr. Rober."

"No," said Max Rober steadily, "but nobody's going to hate you either. Keep the edge off the jokes, you'll be playing to a new America. If you survive the matinee."

Clara said, "Thank you, Mr. Rober."

He smiled at her. "Keep this man of yours in order, Mrs. Viner, and you'll see California."

Harry asked, "Will you be there yourself, at the matinee?"

Max Rober lit one of his Turkish cigarettes. "Wouldn't miss it because I know you are going to be sensible and get the job. Work on the monologue. It could be a clincher. Oh. . . ." He looked at a paper on his desk. "How do you want to be billed?"

"We're still Viner and Viner, Finer and Finer . . . ?" asked Harry.

"Yes," said Max Rober, "but possibly something different?"

"Viner and Viner, as English as Roast Pork?" suggested Harry.

Max Rober looked pained.

Clara said, "Why not Viner and Viner, Man and Wife?"

"Why not Viner and Viner, a Life Sentence?" said Harry.

Max Rober looked pained again.

"I used to be billed as King of Kosher Komedy," said Harry.

Max Rober sighed. "I think we'll say Viner and Viner, Talented Tunes and Talk."

"Well," said Harry gloomily, "nobody is going to object to that."

"That," said Max Rober grimly, "is why I suggested it. I have done a lot of hard work here on your behalf. It's yours for the taking."

"We'll take it," said Harry, "if they offer it."

The Monday matinee was full of people who had come to

see acts fail, and second curtains were few. It was a cosmopolitan audience, and a professional one, partly consisting of agents and bookers and other performers who were not working and, of course, Mr. Darling, representing the Orpheum Circuit, who had a name for his attention to the things that a dollar might buy in this world. Harry had worked hard at a monologue and was to go on first. He asked for an advance from Max Rober and bought a new suit of yellow peg-topped trousers along with a new yellow straw cady and a bright blue coat, high-buttoned. "Nobody," said Max Rober, calling, as usual, courteously to see them before the show, "is going to miss you in that."

"I don't intend them to," said Harry.

"Easy does it," said Max Rober. "Good luck." To Clara: "You look lovely, m'dear," and was gone.

Clara was wearing her blue sailor dress. It was old, but it still looked good. Her shoes were white, and her hooped skirt fell only halfway down her calves, far above what a man might see in the street. "Shall I go higher?" she asked Harry.

He frowned. "What do you think you are, a whore?"

She fell silent. If only you knew, she thought and felt very, very naughty indeed. It was strange to be working again in an atmosphere where to show an ankle might be regarded as risqué. The world was full of audiences, she thought, and no two alike.

A fist rapped the door. "Two minutes, Mr. Viner!"

"Good luck, darling," she said, not kissing him because of the makeup.

Harry nodded. "As they said to the man in the condemned cell."

"You'll do splendidly."

"If I can get my mouth round my monologue, darlin'."

Out on the stage he thought he might not. The musical director was unprepared for a comic who needed only two bars to cover his walk out front and who then was prepared to take the audience on. He motioned his musicians into silence as Harry confronted the first few rows.

Harry had intended to launch straight into his monologue. But the silence unnerved him.

"Anybody here," he asked, "ever been to an execution before?"

There was a small laugh.

"The Romans used to do it as well," said Harry. "They used

273

to set the lions on the Christians. Now they're setting the critics on the Jews—I see you out there, Mr. Sargent!"

For Harry had heard that Chicot, real name Sargent, the top New York vaudeville critic, was in the house.

He got a laugh for that.

"Mr. Chicot didn't like Marie Lloyd, and he didn't like Anna Held, so why should I worry? They may be beautiful and rich and I'm ugly and poor, but like the fella said, who can tell the difference in the dark?"

He got another laugh. Harry's laughs always came from the same people, never the whole audience. Chasing the rest of them, he added, "I don't know if Mr. Chicot has heard about my friend Finklestein. Now, there's a funny fella, Finklestein. He went to this party in a pair of borrowed pants and couldn't sit down all night. Listen, to this party he had an invitation that said, 'Your presence is requested,' and Finklestein says, 'They're asking for the presents already and I ain't even there yet?' . . . So, listen, a fella Murphy, who ain't invited, turns up and picks a fight with Finklestein. Finklestein tells me, 'Who says the Irish can fight? Me and my two brothers and my cousin Isaac had him out the door in less than an hour. . . .' "

Harry got some laughs, nice and comfortable.

He stopped the monologue. "If Mr. Chicot isn't asleep now, he ought to be. He's heard that a dozen times before. I've heard it a dozen times before, and I wrote it. I mean, I remembered it. I mean, I copied it. Well, who's looking?"

The laughs were fewer but genuine and not patronizing.

Harry took heart. "Mr. Chicot, I've been out working Little Time for three years, and right after this matinee I'll probably be working Little Time again. You should come and see me out at Union City, Mr. Chicot. It's across the Hudson, in case you've never been there. You dress in the john, Mr. Chicot. Now, there's something new, a dressing room that is also a john. It's a wonderful modern invention, Mr. Chicot. It saves valuable space, you see?"

There were a few more laughs.

Harry said, "Did you hear about the old vaudeville performer who played Union City and the musical director died. He went to the funeral just to show respect, and when he was standing at the graveside, he coughed a lot and the undertaker said, 'Not much point in you going home, is there, buddy?' "

The musical director looked inquiringly at Harry. Time, he

signaled. Harry told his joke about the cemetery cat. Then he nodded to the musical director, and Clara came on.

The stage lights dipped.

"This is the wife," Harry said. "I went home early one day last week, and a man ran past me out of the house. No clothes on. I said to the wife, 'Who's that?' and she said, 'He's a swimmer just got cramp in the sea, lost his bathing costume, and he's just been in to borrow a cup of sugar. Funny fella.' "

Clara smiled and sang:

I stood on the stage, and the manager said,
'Me dear, I'd just love to take you to . . . .' (Crash of cymbal!)

She talked:

"He *did*, that's what he *said*. . . . But we went to Lüchow's and had meatballs instead, he was ever so *manly!*"

They danced together and sang in chorus:

Naughty but Nice, Naughty but Nice,
Never Been Kissed in the Same Place Twice!

They took one bow, all they were allowed. The applause was good, if not ecstatic. Clara said, "Harry, will you never learn?"

Harry marched moodily back into the dressing room. "Darlin', I couldn't do that monologue *drek*, I just couldn't *do* it!"

Clara sat down, near to tears. "You heard what Mr. Rober said. Keep it nice and clean, and don't offend anybody. Don't ad-lib. Stick to a routine act. Oh, Harry, Harry, we've probably lost our chance!"

"So what?" Harry said. "There'll be others."

"Will there?"

"Of course, there will. *Shut up*, will you!"

It was the first time he had actually yelled at her, and she was shocked. He seemed like somebody else, his face twisted and hateful.

Oh, God, she thought, he hates me.

She was suddenly very angry.

"Well, I can't do *that* again anyway."

"Do *what* again?"

"Get us money the way I have for the past three months."

He looked up. "How did you get money in the past three months?"

Clara looked away. "It doesn't matter. It's nothing."

He was standing over her, his face very set, under the mirth lines he had painted on his face. "What did you do?"

"Nothing, Harry. Nothing."

"The money? . . . It wasn't for dresses?"

"No, it wasn't."

"Did you. . . ." He seemed to be choking. "Did you . . . ?"

"No, I didn't. I posed *plastique*, that's all."

"That's *all!*"

He seemed without words. She said softly, "It was nothing. I didn't mind. Really I didn't."

He slapped her.

She stood stunned, staring at him.

"If you ever do that to me again," she said, "I'll leave you."

"Leave me. Go now. Get out!"

"All right." Her face burned; her head spun. The blow had not been hard, but she was shocked. She would not cry, she was determined. She would clean off her makeup and go back to the room, and she would not talk to him the following day or possibly the following week, and most important of all, she would not cry.

The door opened, and Max Rober came in.

"Welcome," said Harry, "to the wake."

Max Rober looked at Clara quickly, but she turned away, sat down and opened her makeup box. She began to remove her makeup.

Max Rober offered Harry a cigar. Harry had never seen him produce a cigar case before. Plainly it was kept for important clients. "They say a condemned man can have a cigar if he feels the urge," said Harry.

"Eddie Darling did not much like the act," said Max Rober. "But he liked it enough."

"Enough for what?" asked Harry.

Clara sat very still.

"On the other hand, Mr. Chicot liked the act very much."

"Mr. Chicot has taste,"said Harry.

"It was a very risky thing to do, to bring Chicot into the act," said Max Rober. "It could have misfired."

"Being risky is being funny," said Harry. "Or do I mean risqué? Never mind."

Max Rober sighed. "Eddie Darling liked you but wondered how you'd go on the Route. He couldn't make up his mind, and Chicot liking you made it up for him. So he offers a booking on the circuit. . . . You pay your own rooms or hotels, but your railroad fares are chargeable to the company. There is a warning. The management will not allow any changes in your act from the first time you do it on through the end. They can fire you at no notice whatsoever if you do. Or if you use doubtful material. They money is two hundred dollars a week."

They stared at him.

"How much in English pounds?" Harry asked.

"Fifty pounds," said Max Rober, smiling. "But you'll lose half of that in expenses. Don't think you're Mr. Rockefeller. You aren't. Go easy and save what you can." He shook his head, a smile on his lips. "Viner and Viner, you are going to see America!"

Harry met Belle Alvin by appointment in the *Tribune* lobby.

She came downstairs chattering to a group of reporters and seemed perfectly at home with them. They wore large hats and long ulsters, and some had cigarettes in their mouths. This Harry thought effeminate. If a man smoked, a pipe or a cigar was surely the thing.

He raised his hat to Belle Alvin. She broke away from the men, waving to them on an equal basis of work, and smiled at Harry. "Gee, I'm but knocked out, Mr. Viner. Do you mind if we stop off somewhere for a drink or something?"

Harry asked, "Don't you usually go with your colleagues?"

"Yes, I do, but I got your note, and I wanted to talk to you."

These American girls, Harry thought, they say what they mean. Except that Belle Alvin was a working girl, and that surely made a difference. What am I doing here? Harry asked himself. I could get myself into trouble very easily with this girl, and do I want that? He said, "I can't think where to take you, except maybe a hotel."

She grimaced. "I've been sitting in a hotel lobby all day. You know that Albee is bringing Harry Lauder over? Well, the rumor was that he was here already, but of course, he isn't. Apparently they're still arguing about money."

Harry said, "I can believe it. I wish I was."

Belle Alvin whispered, "They say Lauder wants five thousand a week. And he has no contract with his agent, William Morris. They swore a Scotch oath, years ago, nothing on paper."

Harry shook his head. "I wish Bill Morris was *my* agent."

Belle Alvin yawned. "Look, could you bear to come to my

277

place and have a drink? It isn't far on the streetcar. I just have to pick up one or two things to eat on the way."

Belle Alvin lived in Greenwich Village. Inside an hour they had shopped in a delicatessen, and Harry had carried the groceries in a long brown paper bag up two flights of stairs to her apartment. It was roomy and furnished in light, unstained woods of a kind that Harry had not seen anywhere before. There was a white polar-bear rug, but the rest of the floor was polished, like a farm kitchen. Pieces of sculpture stood around (naked men and women, he noticed), and there were paintings on the walls of a kind he had not seen before, menacing and nightmarish. "From Paris," Belle Alvin explained, taking the groceries into her kitchenette. "Do you like them?"

"I wouldn't want to wake up to them," said Harry. "I'd think I was still dreaming."

She laughed. "They take getting used to. Help yourself to a drink. There's bourbon or rye. The ice is in the icebox. Fix me a bourbon, would you, please? Straight, with ice."

Harry did as he was bid and sat down on the long wickerwork sofa with velveteen cushions and was surprisingly comfortable. He drank the bourbon in his glass, decided he liked it and helped himself to another. A woman who drank bourbon straight, with only ice for company, was asking no favors of men. She must have a good head for the stuff. Harry looked around for a sign of a man, but there was none. Education, he decided, Belle Alvin was educated, one of the New Women, and well able to look after her life. She would not need to pose *plastique* to get money. All she would do was go out and write about something. Which was why he was here, to get her to write about them, why else would he be here?

Plastique.

The word stuck in his throat and his mind. Clara and he had not spoken pleasantly to each other since he had struck her. She had closed up, as the Americans said, like a clam. She was hurt, it seemed. That was a joke. *She* was hurt! How did she think he felt at the notion that his wife had gone to a sporting house and taken off her clothes for a lot of lechers to gaze at her naked body?

Clara had insisted she wasn't naked when he had thrown it at her that morning at breakfast, her face white and set at the question.

"Near enough, though," he'd sneered, feeling cruel and defeated. "Showing all you'd got, I know."

"If I did show all I'd got, I did it for you," Clara had declared, putting on her coat and hat.

"Me, me, how could it be for me?"

Clara paused at the door. "Because without the money from my posing *plastique* you would have starved, and so would I." Suddenly she pleaded, "I did nothing wrong, Harry. Honestly."

"I don't believe you." Harry had turned away harshly. "Nobody can pose unless they like it. Posing *plastique* means you have to keep still. I know, I've seen it. You enjoyed it, deny it if you can."

Clara opened the door. "All right. I enjoyed it. If that's what you want to hear."

"It's not what I want to hear; it's the truth!"

"All right, it's the truth then. I'm going out shopping. When will I see you?"

"Probably never. Just get out, you rotten whore."

Clara had stood in silence a long moment. Then she had left the hotel room. Harry had sat for a long time, the bitter word *plastique* running around and around in his head, and then he had put on his own topcoat and hat and followed her out into the streets of the city. He could not stay in the room another moment. He was afraid he might strike her again. She had said she would leave him if he did that. Very well, let her.

Still, he went out, the word *plastique, plastique,* bloody *plastique* running through his head. Once out in the street he had nowhere to go. It was then he had thought of Belle Alvin.

Harry poured himself a third drink. He felt he deserved it. Who would have thought, he asked himself, that Clara Abbott would turn out like that, who would have bloody thought it?

"Going at it a bit hard, aren't you, Harry?" Belle Alvin stood in the doorway. "Something wrong?"

Harry shook his head. "No, nothing."

"Doesn't look like it, the way you're attacking that bourbon." She smiled tolerantly. "Supper's ready, it's on your knee, I'm afraid." She brought in two trays, with broiled steaks and side salads. "Soak up the bourbon, and there's black coffee, if that's to your taste."

"Anything is to my taste," said Harry recklessly. "Anything at all."

"Eat and enjoy." Belle Alvin pointed to the food. "Talk later."

So they ate, and then they talked. Sometime, between the steak and the coffee, Belle Alvin went into what could only have been her bedroom and changed from her stern tailor-made business suit into a Japanese silk kimono. A scent of sandalwood now emanated from her, in soft waves. Harry felt better, sitting on the fragile wickerwork sofa, than he had felt in a long time. He felt like a success. Slightly fuddled by the bourbon, he told Belle Alvin about the Orpheum Circuit booking, which was to follow their half dozen appearances at Big Time Keith-Albee vaudeville houses in the city, before the act went the Route.

Belle sipped her black coffee. "I'll come along to the first— when is it?—and do a piece on you."

Harry told her.

Belle got up and noted it in a large working diary.

Harry said, "That's nice, but I didn't really come to see you just so you could write up the act, you know."

Belle Alvin laid down the diary. "Then why did you come, Harry?"

As Harry Viner was to ask a thousand times afterward, what was he supposed to do, pick up his hat and bloody leave?

Belle Alvin was gone when he wakened. It was already day, and Harry had a thick and throbbing head and very little memory of the night that had passed, except that it had been composed almost equally of sex and deep alcoholic sleeps. He staggered into his clothes and wondered if someday somebody would invent a medicine to take away a headache. He was almost out of the apartment when he noticed a piece of paper propped up against the cold coffeepot on the table. He stared at it blearily:

> Harry, that was nice. Let's do it again sometime if you want to. There are no strings, no obligations. You are a loving, clever man. Belle.

What sort of note, Harry wondered, staring at it, was that for a woman to leave for a man the morning after? It was more like something a man might write to a woman in like circumstances.

Harry crumpled it into his coat pocket and left the apartment. He did not tell Clara where he had been all night, and she did not ask him. A space was there between them for the first time.

To break it, he said, bathed and shaved and relaxed, "Well, like Max Rober said, America, here we come, eh?"

Clara made no reply.

Clara sat in the observation car of the Canadian Pacific and stared at the rain and the hills. Harry wore a long, new ulster topcoat, and Clara had a suit of tweed with the new six inches off her skirt length (very daring and attracting many admiring glances from men everywhere, which she ignored) and high-button shoes. Harry smoked a cigar and drank whiskey from his flask. Clara stared out the window and said to herself: this is a dream; it's dreamland; it hasn't really happened; somebody will come and take it away from us. The previous evening she had cried in the privacy of their sleeping compartment. Harry had asked her why she was crying now, when all was well, and she hadn't even blinked when he had struck her. She did not answer. She didn't know the answer then. She didn't know it now. She put away from her mind the thought that Harry had not made love to her often since she had told him she had posed *plastique*. It happened only when he wakened during the night, when he would take her, suddenly and, she thought, savagely, and go to sleep once it was over. She rarely came during these sudden encounters and felt dissatisfied and miserable. He did not mention her posing *plastique* again, but she knew it was in his mind. God knows, she thought, how he would feel if he knew about the cancan dance. How would he feel if he knew about the incident—which she had all but blotted from her own mind—with John Hyatt in his room above Mooney's bar?

Clara decided she had learned two things.

One, never tell a man the whole truth if you think it will harm your own interests, especially if that man is Harry Viner.

Two, never forget that a man regards a wife as his own property, whereas a girl like the girls at the burlesque had equal rights with a man, not belonging to him by contract.

Yet she loved him, didn't she?

Clara glanced over and saw his intent face—he was playing stud poker with a group from the show and, as usual, losing— and her heart turned over. Don't let me lose him, she prayed; he is mine and the only man I want. Let him want me, too, again, soon, like he used to.

She picked up a letter from her brother, Adam, one of the very few she had received from England.

My dear sister [he had written],

I'm more pleased than I can say that your fortunes have taken a turn for the better. I often see, when I am in London—which I sometimes am, now that Papa is allowing me to do some of his work—American managers in search of talented performers to export. And there you are, all the time, under their noses. The Alhambra is doing well enough, but Papa *will* book people like Sir Henry Irving. I'm against this policy and would prefer we stuck to the old, tried, *low* comedians and singers, but Papa is adamant. Marta is well, and we have a baby girl. I send my felicitations, my dear sister, to your husband and yourself. And trust we will meet again ere long.

Yours,
Adam

Tears came to her eyes.

Dear, dear Adam. How far away he seemed.

But she still had her husband, even if he was a difficult man to be married to. There he was, intense and combative over the cards, hat on the back of his head, cigar in mouth, ready with a joke or a laugh for anybody who was bold enough to engage him.

How brave he is, she thought.

How lucky I am, really.

The train thundered on, warm and lighted, into the chill mountain rain.

They had a week out at Banff when the Edmonton date was canceled because of theater repairs. They decided to stay at the Canadian Pacific Banff Hotel for a week. Clara stood, thrilled by the spectacle of mountain and pine forest. They lurched up the foothills on ponies and were rewarded by breathtaking views. "Isn't it wonderful?" asked Clara, in the high stillness.

"Only if you're a sheep," said Harry.

Yet he seemed to soften, and he smiled more, and he talked about the act less. Back in the large, quiet hotel he ate well. The menu was prodigious, English hotel fare, and offered everything from game to suet pudden, which they both ate in large quantities. They slept deeply, and they began to make love again in their old way. Harry was attentive, and she thought: he loves me again, and was supremely happy.

Harry was happy, too. "Or as happy," he told Clara, "as any comic can ever be."

The Vancouver *Sun* called Clara "The freshest English rose seen in Canada in many a long day." Of Harry it said, "Mr. Viner's jokes are good, if rather well-worn." Harry was furious.

At Seattle Harry was a guest speaker at the Chamber of Commerce. At Portland, Oregon, they all went on a trip down the Fraser River to see the salmon cannery. It was expected of them, the company manager said. On the Route, everybody accepted all invitations. It was good for business.

Business was good.

They played two-a-day, everywhere, to full or almost full houses. The company was a strong one. The headliners were a Japanese act, Kita Banzi, a group of tumblers and jugglers who threw Zenzo, the boy of the act, around the stage, on long ropes, holding jugs of water and never spilling a drop, to rapturous applause.

In San Francisco—they were playing the Orpheum—the rest of the company went out in the steamer on a trip around the Bay, while Harry stayed behind in the hotel, thinking. When Clara returned, he said, "I have a sketch for us."

"For our next tour?"

"For this one."

"Harry, please! We can't do a new sketch on this tour. We have our act."

"I know we have our act, but how many laughs are we getting? Tell me."

Clara sat down and looked at him. She said nothing.

"The Japs are a riot. We are not a riot."

"Harry, six months ago we were playing Little Time."

Harry stood on the hotel-room balcony and looked across the Bay. One of the most beautiful views in the world, Clara thought, and he doesn't even see it. "What we need is a good sketch, and this is it."

"Well," said Clara, "you'd better tell me about it."

"Better than that, I'll show you. Tomorrow."

"Tomorrow?"

"I'm going out now, I have to find the stage carpenter."

"Oh, Harry, please, no!"

Clara stood in the empty theater, smiling at the blackness. Only the manager and one or two of the company sat out there. It was eleven o'clock in the morning, and she felt sick. Harry had not been to bed the night before, nor had she. They had rehearsed the new sketch, despite Clara's protestations that they would never get permission to do it. They had not got permission to do it yet. Such a request was very unusual, the manager had told Harry, in his office, early that morning, but. . . . He smiled at Clara as he said that. Clara had gone into the office with Harry and had stood behind him, smiling vaguely all the time Harry spoke, long and earnestly, to the manager. The manager had listened to Harry, but his eyes had been for Clara.

She had said, "Harry, the manager can't do this; it's asking too much, it's out of his authority."

"What the *hell!*" Harry had turned around sharply.

"Isn't it?" Clara had asked sweetly.

The manager had tugged at his mustache and said no, he had a little more power than that. He could see the sketch himself and wire the head office if he thought it was good enough to include from now on. They might consider it. On his word. They took notice of a manager.

"Of course they do," said Clara.

"What?" said Harry.

"Shall we get ready?" Clara asked the manager.

"Of course, me dear. Of course."

"I'll just go and change, if you'll excuse me?"

When Clara had gone, the manager said, accusingly, to Harry, "Wonderful little wife you have there, Viner. I'm sure you appreciate her." He said it as if he did not feel that was the case.

Now they stood onstage, and Clara wished they were somewhere else. She was sure the sketch was amusing, but it did seem very rude, and after all, you were not supposed to be rude on the Route, not unless you were a headliner and could get away with it. She hoped she remembered her moves.

Harry came onstage to their "Naughty But Nice" music, as if drunk. He wore an oversize dinner suit. He carried a large frankfurter in his hand. He did a pratfall and got up slowly, looking at the large black box the props carpenter had made for him overnight. It was exactly to specifications, and it had cost them thirty dollars. The props carpenter had not been to bed either.

Still holding the frankfurter, Harry weaved toward the box, and Clara, who had been to the wings for three large swords, plunged them into the box, through the prearranged holes, and drew them out again. Three orchestra players, whom Harry had persuaded to come in early, played a majestic roll, a cymbal accompanying the thrust of each sword.

Clara said, "Get in the box!"

Harry said, "What?"

"Get in the box."

"I'm not going in the box," said Harry with the logic of the drunk, "without my little frankfurter."

He held the frankfurter up for all to see.

Out in the darkness the manager laughed.

"All right," shouted Clara, sweating cold down her back. "Then take your frankfurter into the box."

"You're sure?" asked Harry.

"Sure!"

Harry weaved to the box. Stopped. Turned around. "He won't like it in there."

"Why won't he like it in there?"

"Too dark."

"Well," said Clara, "I don't know what we can do about that."

Harry produced a brace and bit from the inside of his jacket.

"Bore a hole?"

"Bore a hole."

He did. A trick hole was already bored. Harry knocked out the piece of wood.

"Get in, please," said Clara.

Harry got in slowly, meanderingly, like a drunk.

Clara shut the lid down and with a flourish got ready to plunge the swords into the box.

The drummer ran a series of rim shots.

Harry opened the top of the box.

"It's dark in here."

"Close the lid! I said, close the lid!"

Harry closed the lid.

Clara got ready to thrust the sword through the box.

The frankfurter appeared through the hole.

It wriggled.

We will never, Clara thought, get away with this.

The manager's laugh had become a loud, choking cough.

Clara moved around the stage. Wherever she went the frank-furter followed her from the hole.

The manager seemed to be in need of resuscitation.

Clara approached the box.

The frankfurter drooped.

She stopped.

It perked up again.

The stage hands had arrived and were laughing loudly.

Clara approached the box from the rear.

The frankfurter was very still.

She raised the sword.

The frankfurter squeaked.

Harry called out, "Don't you dare interfere with my frank-furter!"

Clara thrust the swords through the box. One after the other, to the clash of the cymbals.

The stage lights went out. A long black pause with drums rolling.

Harry was out of the box when the lights went up.

He was putting mustard on the frankfurter.

He explained, as Clara held the frankfurter in her hand, "She always liked a little bit of frankfurter!"

Curtain, for God's sake, Clara silently screamed, holding the frankfurter in the air. The curtain came down.

In the dressing room the manager wiped tears from his eyes. "I'm going to wire the head office by Western Union, asking permission for you to put it in tonight." He blew his nose. "It's rude, but it'll get you laughs. I'll think of some story that your monologue won't work here." At the door he paused. "She always liked a little bit of frankfurter!" He shook his head. They could hear him choking down the corridor.

Harry took Clara in his arms.

"There, what did I tell you?"

"I feel a fool," Clara said. "It's so very indelicate, isn't it?"

"What isn't," asked Harry, "if it's any good?"

The frankfurter sketch stayed in when they played Los Angeles. Nobody at the head office of the circuit had objected yet, anyway, and they got a lot of laughs. One day they made their way to look at the new Mack Sennett film studios at Effie Street. Harry stood at the edge of the crowd of extras (they had got in on the nod of the head, through a friend in the company) and watched the work in progress. It was hot in Los Angeles that summer, and the dust raised by the pantomimers as they rushed to and fro before the hand-cranked cameras—operated by men in cloth caps worn back to front—seemed to Harry a comment on the whole thing. "There was a lot of dust," he said to Clara, "but what are they accomplishing?"

Clara was impressed by a large man with a mop of gray hair who chewed tobacco and spat accurately into a brass spittoon from ten feet away. This, they were told, was the boss, Mack Sennett. He did not direct the performers but seemed to have total, if eccentric, command of things. Seeing Clara standing there in a pretty satin dress and picture hat, he spat a stream of yellow tobacco juice narrowly past her into the spitton and said, "Be here eight o'clock tomorrow morning, young lady," and went into a building which they were told was his office. They were also told it contained a bath. They were also told that if Clara did report the following morning, Sennett might have forgotten about it or he might welcome her with open arms. There was no way of knowing what her reception or money might be. Clara was intrigued, but Harry was indignant.

"The fella's a big Irish plumber, and he's dishing out orders without a by-your-leave to such as us. We're pros, dear, and this is a business for amateurs." He gestured to the stage on which the actors were pantomiming. "Look at it." All around lay props: iron stoves, benches, tables, garden hose, bicycles, quietly rusting in the sun. "They don't even have a props department. They make it all up as they go along. Not like us; we polish and polish till we get it right. No, there's nothing in it for us, dear. We're vaudeville, and this is strictly for the people who never went the Route." A very fat man was doing a funny walk over and over again until he got it right. He wore an old derby hat and a dickey and a pair of wide, baggy trousers. "He moves well," admitted Harry, "but on a stage he'd have to get everything right first time." This, they were told, was Fatty Arbuckle, doing his second short at Keystone. There were high hopes for him.

They were introduced in a short break between filming. Arbuckle had done vaudeville, he told Harry, but this was his future. Hearing some of Harry's story, he said, "You should stay. You'd do good here. If you're good enough for the Route, you're good enough for this." He was called back to the cameras. He moved

287

nimbly, very fast for such a big man, and waved. "Come by tomorrow. We'll talk more."

They never did. Harry said, sitting in the hotel, a large whiskey in front of him to clear the dust of the film lot from his throat, "They might be all right as a novelty, the movies, but they're really only the nickelodeon arcades with a bigger picture. And you can't hear a word anybody says, you have to wait for the caption to know what they're talking about. Why should we take it seriously? We've got a good thing going as it is."

Clara had to agree. They were earning a very great deal of money, compared with anything that had gone before. They ate well and bought whatever clothes they needed and refurbished their costume basket. Harry played a lot of poker and lost some money, perhaps a little too much, but they were both still priding themselves that they had made the Route, so why not?

Harry said, "Of course, if you want to go down tomorrow morning, go. That mad fella Sennett might have meant what he said."

Clara shook her head. They had a contract to honor anyway. What could it mean, a few hours' work at best, and she'd have to go out there by cab and get back in time for the afternoon performance?

Harry said, "That Arbuckle. He's good. He's very good. But he's wasted there. He should have stayed in vaude."

"It would be lovely to live out here," said Clara. "Oranges growing outside the door, blue skies all the time, they say."

Harry looked incredulous. "It's a whole lot of nothing. It's the sticks. New York City is where the big successes are made. Thank God we're halfway through the Route, dear. All we have to do is make it back alive."

Harry was pleased with the way the act was shaping up. They were picking up laughs and some nice notices in the local newspapers, all of which Clara cut out and pasted into a large album she had bought for the purpose. Watching her sitting in the hotel room, doing that, Harry was conscious of how much he loved her and how lucky he was to have her. If he had not realized it for himself, it was forever being pointed out to him by incidents like the one with Sennett that day. Of course, everybody fell for a pretty face and a good ankle, and Clara had both. Not every woman would have gone out and earned money posing *plastique* either, he thought wryly. He would never tell her so, but on a lot of

288

reflection and heart searching, he finally decided he admired her for that. Somehow, the Belle Alvin interlude had canceled out the *plastique*.

Harry felt very protective, looking at Clara across the large lounge of the splendid hotel. Here they were, dressed in new clothes tip to toe, written up, applauded, rich. Harry relaxed and smiled. This was what he had worked for all his life. Shadows moving on a screen? Never.

In Denver the frankfurter was a riot. Offstage, they went to the Museum of Covered Wagons, and they shook hands with Colonel Cody and were shown in the Denver *Star* doing it. At Cincinnati they had a good-natured, rowdy audience, and the frankfurter stopped the show. In Cleveland and Columbus they were getting more applause for the frankfurter sketch than any other act in the company. Harry was pushing the gestures with the frankfurter as far as they would go. After the Friday performance in Columbus, the house manager came in with another man. This was a mild-looking gentleman, very expensively dressed and with an air of quiet authority. He fixed Harry with a cool, amused eye, and he said, "My name is Darling, I saw your act in New York, remember?" Harry swallowed and nodded, his knees suddenly weak. "I've just seen your sketch, which was not in the act then, was it? Mr. Viner, you know our rules. It is *out.* I can't understand how it ever got *in!*"

"But listen," protested Harry, "I'm getting a lot of laughs."

"I don't doubt it," said Mr. Darling, "But Mr. Albee—and everyone on the circuit, too—is insistent that the vaudeville house is for the family. Take the sketch out from now on. We won't dismiss you because I understand that the office somehow gave you permission to include it. It is thoroughly unsuitable. Good night to you."

And he was gone, the manager, a despairing but relieved figure, with him.

Harry sat down. Clara poured him a whiskey. He drank it in one gulp.

"I was waiting to try that in New York," he said, "and now no bugger's ever going to see it."

For the first time since they had been together, Harry deliberately got drunk that night. He did not mention the frankfurter sketch again.

289

Back in New York City they booked in at the Astor Hotel in Times Square. It was heavily overfurnished and comfortable, and they had the special rate of five dollars each for bedroom and bath. They ate gargantuan feasts for breakfast—orange juice, coffee, cereals, steak or mixed grills for fifty cents each. Sometimes, to save money, they went across the street to the Liggett drugstore and had coffee and orange juice and toast and a boiled egg for twenty cents. Harry pointed out, "Why do we have to save money? We're making money. Let's spend and enjoy."

Clara's reply was: "Harry, we have to save something. As it is, all we have at the back of us are a few hundred dollars. It's going out nearly as fast as it's coming in."

Harry frowned over his *Tribune*. "It's all right for you, dear. You've had plenty of everything most of your life. I haven't. I want to live a bit."

Clara could find very little to argue with in that. Still, she made all the small economies she could. Harry pointed out that engagements were coming in regularly, as indeed they were. They hardly ever had a free week. They grew used to taking cabs and eating in the best restaurants. They went to Hammerstein's Roof Garden and to Lüchow's and to Delmonico's, and they savored the delights of the city. Their days of poverty were behind them, and they basked in the full rich glow of success.

It went on for a year, the solid bookings, the good notices, the serenity of knowing exactly what they would be doing week in, week out. Max Rober was delighted for them and made himself available to see them, sometimes at short notice. They had become valuable clients. Clara liked the steadiness of this period; she was learning all the time; much of the applause was for her song; they were a well-balanced team. She was doing what she had hoped to do when she had left the Alhambra with Harry that night long ago, and she was profoundly content.

Then she got pregnant.

Harry could not believe it when she told him.

"Darlin', how could it happen?"

"It happened because you made love to me. During the night. When I was tired. I went to sleep again. I didn't use my douche. It was my fault as much as yours."

"It's nobody's fault." Harry sat down on the bed in the hotel room, his head in his hands. "But what a time for it to happen.

Just when we were getting ourselves known."

Clara sat down, too, and smoothed her satin housecoat. Harry was in shirt sleeves. It was a Sunday, the day they rarely worked; she had chosen it especially. She had known for two weeks. "Harry, a lot of showfolk have children."

"What can we do with a kid," Harry asked despairingly, "when we're on the road?"

"I think we'll have to try for bookings in the city only for a year or so. Then the baby can tour with us."

"You've seen kids touring." Harry looked at her, shocked. "I don't want my kid hanging around stage doors, short of sleep, going into the act at four years of age. I wouldn't wish this life on a kid."

"You want it for yourself."

"I'm me. How do I know the kid will want it?"

"You don't. But people like the Foys and the Ashtons seem to manage."

"They're theatrical families; it's the way they've always lived." He took her hand. "I wanted something better for any kid we might have. I always thought of a house."

"A cottage in the country, roses round the door?" Clara smiled. He was worried, but that was only to be expected, surely. "We can manage, Harry, I know we can."

He looked doubtful. "Do you think so, really?"

"Yes, I do. And, Harry, I can't do what I did before, I just can't.

Harry was silent a long time. The city was very quiet on Sundays; only the cries of cabbies and the odd roar of an automobile filtered into the room. Then he kissed her and said, "Whatever you want is what we'll do."

"Do you mean it?"

He kissed her again. "Of course, I mean it." He grinned. "Just make sure it's a boy. He'd be more useful in the act."

"Oh, Harry!"

Clara was astonished, thereafter, at his gentleness. He pressed her to lie down between houses, and although they could tell nobody, in case of canceled bookings (nobody would employ a pregnant performer at all if he knew about it), Clara guessed that Harry was secretly very thrilled about the whole business. At Christmas he came into the hotel loaded with presents: a huge teddy bear, a wooden rocking horse with a real leather saddle, a large pot doll with eyes that blinked and genuine hair, a toy drum in red and gold, with drumsticks.

Clara protested, "But a girl won't want a drum and a boy won't want a doll."

Harry kissed her. "What if it's twins?"

Clara laughed and loved him more than ever. She saved assiduously and began to inquire about unfurnished apartments, somewhere central where children were not objected to. The prices of such places were high, being designed for gentlemen in responsible business positions, with families, but Clara was determined they would have at least a year in the city. After that they would do their best to cope with the baby on tour. Other acts did it. So could they.

Unknown to Clara, Harry took Max Rober into his confidence.

Max Rober fell silent, taking time to light his Turkish cigarette. He's thinking exactly what I thought when I heard the news. Harry said, "You don't know whether to congratulate me or tell me I'm a bloody fool, do you, Mr. Rober?"

Max Rober extended his hand. "First, congratulations. Next, you are, as you say, Harry, a little bit of a bloody fool because you are in a very good position now, and it might have been better to consolidate." He surveyed his cigarette. "However, we must do what we can."

"As many bookings in the city as you can till March. Then it'll begin to show."

"Not before then?"

"She says not." Harry shrugged. "I have to take her word on that."

Max Rober nodded. "I think we can arrange that. Of course, you'll have to be prepared to face a few weeks out during that time, but I expect you can manage." He looked at his bookings diary. "How long will Clara be unable to work?"

"She says a month, but I'd make it two."

"So I should think." Max Rober looked stern. "It's a heavy responsibility being a mother."

"Being a father's no joke." Harry smiled, but he did feel very strange when he thought of himself in that capacity.

Max Rober poured them both a glass of whiskey. "It's pretty painless, Harry. It starts to get difficult when the bills roll in."

292

They drank to the coming child. Max Rober said, "Talking of money, how are you circumstanced?"

Harry shrugged. "I leave all that to Clara. She's the paymaster."

Max Rober nodded. "I suppose you'll have to economize a bit, now you know how things are." He was looking at Harry's newest suit, a seventeen-ounce worsted, cut close in the calf and waist, a hundred and twenty-five dollars. Many people had remarked on it, especially women. Women, Harry knew, always liked new clothes on a man. Except Clara. Clara asked the price first these days.

Harry said, "I bought this before I knew about Clara." Jees, he thought, if being a father has me apologizing now, how will it end? He laughed uneasily and said, "I could work single act while Clara's in the hospital."

Max Rober pursed his lips. "Not worth it for a short time only, Harry. People know Viner and Viner. Best to leave it alone."

Harry sighed. He had tried. What else was he supposed to do?

Max Rober shook his hand again and said, "Anything I can do at all, don't forget to ask me. And once again, congratulations."

Harry thanked him and walked out into the snowy winter street. A father? Was he really going to be a father? Was it possible that it was going to happen to him? He'd never wanted it, never even thought of it, and now here it *was*. A sudden male exhilaration coursed through him, and he threw his velour hat into the air. Several people stared at him as he caught it. So he put it back on his head and walked on down the street.

Clara felt very well during her pregnancy. She saw a Dr. Hartz, and he told her she seemed in good shape. He asked her if she had any history of any sort, but she did not tell him about the abortion in London. Somehow, as she sat in this Fifth Avenue office, with the wintry sun filtering through net curtains onto solid mahogany and thick carpets, it all seemed so very far away. Dr. Hartz was very satisfied with her, but he warned against continuing to work too long. "You are a fit young woman," he said, "but you lead an exacting life. Make next week your last."

Clara promised she would, and she stuck to the promise. They told Max Rober that there would be no more bookings after that week, the Colonial on Upper Broadway. They were on a good bill and had nice notices, including a very friendly one in the

Tribune, signed B. Alvin, which referred to the brilliant comedy of Harry Viner, "who refuses to take the easy road to cheap laughs." Harry cut that one out and put it in his pocketbook. He could not have said why, except it seemed somehow private. It contained his entire philosophy about comedy. Do not go for cheap, easy laughs. Do not ask, "Gimme your kind applause." That girl had seen the truth about him if nobody else did. He was impressed. He thought of writing a letter of thanks to her but decided against it. What could he say? Besides, he had a feeling he might be more interested in her than in the things she wrote. At some level, he knew that much. And everybody knew that men whose wives were pregnant were very susceptible, for obvious reasons. So he did nothing and felt furtively proud of himself.

In truth, he was more nervous than Clara was. It was Harry who felt sick most mornings and Clara who laughed off her own very real nausea. It was Harry who woke in the night, sweating, with stomach pains. It was Harry who ticked off the days and weeks on the calendar. It was Harry who finally said, "This week is our last."

Clara first felt the pains while still onstage. They came suddenly, frighteningly, in the middle of their last chorus of "Naughty But Nice."

> This very nice boy in Central Park,
> He said, "Me dear, let's go for a walk. . . ."

Clara staggered, and Harry paused and suddenly took her in his arms and walked her to the wings. He hissed, "Get a doctor, for Christ's sake!" and turned back to the audience, finished the chorus, took one bow and then held up his hand to still the applause. "If there's a doctor in the house, will he please go to the stage door and then to dressing room number two? It is very, very urgent. Thank you." He bowed to a rumbling and mystified house and ran, coldly sweating, past silent stagehands to the dressing room. The doctor, a young man, was there a moment later. He took one look at Clara, turned to Harry.

"You her husband?"

"Yes."

"We'll take her to my clinic."

"The hospital—"

The young doctor grimaced. "I'm just around the corner. The hospital's miles away. You got anything we can use for a stretcher?"

They used a property door as a stretcher and the stagehands carried Clara, still in her "Naughty But Nice" sailor-boy dress and covered by blankets and Harry's fur coat, out of the stage door of the theater.

The clinic was well appointed and quiet and obviously well-run. The young doctor, whose name was Blake, disappeared into the inner office with a nurse, while Harry sat, mute, in a waiting room. He sat there all through the night and into the bleak morning. Twice in the night young Dr. Blake came in to tell him personally that things were going as well as they could hope for. He put a decanter and glass at Harry's elbow and patted his shoulder. Harry found himself, for the first time in many years, saying the prayers his mother had taught him as a child. The response was automatic. He did not think about it. He just did it. He supposed everybody did, in a case like this. Don't let her die, Lord, he prayed, anything, anything, but don't let her die.

He sat, numb and suffering pain he had never imagined he could feel.

At seven o'clock in the morning Dr. Blake came in. His face was gray, and he looked much older than he had in the dressing room nine hours before. Harry tried to stand up, but he found his legs would not bear his weight.

Dr. Blake said, "She lost the child, but we've saved her life. She'll be weak, and I doubt if she can have another child, but at least you have her."

"Thank you, Lord," Harry said. "Thank you."

"What?" said Dr. Blake.

Harry shook his head. Tears ran down his face. He had not cried since Beckie died.

Clara lay in the clinic for four weeks, hardly moving. She did not weep; she just lay there mute, feeling nothing. When Harry came to visit, as he did each day, carrying bunches of flowers she never smelled and cartons of fruit she never ate, she could find nothing to say to him, except: "It's nobody's fault. It's life, that's all."

Harry sat hunched at the bedside, his face ashen and bleak despite his brave attempts at humor. "Come on, gel, cheer up, we'd have been a pair of shocking parents, right? Now then, what sort of an old man would I be for a kid? Terrible! So he's been saved all that. And you're young, there's lots of time; we don't have to believe everything the doctors tell us, do we? These things are never definite, are they? No, they're not, so all we have to do is rest and not think about anything except gettin' well, right? Just lie there an' let it all wash over you, and eat your grub and drink your milk, and we'll soon have the roses back in your cheeks, all right?"

Clara would try to smile, but it was a wan, little effort, and she knew that Harry was not deceived, any more than she was deceived by his act. They were both shattered, and they both knew there was nothing they could do to help the other, except, possibly just *be* there.

Dr. Blake was sympathetic and more concerned, he told Harry, about Clara's mental state, once the danger was over. Was it possible for her to go away for a vacation? She would need a period of recuperation; he would recommend at least three months and ideally six months out of the kind of strenuous work he understood her to do. Was there any possibility of that?

Harry, standing in his waiting room, told them bleakly that he would try all he could. To himself he said: how can she be out of the act for *six* months?

"The problem is that she is in a very low state, bordering on neurasthenia." Dr. Blake was a kindly young man, and he had never once mentioned money to Harry. "It's usual in these cases for a woman to be extremely depressed, you see, Mr. Viner?"

A woman to be depressed, Harry thought; has he any idea how I feel? He was drinking a bottle of Irish a day at the time and hardly eating at all. He stayed in his hotel room and talked to nobody, not even Max Rober. It had been going on like that for four weeks. The only time he left the hotel room was to go to the clinic to see Clara.

"The sun would do her good," said Dr. Blake. "But a complete change is the important thing. Get her away physically from it all."

"If I could do it," said Harry, without hope of doing any such thing, "I wouldn't be able to go with her. I'd have to work."

Young Dr. Blake nodded. "That might not be a bad thing. Let the wounds heal. Perhaps being apart for a while might help you both."

"It was my fault, all of it." Harry knew it was, in the awful night hours, when it would not leave his mind. "If I hadn't got her that way, none of this would have happened."

296

Dr. Blake took Harry's arm. "Mr. Viner, you are not God. You are a man. You can't blame yourself for that, any more than your wife can blame herself for miscarrying." He looked concerned. "You mustn't say any of this to her, you know. The best thing to do is keep cheerful, or anyway, don't let her see your own grief too often. She has enough misery of her own to bear."

Harry shook the doctor's hand. "You'll have to send me a bill."

"All in good time," said Dr. Blake. "No hurry at all."

"But there is," Harry insisted. "You see, I may not be able to pay you right away. We didn't have a lot of money saved and—"

Dr. Blake said, "It is all taken care of. Mr. Rober has been in. He has paid my bill in advance."

"He *has?*"

"He said only to tell you if you insisted. He also said. . . . I understand you haven't answered any of his letters or telegrams?"

Harry shook his head. A pile of unopened letters lay on the hotel-room table. He had not looked at them, or at a newspaper, for weeks.

"Well, Mr. Rober said get in touch when you can."

"He's been here, to see Clara?"

"He came on the second day. As soon as he heard. She was not well enough to recognize him. He's been in constant touch. He's a good friend."

"He is," said Harry. "He is."

Dr. Blake smiled. "Go around and see him, why don't you?"

Harry shook hands again and said he would do that, but once out in the street, he found that his steps led him back to the hotel. He could not face a busy office full of cheerful people going about their business. He had heard all the legends about showpeople carrying on, no matter who died. It wasn't the truth. Anyway, not for him. He could not have stood on a stage and told a joke; the words would have choked him. To laugh would be an obscenity. He would go to see Max Rober when he knew he was able to work.

Until then he would hide.

In the hotel room Harry took a slug from a new fifth of whiskey. He grimaced; he did not even like the stuff, but it deadened the pain, as the laudanum deadened Clara's pain, behind the drawn curtains of the clinic.

He sat at the table, loosened his collar, kicked off his shoes and took another slug of the alcohol. He pushed aside the issues of *Variety* that had piled up and that once he had perused line by line. He frowned at the letters (at least three, he recognized, were from Max Rober) but did not open any of them. He ignored the room maid's knock to come in and tidy the room and her plaintive call of "You sure you're all right in there, Mr. Viner?"

The girl knew about Clara and sympathized. Everybody in the hotel did.

Harry did not want sympathy. He just wanted to be left alone.

He drank again and again, as he prepared to face yet another black night, alone in the room.

Clara still felt drowsy from the laudanum, but she tried very hard to smile when Max Rober came in. Dr. Blake had told her the bill had been paid, only because she worried him about it.

"I don't know how to thank you, Mr. Rober."

Max Rober smiled. "I'll take it out of your earnings the year you top two thousands dollars." He patted her hand. "I was privileged to do it, for a lady like you."

"I could wire Papa." Clara felt her own voice was far away, almost as if it belonged to somebody else. "But he and Harry. . . . He would think Harry wasn't looking after me properly . . . or something silly like that."

Max Rober said, "Harry's very upset. I haven't seen him. I've left messages. He'll come around in his own good time."

Clara asked, eyes closed, "We only have a few hundred dollars, and if we aren't working, it'll all go—"

Max Rober put his finger to her lips. "Don't concern your pretty head about that, m'dear. I'll see he is all right."

"I'm not sure when Dr. Blake will let me work." Clara was saying the words because she knew they had to be said, but she felt nothing; she just wanted to lie there, do nothing, see nobody, not even Harry.

"Harry can do a single for a while," Max Rober said soothingly. "I'm sure I can get a few dates for him. Of course, the money won't be. . . ." He stopped quickly. "He was a single act before he met you, wasn't he?" He laughed. "He won't have forgotten how?"

"No," Clara said, facing the truth of it. "I'm not sure he ever really wanted me in the act. I forced myself on him, you know."

"I'm sure that's not true."

"It is. Like I forced the baby on him. He didn't want it. I

298

could have avoided the pregnancy, but I let it happen because I loved him and I wanted something of his. It was all my fault."

Clara closed her eyes. There. She had said it.

Max Rober was silent for a long time, and then he left the room, on tiptoe. To Dr. Blake he said, "Is she going to get over this?"

Dr. Blake nodded seriously. "In time, but it might be quite a time, Mr. Rober."

Max Rober put on his hat and went out into the snow.

Harry sat in the hotel room at the Astor. He ate almost no food, just an occasional sandwich. The alcohol was his meat and drink. He went out for his whiskey, and he only washed and shaved to go to the clinic, which Dr. Blake had said should be on alternate days. Harry did not mind. He was finding the task of being cheerful harder to bear, and anyway, Clara just lay there, smiling that polite, faraway smile, as if listening to the babble of an idiot. I'm suffering, too, he wanted to yell at her, I'm suffering too—can't you see that?

But of course, he went on telling his jokes and badgering her to eat her food, it was paid for! The nurses told him that she was eating practically nothing at all, just enough to keep her alive. Finally, he had fallen silent in the face of Clara's apathy, and the last few days he had just sat there miserably, holding her hand, saying nothing at all.

There was a sudden knocking at his hotel door one evening.

"It's all right, Brigid, I'm all right, the bed's made."

Max Rober's voice answered, "Harry, it's me, Max. Let me in, we have to talk."

"Nothing to talk about, Max. Not yet."

Harry took a slug of his whiskey. It was eleven in the evening. He guessed Max had just come from some downtown hall, where he had been watching one of his acts. Well, he didn't want to talk to Max Rober about acts or money. All he wanted was to be left alone.

"Open up, Harry. Please."

Harry called, "Max, thanks for all you've done. I'm all right. Just let me be."

"Harry, I have to talk to you. Clara comes out of the clinic on Monday. It's Friday today. Please, Harry."

Blearily Harry got to his feet and fumbled the door open.

Max Rober stood there smartly dressed, as always a carnation in his buttonhole and the Turkish cigarette in the holder. Harry thought: he doesn't know what sorrow is. He ushered Max Rober in with a flourish. "It isn't what you're used to, Max, but I call it home."

"Sit down, Harry," said Max Rober, closing the door behind him, "before you fall down."

Harry shouted suddenly, "Look, I know you've helped us, and thanks for that, but don't come in here and tell me what to do!"

"Harry," Max Rober said, cuttingly, "sit down before I knock you down."

"What?" Harry swayed. "You'll do what?"

"That girl is in the clinic, just lying there. She thinks it's the end of her road, and maybe it is in a way. She needs to come out to a man she can lean on, not a drunk." Max Rober took the fifth of whiskey and, before Harry could stop him, went into the bathroom and closed the door. Harry could hear him pouring the precious liquid away. Harry beat at the door with his fists and his feet, but when Max Rober came out, he had slumped back at the table.

"I can always go out and buy another bottle, Max."

"I know you can, and after I'm finished talking to you, you probably will. There is a chance you might not, which is why I'm here." Max Rober sat down opposite to Harry and began to open the piled-up letters and to read them. Harry watched him foggily.

"Three of my own letters asking you to call me. Three statements from the hotel manager about his bill, we'll pay that. Two tailor's bills and two costumer's bills for Clara's costumes, we'll pay them, and a statement from Clara's bank saying you have three hundred and forty-two dollars in the world."

"There should be more than that," Harry said.

"There isn't. When you've paid these bills, there'll be one hundred dollars."

Harry shook his head. "I thought we saved more than that."

"It's very hard to save on the Route. I don't blame you for that. Headliners can save; some of them even do. For a standard act, it comes harder."

"Standard act," Harry shouted, "standard bloody act. I'm better than that, *standard* act. That's rubbish, and you know it, Max."

"Yes, I do, and there's still time to capitalize on your success on the Route."

300

Harry blinked. "I never knew we were a success."

"You were. You have been noticed in all the things you've done since, too. I can even get you bookings as a single comic."

Even, thought Harry hazily, what's all this *even* stuff?

"I don't want any bookings as anything. I couldn't go out and face an audience. I'd die."

"Yes, you would," said Max Rober, "as you are now. Once you've been to the Turkish bath on Forty-second you'll feel different, especially when you've been there all night."

"I have two questions for you, *Mr.* Rober," said Harry. "One, who's going to get me to this bloody Turkish bath, and two, who's going to keep me there all night?"

"I am," said Max Rober grimly.

The day before Clara was due to leave the clinic she had a visitor. It was John Hyatt. He came in awkwardly, holding a large bunch of white hothouse roses, and he sat on the edge of his chair at the side of her bed.

Clara thought, through her laudanum haze: how sweet, how very sweet.

She said, "John, I'm sorry. About that night!"

"It's all right. I'm the one to apologize."

"How did you find out I was here?"

"Sure, hasn't the man called three times already," said the nurse, taking the flowers from John Hyatt's hands. "Let me go away and put them in water for you; sure, you've nearly crushed the poor things to death, so you have!"

John Hyatt released the flowers with a gasp of apology and laughed, embarrassed. He's a nice man, Clara thought, he still colors up easily, and he looks older, but nicely older, he's put on weight, he has a cared-for look.

"I saw it in *Variety*," John Hyatt said. "About you being in here, so I came along. How are you, really?"

"I'm fine. I'll be fine." Clara was sitting up now, the pillows piled behind her.

"You don't look well enough to come out yet. Not to me."

"I've been here four weeks, John, I have to come out sometime. Besides, this place isn't cheap."

He looked at his feet. "If it's money, can I help?"

Tears came to Clara's eyes. She reached out and took his hand. "Thank you. That was very nice. The bills are all paid. I'm quite fit again. I walked around this room yesterday."

"You're not going back to work or anything?" He looked uncertain. "Is Harry around? The nurse told me—"

"He won't be in today. He's coming tomorrow to collect me." Clara saw a sudden cloud on his face, and she thought: the man doesn't feel anything for me still, surely? "Tell me about yourself, what's happening to you?"

John Hyatt grimaced. "Shows you don't read the small print in the musical press."

"We'd just come back from a tour."

"I wanted to write to tell you I was ashamed of myself that night." John Hyatt looked at his shiny brown boots. "I had drink taken, but that's no excuse."

"It's all right. I've forgotten it, please forget it, too."

John Hyatt sighed and nodded. He looked relieved.

"You look prosperous, John." His suit was a good dark serge, and he had a high white collar and a heavy silk tie. A silver shamrock tiepin held it in place. She knew it was a present from a woman. It was something the John Hyatt she knew would never have bought for himself.

"How's the songwriting?"

"Going very well. I have a partner; Harry always said my words were no good, and he was right. We've sold a few songs, and we're doing very well. Making progress. It's hard work, but I think we'll get there."

"Tell me what you've written?"

"Well, 'Dream of Summer' and 'Sullivan's Daughter Ruth' and. . . ." He grimaced. "And 'Ragtime Irish Mary.'" He shook his head. "We write what people will buy."

"Do they buy this ragtime stuff?"

"Yes, the young people. Of course, the ballad is still the big seller. Jimmy, my partner, he's the one thinks ragtime's here to stay, as much as anything ever is. I'm not sure. I can do it, but I'm not sure I like it as much as the ballads. Still, we eat."

He did not ask any questions about Harry, and Clara thought: he's been talking to the nurses; he knows how things are. She felt touched. It was exactly the thoughtful kind of thing he would do. Looking at him, she thought: why did I never see his interest, why was I never really drawn to him, much as I like him?

He doesn't excite me, she thought. Harry does, that's all.

She wondered if she would ever be excited by anybody ever again. She doubted it.

"I like the tiepin."

"It was a present."

"From a lady?"

"Well, yes, it was." He looked uncomfortable and said no more.

Clara smiled, for the first time since she had come into the clinic. "You're a dark horse, John. Who is this you have, tucked away somewhere?"

"My wife," John Hyatt said painfully. "I'm married now."

Clara felt surprised and in some small way let down. Good Lord, she told herself, I am very low, the poor, dear man is entitled to marry somebody if he wants to; what on earth am I thinking about, for goodness sakes?

"Oh, I am glad," she said. "You'll make a wonderful husband."

"I'm a father as well," John Hyatt had said, and could have bitten his tongue off when he'd said it. "A boy. . . ." He faltered. "He's just three months old. . . . I'm sorry. . . . I shouldn't. . . . I forgot. . . . for a minute. . . ."

"That's all right. . . . You meant nothing. . . . I know. . . . I'm just silly." The tears ran steadily down her face.

John Hyatt went out quickly for the nurse, who came back in and said, "There, there, my love," and took Clara's hand. "It's what she should have done weeks ago. She needs this." The nurse indicated the door with a nod of her head. "You've worked a miracle, sir, but you'd better leave, I think. This is going to go on for a while."

John Hyatt stood at the door and watched Clara as she cried. On the way out of the clinic he inquired at what time Mr. Viner was expected to collect his wife the following day.

Their room at the Astor was full of roses. There were get-well cards spread around and fruit in bowls. It was as cheerful and homely as any hotel room could be. Harry looked at his watch, put on his melton topcoat and the velour hat he had thrown into the air in Central Park and tried to control the shaking of his fingers as he pulled on his soft brown kid gloves. He looked good in the mirror, but he felt awful. He had not taken a belt of Irish in three days, and he was feeling it. Those three days had been spent sweating it out in the Turkish bath, apart from the business meeting with Eddie Darling, Albee's booking manager, in Max Rober's office. Mr. Darling, who was as charming and sympathetic as Mr. Albee was said not to be, had indicated with a gesture that he did not need to see Mr. Viner's act, he had seen it already. He was very sorry to hear of the indisposition of Mrs. Viner, and he wished her a speedy recovery. If Mr. Viner wished to start, rather low down on the bill, he was afraid, but it was a case of walking before running, he could offer him, on behalf of Mr. Albee, a few dates, not unfortunately all in New York City, in the next months, just on speculation, see how it all went. He would work out details with Max Rober if they were interested. Of course, the money might be lower, but Mr. Albee was generous if one was a success.

Harry had said he certainly was interested. He had shaken hands almost too gratefully with Eddie Darling, and Max Rober had seen Mr. Darling into the outer office. Harry thought he heard the words, "Very good of you Eddie, I appreciate this. . . ." Max Rober came back into his office, looking pleased. "I'm glad it's tomorrow you go and get Clara. I'm getting very tired of Turkish baths!"

Harry shook his hand. "Thanks, Max. I mean it."

"I know you do, Harry." Max Rober looked as if he might say more, but he contented himself with: "Look after her."

"I will," said Harry, meaning it more than he'd meant anything else in his whole life.

At the clinic Harry was astonished to see John Hyatt.

"Good God, what are you doing here?"

"No time to talk. I saw Clara yesterday."

"Oh. . . ." Harry shook his hand. He felt like death. He was finding it hard to think straight. "Why are . . . I mean I'm glad to see you but. . . ." Harry closed his eyes.

"Are you all right?"

"Of course, I'm all right." Harry looked around the waiting room uneasily. "Look, I have a cab waiting outside, John; why don't I get Clara home and you come and see us tomorrow or something?"

John Hyatt took a long time before he replied.

"How are you for money?" he asked.

"I don't know what that has to do with you," Harry said harshly.

"How are you for money?"

304

"No bloody business of anybody's how we are for money!"

"Harry, it's John Hyatt. How are you for money? I know the clinic bill is paid, but how are you for money?"

Harry said slowly, "Why should you care?"

"Never mind. I do."

"It's her, isn't it?"

John Hyatt paused. "I'm a married man now myself. I want to help. That's all."

"Married yourself?" Harry peered at him. "You're a man of surprises, John." He slapped John Hyatt on the back. "And you're a hell of a friend. I'll tell you how we are for money. We have enough to last us till I get my first pay packet; that's how we are for money. My agent's been a brick, but I can't ask him for another dime."

John Hyatt took a long white envelope from his inside pocket. He shoved it into Harry's inner pocket and buttoned up his topcoat. "It's only a loan," he said, and started for the door.

"It's always only a bloody loan with you," Harry called after him. "You never get paid bloody back!"

"I know that," came John Hyatt's voice as he left. "It doesn't matter."

Harry told Clara nothing of the incident.

Clara was very weak, and her legs seemed to be made of rubber. She was glad, she told Harry, to get to the hotel. She sat gingerly in the soft chair and smiled feebly. Harry said, "Can I get you anything at all? Coffee? Anything?"

"No, thanks. You look pale, Harry."

"I'm all right."

He didn't kiss her. He didn't feel she wanted him to or that he had the right. Dr. Blake had warned him anyway against any form of sexual passion for a matter, conservatively, of several weeks, possibly longer. Harry did not feel he would ever be able to touch her again, after what he had done to her.

Clara slept alone in the big bed that night, and Harry had the couch.

Gradually, over the first couple of weeks, Clara began to use her limbs again. Some strength returned to her body, but very slowly. She did not feel any emotion whatever, about anything. Between them there was a wall. They both knew it was there, but neither of them admitted it. They spoke rarely, as if to a stranger, and Clara wondered how long this would last and if she would be able to bear it.

Harry went out a good deal and returned late, sometimes the worse for drink. She did not question him as to his doings. In fact, he had been playing poker a little and drinking a lot. Without the drink he would not have slept at all. He had no work yet. Max Rober had told him to rest up for a month before he took on any engagements. He felt lost and alone. It was all his fault. All of it.

Belle Alvin was surprised to see him.

"Well, hello, stranger." She held the door open, and Harry walked in. He was conscious of her curious eyes on him. He sat down on the wickerwork settee without taking off his topcoat.

"You look as if you need a drink."

"I need a lot of things, but a drink will do for a start."

She asked no questions and poured him a large one. He sipped it slowly, looking at her. Belle was wearing a long silk housecoat he had not seen before. A smell of broiling meat came from her kitchen.

"Am I interrupting supper?" Harry asked, starting to his feet. "Are you expecting somebody?"

Belle nodded. She looked poised and attractive and healthy. Her breasts pushed against the housecoat, a plump brown leg swung free up to the thigh. She saw his look, returned it and did not cover the leg. Harry thought guiltily of Clara, lying in the darkened hotel room, a handkerchief soaked in water and vinegar over her forehead to ward off the persistent headaches she seemed to have most days. "If they're due, I'll go. I thought I'd call in. I was passing the door." He swallowed his drink and got to his feet.

"No, you weren't passing the door, Harry, and no, you aren't leaving. You look like hell. Sit down, have another drink and excuse me while I make a telephone call."

"You got a telephone in now?" Harry was surprised.

"I need one for my work. Comes in useful socially, too." Belle got up and went into the kitchen, closing the door behind her. Harry heard her voice indistinctly, but from what he heard of it, she was irritable with whoever was on the other end of the line, and finally, on a rising note, she terminated the conversation, the telephone being replaced on the hook with a decisive and final click. She's been talking to a fella, Harry thought; she's put him off, and he's mad about it. Nobody as ruthless as a woman when she wants one fella and doesn't want another. He drank his bourbon. It was nice to be wanted.

Not that he felt like doing anything about it. He was here, he realized, for sympathy, not sex.

Belle came back into the room. She poured them both another drink and waited.

Harry said, "Clara got pregnant. She had a miscarriage and lost the kid."

"I'm sorry. Truly." Belle Alvin sounded sorry. That puzzled Harry. Women, he thought, one minute they're at each other's throats, but on a thing like this they're sisters.

"Anyway, she's still pretty sick."

"You look pretty sick yourself."

"I'm all right. I have to start work soon."

"Do you want to?"

"I couldn't tell a gag to save my life," said Harry truthfully. "It would stick in my throat. But it's a case of having to."

Belle Alvin asked, "When is your first date?"

"Three weeks."

"You'll be ready by then."

"I doubt it, the way I feel."

Belle Alvin was silent a long time. "She doesn't blame you or anything, does she?"

"If she did," said Harry, "I wouldn't mind."

"Well then?"

"It's worse. I blame myself."

Belle got to her feet and made for the kitchen. "When did you last eat?"

"I dunno. Sometime yesterday, I s'pose."

"You're going to eat now. Supper's ready. And you can cut out the self-pity. It isn't like you. Finish your drink while I dish up."

"I'm not hungry," Harry protested, but he was.

He ate the steak and salad and drank a good deal more bourbon, and at some point he made love to Belle Alvin on the wickerwork couch, and then he slept. He did not remember very much about it, except that it was not a sex scene in the ordinary way with Belle (and that was unusual, since she was a very sexy lady) but more a loosing of pent-up emotion, a sudden release, like a crying jag for a woman. He felt very grateful, and he actually

307

thanked her, a thing he could never remember doing with a woman ever before in his whole life. At midnight Belle finally put him in a cab.

Clara was asleep when he let himself, on tiptoe, into the hotel room. She looked very pale, lying there in the moon's silver wash, and he had an insane desire to waken her and tell her how much he loved her. Bloody stupid, I'm drunk, he told himself, what are you on about, get to bed and get to sleep before you do something stupid, like tell her about Belle Alvin, you silly bugger!

He went to bed and slept deeply, for the first time in many days.

It was only with a great effort that Clara made herself do any work around the apartment. She reproved herself: you have to do something to break yourself of this depression. You must. Or you will be no use to Harry or yourself or anyone else. She took Harry's clothes out of the wardrobe and began to sponge and press them, including the old brown check he had not worn since the previous winter. He would need to look smart, on and offstage, now he was working on his own, and there was no money for new clothes, for street or act. She got out the trouser press and ran her hand through his suit pockets to clear them. It was then that she found Belle Alvin's note.

> Harry, that was nice. Let's do it again sometime if you want to. There are no strings, no obligations. You are a loving, clever man. Belle.

Clara read it with a heart of stone, recognizing it for what it was and much much more. Then she put it back in the pocket and put the suit away.

I am married to this man, she thought, and yet do I know him at all?

Did this happen, she wondered, while I was in the clinic?

Surely not.

Was it still going on?

Who was the woman? She seemed to have heard the name Belle before. When, where, she could not immediately recall.

She sat down to think about it, to try to remember.

Belle Alvin looked at Clara standing there, white-faced. She listened to Clara's name and then stood wordlessly aside and let her into the apartment. Clara sat down on the wickerwork couch and gazed, dismayed but trying not to show it, at this exotic creature Harry Viner had found more attractive than herself. Belle was smoking a cigarette in a long jade holder and wore a Chinese kimono, and she was of a piece with the room. She offered Clara a drink as if she were a casual caller, not the wife of a man she had slept with.

"I'm having bourbon, what about you?"

Clara did not have to like her, but she admired her nerve.

"No, thank you."

Belle poured the liquor over the ice in her glass and sat down opposite Clara.

"I suppose you're here about Harry?"

"You suppose right."

"How did you find out?"

Clara did not answer that. She was here to ask questions, not answer them. "I got your address from your newspaper. I had to say it was urgent and personal. Which it is. Do you love my husband?"

Belle laughed. "Yes, I suppose I do, in a way."

"That's a curious answer."

"It's the only one I have."

Clara looked around the alien room. She could not picture Harry in it. "How long has this thing between you been going on?"

"Shouldn't you be asking Harry that?"

"I'm asking you."

"Have you talked to him yet?"

"No."

"I think," said Belle Alvin, toying with her drink, "that you'll find he loves you, not me."

"I can't believe that." Clara fought back the tears from her eyes. She must not show weakness before this woman. "I wish I could, but I can't. I asked you how long this has been going on."

Belle Alvin sighed and then leaned forward. "Don't play the wronged wife. Not with him. It won't work with him. Be sensible, go home and forget you ever came here."

"Please don't give me advice about my own husband," Clara said icily, feeling numb and bereft. "I take it you want him for yourself?"

309

"Yes, I do," Belle Alvin said. "But I'm not sure he wants me. Why don't you go home and leave him to do the deciding?"

This woman says she loves him, Clara thought, but she can't love him. Where are the tears; where is the terrible tearing pain; where is the bleak loneliness?

She said, "The person who will do the deciding is me. I have been wronged, and I'm not impressed by clever, sophisticated talk from whores."

Belle Alvin made a face. "I'm sorry you think that. The man made up his own mind. I didn't drag him into bed."

"Any woman can get any man into bed under certain circumstances," Clara said coldly. "All she has to do is take off her drawers and lie down with her legs open."

Belle Alvin smiled, but she looked surprised.

"I can see why Harry likes you. Go home and forget it. Take my advice."

"You have a career," Clara said, "and now you have my husband."

"What?" Belle Alvin looked startled.

"His baggage will be here first thing in the morning." Clara stood up. "And he'll arrive shortly afterwards, I should think."

"Are you serious?"

"Never more so."

Belle Alvin shook her head. "I'm sorry about the baby, I know you're upset, believe me. Harry told me about it—"

"Please don't talk about it," Clara said, feeling sick. Had Harry talked about *their* child, with this woman, in this room, amongst all this silly furniture and the obscene statuettes and the pictures she couldn't understand? The very thought turned her to ice. "I'm going now. I can't say it's been nice to see you. Good-bye and remember me when my husband goes off with another woman, because he will!"

"Mrs. Viner"—Belle Alvin tried a last time—"don't be a fool to yourself."

Clara slammed the door and stood trembling on the other side of it. She did not cry until she was safely back at the hotel.

The hotel staff were surprised when Clara took another room and even more surprised when she said that under no circumstances was Mr. Viner to have the key. It did not take long for Harry Viner to find out where she was (on the same floor, as it

310

happened) and bang on the door for admittance.

"Go away, Harry, I have nothing to say to you. Your bags are over at Miss Alvin's. She's expecting you."

"*What?*"

It was nice to hear his anger. It fueled her own.

"I'm going back to England this week. I will wire Papa for the fare. Please go. I don't want to talk anymore." Nor did she. She stood on the other side of the door, in her nightgown, and trembled with suppressed anger and loathing. To have done *that* while she was pregnant, to have talked to *that woman* about their child!

"Look, love," Harry Viner said in a different voice, "open the door. Let's talk."

"No."

"Please."

"Harry, you are a fraud and a lecher. I loved you, and I trusted you, and you let me down. You went with that awful woman, Harry—"

A long pause. Then: "It was nothing, I tell you it was *nothing!*"

"It's never nothing."

"I got fed up with your *plastique—*"

"All I did was pose. You slept with her."

"It's the same."

"No, it isn't the same, and you know it."

Harry breathed in. "What am I supposed to do, go to confession or something? All right, I slept with her. All right, I've slept with one or two other girls. Or anyway, I've rogered them. So what! It means nothing!"

"It does to me. Go away, Harry, I don't want to talk to you. You sicken me."

"What about me?" He was hurt, she could tell that. It was good to know he was in pain, too. Hurting herself, she said, "I don't want any more to do with you, Harry. I loved you. I trusted you. It's over."

There was a long silence on the other side of the door.

"Who asked you into my life?" Harry Viner asked. "I didn't. You volunteered into it. You've been round my neck since the day I first saw you. I don't want any woman round my neck."

She said nothing.

"Your passage money home is under the door. It's all right.

311

It isn't my money. John Hyatt gave it to me. Take it, and good luck."

His footsteps receded down the corridor. Somewhere a door slammed.

Clara thought she would die. She looked down. A long packet was half pushed under the door.

Clara sailed on the *Berengaria* for England the next day.

Are We to Part This Way?

Papa met her at the dockside.

He looked older, she thought, shocked. He's gray, and he's heavier around the middle. His topper shone, and so did his black boots and his gold watch chain and the pearl stickpin in his tie. He had on his lavender gloves, held his silver-topped walking cane, wore a crombie topcoat and bore in his hands a bunch of English garden roses. That makes two men, Clara thought, who have brought me roses, John Hyatt and Papa, both of them big, responsible men. Why is it that I am not always at ease with them?

He took her in his arms. Tears came to his eyes.

"My dear girl, how pale and thin you are!"

"I have been ill, Papa. But I am well again. The sea voyage has done me a world of good." At least she had stopped taking the laudanum three days out.

"Soon have you well, soon have you well again. Come along, let's get these lazy porter fellows to get your stuff, hope you haven't brought your entire wardrobe."

"Only one small trunk."

"Traveling light, like the light infantry, eh?"

"Well, I came on the spur of the moment."

Papa paused. "All over with that fellow, is it? We'll talk later, what? Now, where are those porters?"

Papa was in good form. He seemed more cheerful, to be treating her as a woman of the world, as if she merited that now. He did not seem so stern and unbending as she remembered him, anyway toward her. This did not extend to anything else. He criticized the seating arrangements in their dining car to Victoria, and he was not impressed by the quality of the food served on the train, which seemed to Clara excellent. They ate oxtail soup and whitebait and roast beef with fresh spring cabbage and spotted dick with custard sauce, with claret to drink and brandy to follow. Papa had a cigar.

"Enjoy that, my dear?"

"I haven't eaten as much as that for years, Papa."

"Do you good. Don't suppose the food was much on the boat?"

"It was excellent, Papa."

"Glad to hear it. The thing is, if they're not up to scratch, complain. That's the ticket. Always make a fuss. You're paying good money out. You're entitled to good service."

The train pounded through the green English countryside, and Clara saw the red of the pillar boxes and the tiny fields and the deep green trees and the policemen on bicycles with a deep feeling of home.

Papa said, "I behaved badly, I admit it, but I have had second thoughts. You are coming home, and you are coming as my daughter." He waited. "I take it, everything is over with Viner?"

"It seems to be, anyway as far as he is concerned."

"You don't love him anymore, or he you, is that the way of it?"

"Something like that."

Papa patted her hand. "You're home now. It's all over. Let's talk about it no more."

Clara nodded. It seemed as good an idea as any.

Papa raised his *Times* and read for a while. From time to time he took a pinch of snuff from his old Japanese snuffbox.

At length, he lowered his paper and followed a new train of thought. "My whole intention, Clara, is to improve the standard at the Alhambra. I am only booking those acts that I feel will add tone to the place and reflect credit upon the person who presents them, to wit, myself."

Clara didn't know whether it was the wine or the food or both, but she began to feel better. It was indeed good to be home. "Does Adam agree with you about that?"

314

"Adam," said Papa, "does not run the Alhambra yet."

"How is his marriage?" Clara asked curiously.

"How should his marriage be?" asked Papa. "It is like all marriages; it has its up and downs. As Adam, I believe, wrote to you, he is now the father of a small girl, named, I am proud to say, after your dear mother." He looked at her delicately. "The possibility of anything in that direction, circumstanced as you are, is not, I suppose, on the cards?"

Clara shook her head. She felt suddenly very, very tired.

"No, Papa. I'm afraid, as you say, that it isn't on the cards."

Papa nodded as if it was what he expected to hear, but he said nothing. He just pressed her hand.

"Can't pick up a good hand every deal, me dear, can you?"

She could have kissed him, but she knew he wouldn't have wanted that, and besides, he was already complaining to a waiter about the brandy being served in a wineglass.

The house in Leazes Crescent looked exactly the same. Except that Jean, her old nurse, was gone.

"Good old soul." Papa blew his nose. "Died in harness. In her kitchen chair. God rest her." Papa blew his nose. "Sixty meself this year. Beginning to count the days, me dear. Beginning to count the days."

Clara felt a sudden fear. "Nonsense, Papa, you'll live to be seventy-five."

"Might, might, y'never know." Papa helped her out of the cab. "Not many do, do they?" At the door as they went in, he added, "Hope you get on with Marta. She's the woman of the family now."

Marta was indeed the woman of the family. A mother, too, but only of a girl, which reduced it all somewhat. Nonetheless, as Papa said, in apology, "There's plenty of time for boys, what?"

Clara and Marta kissed on the cheek, and Marta said how very thin Clara was. Clara said that motherhood suited Marta and admired the baby, brought downstairs from the nursery (Clara's old room, to her consternation) for inspection. "It was the lightest room, and we didn't think you'd be back, well, not to stay," said Marta, dismissing the young nurse and showing Clara to her new room at the back of the house. "I hope you'll be comfortable here; it's our number one guest room, not that we have many guests."

"It looks very pleasant." Clara smiled, trying not to let her

315

eyes show anything. The room was chill, despite a small fire in the grate. I want my old room, she almost cried. "I wonder where my personal things are?"

Marta laid her hand lightly on Clara's arm. "I think Papa put them in the attic, if you mean your dolls and such?"

"Yes, I do, actually."

"I'll get one of the maids to look for them later, if you like."

"No. I'll have a look myself."

Marta frowned. "I don't think members of the family should root around in attics, Clara. The servants would think it very odd."

"I lived in this house before you married my brother," Clara said. "If I want to go and root around the attic, I will go and root around the attic, thank you very much."

"I see that your adventures have not crushed your disposition," declared her sister-in-law.

"My adventures, as you choose to call them, have made me perfectly capable of looking after my affairs, dear Marta."

"I would not have thought that," replied Marta huffily, "or else why are you here without your husband? But perhaps I should not ask such questions. I'm sorry. You do not look at all well."

"I am not at all well." Clara took off her hat and laid it on a chair. "And my husband is not here with me for reasons that are his and mine."

"I do not wish to pry," said Marta, "but is he still in America?"

"Indeed he is; he is working there."

"And shall you be going back?"

"Marta, I am hardly here."

"I know, but since I have to run this house, it would be some kind of courtesy to tell me your plans. Dear Papa and Adam are merely men and would never ask. It is not that I am vulgarly curious, simply that I need to know what foods to order and what household arrangements to make."

"If what you want to know is why I have been ill, it is because I lost a child. If what you want to know is will I ever go back to my husband, the answer is I do not know, probably not. Now, may I please rest? It has been a long journey."

"Of course." Marta stood at the door, and her voice softened. "I am very sorry, my dear." After a pause she added, "It just goes to show that one should be content with what the Good Lord freely giveth and not strive for more."

316

"You really believe that, don't you?" Clara asked, tired now to the very bone.

"Yes, dear sister-in-law, I really do."

Marta closed the door gently, and Clara took off her shoes, dabbed some eau de cologne on her temples (she had developed a slight headache in the last moments) and lay down on the bed. The firelight danced on the walls, and despite her misgivings, a sense of home came over her, and closing her eyes, she slept until suppertime.

Adam was in good form and looked older and heavier. He kissed Clara warmly and commented on her appearance. "Lost all your puppy fat, I see. And a good thing, too." Plainly, he had been told the facts of her life by Marta. Adam had been looking after things at the Alhambra while Papa was away, and he seemed knowledgeable about the business in a way that surprised Clara. As they ate (pea soup, grilled sole, saddle of mutton and red currant jelly, baked potatoes, brussel sprouts, peas, cabbage, jam roll and custard, Stilton cheese, fruit and nuts), he asked many general questions of Clara, but no personal ones at all.

"Tell me, do the American acts strike you as generally good? Is it usual for a family to attend together?"

"As if to church?" Clara asked. There was hock and claret to drink, and she had taken her share, and her spirits had lifted in consequence.

"No reason why a man should not take his family to the Alhambra," grunted Papa. "Raise the standard, that's the thing. Give the people good quality; let them see something above the streets they live in."

"Papa," said Adam, grimacing at Clara, "is determined to ruin us with his thirst for gentility. We have played to some very poor houses both last winter and this one, owing to his booking playlets featuring eminent London actors as our main attraction."

Clara waited for the storm.

It did not come.

Papa glowered into his claret. "The people aren't used to it, that's all. Give them time." He coughed, almost apologetically, Clara was astonished to see. "By the way, I booked Henry Irving for another week in February."

Adam flushed and looked as if he might say something, but he took a deep breath and merely nodded.

317

"Did well last year for us," said Papa, an unusual pleading note in his voice.

"Yes, he did," agreed Adam. "I suppose contracts are not yet exchanged?"

Papa looked affronted. "I spoke to him meself. Gave the fellow my word."

Adam rubbed his eyes. He looked suddenly older than his years. "Yes, yes, of course, Papa. He'll do excellently. He always does."

"*The Bells,*" said Papa, his eyes alight with enthusiasm, "you've heard him in *The Bells,* Clara?"

"No, Papa."

"A feast." Papa crumbled a slab of very ripe Stilton onto a cracker biscuit. "Art. Not stuff made up by barrow boys. The real thing."

"I shall look forward to seeing it, Papa."

"Trust you'll still be here, glad you're home."

"Thank you, Papa."

"I have no doubt some decent fellow will want you sooner or later, what?"

Clara laughed. Papa frowned. He was only trying to help.

"It sounds, Papa, as if you are trying to get rid of me."

"Me dear girl," said Papa, "if you'd listened to me, you'd never have set foot out of this town, would you?"

"No." Tears, Clara knew, were not far from her eyes.

Papa saw this and quickly changed the subject. "Still, all's well that ends well, eh?"

"Papa," interposed Marta, "I wonder if a glass of your special port might not help Clara back to health."

"Capital," said Papa, and poured a liberal measure both for Clara and himself. "Got to get you back to scratch again, eh?"

It was a pleasant dinner, but Papa retired early, pleading exhaustion. "London wears me out these days. Ain't what it used to be." He kissed Clara on his way to bed. "Stay as long as you like, me dear. Stay as long as you like."

Clara did not cry, but it was a near thing.

Marta excused herself, saying, "I must see to Clara's room," and she was alone with Adam.

"Nice to see you back home," he said.

"It's nice to be back home."

Adam did not pretend. "Marta's told me how things are with you and Harry. My advice is, get well, take your time, no hurry for anything."

"Thank you. I think you're right. I feel drained and dead." The words began to tumble out. "I don't think I could have gone on another month. I suddenly ran out of steam, as they say."

"Don't suppose losing the child was Harry's fault?"

"No, it wasn't." Clara shook her head. "I just had to get away from it all, from him, too, from everything. I did a lot of things in a hurry, running off with him—"

"Yes, dear little sister." Adam puffed on his cigar and laughed. "You have no idea the fuss that caused. House wasn't worth living in for a year."

"I had to do it."

"I know. I know. And if it hasn't prospered, well, there it is. It isn't the end of life, is it?"

Clara looked at her brother, astonished. "Isn't it?"

"No, of course it ain't. Marriage is a lottery. You've no idea how it'll work out when you go into it. And whatever happens, it's never what you expect, I'll lay odds on that."

"How is your marriage to Marta?"

Adam's face clouded imperceptibly. "She is a splendid woman and a good and true wife. No man could ask for more."

Clara said nothing. Adam poured himself another glass of port. The fire fell in the grate, and the wind howled outside. There was a silence.

"Papa seems a little . . . less robust?" Clara hazarded.

Adam nodded. "He would like a knighthood, y'know."

"Would he? Really? I never knew."

"Oh, yes. Not going to get it, though, is he, as the owner of a music hall putting on low comedians? Might, as the promoter of concerts, featuring great and famous players, just might."

"Oh, then let him have them," cried Clara. "Poor, dear Papa."

"Can't, unfortunately." Adam cracked a walnut and prized out the fleshy nut. "We don't altogether own the Alhambra anymore, you see."

"Don't own it? But Papa always—"

"I know." Adam smiled tiredly. "Papa always held the reins himself. 'Tain't so any longer, I'm afraid." He sighed. "I hate to burden you with all this, but Papa has been presenting special

319

Sunday concerts at the Alhambra, booking actors and actresses from the London stage. Not one single concert covered its costs. Most lost a great deal of money."

"But Papa has reserves—"

Adam shook his head. "He had to go to backers to get enough money to keep the Alhambra running as a music hall. His backers, all of them friends of his, have loaned him the money on consideration there are no more of these concerts and that the Alhambra is run solely as a music hall. And that I am to approve all bookings." Adam drank his port. "I hate that obligation as much as Papa does, though he never speaks of it. But it was the only way to keep out of bankruptcy."

"Bankruptcy?" Clara felt cold at the very word.

"That or agree. So I agreed, and Papa agreed." Adam crushed out his cigar. "I will have to write Sir Henry Irving, for example, and cancel that booking, with many apologies, naturally."

"Oh, my Lord," exclaimed Clara. "Nothing stays the same."

"No, it don't," said Adam, "does it?" He took her hand. "But we shall win through, never fear." He stood up, as if to attention, and saluted, knocking over his port. "We're Englishmen, after all, are we not?"

At which they both roared with laughter, and when Marta came in, they were still laughing. Marta frowned a little at the spilled glass, but Clara did not care. It was the first time she had laughed since she lost the child.

Clara recovered slowly. She stayed in bed late most mornings, at Papa's insistence, and ate her breakfast in her room. Porridge, finnan haddock or kippers, or kidneys and bacon, or coddled eggs. Her appetite returned, slowly, too, and there was almost no pain any longer. Simply, her senses had dulled. She walked in the mornings around the nearby park and sat in the warm spring sun and tried to think of nothing at all. She endeavored to help Marta around the house, but her sister-in-law had the wheels of domesticity running smoothly and well. Marta seemed to be saying, in her polite refusal of help, "I have my life, husband and child and house; you have yours, performing, disporting yourself before men. You cannot have both." It was as if she had spoken the words aloud, so clearly did they register in Clara's mind.

Indeed, Marta did ask her, as they stood outside the Alhambra on one of their shopping jaunts, "Do you not miss performing at all?"

Clara shook her head wonderingly. "No. I don't think so."

"But you were so desperate to do it?"

"Was I? I suppose I was. It seems such a long time ago."

"Do you not think of your husband, all those thousands of miles away, working at a place like this?"

Clara shook her head again. "I never think of him at all. And that is curious, for once he was never out of my thoughts."

Marta looked puzzled. "What do you think of then?"

"My baby sometimes. What he would have been like."

"Oh, my dear," said Marta, tears coming to her eyes.

"And sometimes of nothing."

Marta took her gently. "Let's go in. Adam will get us seats for the first house. It's on in a half hour."

Clara shook her head. "No. I don't want to. You can if you like."

Marta shrugged. "I don't like the music hall. I never go. I think it panders to low tastes, and I have told Adam I think that. Let's go home, shall we?"

And they did.

The summer came, and it was time to sit on the lawn, in the trees' shade against the harmful rays of the sun. It was a time for silk dresses and glasses of sharp lemonade and soft nights with the bedroom windows wide open. It was a long and languorous season, and Clara grew brown despite her war against the sun, and the color returned to her cheeks. One day in July, as she lay half asleep in a striped hammock chair, Papa interrupted her. He looked hot in his striped blazer and strawboater hat, and there was a pile of unopened letters in his hand.

"Marta tells me these are all from your husband?"

"Yes. They are."

"Haven't you replied to a single one of them, girl?"

"No."

"Why not?"

"Papa, I don't know. I really don't."

"What," demanded Papa, "is the fellow to think? That you're dead?"

"I don't know," said Clara. She didn't.

"Well." Papa blew his nose loudly. "He knows you're here

321

anyway. Wrote me yesterday. I wrote him back this morning. That's why I looked in your room for these letters." He paused. "Are you going to answer them now?"

"I don't know, Papa."

"Seems to be a lot of things you don't know," declared Papa, thoroughly angry by now. "At least read the damn things. He's entitled to an answer!"

And he stomped out of the garden into the house.

It was the only time Clara ever heard him swear in front of a lady.

But she still did not read the letters.

Harry took Belle Alvin to the opening of the New York Palace, at Broadway and Forty-seventh Street. They sat in the vast auditorium and marveled at the depth of the carpets, the sparkle of the chandeliers, the plush of the seats. Marble floors in the lobby and, it was said, in the coal cellars beneath the theater. His tickets had been provided by Max Rober, who had told him privately that the house was at least half "paper." There had been two tickets, and he did not fancy sitting next to an empty seat all evening, so here they were, early-doors like a couple of vacationers from Bismarck, North Dakota.

"What a place!" Even Belle was impressed. "The press releases say it cost Beck over a million dollars to build it. Albee's in it, too, they say, but he isn't admitting to it, in case it's a flop." She shook her dark head and pressed Harry's hand. "I'm really glad you asked me. It's like something from the *Arabian Nights.*"

"Two dollars a seat," said Harry. "All the Times Square wise-acres say it will never pay its way. Look at all the empty seats upstairs!" She craned her lovely neck. Harry thought: why did I ask her? It will only lead to trouble.

Belle flashed a wide smile at Harry. "Cheer up, comic. Enjoy yourself. The managers are losing money, why should you worry?"

"I don't worry. I only wish they'd spend some on us, instead of four thousand dollars on advertising for this week alone."

"Don't tell me you wouldn't want to play this place?"

"Of course I want to play it, who wouldn't?" Harry sighed. He was used to Clara, to whom he did not have to explain himself. This girl asked a lot of questions and did not seem to hang on his answers either. She was not as beautiful as Clara, but she was more than passable, with her large mouth and bold stare. The

322

dress she was wearing was of a rather dull handloomed material, with heavy beads. Her jewelry was of silver, large and of a foreign design, she said Mexican. Harry was not impressed. If you could afford gold, then you should wear gold. Gold, said Belle, was vulgar. Anybody could wear it; just look at the people who did.

Harry took out his new gold Russell hunter and consulted it. The feel of gold suited him very well; Belle could keep her silver. So, too, did the dark tweed suit, custom-made, and the silk shirt. A gold pin plugged his large Macclesfield silk fringed necktie, and his gloves were of the best kid leather. Belle had looked at him in an amused way when he had picked her up at her apartment. "Very smart. Anybody can see at a hundred paces that Harry Viner is doing very well."

They had taken a bourbon to help them on their way. Straight with ice, as Belle Alvin always drank it.

"Never expected to hear from you again," had been her first statement, delivered with no sense of rancor. "How long's it been, three months, since you claimed your baggage and went back to your hotel?"

"I've been working hard, Belle."

"Do you hear from your wife?"

"No."

"I thought when your baggage arrived, you'd arrive, too."

"I had to think, Belle. I was feeling very sorry for myself. I would have been lousy company."

Belle freshened their drinks. "What was the trouble between the two of you?"

"She lost the child, you know that."

Belle touched his arm. "I didn't mean that. I meant, what was the trouble between you?"

Harry shook his head. "She got fed up with the life, I suppose. I'd been a bit hard on her, I don't know." He didn't. "She doesn't answer my letters. I think she's given up."

"If she has, she's a fool," said Belle Alvin with conviction.

Harry was irritated. "Anyway, that's all water under the bridge. What about you?"

"Oh, I'm doing all right. I get nice interviews for the women's page, and sometimes I'm allowed to do a real story." Belle grimaced. "I'm not doing show-business stuff anymore. Unless there's a woman's angle, and in your case plainly there isn't, so I'm no use in that way, I'm afraid."

"I don't want you to be of any use," said Harry. "I don't want any favors from you, darlin'. I wouldn't know how to treat you if you did that."

Belle studied him seriously. "How do you want to treat me, Harry?"

Harry put his hand around her neck, very gently, and kissed her on the lips.

"Like that."

"Just like a woman?" She sounded disappointed. "Is that all?"

"Well, you are a woman, or am I mistaken?" Harry laughed, genuinely puzzled.

Belle smiled quickly and kissed him back, but on the cheek. "Of course I am and sometimes not too proud of it."

Harry was totally bemused now. "What's wrong with being a woman?"

"A lot of things. Too many to go into now." Belle finished her drink. "We'd better go if we're going."

"We could stay." Harry indicated the bedroom. "I'm game."

"What, and miss the first night of the Palace? We will not!" declared Belle, and slipped into her coat. "This is the big night of the season, and besides, it would take you an hour to get out of that outfit."

"What's the matter with my outfit?" Harry asked, but he did not get a real answer, only a series of giggles. Belle was a girl who found a lot of things amusing. Harry was never sure whether she was laughing at him or with him. Anyway, here she was, at the Palace, and seemed to be pleased to be with him. He looked at her as she craned around to take in the brilliant, chattering, bejeweled first-night audience, and his loins stirred at the thrust of her breasts against the hopsacklike material of her dress. He was glad of the stirring; he was beginning to think he had lost his manhood. He had slept with no woman since Clara had gone away, had not wanted to (and that was new) but had simply drowned himself in his work, refusing the invitations of dancers and hungry stagestruck women on the long jumps out in the sticks. A hotel room and a bottle had been the form. He had been grieving for Clara and the child, and it had taken a long time.

But he had been lonely. Lonelier than he had ever been in his life.

He had written Clara to say so. He had written Clara to please come back.

He had pleaded.

She had not replied, not a line, nothing. Even when he had written to her father, who had replied asking why did he not come home to England, see her, talk to her, if he was so concerned about her. It had been a fair letter, Harry thought. Edward Abbott was a fair man. He might not like you, but you would get a decent shake from him.

How could he go back to England when, for the first time in his life, he had bookings six months ahead?

It was over between himself and Clara. No doubt of it. He had to face the facts.

Over.

Harry took Belle's hand and quietly kissed her palm. She was suddenly still and serious. "What was that for, Harry?"

"I don't know, I just felt like doing it."

"It is the first time you've done anything tender to me." Her gaze was level; what was she reading into it? "It was very nice, thank you."

"Look, Belle, I—" said Harry desperately. He didn't want her to get hold of the wrong end of the stick. He didn't love her. He didn't love anybody. He didn't think he'd ever love anybody again.

"Shush, curtain's going up." Belle held his hand in hers, and Harry looked around uncomfortably. Max Rober was seated somewhere in the vicinity, he knew, and so were, no doubt, many other people who knew Clara. He need not have worried. Everybody in the vast concourse was looking at the stage, with wide-open eyes. It was the biggest night in vaudeville history. Nobody cared who was holding hands with Harry Viner.

It was a big night indeed. Thirty dancers played "The Eternal Waltz"; Taylor Holmes told a monologue; the Four Varvis did a wire act. The huge audience leaned forward, holding its breath. The applause was loud and long for every act.

At the intermission Harry, getting drinks at the bar, was jostled by a man, turned around and saw it was John Hyatt.

"Harry, hello. . . ."

"John. . . ."

They shook hands. John Hyatt looked the same. As if he should be behind a plow. Harry was glad he was doing well himself. He said, "John, I owe you some money." He reached for his pocketbook.

John Hyatt laughed. "I meet the man, and the first thing he

talks about is money. Forget the money. How's Clara?"

"I meant to write." Harry felt guilty. "But you know how it is on tour."

"Is she recovered?"

"I think so."

"What sort of answer is that, Harry? You *think* so?"

"She's in England." Harry could not tell John Hyatt the truth in a crowded place like this. "She's staying with her family. Recuperating."

"Oh. I see. I'm glad to hear that." John Hyatt looked surprised. It occurred to Harry that he might think it unlikely Harry would *allow* her to go away like that.

Harry said, "I'm doing a solo these days."

"I saw the write-up in *Variety,* and I wondered." John Hyatt got his drinks, and Harry got his, and John said, "Come and meet my wife."

"I do have somebody with me." Harry thought: now he'll think I'm a rotter because I didn't tell him Clara has left me and won't even reply to my letters. He sighed and signaled Belle Alvin to join them. She did quite coolly, and Harry was pleased to see John Hyatt's flicker of sexual alarm at the poise and easiness of the girl.

John recovered and made introductions all around. "This is my wife, Patsy, and my friends Jimmy and Mamie. This is Harry Viner and Miss Alvin."

Belle Alvin said, "Belle, please."

"Don't you write for the *Trib?*" asked Mamie, a forward and pushing young woman, Harry noted. He was a shade uncomfortable with her. She asked him where he was playing next, and when he said the Bushwick, Brooklyn, promised to come out and see him with some songs that John Hyatt and Jimmy Cowley had written.

Jimmy Cowley said, "Mamie, look at the man's face. He doesn't *want* any songs."

"How does he know he doesn't want any songs until he hears them?"

"He doesn't want to hear them, right, Mr. Viner?"

Harry laughed. "Depends on the song."

Belle Alvin talked to John Hyatt and his wife. She seemed to be at ease with them, but Harry could not hear any of their conversation. He hoped that Belle wasn't saying anything embarrassingly truthful. Women, he knew, were bad liars about things that were personal to them. They told the truth about their feelings as naturally as a man did not. He began to think that it had not been a very good idea to bring Belle Alvin along to this glamorous and epoch-making evening of vaudeville.

The pushy girl, Mamie, was asking, "Didn't you used to have a girl partner who sang songs? I thought I heard John say that?" and Jimmy Cowley was adding hastily, "When you want a song, you know where to come, right?"

"I used to have a partner. I don't now." That, anyway, was true. "But if I ever need a song, I will come to you, I promise. Are you doing all right?"

Jimmy Cowley grimaced. "All right, yes, I guess all right. You heard 'Dream of Summer'? That's our best to date."

The bell rang for the second half of the program, and Harry turned away to rescue Belle Alvin from John Hyatt and his wife, or was it the other way around? He heard Mamie say, "The man's right, Jimmy, stop pushing for the fast buck, and invest some time in a ballad or two. . . ."

John Hyatt said, "Can I ask you both to supper?" but Harry answered quickly, "Sorry, we have a date," and shook hands with Patsy Hyatt, who seemed a pleasant, quiet woman, and ushered Belle Alvin back to her seat.

Once seated, Belle frowned and said, "What's the matter, Harry, don't you want me to meet your friends?"

"They aren't my friends. I only know John Hyatt."

"He seems a nice man."

"He is."

"But you're not sure, no?"

Harry said, "John Hyatt's a very nice man, he's too nice, he's done me a couple of favors, and he won't let me repay him. I don't like owing people favors in this world."

"You're a hard man, Harry Viner."

"Never been accused of anything else."

"You're hard on other people, and that's bad. But you're hard on yourself, too, and that's better." She patted his hand. "Don't worry, I still like you."

"Darlin'," Harry Viner said grimly, "when I worry about whether a woman likes me or not, that'll be the day. Let's watch the show, shall we, somebody paid for these tickets."

Ed Wynn was the headliner, playing his "Perfect Fool" sketch. Harry liked him but confessed he had seen better supporting bills.

It did not seem to matter, the audience applauded everything. Vaudeville would go on forever; the opening of the Palace was merely the confirmation of the fact.

In the crowded foyer, leaving the theater, Max Rober spoke to them. His eyes flickered over Belle Alvin, but he said nothing, merely smiled politely and said, "We must get you on here one day, Harry."

"Any chance of it?"

"Mr. Beck is going to run Monday matinees. Do you want me to put your name down?"

Harry nodded. He could not speak. To play to *that* audience, in *that* theater. . . . He bade Max Rober good-night and pushed through the crowds out onto Forty-seventh Street. He was hardly aware of Belle Alvin at his side as he strode along Broadway. She tugged at his arm. "Harry, please slow down; it's me you're with, Belle Alvin, remember?"

Harry stopped. He had genuinely forgotten, his mind filled with the dream of playing the Palace. "I'm sorry." He took her arm. "Let's go and eat supper somewhere, shall we?"

Belle shook her head. "No. Let's go home to my place, shall we?"

They took a cab.

Harry thought: she always makes the moves, and that can't be right. But sitting in the cab, her head on his shoulder, he did not care. Or he told himself he did not care.

Lying naked in bed, smoking a cigarette in a holder, Belle asked, "Is it really all over between you and your wife?"

"I don't know." Harry was sleepy. Belle was an exhausting and inventive partner. There was nothing she would not do, and while that pleased and excited him at the time, and while there was no doubt a man could do things with a woman he did not live with that he might not do with one he did live with, when it was over it was over. Besides, he was not used to long conversations in bed. "I write to her; she never writes back. I'm not chasing her anymore. It's up to her."

"But you want her back?"

Harry frowned. "I didn't say that."

"No, but you sound as if you do."

"She is my wife, after all."

328

"That makes her somebody special, doesn't it, being *your* wife?"

"Well, of course it does, be sensible."

"You mean, you own her?"

"No, I do not own her. I'm married to her. It's a different thing."

"How is it any different from you and me? We are in bed together, after all?"

Harry opened an eye. She seemed serious. There was no doubt, Belle Alvin had some very funny ideas. "I know we're in bed together, dear, but it's not the same, is it? I mean, you want it as much as I want it, there's no strings attached, we get up and each go our own ways, don't we?"

"Yes, all that's true." Belle Alvin's voice held some regret and some annoyance also. "But I can't see how having a piece of paper to wave about makes any difference to the feelings a man and a woman have about each other."

"Darlin'," Harry said, "if you can't see that, you can't see anything. Of course, it makes a difference. Sometimes not for the better, I grant you, but a difference, certainly. It's the difference between people shaking hands on a business deal and putting it in writing."

"You mean," Belle Alvin said, "it's legal, not just a matter of mutual trust?"

"I dunno anything about mutual trust between a man and a woman." Harry sighed. "A woman might have a lot of this mutual trust you talk about, but most fellas don't. I don't." Harry thought: she ain't my missus, so I can be more truthful with her, and that's a funny thing. "I wish I was better than I am, but I ain't. I'm about average, I reckon. I have a lot of mutual trust for everybody, but I ain't married to them, am I?"

Belle Alvin laughed.

She's a funny woman, no doubt of that, Harry Viner thought with a slight irritation. Then he slept.

Things were not going well at the Alhambra, Adam told Clara.

It was winter again, and they sat before the deep red fire in the drawing room. Outside, the prevailing nor'easter blew, and the last leaves flickered against the windowpanes. Another winter, Clara thought, and still, I sit and wait. For what? she wondered.

329

"What's gone wrong?" she asked. She did not feel any alarm at his words. She had been home almost a year now, and nothing had happened. I grow stronger each day, she thought, my body does anyway, but I feel less able to go out and do anything than I felt the first day I came back home.

"Those last concerts Papa did cost us our reserves of cash. We are in the red again."

"No?" This time Clara was shocked.

Adam bit on his cigar. His face was pale and lined, and he looked like the elder brother of the young bridegroom she remembered. "Papa meets his backers next week at his solicitor's office, and he is going to have to do some very fast talking indeed." Adam shook his head. "I want to go with him, but he's refused to have me there. Doesn't want me to see him begging for money, I suppose."

"Is it as bad as that? Summers are always down, Adam."

"Yes, they are," answered Adam soberly, "but they're not usually as bad as they've been. Halls are doing well all over the country. It's Papa's booking policy. It's wrong."

"He built the Alhambra, Adam. He even designed it, got the plans passed when nobody else could. It's his music hall, not ours."

"You're wrong," said Adam. "It isn't even his, unless he gets that loan. And he still has one more concert, on Sunday. It'll lose money, but I suppose we have to live with it." He put out his cigar and stood up.

She said, "Everything will be all right, won't it, Adam?"

"Of course it will, little sister. Don't know why I bothered your head with such things."

"I am a grown lady, Adam," she protested.

Adam laughed and patted her cheek. "Not really grown, not yet." He smiled like the old Adam before the cavernous look came into his features and bade her good-night. His step up the stairs seemed slow and weary. Poor Adam, the weight of marriage and family and business on his shoulders and not yet thirty. There was no doubt, Clara thought, a man had to like responsibility to embrace it. Or did he never think of it, was he into it before he knew it, and forced by circumstances to contend with it, as Adam plainly was?

Had Harry been like that, forced into something he didn't really want?

330

Was it her fault?

She pushed the thought away.

It is time, she thought, that I stopped dreaming of Harry Viner and *did* something for myself!

Papa was evasive when she asked him about his special Sunday concert. "Not doing as well as all that, m'dear. This has to be the last one, I'm afraid."

"I wonder," Clara said, "if I could help, Papa."

"Can't see how." He shook his head. "Adam's against the concert, he'd cancel it if he could, but it's too late."

"Yes, I know. . . . Well . . . let's see, shall we?"

Clara went to Adam and made her suggestion. Adam was surprised but puffed on his meerschaum and said at last, "It could work. Let's go along and see the newspaper people, shall we?"

Clara took the *Journal* in to Papa herself the next day. She handed it to him with a flourish. "Look at the back page, Papa."

"What's the rush? I'll read it later."

"No. Now."

"What?" He turned the paper around and looked. " 'Edward Abbott presents, by Special Arrangement, Sir Henry Irving in his Famous Rendition of *The Bells*'? That's what I told them to put."

"Read the rest."

He frowned. " 'And also presenting, by Special Arrangement, Miss Clara Viner (née Clara Abbott), who has Just Returned from her Successful American Tour.' " His mouth opened. "You're mad!"

"No, I'm not, Papa. It will fill the hall, you'll see! Look at the inside pages."

Papa looked. There was a story about Clara, carefully leaving out any mention of Harry Viner. It was a local-girl-makes-good story, and Adam had told her that the demand for tickets at the box office since the newspapers had been on the streets had been exceptional, double what was usual.

Clara said, "I think it's about time I got back in harness again, Papa."

But Papa was on his feet. "First you run off and marry that fellow, Viner. Now you want to perform at one of my special concerts, no doubt doing a leg show!"

"Papa!" This was all going wrong. "You have leg shows all the time!"

"Maybe I do, but it isn't my own daughter showing her legs!"

"I only did it to help," Clara cried.

331

But Papa had gone out, after throwing the *Journal* down on the leather sofa.

Adam touched her arm. "All my fault. I should have known the old man would hate the idea. He's scared you'll lower the tone of the concert. He still thinks it matters."

Clara shook her head. "It was a mistake then."

"No. We'll have a full house."

"Oh, dear. I've done it all wrong."

"No, you haven't. At least we won't lose money, and some of Papa's creditors may be in. If they are, they might be impressed."

Clara frowned. "Shall I make my act nice?"

Adam laughed. " 'Naughty but Nice' is what they're paying for. Never mind Papa, that's what you have to give them, ain't it?"

Clara supposed it was.

The Alhambra was full for the special Sunday night concert. The audience was posh; there were many gentlemen in evening dress and ladies in long gowns. Only Papa could obtain permission for such an occasion on a Sunday. The profits, if there were any, were, Adam told Clara wryly, for charity, part of Papa's attempt at a knighthood.

"Where is he?" asked Clara.

"Haven't seen him all day." Adam shook his head. "The old chap's sulking. He thinks you're lowering the tone of his damn concert."

Sir Henry Irving had to catch a train back to London that evening, so he was on first. He boomed his way through the famous monologue, the guilt and the madness of the murderer and, finally, bathed in sweat, took a standing ovation and was preparing to go, with a handshake for Adam. "Can't see your father, give the dear man me best, must rush, this damn train." The great man smiled at Clara. "Good luck, me dear. They'll have simmered down after the intermission. Forgotten me by then. Ready for you, eh?"

And he was gone.

The intermission seemed to last forever. But Sir Henry was right. They had settled down by the time she stood in the wings, waiting for her cue and for the old excitement and fear. She had expected it to come when she changed in the dressing room, but it had not.

332

"Not an empty seat in the place." Adam appeared at the side of the stage, squeezed her arm. "Excited?"

"No. I ought to be, I suppose. But I'm not."

"You will be once you get out there."

"Perhaps. It all seems like a dream."

Am I still sorrowing, she wondered, listening to the swell of her music from the pit orchestra, for Harry? Will I never feel anything again?

And Papa, where was Papa?

"You're on," Adam whispered. "Good luck."

Clara danced out onstage, feeling sad and sorry. Papa would never see her now.

The limelight held her. She twirled her parasol. I'm all right, she thought, I've learned to do everything *slowly*, to make them wait for me. "It's like making love, darlin'," Harry had told her. "Don't rush it. Enjoy it. There's no hurry. Tease them along. Let them look at you. Let them see you're enjoying it as much as they are."

So she did.

Then she froze.

Papa was out there somewhere, and he was hating this. He was ashamed of her, disporting herself like a whore. She faltered. The audience, sensing something wrong, hushed. The musical director looked up at her anxiously. She felt panic, this had never happened to her before. . . . She tried to sing on cue, but no words came. The audience started to rumble curiously, not yet ominously. Clara wanted to faint, she willed herself to faint, it had been too long, she had forgotten how, she could do nothing without Harry Viner, not even this, it was as simple as that. . . . The stage spun.

"Come along, girl! *Sing!*"

She opened her eyes.

Papa stood in the wings, a gold watch in his hand, a cigar in his mouth. His voice reached her, in a strong and audible stage whisper. "You only have eight minutes!"

She stared at him.

"Sing!" he whispered in what sounded like a shout.

The audience waited; it was ready to applaud her; she was, after all, Papa's daughter. Clara felt her nerves quiet. Gallery, circle, stalls. One, two, three. Take your time. She could hear Harry Viner's voice, all the time she was onstage. No hurry, no hurry

333

at all. They're watching. Let them watch. Lift the dress, not too high. Whoops! A little smile, you're innocent, you're playing with fire, but you don't really know it. Smile back at them, and they'll forget you made them feel randy. They'll feel guilty then, they'll remember you're a nice little girl from along the street. The smile, then the song. . . .

> I went for a stroll upon the Town Moor,
> A young man he spoke to me, said, "Are you *sure?*"

She talked:
"You're very young to be out on your own, my dear. . . ."
Oh, he was ever so manly. . . ."
Here she did something new, on the spur of the moment. She leaned forward and asked innocently, "Are all gentlemen manly like *that?* I wonder."
The audience chuckled, deep and cynical.
Clara sang:

> Naughty but Nice, Naughty but Nice,
> Never Been Kissed in the Same Place Twice!

She sang three choruses and took three bows, to loud and prolonged applause.
Clara sat in her dressing room and looked at herself in the mirror. They said that once it got into your blood it stayed there. They were right. It has been wonderful. The fire was racing through her veins, and she could hear the congratulations of the other performers still, and Adam's enthusiastic "You went marvelous, Clara, I hardly knew you!" She began to clean off the makeup. I was good, she told herself. I always knew I could do it on my own, and I can. I need Harry as a friend, as a lover, as a partner. Or I did. But I can work on my own, I can, I can, I can. . . .
She smiled into the mirror. I'm free, she thought. I'm free. If I want to be.
Clara smiled to herself as Harry's words came back to her. "Don't believe them when they say you're marvelous, darlin'; then you don't have to believe them when they say you're rotten!" She went on cleaning her face.
Papa was waiting for her when she got home.
He had been nowhere to be seen when she came offstage. Clara had been disappointed by that. She had finally broken away

from a crowd of well-wishers, leaving Adam to pacify them, and taken a cab back to Leazes Crescent.

"Papa. . . . That was good of you. To prompt me. I'd frozen. I don't think I could have gone on."

"Nonsense. You're a professional, and a damn good one." He stood up and kissed her. "I was wrong. I'm a silly old buffer. Wrong about these concerts. I'll never get a knighthood now, and I don't care, all of a sudden. But nothing wrong about you. You're a trouper, me dear; you were very, very good indeed tonight."

"Papa," said Clara, "you're only saying that."

"Indeed, I am not," said Papa. "And to prove it, I'll book you at the Alhambra all next week." He blew his nose. "That is, provided I still own it."

"Oh, Papa."

Clara kissed him, and he held her for a long moment. "Had to come away and wait for you here or I'd have disgraced meself." He blew his nose again. "Think I'll take meself up to bed. I'm tired, and I have a busy day tomorrow."

"Yes. Of course. Good night, dear Papa."

"Good night, my dear. And I meant it. You were very, very good. I'm proud of you."

Clara tried not to cry, but she did not succeed.

Adam and Marta came in and said good-night and went up to bed, Adam adding, "We broke even, and you were the success of the night. We might even get our loan now."

Even Marta said, "It was quite pleasant, really, Clara. Not at all offensive."

"Good night, Marta." She kissed Adam. "Good night, and thanks. I know I can do it now."

"What did Papa say?"

"He was pleased."

Adam pressed her hand. "So all's well!"

Then the house was quiet again.

Clara sat in front of the dying fire, neglecting to use the bellpull to summon a maid to build it up. She needed somebody close, to talk about the events of the evening. She needed Harry Viner. No, she didn't; what was she thinking about?

The fire fell noisily in the grate, and she came out of her reverie. How foolish she was being. There was no point in thinking about Harry. The fact that she had not answered his letters and that he had stopped writing said it all. He regarded the marriage

335

as over, and so did she. Tonight she had done something on her own. It was a step away from Harry Viner. There would need to be more before she was utterly free of him.

The door opened gently, and Papa came in, in his dressing gown. It was a large checked-blanket garment like a heavy overcoat, made for icy bedrooms. He looked surprised to see her there. "Ah, me dear. Thought you'd gone to bed with the others." He gazed at the fire. "Nearly out, I see." He stooped and took up the coal tongs and threw two sizable pieces upon the embers. "That should burn up in a few minutes." He moved to the sideboard. "Forgot me nightcap. Can't get off to sleep without me nightcap." He poured himself a liberal measure of scotch. Clara knew that this was his second nightcap, for she had seen him take one up an hour earlier when he officially retired to bed. "Can I get you anything at all?"

Clara was astonished. It was almost a blasphemy, Papa asking a woman, above all, his daughter, if she would care for a nightcap. Gentlemen had nightcaps. Ladies did not.

"I think I will perhaps have a very small glass of your fine port, Papa," said Clara. "To be sociable."

"Excellent," said Papa with obvious relief. He poured her a good glassful and brought it across. "You have your sorrows as well, me dear, I know. We will not drown them, but at least we can dampen them a little, um?"

"Yes." Clara sipped her port. "If drink would wash it away, I would finish the bottle."

"Here, steady on." Papa looked stern. "No good getting at the bottle like that. You aren't an old spinster woman, tipplin' in the afternoons when nobody's looking, are you?"

"Sometimes I almost wish I was, Papa, but no."

"Glad to hear it." Papa swallowed his whiskey and poured himself another. "Anythin' I hate, it's a woman toping. Can't stand to look at it. You know how I'm circumstanced, Adam is bound to have told you? He has, hasn't he? Save me doing it again if he has?"

"He's told me, yes," Clara said.

Papa exhaled and helped himself to more whiskey from the decanter. "This is a Scotchman's drink to be sure, but you can get used to it if you drink enough of it." Papa took up the long iron poker and rattled it furiously between the bars of the grate, making a great deal of noise, which seemed to please him. "You sometimes have to do that to life, have you noticed, me dear? Give it a good old stir-up like that. You did that when you ran away with Harry Viner. I did it when I opened the Alhambra. Everybody said I would lose money, every penny I had, every penny I'd saved and your poor dear mother's money as well. I didn't. I proved them wrong. Like you proved me wrong at that concert tonight. They said no decent man would take his family to a music hall, but we needed six strong men at each door to keep the crowds back the first night. They said it wouldn't be a success, and they were wrong. They've been wrong for thirty-five years. But it's beginning to look as if they might be right tomorrow."

Papa sat looking into the fire.

"Dammit," he said, "I've been to sea as a young man. I've been round the Horn twice as a purser on the old sailing ships. I've fought ten rounds with a professional boxer—old Jem Mace—and never been afraid." He shivered. "But I'm afraid now. Afraid of going into that room tomorrow and being treated like a naughty schoolboy." Clara put her hand on his arm, but he did not seem to feel it. "For the first time in my life I have to go cap in hand to a lot of miserable solicitors and such, that have never been out of this town in their lives and have never done one single risky thing, and ask them for money. It beats all, it does, me dear, it most certainly beats all."

Softly Clara poured him another whiskey.

Papa sat there, the drink in his hand, not moving, just staring into the fire. "I don't want Adam there," he said slowly, "but I'd like you with me tomorrow. Will you come?"

Clara was touched. "Of course I will, if you think I can help."

"I want somebody with some guts, somebody who ain't afraid. You ain't afraid; you've done what I did. I ran away to sea to make me fortune, and I did it. Came back home, built the Alhambra. That's my monument."

"At least you have a monument, Papa," Clara said. "I don't have anything at all, not even a husband, do I?"

Papa squeezed her hand. "It'll all come right. Promise me you'll try anyway."

"I can't promise, Papa. You shouldn't ask that."

"No, I shouldn't. You're right. Foolish of me."

"You mean well, I know, but I'm not sure I can ever bear to look at Harry Viner again. There was another woman, you see, and that was inexcusable. I was pregnant, and he went to another woman. I cannot forget that, I know men are very easily tempted, and no woman should tempt them in that way because of their weakness, but surely you understand I cannot have anything further to do with him while these awful thoughts of them both are still in my mind?"

Clara turned to Papa guiltily. She had never intended to say those words, to him or to anybody else. No doubt it was the lateness of the hour and Papa's frankness and the port, but all the same, it had been wrong to do it.

She need not have worried. Papa was asleep, the glass in his hand. Clara took it gently, laid him down on the cushions, then went upstairs for blankets. She covered him up, and then she built up the fire and tiptoed out of the room. He lay there, still as death.

Clara woke to an unnaturally still house and the sound of quiet sobbing.

Quickly, fearfully, she got out of bed and ran down the broad staircase in her nightdress. Adam, in a dressing gown, his face very pale, stopped her as she ran toward the drawing room.

"Don't go in there, Clara."

"Please. I must."

"No!"

"Is he . . . is he. . . ?"

Adam nodded. "The doctor's in there with him now. He went in his sleep, it seems. A stroke. No man could ask for a quicker way to die."

Papa *dead.*

Clara looked at Adam. "I knew last night when I left him. Adam, I knew! And yet I went upstairs to bed and I slept. I knew this was going to happen."

"No, you didn't. You just think you did, now it has."

"No, I knew."

He put his arm around her. "It doesn't matter. Maybe it is all for the best in a way."

"Why?"

"I don't think he would have got that loan. And that would have been worse. What's more, I believe he knew it. He's lucky in one way. He is out of it. I have to go and face those people in his place."

"They cannot refuse you after this, Adam." It was the voice

338

of Marta, standing behind them, her voice cold but her eyes red. "They would not dare."

"We shall see," said Adam. "There are the funeral arrangements to think about first."

"I will do those," said his wife. "You get ready and go to that meeting. Clara and I will do all that is necessary here."

Adam stared at her. "You don't mean that?"

"I do. Go upstairs and put on your best suit. It is all laid out for you."

"She does mean it," said Adam in a low voice.

"Yes, I do. Go now. Hurry. I will get the cab ready. You might as well go in style."

"But Papa?"

"The best thing you can do for Papa is keep the Alhambra going. The best way to do that is to go to the meeting this morning and break the news of your father's death first, then ask for the money immediately afterwards."

Adam looked at his wife as if he might hit her. Then he released Clara and went slowly up the stairs. Clara stood in the hall as Marta, without another word, went into the drawing room. She was still standing there, unseeing, as the doctor came out with Marta. He was an old man who had served the family for thirty years. He looked at Clara and said, "You ought to be in bed, young woman."

Marta asked, "Do you want to see dear Papa?"

Clara shook her head. "No. I want to remember him as he was." He saw me work, she thought, he saw me work, at least I have that.

"Best thing," said the doctor, and wrote out a prescription for a sleeping draft for everybody in the house. Not for the servants, of course, who could be heard sobbing in the kitchen. "Take this at night. You'll need your sleep. Your dear father had a lot of friends. It is going to be a big funeral."

It was a big funeral, very big.

There were sixteen carriages, drawn by black horses with black plumes, and the people walking behind the coffin stretched for almost half a mile. They were all men, some of them knowing Papa only by sight. Many of them had visited the Alhambra once a week, regular as the visiting acts, every week of their adult lives.

They walked soberly, though some of them were not sober. No woman walked behind a coffin. It was not a thing a woman should do.

The service, at St. Nicholas's Cathedral, had been crowded and sympathetic, and the bishop himself had given the address. There had been tears in his eyes, Clara saw, from the family pew, and they seemed genuine. He had known Papa as a friend. So had the entire city. He belonged to them all, rich and poor alike, because he had owned the Alhambra, and they were here to see him to rest.

At the graveside Clara was dry-eyed as others wept. Papa is gone, she told herself, but she did not believe it.

At last the funeral party was over. The last mourner had departed, and the maids were collecting the glasses and plates.

"At least," said Adam softly, "we could afford it all."

For he had obtained the loan, exactly as Marta said he would.

It was then that Clara broke down and sat on the very sofa on which Papa had died and cried as if her heart would break.

Adam and Marta tiptoed out of the room.

"Oh, Harry, Harry," Clara whispered to herself over and over. Nobody heard her.

Clara went to Adam's office at the Alhambra. Adam looked calm and purposeful, and he seemed to be busy. He had a pile of letters and contracts on Papa's old desk, and he was working his way through them as she knocked and entered.

Adam smiled. He was always pleased to see her. Clara felt like kissing him, but she sat down at his invitation and simply said, "Adam, it's been nice, but I think it's time I moved on."

He sat up. "Moved on where?"

"Oh, I don't know. London perhaps."

"But why? Is it something Marta has said?"

"No, it isn't." Not strictly true, Clara thought. Marta had made one or two remarks in the three weeks that had passed since Papa's funeral. Nothing direct. Just hints that a woman should not grieve over a man forever. That pain and separation and grief were a woman's lot, and she must learn to live with them, with dignity. And of course, the fact that a woman's place, no matter what, was at her husband's side, even if he was the greatest blackguard in the whole wide world. "Marta," Clara added, "is a fine wife for you, and naturally she would like you all to herself. While Papa

340

was alive, it was his house, and things were different. Now the house is yours—"

"And yours," interrupted Adam. "Come anytime you wish, stay as long as you like. That's what Papa would have wanted, and so do I."

Clara felt near to tears, but she fought them back. "Thank you. But really, I think I must make an effort, or I will be with you forever, the spinster sister of Leazes Crescent. Can you imagine that?"

Adam laughed. "No, I can't." He spoke slowly, seriously. "But what if you stay with us and eventually divorce? Was that in your mind?"

"I don't know for sure," said Clara, "what is in my mind."

"If you had thought of that," Adam went on, "I should think that sooner or later you would find a suitor. You are still a young woman, and divorce is not the disgrace it used to be."

"Very nearly," said Clara.

"Well, yes, but some older man might not see it like that."

Clara thought: some *older* man? Who? She felt a shudder of revulsion pass over her. I am a one-man woman, she thought, I really *am*, and I must live with it even if I don't live with the man.

"Adam, I don't want an older man. I just want to get on with my life. I think it is about time I did, don't you?"

Adam debated this. "What will you do?"

"I have some money Papa left me."

"Only a hundred pounds. That will not go far."

"It was so good of Papa, that. Even when everything was going wrong, he thought of me."

Adam sighed. "I wish he'd thought of the Alhambra. We are going to need some good houses this winter to get ourselves on an even keel again." He indicated the papers lying on the desk. "Artistes' salaries have gone up alarmingly since the strike. One hundred pounds a week, not a bit out of the way." He touched his mustache. "Kate Carney is top-of-the-bill next week. One hundred and ten pounds. I only hope she's worth it."

"I know a very good act you could get for nothing."

"Who?"

"Me. I could work for you next week. As a going-away present. Papa actually asked me the night he died."

Adam stared at her. "Did he?"

"Yes. And I have been making my living at it for years, you know."

"Marta won't like it." Adam put down the pipe, unlit. "She's a devil for appearances. Once for a special concert, yes. But as a regular performer?"

Clara said, "Do you have to have her approval, or are *you* managing the Alhambra?"

"What?"

"Would Papa have asked for her approval or any woman's approval?"

Adam looked shocked. Then he grinned. "No. He wouldn't." He took a deep breath. "All right. You're in. I'll put you third. . . ." He peered at a list in front of him. "Yes, I'll put you on as third turn."

"No," Clara said. "Put me on at next-to-closing if you're putting me on at all."

Adam smiled. "All right. Twice nightly, matinees Wednesday and Saturday. Salary, thirty pounds."

"No," Clara said. "No money."

"My dear," said Adam, "the laborer is worthy of his hire. You get paid like everybody else."

He stood there, looking careworn and yet still so young. Clara kissed him. "I won't let you down," she said.

Adam lit his pipe. "That isn't what's worrying me. How do I tell Marta, that's what's worrying me."

Marta did not take the news well, but she mellowed when Clara explained privately, "This is to be my last week here. I'll be going away once the week is over."

Marta had looked shocked. "You're going back to America?"

"No."

"But where?"

"I don't know. London probably."

"To work in the music halls?"

"If anybody will give me a job."

"But I thought you had left all that behind you."

"I thought I had, too." Clara shook her head. "But after Papa's death I realized I had to do something, not just sit about and mope."

Marta took her hand. "Why not go back to your husband?"

"No."

"Why?"

342

"I don't think I love him anymore."

Marta looked annoyed. "You do not stay in love with people all the time you are married to them. That is not what marriage is about. Adam and I have only been married as long as you, but already we have settled down to a routine. We get on with each other. We accept each other's faults and virtues. Couldn't you do that?"

"No," said Clara. "I can't just *get on* with Harry. Either I love him or I don't. If I don't, I can't live with him, now or ever."

Marta looked sad. "You still love him, I think you do."

The bill at the Alhambra that week was a good one. Kate Carney, coster girl, no longer young, forty-five now, was singing her famous love song of the halls, as she had been singing it for years:

> Are we to part like this, Bill,
> Are we to part this way?
> Who's it to be, her or me?
> You've only got to say.

Clara told Kate, "You were wonderful. I wish I had a song like that, but my husband said I'd have to live a full life to know how to sing it."

Kate Carney said nothing about the current absence of a husband. One of the nice things about people on the halls was the fact that they never asked personal questions. "Don't you, neither," Harry had told her. "If anybody wants you to know their private business, they'll tell you. And another thing, never talk about a pro to an ordinary person, never, especially scandal. That's an unwritten rule that is, like never piss in the dressing-room sink unless you're a top-of-the-bill, and not very often then."

Kate Carney asked, taking off her huge "pearly" hat, "You been working in America, how was that?"

"I liked it, but we had some hard times."

"Coming back into the business here, are you?"

"I was going to London next week, see if anybody would give me some jobs."

"You'll get jobs. You've a lovely voice, dear." Kate Carney looked at her shrewdly. "You been working double, have you?"

"With my husband. He's in America."

"I see."

343

"We parted. I don't know if we'll get together again."

"Like my song, eh?"

"Something like that, yes."

"Let me see," said Kate Carney, "what I can do, eh?"

And she patted Clara's hand sympathetically.

Kate Carney's introduction to Walter de Frece was all that Clara needed. The top London agent, husband of Vesta Tilley, one of the best-dressed and most influential agents in the capital, he seemed to know all about Clara, as they sat and talked in his Shaftesbury Avenue office.

"You want me to obtain bookings for you?"

"If you feel able to."

"Oh, I think I can do that. You aren't the usual type of artiste, Miss Viner. I don't want to book you at any of the rougher halls."

Clara said, surprised, "I didn't know you'd seen me."

Walter de Frece laughed. "I haven't, but my spies have. Where are you staying?"

"I'm at the Cadogan Hotel, in Sloane Street."

"That is a very good address."

"It wasn't my idea. I'll have to move, I expect. My brother booked me in there. He seemed to feel better when he did that. He likes my act, but he does not like the idea of my being in this business any more than my dear papa did."

Walter de Frece smiled as he showed her to the door. "I can't afford to be prejudiced, can I?"

He shook hands and promised to be in touch.

How very easy it all is, Clara thought, walking along Sloane Street toward the very grand Cadogan Hotel, where, the housekeeper had told her, in a shocked whisper, Mr. Oscar Wilde had been arrested. In the *Cadogan*, she had whispered, scandalized. Clara liked the Cadogan. It reminded her of Papa. He had often stayed there. It was, he had said, quite without any kind of snobbery, a hotel for gentlemen.

Everything I touch turns to gold, Clara thought, everything I always wanted is about to come true: to play at the best halls on my own, to be recognized as an artiste in my own right. It is all about to come true, she said to herself.

Why am I not more excited?

Clara booked herself a rehearsal room in Lisle Street and worked hard. She obtained two new songs, "By the Light of the

344

Silvery Moon" and "The Band Played On," both American successes but rarely sung in England, and rehearsed them daily with a voice teacher. She polished up her dance routines with the aid of a very good dance coach. She designed new dresses and bought new tap shoes and a new skip basket. It looked very strange, lying in her hotel room, brand-new, the wickerwork bright yellow.

Finally, she had the act as polished as she thought it would ever be. Walter de Frece came along to the rehearsal room and approved it. "Very charming, my dear. I think you're ready."

"Am I?" Clara asked. "I don't know, I really don't."

Suddenly the idea of going on alone, not at the Alhambra for a week, but forever and ever was a fearful prospect. Walter de Freece was watching her keenly. "Don't you want all this?"

"Yes. Of course. It's just . . . I'm not sure of myself."

He took her hand. "Well, I am."

Clara went back to the hotel and sat looking at herself in the mirror; her looks were still there. She was conscious of men's eyes, in the rehearsal room and the street. Conscious but not interested. Would she ever be interested again?

She took a glass of port and went to bed. The port helped her to sleep. Sometimes it took two glasses.

Walter de Frece booked Clara exclusively into the best London halls.

The first was the Empire, Liecester Square. A huge hall, reputed to be one of the most difficult in London. The gallery shouted, "Speak up!" to an artiste they could not hear clearly. "Speak up or get off!"

Clara should have been nervous.

She wasn't.

She should have been worried about the audience.

She wasn't.

She should have felt that if she failed here, she would fail everywhere in town, because news of her failure would have gone before her.

She didn't care.

The roars of applause that came out of the black auditorium at the end of her act pleased her greatly, but she was not "out of her mind" with delight, as she knew she would have been a year or two before.

I don't give a damn, she thought, surprised.

I really don't.

345

One after the other, she played them. The Oxford, the Canterbury, the Met, the Bedford, the Tivoli. The London *Star* said, "Miss Clara Viner has a wonderful way with a song. . . ." The *Sunday Dispatch* opined, "Miss Clara Viner brings a vivacious innocence to the music halls, not a place renowned for those qualities. . . ."

Clara played right through it all, feeling everything short of total happiness. There was always an ache when finally she had to face her lonely room at the Cadogan Hotel. She had stayed on there, expensive as it was. There was no point in saving money. She was earning fifty pounds a week now, and she had no other expenses. Adam and Marta came down for an evening, late one Saturday, and were thrilled at her success. Adam reported that things were picking up at the Alhambra, and with another good season behind them they would be out of the wood.

Life, altogether, should have been wonderful.

It wasn't.

Harry said no to Belle Alvin's offer that he move in with her.

Harry, sitting on the cane and wickerwork sofa, looked over the spectacles he had just started to wear for reading. "I'm all right at the Astor. Stop arranging my life." He did not like the spectacles and took them off whenever he could. Since, as Belle pointed out, he rarely read anything except the *Morning Telegraph*, a popular daily that combined show-biz gossip with racing tips, he did not use the spectacles often. Belle was constantly attempting to get him to read books and improve his mind. Novels by Wells and Bennett and Galsworthy and other fashionable writers were always lying around, opened invitingly. "Darlin'," Harry told her, "if I improve my mind, I'll stop being a comic. To get laughs, what I have to do is disimprove my mind."

"No such word as disimprove," said Belle, chewing on her supper, which always contained a salad of some sort. Rabbit food, to Harry's way of thinking.

"If I was an educated feller," said Harry, "I couldn't be a comic. I have had no education. So I just have to use my brains."

"Oh, very funny," said Belle. "And anyway, you're off the subject. Why not move in here? You're booked solid into New York City for the next six weeks."

"So I am," said Harry. "But I like my own company when I come offstage. I'm not fit to converse with lovely ladies."

"So I've noticed," said Belle. "But you're very manly in the mornings, and most mornings you're at the Astor Hotel."

"I need my sleep," replied Harry. "And so do you. You work hard on that paper. A bout of wrestling every morning would put a big strain on both of us."

Harry Viner finally played the Palace, New York.

The reviews were very good, too. *Variety* had said, "Harry Viner has arrived at last, and he has done it his way. The King of Kosher Komedy does not care if you like him or not. That is why you like him. He isn't a headliner yet, but how long can he be denied?"

That review sent John Hyatt to the Palace. He saw Harry take three curtain calls. Patsy would not come. She had turned into a full-time mother and very properly, too, as his father had said in a letter from Dublin: "You seem a bit surprised your wife doesn't want to go out to all these theatrical evenings and things. The good woman has two children to look after; she's not going to leave them to the care of some old nurse. You ought to be grateful, son, instead of grumbling."

John Hyatt had been mildly shocked by that letter. He had not been aware he was grumbling. Yet truth to tell, he was sometimes disappointed that Patsy showed so little interest in the work he did. He could have been a publican for all she cared. He was a good husband to her, and as far as Patsy Hyatt was concerned, that was enough. John shook his head. What was he going on about at all? They had a nice house now, and enough money, and the two boys. What else did he expect from life?

Love?

The dressing room was full of people John did not know, socialite women dressed in the modern style, smoking cigarettes in holders, men with longish hair and green cravats, plainly friends of Belle Alvin, who stood in the middle of the room, distributing opinions, "I don't think you can call vaudeville an art, more an event really, but it does speak directly to the ordinary people, and what else does? I mean, does the legitimate stage? Well, hardly. Do books, novels? Who, amongst our toiling poor, reads them? The nickelodeon arcades? Perhaps, eventually. No, I think there's a lot to be said for vaudeville; at least it's spontaneous and genuine even if a lot of it is absolutely childish and silly. But then a lot of people are absolutely childish and silly, wouldn't you say?"

The artistic-looking man she was talking to nodded politely.

John Hyatt understood. She was apologizing for Harry Viner.

The man was a rave at the Palace, and it was not enough? What did she want him to do, write a volume of poetry? He said, "Hello, I'm John Hyatt. We met here about six months ago. Harry was terrific tonight, wasn't he?"

Belle Alvin looked at him a very long moment. There did not seem to be any supporting garments under her dress. He could see the actual shape of her breasts. Her arms were bare and beautiful. John was conscious of her sexuality. It's a challenge with her, he thought. She doesn't want any man to think of her as just a woman, but she screams it with every word and every gesture. He felt more than slightly envious of Harry Viner. He can certainly collect the women, he thought, and hated himself for the envy.

"Oh, yes. You're the songwriter." Belle indicated Harry sitting on his stool, removing the last of his makeup. He was the only person in the dressing room not in deep conversation with somebody. John Hyatt thought he looked rather sad.

"Do talk to Harry; he's always a bit down after a show." Belle turned back to the young man with the green cravat. John Hyatt pushed through the chattering crowd to the dressing table and sat down on a stool next to Harry.

"Hello there," he said through the mirror.

Harry Viner looked back. "John, well, I'll be damned!" He went on removing the eye black. "You got a drink?"

"I'm all right. I saw the show. It was better than any drink."

Harry Viner was still. "You really think that?"

"I do. You had them in your hand."

Harry Viner went on working on his face. "They were good tonight, but they can be bastards here. I have a long way to go before I'm a headliner, but closing the first half isn't bad, for a foreigner."

"I enjoyed every minute of it, even the jokes I'd heard before."

Harry Viner grinned, took his hand and shook it. "Thanks. Sorry I don't need any songs."

"I noticed."

Harry said, "They've given in. I walk on, tell the jokes, walk off. No songs. No monologues. I'm working as a patter comic. If they hate you, it can be bad. I worked Philadelphia in total silence." He shook his head. "I have no insurance. No songs. No pretty lady any longer. It's all me, love me or hate me."

After a pause John asked, "Do you hear from Clara?"

It was, after all, the question he had come to the Palace to ask. Seeing Harry's show had just been an excuse. John Hyatt sighed. He might as well face it. Marriage had changed nothing. The sound of her name still affected him. He was a fool; she didn't even *see* him. He hung, nonetheless, on Harry Viner's reply.

"I've written her twenty letters. She hasn't replied to any of them."

John Hyatt kept his voice very low and even. It was an effort. "Then it's all finished between you?"

Harry Viner's eyebrow lifted. "You always liked her yourself, didn't you, John?"

John Hyatt reddened. "I'm a married man now, Harry. I'm just asking."

"Yes." Harry nodded. "Just to be polite. I know."

John looked at him hard. This man does know, he thought. Yet he's friendly; he doesn't hate me. It would be easier if he did. Perhaps he didn't care for Clara anymore.

"Have you thought of going to England to see her?"

Harry looked surprised. "No. Why should I? I'm her husband. Her place is here with me. Why should I chase across the Atlantic?"

"I don't know," John Hyatt said, "except then you'd know for sure, wouldn't you?" He took a copy of *Variety* from his coat pocket. "She's been doing music hall in London. Did you know?"

Harry Viner did not know, and he was astounded to read the notice.

"Hey, that's good, she learned something with me. Well, who would have thought she could do it?"

"Not you?" John Hyatt ventured ironically.

"No, never thought she had it in her to go solo."

Harry was genuinely surprised and, to give him his due, apparently pleased. It was the last reaction John Hyatt would have expected from him. Harry looked thoughtful. "If she's taken up her career again—and this is a nice little notice, right?—then that's a good reason why she ain't written, isn't it?"

"You don't mind her going off on her own?"

Harry shook his head. "Shows guts, that does. I knew she had guts. The thing was, she never had to struggle in her life till she met me. Maybe that helped a bit. Taught her to stand on her own two feet. Good luck to her."

John Hyatt said, "Keep the paper. I brought it to show you."

Harry put it in his pocket. "Fancy going out for a drink?"

John Hyatt looked around. "These people?"

"They're Belle's friends, not mine. She invited them, I didn't. Let her look after them. Come on."

Harry got to his feet and pushed his way through the crush, touching Belle's arm as he left. "Just having a quick private drink with my old mate here." Harry smiled. "See you back at your place, all right, darlin'?"

"Harry, there are a lot of people here who would like to talk to you." Belle's lips tightened. Harry was, John Hyatt saw, something of a challenge to her as well.

"I'll see them again, dear. Got to talk business to John. Ta-ta now." When they were in the street, Harry breathed out. "Thank Gawd. I never know what half of them are on about."

In the bar, Harry drank bourbon straight with ice, and John Hyatt had a beer. "How's the songwriting game?" Harry asked. He ate pretzels and seemed happier in the bar than he had been in the dressing room. The bourbon, for one thing, kept coming. Harry was plainly tired after three houses that day.

"I'm selling a few songs. My partner, Jimmy, and me and his wife, Mamie—you remember her?—we started a small publishing business of our own. Mamie runs it, she's the business brains. Jimmy and me do the creative work. If you can call it that."

"Well, of course, you can call it that. What else would you call it?"

John Hyatt hadn't meant to tell Harry Viner his troubles. But he found himself doing just that. "We do all right. Mainly, we feed the market. We write a lot of topical songs, ragtime, novelty songs to order, for performers, that kind of thing. We never sit down and write for ourselves, and I think we should sometimes because that's the only way anything very good ever gets done."

Harry finished his bourbon and raised a finger for another. "You know what you said about my walking on and off without a song?"

"I say it's a miracle."

"If I find a song," Harry said absently, "the right song, I wouldn't be above singing it."

"But I thought—"

"I've proved my point, right?" Harry frowned as he wrestled with the thought, straightened his splendid silk tie and tugged at his tweed vest. A large diamond ring glittered on his finger. "I'll never headline unless they can be sure of me. They'll never be

350

sure of me unless I have a song to get off with. My agent, Max Rober, tells me that, and I believe him. So. Sooner or later, I'll have to find a song."

John Hyatt was disappointed. He could not have said why. "I thought you'd made it on your own terms, Harry?"

"I have, but I'll stay last-before-intermission unless I find a song. I don't mean a love song or a ballad or anything. I think it has to be funny. I think it has to tie in with the act I do." He grinned, but he did not seem to be amused. "I'm open to offers, John."

I come here, John Hyatt thought, to find out how things stand between him and Clara, and what do I go away doing? I go away writing Harry Viner a song he doesn't really want.

It was, he reflected, about par for the course, as far as his relations with Harry Viner were concerned. He got to his feet. "I'll be in touch," he said, shook hands and walked out of the bar.

The old stage doorkeeper looked into Clara's dressing room at the London Pavilion.

"Hello, Jack," said Clara. "How are things?"

"Bloody awful," said old Jack. "I reckon we'll be at war soon."

"Just another scare?" said Clara.

"I dunno." He shook his head. "A Mr. Hyatt's at the stage door, miss. Can he come in?"

Clara could not believe it at first. Yet there he was, smiling and healthy-looking as ever, still dressed in tweeds and smoking a pipe (*and* carrying a great bouquet of roses) and telling her how wonderful she had been, how much she had learned since he had written that song for Harry, did she remember?

John Hyatt sat and gazed at her in adoration as they drank champagne (there was a bottle tied inside the bouquet), and she sat, drinking in both the champagne and the adoration, and felt that life, perhaps, was going to be all right once again.

"What are you doing in London?" she asked.

"I had to see my mother," John Hyatt replied, looking at his hands. "She isn't well. Nothing desperate, but I felt I should come over. Once I was in Dublin I thought I'd come on to London, take in the shows."

"It's lovely to see you. How are you? How are your family?"

John Hyatt blushed. He actually blushed. "We have two

children. The songs have been selling, and we have a little house. We are doing all right."

"I'm glad." She was. The thought crossed her mind, as it always did when she saw him, what a very pleasant man he was. "Have you seen Harry at all?"

John Hyatt looked at his hands again. "I saw him a couple of weeks ago. He's playing the Palace. He's had top reviews in *Variety* and *Billboard,* and well, you name it."

Clara felt pain. Harry Viner did not need her or her songs. He could do it on his own, his way. Well, so could she. She had proven it here in London this very night. It still hurt to ask, but something drove her on. "Is he happy?"

"He seemed to be when I saw him." John Hyatt looked embarrassed. "Of course, it was just after a show, like I'm talking to you now. You're both doing very well apart, aren't you?"

"Yes, we are." Clara thought: perhaps he's trying to say we should stay apart, but why would he say that?

"Where is he living now?" she asked.

"He didn't say." John Hyatt hurried on. "We only went for a beer. He asked us to write a song for him—he needs one if he's ever to be a headliner."

"A headliner?" Another jolt, thought Clara. Harry Viner a headliner? He doesn't need me, he really doesn't, he probably wouldn't want me back in the act, why should he, if he's prepared to sing a song to be a headliner?

"Is that woman Belle Alvin still with him?"

It was out before she knew it, but she could not take it back once said.

John Hyatt mumbled, "I don't know, Clara. It's none of my business, is it?"

"Then she was there?" Clara felt cold. "In his dressing room? After the show?"

"A lot of people were there," John Hyatt said. "It didn't have to mean anything."

"Then she is still with him?"

"Honestly, I don't know, Clara."

"Yes, you do. You were there. You saw. She was, wasn't she?"

Beads of perspiration stood out on John Hyatt's forehead. "That time, yes, but how do I know whether—"

Clara cut in, "Where are you going to take me to supper?"

John Hyatt looked bewildered but pleased. "Are you free? What about the Café Royal?"

That was where they went. To sit at a marble-topped table and watch bookmakers and chorus girls and writers and singers, all sitting, eating, drinking, in the large public rooms. They had champagne and caviar and fillet of sole.

John said, looking around the mirrored and gilded hall, "There's nothing like this in New York."

"No, but we haven't got the Palace."

Mention of the Palace reminded them both of Harry Viner, and they fell silent for a long moment. Then John Hyatt started to talk about how London seemed so different, with taxicabs and automobiles in Piccadilly, hooting and snaking through the horse-drawn cabs and drays. Newspaper placards said: "European Crisis." Nobody took any notice. "People seem as poor or rich as ever, though," he said, "but since we're rich tonight, I don't suppose that matters."

They walked a little, after supper, along Piccadilly, through crowds, past the flower girls, who cried their wares deep into the night. John was astonished as always in London by the large numbers of streetwalkers with expensive finery and painted faces. There were a lot of soldiers in uniform, too, a sight rarely seen in New York. The city looked both very rich and very poor, with beggars at most street corners, as if anything and everything was for sale. There seemed to be a strange atmosphere in the air. "It's all this talk of war," Clara said.

"Will it come?" John Hyatt asked.

"Nobody thinks so." They walked on until Clara finally said she was tired, and John Hyatt instantly hailed a hansom. They rode in silence to the Cadogan Hotel in Sloane Street, but once there John Hyatt bade the cabby to wait and put his hand on hers. "I'm a married man," he said, "and I shouldn't be saying this. I love you, Clara, and I always will. I think you know that. No need for you to say anything. There's nothing to say. I'm not the kind of man to do anything about it, and you are not the girl to let me. I just wanted you to know, that's all. I didn't want you to think that incident in my room in New York was all there was."

He sat, silent, looking straight ahead down Sloane Street.

Clara should have been shocked, but she wasn't. She leaned

forward and kissed him on the cheek. He stirred as if he would embrace her, then pulled back.

"You can kiss me," she said, "if you like."

She was not prepared for his kiss to be so passionate, and she was not prepared for the fact that she responded to it. If he asks me to go to his hotel with him, I'll go, she thought, feeling his body urgent against her own, I'll go, I will, and to hell with Harry Viner. But he was pulling away from her by what she knew must be a sheer act of will. "It's the puritan Irish in me," he apologized. "I mustn't."

"No. I know."

"I have to go back and face Patsy."

"Yes. I understand. You're right. It wouldn't be any good."

"Perhaps . . . in the future?"

Clara said, "Who knows?" She kissed him softly on the cheek. "Don't come and see me again. It's been lovely, but don't. Good night, dear John Hyatt, and thank you."

In her hotel room she drank two glasses of port (to the devil with whether it mixed with champagne or not), and then she drank a third. Suddenly she heard shouting in the street. She went down into the hotel lobby and asked what had happened.

The night porter looked serious. "They're calling up the reservists, miss. It looks like war to me."

"War?"

He nodded. "I'm going myself tomorrow. God knows when I'll be back here again, miss."

Clara's first thought was: a war? Would Harry be in it?

Of course he wouldn't. He was too old—forty-three now—and besides, he was in the United States.

And anyway, what was it to do with her any longer, what he did?

Outside, the crowds gathered. There was a strange expectancy in the air. She shivered.

Clara went to bed, but she did not sleep.

Give My Regards to Broadway

Harry was playing the Colonial Theater on Upper Broadway when he heard that war had broken out between England and Germany. He sat staring at the *Trib*'s headline for a long long time.

Max Rober was surprised to find him waiting in the office first thing the next morning, and very depressed but understanding about Harry's plans.

"You'll have to play the Colonial out. I suppose I can cancel your other bookings, but think, Harry, how long it's taken you to get this far. Are you prepared to throw it all away because that is what it could amount to, you know? People have short memories in this business."

Harry said he was sorry.

Max Rober shook his hand and wished him good luck.

At the Cunard shipping office they told Harry there was a waiting list, and he would have to take his place on it, unless he had special priority on war business, which he did not. The clerk in the office looked over his pince-nez and dropped his voice. There had been sinkings in the Atlantic, more, many more than the newspapers reported. Mr. Viner might like to think again?

Harry shook his head.

"I admire you, sir. Joining up, is that it? Enlisting?"

"Something like that," Harry said.

"I'll get you the first passage I can. Don't worry."

"Thanks." Harry nodded.

The clerk said wistfully, "I don't suppose we'll ever get in it."

A month later he pressed the boat papers into Harry's hand. "Don't tell anybody. There was a cancellation. It's murder getting berths, even for people going home to fight, like you."

Harry shook his hand. Was he going home to fight, or was it just an excuse?

"I admire you, sir," the clerk said, "I really do."

That night Harry debated telling Belle Alvin his plans but decided against it. Belle would not understand. She disapproved of war of any kind (she described it as legalized murder), and she was outspoken in her condemnation of both England and Germany. "Thank God we're out of it" was her view.

"Darlin'," said Harry, "I'm English. I'm not out of it."

"Well, of course you are, don't be silly. You're over here."

"Yes," said Harry, "so I am, aren't I?"

Belle asked, "You worrying about your wife?"

"Why should I do that?" asked Harry. "I ain't heard from her since she left, have I?"

Belle looked at him a long moment. Then shook her head. She knows me a bit, Harry thought, but not a lot, really. They went to bed early, and Belle slept at once. Harry lay awake until dawn, wondering if he was doing the right thing. It didn't matter if he was or not. He was doing what he had to, that was all.

He slept until Belle brought his coffee. She was clothed for work and the city.

"Bad night?"

"Been thinking, that's all."

She hesitated. "You all right?"

"Yes, Fine."

Belle kissed him. "You're a delicious man. I love you. Got to rush. Bye now."

Harry lay in bed, drinking his coffee and smoking a cigarette, a habit he had lately picked up. Once he would have thought it feminine, but Belle had complained about his cigars. They left a smell, she said, all over him, hair, underclothes; even the curtains reeked of the tobacco.

Slowly Harry got up, shaved and dressed and looked at the

356

apartment for the last time. He left a note, with the door key, propped on the table. It read:

Belle, you lovely girl. I have to go, love, but I will write and explain it all when I get there. It's been nice, hasn't it? Love, Harry.

Then he went out into the street and called a cab.

London was full of uniforms that first week of the War. Most shows in the capital closed and then reopened. Clara worked steadily (she was now second-top-of-the-bill) and made short patriotic speeches and sang patriotic songs at recruiting centers and public meetings. She was much in demand and very busy in those first hot weeks of War, and only once (on Victoria Station, cheering the boys off to the front with a song sung with a portable piano as sole accompaniment) did she stop to think what it all meant: wounds and dirt and death. But the boys were smiling and waving, and she smiled and waved back. If they could be brave, so could she.

Clara was busy, and in the hectic hot-blooded rush of war she tried to forget Harry Viner. She almost managed it.

Harry Viner had to buy a ticket to get into the Tivoli in the Strand. It went against the grain to do it, but nobody knew him anymore, so there was no possibility of any kind of free ticket. He could not remember when he had last paid for a seat anywhere. He was lucky to get it apparently; it was a sellout. The stalls were packed with officers and their ladies, the gallery with Tommies and their girls. He felt light-headed, and he by no means had his land legs back. Three weeks on the ship seemed a very long time indeed. Expensive, too. He had traveled first class. It had been a long jinking voyage home, the huge liner blacked out, constant changes of course, and fogs and U-boat scares. He had been relieved to dock at Liverpool, touched to see old England again, dressed for war.

He sat and waited for the curtain to rise and felt an expectation so strong that he could hardly bear it. Why hadn't he gone around to her hotel and talked to her there, as a sensible person might, instead of sitting with a lot of punters in an audience?

Surely not because he was afraid of her, surely not because he was getting up his courage, by seeing her first, getting around

357

to the look of her again, perhaps even (the thought chilled him) *trying her out* to see if he still wanted her, giving her an audition, as it were? His thoughts and emotions were jumbled, as they had been ever since he had seen the advertisement in the *Daily Mail* that Miss Clara Viner was playing this week at the Tivoli. Harry's feeling of panic was such that as the curtain rose, he very nearly got up and walked out of the place. This was no way to see her again after all this time, no way at all.

But he didn't get up. He waited, and suddenly there she was.

Two hours later he was outside, in the cool night air, mingling with the home-going crowds. He walked around the block twice, his mind full of sharp impressions, the major one being: she was good, she was very good indeed on her own.

She had lived, as the Cockney saying went, without him.

It was a sobering thought.

So was the fact that he wanted her very much, so much that his loins ached and his thoughts were full of grace and poise, but above all of these was the principal reaction: he was proud of her, bloody proud; it was as simple as that.

In this frame of mind, he presented himself at the stage door.

The ancient stage doorkeeper demanded his name in a brusque fashion and, when he refused to give it, refused in turn to go and see if Miss Viner would see him.

"All right," said Harry. "It's Mr. Smith."

"You sure it's Smith?" demanded the stage doorkeeper, a much more belligerent creature than usual.

"It always has been," said Harry.

"Don't I know you?" asked the old man.

"No," lied Harry.

The stage doorkeeper came back in two minutes. "She doesn't know any Smiths, so go and get yourself a beer and cool down. She's a lady, Miss Viner is, you've got no chance with her, a masher like you."

Harry put two pound notes in the stage doorkeeper's hand and asked which hotel Miss Viner was staying at. The stage doorkeeper said he couldn't tell him that.

Harry Viner made it a fiver.

Clara took off her dress when she got to the room in the Cadogan Hotel and bathed in warm water in the deep iron bath. It was absolute heaven, the best moment of the evening.

There was a sudden knocking on her bedroom door.

"It's open," she called. It was obviously the maid who came to turn the covers down.

No answer.

"Come in," she called. The maid must be deaf.

Harry Viner stood in the doorway.

Clara stared at him.

"Hello, Clara."

"Harry, what are you doing here?"

It was a stupid thing to say, but what else?

"Looking at you. You look very tasty an' all."

"Tasty?" What a word for an occasion like this!

"Very."

I'm not sure, Clara thought, that I can get out of this bath. She stood up, turned away from him and reached for the large white towel. How would she get through the next ten minutes? she wondered, her cheeks burning (after all, she was *naked*) and her body suddenly chill.

Harry Viner solved her problem for her. He reached out and picked her up in his arms.

"Harry, don't be a fool!"

He carried her into the bedroom.

"Harry, don't, you have no right—"

He laid her on the satin coverlet.

"Harry, we have to talk, you can't do this, I'll scream."

"Scream then," said Harry Viner. "Tell them your husband is raping you."

"I will," she promised, white-faced and trembling.

"You won't." He took off his boots, shirt and trousers in quick movements, holding onto her arm with his free hand. She struggled and bit his arm. She beat at him with her fists. He took no notice. She squirmed away from his body as he lay on her. It was only when his lips met hers that she stopped struggling.

They made love four times that night, and she came each time. Harry said he loved her as many times and more.

She believed him.

"You have a nerve," Clara told him next morning. "You come into the hotel, make love to me and then send for breakfast as if this happens every day."

"I wish it did. I've been waiting for last night for over a year."

359

For Harry had rung for breakfast in bed, and that is what they had got. The nice chambermaid had been scandalized to see Harry in bed with Clara and even more astonished when he had explained. "It's all right. I'm her old man. Got a room along the corridor I won't be using now. Can we have the best and biggest breakfast you've got?"

The breakfast had turned out to be ham and eggs (even with a war on!), and Harry had eaten it all and drunk pints of coffee, and so had she, and all they had really done, she thought, was make love, laugh and eat; they had not talked at all.

"We haven't talked yet," Clara protested. Surely that wasn't just it; he didn't really expect them to pick up exactly where they had left off?

"What's there to talk about?" He kissed her. It seemed odd that he had no mustache now. "I can talk to anybody."

Clara disengaged herself. After all, *four* times, really, it was very nearly indecent. "How did you find out I was here?"

"Stage doorkeeper told me."

"Oh. You didn't see the show?"

"I did."

Clara ached for his view of it but resolutely refused to ask.

He grinned. "You're marvelous. First-rate."

It was her turn to kiss him. "Oh, Harry, do you really think so?"

He opened the *Daily Chronicle*, put on his reading glasses. She was shocked. Harry in specs? He looked over them and said, "I'm short of the old lamp oil, so I had to get these, duck. Suit me, don't they?" He turned the pages of the *Chronicle* curiously. "Hey, what's happened to the paper? Only six pages?"

"Harry, why did you come? Was it to see me?"

"Course it was!"

"Not the War?"

"What War?"

He did not look up. She admired his nerve, dismissing her performance with less than half a dozen words! Mind, they were good words. *First-rate, marvelous!* Did he mean it? Oh, yes. He meant it. Harry never said anything about the business he didn't mean. Give him credit for that. Still, he could spend a little longer on it.

"Did you like my dresses?"

Harry looked over the paper. "Very nice."

"What about the songs?"

"Not wonderful, but you sold them lovely."

"By the way," she said, "John Hyatt was over."

"Oh, yes?"

"He wrote me he got back to the States safely."

"Nice for him."

He returned to the newspaper. Suddenly she felt very angry. "What makes you think you can walk straight back into my life and into my bed like this?"

He smiled. "Because I've done it, love."

"No, you haven't," she suddenly screamed. "Get out, go on, you rotten lecher, you were sleeping with that newspaper tart while I was pregnant, which I was in that clinic, you rotten, lousy swine, you, you haven't even asked me why I ran away from you, you think all you have to do is put your cock inside me and all's well with me, you and the world!"

Harry took off his spectacles and laid down his *Chronicle.*

"Well, it is, isn't it?"

"Stop joking, you rotten swine, I mean it." Tears ran down her face as she thought of the months of separation and despair. "I was a fool, and I knew it, to let you do what you did last night, but it isn't going to happen again! Get out!"

Harry sat very still. His face had gone white. That, she thought, trembling violently, was something at least.

"Let me say one or two things." He didn't try to touch her. He seemed turned to stone. "I had no idea why you ran off to England, but I thought it was because you'd had enough. Enough of being without, of losing the child, of me."

"I hated losing the child, I could live without, but I wasn't sick of you till I found a letter—by accident—from that woman! *That's* why I ran away, the main reason anyway. Oh, I expect you'll tell me it was nothing at all, but it *is!* It was the last bloody straw."

"You've learned to swear, I notice," Harry said.

"You taught me."

"A man sometimes goes with women, and it means nothing. I thought you knew that."

"Men always say it means nothing. That's all I know."

"Well, for your information, dear, I had one night with Belle Alvin before you went into the clinic. A long time before, after we'd had a row. And once after you came out of the clinic. Don't ask me why I did it, I don't know. It wasn't important, and she wasn't important then."

"You were with her in New York only a few weeks ago. She was in your dressing room at the Palace, deny that if you can."

"Yes, she was," Harry said patiently. "I started seeing her after you didn't reply to my letters. I sent you thirty-three letters, if you remember."

"I burned them."

"There you are, you burned them. Anyway, you didn't write back. You were in England. I was in the States. What was I to think? I thought it was over. I was sorry—"

"So you jumped into bed with this Belle Alvin."

"Six months after you left I did. What do you think I am, a eunuch?"

"Oh, I know you're not *that.*"

"Well, that's all there was to it, on my side. I've said good-bye to her, and I've chased you from New York, come across the Atlantic for you, and that ain't no picnic at the moment, let me tell you, and if that doesn't prove to you that I love you, then I don't know what will!"

Harry got out of bed and stood staring out the window.

"And I'll tell you another thing. Before I came here, I went to a recruiting office and volunteered for the army. No chance, I have a perforated eardrum. So it's been a very mixed day, dear, very mixed indeed."

Clara looked at him standing there, naked, plainly very, very angry indeed. She did the only thing she could under the circumstances.

"Harry," she said softly, "come back to bed."

"Not likely."

"Come on. I'm sorry." She stretched out her hand.

He remained staring out of the window. "On one condition. It's all over. We don't talk about any of that, any of it, anymore, not a single bloody word, ever. It's all over, done with, finished. We start again from now, this morning, or I catch the next boat back to the States. Make up your mind."

"I had it all wrong. I thought—" Clara stopped. What did it matter what she thought? Either she accepted the terms, and they were reasonable, Harry sounded as if he was telling the truth about Belle Alvin, which was all that mattered, really, or she didn't. If she didn't, it was the end. Anyway, what more was there to say? She had said it already; she was still trembling from the violence of saying it.

"Harry, not another word. Come to bed." That was all, she realized, she had ever wanted to say.

Walter de Frece was pleased to take on Harry and Clara as a double act. No audition was necessary; Harry's status in New York and Clara's in London were recommendation enough. There was a number one tour going out after four weeks in London halls. Would they consider headlining?

"What will you call yourselves?" asked Walter de Frece.

"Viner and Viner again," said Harry. "What's the show called?"

"Giggles and Girls," said Walter de Frece without a smile.

"Oh, Lor'," said Harry.

Giggles and Girls was full of patriotic songs and sketches. It began with a chorus of girls in a kick line, singing the song that Florrie Forde had made famous, "It's a long, long way to Tipperary," on a stage festooned with Union Jacks and a cheering cast waving other Union Jacks.

Clara led the chorus, dressed as an infantry officer in cap and tunic and Sam Browne belt and stick, with her lovely legs, encased in tights, spreading out from beneath the khaki of the uniform. She was singing a song that Harry had heard the white-faced soldiers in the bars laughing at amongst themselves. There was a private bitterness in their laughter. Only when he had bought them many drinks had they talked about how things really were in the trenches. Their voices were hollow and defeated and, although they were young in years, very, very old. Harry listened to their words and looked in their eyes and said nothing. There was nothing to say. In the end they had stopped talking abruptly and turned away, as if he could not possibly understand; they were disloyal fools for talking of such things to somebody who knew nothing but Blighty.

Clara was receiving generous applause for her song, nonetheless. Harry watched her move. She was a lovely mover, and he liked to think he had taught her a good deal there. She sang well, too, and the martial air suited her:

> I'm going back back back to the firing-line,
> This fighting business suits me fine,

> Far away from all the wenches
> I'll be safer in the trenches,
> Going back back back to the firing-line!

Clara saluted, the Union Jacks waved all around her, the chorus kicked high, the music crashed to a crescendo and the applause came solid, from all over the house. Harry wet his lips, preparing himself, as the dancers skittered off, perspiring, into the wings. Harry marched out as if on parade, did a pratfall and stood up again. He surveyed his audience and said, "I'm sick of the army! I am! I've only just joined today, and I'm sick of it. Look at the uniform they've given me. When I stand at attention, I look as if I'm at ease. Except you never are in the army, are you? I mean, you're on the go, morning to night, aren't you? March here, march there, it's awful, isn't it? You don't know where you're going until you're there, do you, and not always then? I mean. . . ." Harry paused; this was his new piece for the night, and he wondered how many soldiers there were in the audience and if they would get it. The house had looked a bit thin on uniforms when he had glanced through the peephole in the curtains fifteen minutes before. There was a big push on in Flanders, and it was said men had been recalled from leave in their thousands. "They're keeping me back for the big push," he said. "Not the one that's going on now." There was a sudden silence. "Or the next one." More silence. "Or the one after that. No, the very last one. When there'll be nobody left but me to send."

There was total silence.

Then a voice from the gallery: "Too bloody true, mate!"

Harry called up to the man, plainly a soldier, "Well, if you apply in writing, I might let you go in my place."

"Not bloody likely," replied the voice in the darkness.

There was a quiet, conspiratorial laugh at that, from many different parts of the hall. The soldiers know what I'm talking about, but the civilians don't, and they don't want to. The white-faced soldiers were right. The War was a well-kept secret.

Harry saluted and almost fell over and said, "The girls love me in my uniform, you know. Oh, yes. It's the size of my bayonet. I've got a big bayonet." The audience tittered, especially the women. This was safer ground. "Shall I show you my bayonet? Shall I?"

"Yes, go on," shouted the women, many of them, he knew,

munitions girls with soldier husbands at the front, earning a tenth of what the girls got for filling shells.

"You have to ask me nicely," Harry Viner said. "You have to say, 'Show me the size of your bayonet.' Say it nicely for me, girls!"

They screamed it for him.

Harry brought an enormous scabbard from down his trouser leg and held it up innocently in front of him. "They say it's the biggest bayonet in the army."

The stalls screamed. The gallery roared.

He stood and let them settle down.

Harry said, "I was walking down the street, and this lady gave me a white feather. 'You're a coward,' she said, 'you should be in the army.' I said, 'I'm in the army, but I wear my uniform back to front.' 'Why do you do that?' asked this lady. I said, 'So when I'm retreating, they think I'm advancing.' "

Total silence now, but not hostile, with again some soldiers' laughter.

Harry said, "Well, this lady who gave me the white feather, I won't tell you what I gave her. But if you're around in nine months' time, I might."

The whole audience laughed tolerantly. The ladies who handed out white feathers were not generally liked. Before he lost them altogether, Harry called, to a bugle note, "That's for me, I'm off to the war." He saluted. "If I never see you again, it'll be too soon!"

He started to walk off, to a roar of applause, and did a pratfall at the curtain.

The reviews were ecstatic. " 'Viner and Viner' are the funniest and most melodious act to be currently seen on the London halls," thundered the *Times* which normally never reviewed music hall, but, since *Giggles and Girls* was a patriotic revue, made an exception.

Clara and Harry sat in their room at the Cadogan Hotel and bathed in the success. "I never thought we'd make it as big as this," said Harry. "I knew we could do it, of course, but I don't care if we never have it again; this has been worth waiting for! I keep expecting to wake up and find it's only a dream."

Clara loved him most then, loved his bravery. A lot of people thought his "coward" jokes in bad taste, and there were even complaints to managements. They were ignored. People knew the truth about the War. As they traveled with *Giggles and Girls* from town to town, staying always in the best hotels, recognized everywhere they went, Clara was truly happy. They made love often, with much tenderness. They did not think of the future; they were too busy enjoying the present. Harry felt guilty about that and tried twice more to enlist. "Go and entertain the troops, Mr. Viner, sir," said a recruiting sergeant. "When we need yer, we'll send for yer!"

"I feel a fraud, tellin' gags and all those fellas dying," Harry grumbled. Clara said nothing to that but thanked God he wasn't going to the front. They were into the second year of the War, and the casualty lists were getting longer every month.

Inevitably, they played the Alhambra, top-of-the-bill. Adam was delighted to see them, Marta less so. Harry said, "Proper tight-ass she is, isn't she?" Clara thought: if Papa only could have seen me now. She cried a little at the thought, but Harry just laughed kindly and said, "He'd have cut your wages because you were his daughter!"

Harry never told his innermost thoughts. She knew that. She took no offense.

Adam took Harry aside and told him that it was only a matter of weeks before he would be in uniform. Marta would carry on the Alhambra with the aid of a house manager.

"Good luck, old mate," said Harry hollowly, shaking his hand. Poor old lad, he thought.

Clara was invited to Miss Wilson's Academy for Young Ladies to take tea with the staff. Since she was now married *and* a success celebrated in the "One of the Great English Beauties" series in the *Illustrated London News* no less, she was *almost* respectable again. Her presence in the leafy, spacious school was soon known, and the girls peered at her as they changed classes. Miss Wilson was the same, gray skirt, gray cardigan, steel gray hair. "You were always one of our more vivacious gels, Clara; no doubt I am an old fogey and not in touch with the great changes that this dreadful war has brought about."

Clara, who had "dressed down" to absolute dowdiness, a dark costume, skirt four inches from the ground (the War had brought in the fashion generally) smiled. She was certain of a place in the school's private honors list: the girl who had run off to go, not even on the stage, but on the halls!

"I understand your brother, Adam, is now in charge of the family fortunes?"

"Yes, he is, and doing very well, I'm glad to say, Miss Wilson."

"I'm pleased to hear that," said Miss Wilson.

So long as there are family fortunes, Clara thought. She waved to a group of girls at the school gate and called, "Get your papas to bring you to the show, tell them it's very naughty. That should bring them." And she hitched her skirt up. The girls laughed, and the teacher frowned but said nothing, and Clara thought: why did I do that? I get more like Harry Viner every day. I'm simply not respectable any longer!

She had even seen her old school chum Agnes Thorburn in Grainger Street, hanging onto the arm of a naval lieutenant. Agnes Thorburn was married now, with two children. Her husband was on Atlantic convoy duty, returning to sea the next day. Agnes had seemed envious of Clara but had pressed her hand in parting and said in a longing voice, "I wish I had your courage, I'd have run off with you!" Then she was gone, her husband also (a local boy Clara half remembered), and Clara was alone again in the city street.

Yes, it was nice to be home and famous.

Adam was eventually called up, in the army. He came to the Metropolitan, Edgware Road, where they were playing that week, bronzed from his training on Salisbury Plain and looking ten years younger than the last time they'd seen him. He had with him Jack Lewis, a young subaltern, who was plainly overawed to be backstage in an actress's dressing room and who blushed whenever he spoke. Gold-haired and blue-eyed, he was eighteen and had a very slight stammer.

They wouldn't have known he was eighteen if Adam hadn't said so, explaining Lewis was straight from school into the army.

"You don't need to tell your sister that, you ass," he reprimanded Adam. "She's upset enough already, seeing you in uniform."

Which Clara certainly was. She had seen enough wounded men, in white shirts and blue invalid jackets, to have any illusions about what might happen. Harry had gone, still in his makeup, to send the stage doorkeeper for drinks. They had none in the dressing room. Alcohol was getting hard to come by. The pubs were open only a few hours a day, and it had been made an offense to buy drinks for friends. It was a rule everybody ignored. "I'm sorry." Clara dabbed her eyes with her cambric hankie. "It was such a shock, seeing you there, in your uniform."

"They train you in six weeks now," supplied young Jack Lewis. "Then it's into the trenches." He blushed. "I say, I'm sorry, I'm saying the wrong thing now, aren't I?"

"Jack," said Adam, "for God's sake, just sit down and stop wearing my sister out with your eyes."

"Oh, I say, draw it mild, dear boy," said Jack Lewis, very red about the ears. "I w-wasn't really staring, Miss Viner. It's just I thought you were absolutely w-wonderful out there tonight. I mean, I think you looked ma-marvelous."

Adam laughed, sprawling there in his boots and puttees and Sam Browne belt. "What he means is, he's never seen a girl's legs before. It's the first time he's been to a music hall."

"Is it really the first time you've seen a girl's legs?" Clara asked.

"I do have four sisters," said Jack Lewis stoutly, blushing pinker than ever.

"No," pressed Clara, she didn't quite know why. "I mean, is it?"

"Well, yes, I suppose so. I've been at school till this term, and in the hols my pater would never take us to a music hall. He's a parson, you see." He blinked. "I do wish your brother wouldn't tell all my secrets. It's so t-terribly embarrassing."

"Not to me." Clara touched his arm. "I think you're very nice."

Adam laughed, and Clara laughed, too, but there were still tears in her eyes. Harry came back in with a bottle of whiskey. "I won't tell you what this cost because you won't believe me." He found some glasses, and they sat around, drinking and smoking, Adam his pipe and Harry his cigarette. Jack Lewis accepted one, but it made him cough, and he held it gingerly, as if it might explode. Clara smiled at him, and he smiled back. Eighteen, she thought, fifteen years younger than I am, and he might be dead this time next week. She pushed the thought away. They could both be dead, Adam, too.

"Is Marta carrying on the Alhambra?" she asked quickly, to drown the awful thought.

Adam nodded. "How long for I don't know. I've got somebody to manage it for her." He looked at Harry. "Perhaps later, you might be able to go back, give her a hand?"

"Yes, of course," said Clara.

Harry said nothing. Clara knew what he was thinking: how

would they get on with Marta if she was the boss? Clara kissed Adam and said, "Could you boys finish your drinks and wait for me at the stage door while I get decent?" This was a reference to her legs, encased in black tights, which young Jack Lewis had been painfully averting his eyes from ever since he came into the dressing room. Now he jumped to his feet, upsetting his drink, apologized and finally got out of the door.

Harry said to Adam, "Where did you find him?"

"He's the youngest in the draft," Adam said. "I'm the oldest."

Adam was thirty-six.

They ate at the Café Royal, and Clara, who was fearful, made a great thing of being gay. They drank champagne at three pounds a bottle (the Café Royal never ran out of champagne) and ate Dover soles. Harry told them that he had met Mae, from the original sea lions act that had been on the bill with him his first night at the Alhambra. He had asked her how the act was going, and she had told him the seals had starved to death. There was almost no fish being caught, and certainly none for seals. She had cried as she told him. Harry had been shocked, both at the story of the seals and at Mae's appearance. She looked twenty years older, a stout and hennaed lady. She was working in a war factory, and so was her husband. She had pressed Harry's hand. "I often think about the old times, Harry," she had said. "I'm so glad you had the luck." Then she was gone, into the crowded Strand, lost in the vast crowds of soldiers and sailors and marines trudging around the streets of the West End, looking for a drink or a woman or both.

"And here we are," Harry said, "eating Dover soles. The poor old seals could have done with these."

"Harry, I didn't know about the seals," Clara said. "You didn't tell me."

"Didn't want to depress you, love," said Harry, but Clara knew it was because he had slept with Mae before he knew her.

Harry thought: I wish I'd never told that story, and I also wish I'd given Mae a few quid. Not that she'd have taken it, no. She had her pride. A munitions factory, just the same, it was a hard world, as if he'd ever doubted it. He talked to Adam about the possibility of going back to the Alhambra, but his heart was not in it. He told Adam the truth, something he had not yet confided even to Clara. "I'm trying to get in on a tour of the troops over in France. I saw Seymour Hicks, he's doing all the arranging. You go with a party for a couple of weeks, play hospital and troop concerts and so on. We're down on the list, and I got a tip we might go in a week or two." Harry tried to look sorry, but he wasn't really. He could not see any hope of running the Alhambra with Marta for a partner. He felt sympathy for Adam, though, sitting there, bronzed and fit, with a furrowed brow.

"I just don't want it to close," Adam said. "Once a theater closes, people never come back to it."

Harry knew he was right, but he said no more.

Jack Lewis was enjoying himself. The champagne, on top of the whiskey and the food, had eased his embarrassment to the point that his stammer was hardly noticeable.

"I've been planning to go to nearly every music hall in London," he was confessing to Clara, "but we're going over to France tomorrow, there's been a change of plan, so really yours is the only show I'll see. I wanted to see Violet Lorraine and George Robey in the *Bing Boys*, I do so like "If You Were the Only Girl in the World"—it's very nearly my favorite tune, you know. . . ."

"What is your favorite song?"

He blushed, and the stammer came back. "I suppose it's . . . 'The Garden of Your Heart.' It's n-not so well known as the 'Only Girl in the World,' but I like it even better. Do you know it?"

Clara smiled. "Everybody knows it. I'll sing it for you one day when you're on leave. You'll get leave, you know."

The young face sobered suddenly. "That's what they say."

Clara laid her hand on his. "Of course you will. And I'll sing it for you, I promise."

"Will you? Really and truly, Miss Viner?"

"Really and truly." Clara took a photo card of herself (head and bare shoulders) from her handbag and wrote across it, "To Jack Lewis with love, Clara Viner."

He took it gingerly. "I'll treasure it," he said.

They ate and drank till late, and then they all took a taxi to Waterloo Station for Adam and Jack Lewis to catch their troop train to France. Clara and Harry watched them leaning out the window of the packed train until they went out of sight and all that remained in the dark and eerie station was the sound of medical orderlies' voices and the revving of the ambulance engines outside. For the train that took men back to the front had brought the wounded in earlier.

Suddenly Clara was cold and afraid and hopelessly angry.

370

She put her arm in Harry's.

"Let's get out of this awful place," she said.

Slowly they walked out into the dark night.

Marta did not want any help at the Alhambra, she wrote. It was now 1917, and the War could not go on for very much longer, surely, and no doubt Adam would be home again soon. She appreciated Harry and Clara's offer, but she would keep the Alhambra going, as best she could, with the aid of Mr. Sykes, her husband's assistant manager, and they would just have to see how things turned out.

"She must think Adam's going to win the War all on his own," said Harry, sitting in their hotel, a *Daily Mail* in front of him with a headline reading "Setback at Arras." "This War could go on for another ten years, unless the Americans come in."

"Do you think they will?" asked Clara.

"They'll be fools if they do, but yes. Whether it'll be this year or next, who knows?" He laid down the *Mail*. "Clara, I saw Seymour Hicks yesterday. He says we can go over to France in two weeks' time."

"What?" Clara knew Harry had been dallying with the idea, but she was still shocked. The War was nearer in London than it had been up North, but in a way it was not real; it happened over there, in another land, where people spoke a different tongue. She wondered if she was up to the strain of singing to soldiers under the conditions out there. "Did you say we'd go?" she asked.

"Yes." Harry stood up, and put his arms around her. "Adam and that boy Lewis going decided it for me. We can always cry off, though, if you want to."

"No," Clara said. "We should have gone before this. We could have."

"Yes, we could, but better late than never. You're trembling, love, are you scared?"

"Yes," Clara said. "Yes, I am."

"Of what, the shells?"

"I don't know," Clara said. She didn't.

They went over with a full concert party on the troopship *Aries* and entrained at Calais for the base camp at Étaples. They could already hear the guns. At Étaples they played in a huge marquee to several thousand men on their way up or down from the line. They were a pretty ragbag outfit, including two girl tap dancers, and two singers. There were no animal or wire acts. Their sole instrument was a piano which went everywhere with them, on the back of a lorry. They got used to working in the open air and learned to yell much louder even than usual at the huge and motionless crowds of men sitting or standing on the lawns of châteaux (converted into hospitals) or standing around the Hôtel de Ville of some half-ruined French provincial town. They learned to play in hospital wards (singing and pattering very softly then) to men without arms, legs or eyes or sometimes simply without hope.

The concert party was billeted in officers' messes, and they ate what the officers ate. Corned beef and bread and sometimes whiskey or beer or brandy to drink. There were no fresh vegetables or fruit to be had. "The whole of France is one bloody great mud heap," Harry said, gazing around the shattered landscapes, the broken and splintered trees and the pockmarked earth. "It is, it's one bleeding great cemetery." He was so depressed by it all that he drank a good deal (when he could get it) and fell silent for days at a time.

When he worked, he came to life. Clara thought it was because he felt he had to do something since he could not fight. He worked harder than anybody else, and he never grumbled about the conditions. They had reason; they became lice-infested and dirty, and they drank only chlorinated water. "These fellas are here till they die or get wounded," Harry said. "They have a reason to complain. We haven't. We're going back home to clean beds at the end of the week after next."

The audiences of soldiers must have sensed something of this, for Harry's act always went well. He encouraged them to sing the songs they had made their own, like:

> If you want to find the Colonel I know where he is,
> I know where he is, I know where he is.
> If you want to find the Colonel, I know where he is,
> He's hanging on the old barbed wire!

The manager of the concert party, Mr. Crook, asked Harry to go easy on that song. "It's not quite on, old boy," he said, pulling his mustache, elegant in a tailored khaki uniform. "Not liked, d'you see?"

"The troops like it," said Harry. "I thought we were here to cheer them up."

"Not with that song," said the manager firmly.

"Jesus," said Harry, and went on and did his comic soldier who was being held back for the big push. "I've ordered my wooden leg in advance," he told the troops. "But if I don't need it, you can have it." The troops cheered.

He was reprimanded about that, too.

Clara, on the other hand, hardly altered her songs at all. She sang them "Naughty But Nice," giving them new verses:

> The young soldier kissed me at somewhere near Loos,
> He kissed me again at . . . do *you* parlez-vous?

She talked:

"I must say he was very manly, I hear he got a medal that night."

The troops roared. In their parlance, getting a medal meant, as Harry had *not* pointed out to Clara, contracting a dose of the pox. Riding laughter she did not understand, she sang with Harry:

> Naughty but Nice, Naughty but Nice,
> Never Been Kissed in the Same Place Twice!

"You might have told me there was a laugh coming," she said, wiping off her makeup in a bell tent.

"No, dear," said Harry. "If you'd known, you wouldn't have done it half so well."

"Is there anything you won't do for a laugh?" she asked him.

"Die?" said Harry.

They went back to London, exhausted and dirty, but with a feeling of accomplishment. They put their names down for another tour in three months' time. They slept solidly for two days, bathed, got rid of the dirt and the insects and went to work again. They did not speak of the experience, but it had left a mark on them, of horror at what was happening in France and of pride that men could put up with it, with only a cheerful word and a cigarette to help them.

"Least we can do," said Harry. "Go again, right?"

Clara agreed. She knew he was thinking about Adam. Doing this helped, or seemed to. A letter had arrived marked "Somewhere in France," and it said simply that he was well, and so was Jack Lewis and that Jack Lewis was looking forward to hear Clara sing "The Garden of Your Heart." Clara wrote back and could only hope the letters got there.

House managers complained, without hope, to Harry, asked him to cheer up his act, which was full of references to war profiteers and people avoiding military service. He asked, in turn, "Can you see anything to be so bloody cheerful about, mate?"

There was one thing. The Americans came into the War.

London was suddenly full of tall young men (they all seemed six inches taller than Britishers) in wide-brimmed hats and button-up coats and gaiters. They did not stay long, for their destinations were Belleau Wood and the Argonne.

A card arrived at the theater—it was the Palace, Leicester Square, that week—for Clara. It was from John Hyatt. Would she and Harry come to a concert at Richmond Park for American troops the following Sunday afternoon? He was organizing the concert. Would they send a reply by the sergeant who had brought the message? Clara wrote across the card. "We'll be there," and gave it to the gum-chewing sergeant herself. He saluted and got back on his motorcycle. Clara called to him, "Where are you from, Sergeant?"

"Brooklyn, miss."

"Know the Bushwick Theater?"

"Do I!"

"I've played there."

"Wish I was going there next week, instead of over there."

"Do you?"

He grinned. He was a large, beefy man. "Not really, miss. Let's get this War over, shouldn't take too long, huh?"

He saluted and roared off into Leicester Square. He looked fit and confident and well fed, amongst the gray and shabby Londoners in the square, half of them wearing black armbands for lost sons or husbands. Clara went back into the Palace to get ready for the next show.

Harry smiled when she told him but said nothing except: "John Hyatt in the army? He'll do anything to get over here to see you, won't he?"

John Hyatt was a captain in the U.S. Army. He looked very splendid in his uniform, and Harry said, "I don't know whether to shake hands with you or salute you."

Clara kissed John Hyatt a little too warmly for Harry's taste, but he was tolerant. He said, staring out at the solid ranks of young men squatting on the grass in the sun, waiting for the performance to start, "You're running the show, are you?"

"They're letting me do it. In fact, they've taken me off military duties to do it."

"You should be so lucky," said Harry.

"Is it that bad?"

"It's worse. I can't think why you joined."

"A fight and an Irishman not in it, come on, Harry!"

"What about your songwriting business?"

"My partner and his wife are carrying it on. This war won't last long anyway."

"Well," Harry said, looking at the lines of young men stretching back as far as the eye could see, "you've brought a few friends, and do we need them!"

Later, standing on the makeshift stage, he shouted at them, hoping his voice carried in the open air, "The Tommies in the trenches say that a hundred thousand monkeys could win this War, everybody's so tired. I can see you've arrived!"

The doughboys loved it.

The one-liner was something American audiences had always liked. Harry thought, as he worked: oh, if only we'd gone back to the States. The trouble with this business, he thought, *if only.* . . .

He did his comic soldier sketch for them, but it flopped. They had not yet experienced the trenches, and it meant nothing. They were like the British volunteers in 1914. He felt like crying. Instead, he peppered his act with references to ball games and —greatly daring to such a big audience that might not *see*— a version of his old frankfurter routine. It was the hit of the afternoon.

Clara sang:

> I went for a walk with a doughboy today,
> He was a top sergeant, and to me he did say. . . .

Clara talked:

" 'Lady, *please* don't stand at attention.' . . . He took me and kissed me in Richmond Park, oh, it was lovely, oh, such a lark, If I hadn't been a lady, I might have. . . . He was ever so nice, in his uniform. . . . Or out of it. Oh, I am *naughty,* aren't I?. . ."

The troops roared. The complete company sang, to close the show:

> Give my regards to Broadway,
> Remember me to Herald Square,
> Tell all the gang at Forty-second Street,
> That I will soon be there. . . .

Clara said good-bye to John Hyatt and kissed his cheek. "Thank you for asking us, and take care over there."

John Hyatt grinned. "I never thought you and Harry would get together again, but I saw in *Variety* you were doing well over in England here. So then I knew. Just I felt I had to see you again before I . . . went to France."

She kissed him. It was different now. Kinder. Perhaps it was because they were older, just that.

Harry came in, and they shook hands with John Hyatt and his colonel, who said to them, "Come back to the States, you'll do great."

In the summer they went once again on another trenches tour. They were luckier this time, and Clara got lifts in the back of a staff car assigned for the purpose. She had expected summer to be nicer, but of course, it was not. A sweetish stench hung over everything, seemed to get into the nostrils and stay there, despite the liberal use of chloride, in water and trench. It was the smell of death. After a while one got used to it. They racketed along the potholed roads, and once they got near enough to the line to be within shelling range. It was nothing planned, it just happened, and Harry fronted it out, as usual, by standing amongst a crowd of artillerymen, during a lull in the battle, and telling them a lot of jokes, sitting on a gun carriage. They got three hearty cheers when they left, but as Harry said to the driver, "Corporal, just go in *that* direction, fast!"

The corporal driver grinned. He had three wound stripes.

Harry, though, went up into the line and saw for himself the very next day. How he managed it, Clara never knew, and it was certainly unofficial. He borrowed the corporal's greatcoat and hat, and when he came back to the billet (they were six miles behind the lines, at Lorraine), he was very shocked. "I knew it was bad," he said. "Not as bad as that."

Clara was afraid for him and angry. "Were they fighting? It

would have served you right if they were; you might have got killed."

"No. It was quiet. They were just standing about in the trenches, smoking, waiting. Like people at a funeral. Theirs."

"Oh, Harry." She kissed him. He felt things so much, she thought, though he'd die rather than say so. It was what made him a good comic.

Harry worked harder than ever at the concert the next day. It was at the Hôtel de Ville, and the troops were mostly from a rest camp nearby. There were some Americans, looking dirty and tired now, the lack of sleep etching lines on their young, farm-fresh faces. The few French civilians left in the town stood around in jabots and shawls. They were mostly women. It was rare to see a man of any age in France. Only old men. Everybody else was dead or in the army. It was said that the French took conscientious objectors to the front line and threw them over the parapet, saying, "Go and join your friends over there."

Harry and Clara stood in this wreck of a town (the shattered cathedral looming over them) and worked hard to please the crowd, who stood in the sun, inhaling the sweet stinking air, ready to applaud, grateful to be, at least for another day, alive. When it was over, they were astonished to see Adam and young Jack Lewis in the crowd of soldiers pressing forward.

They looked very tired and muddied, but they were grinning. Adam had an extra two pips on his sleeve. Clara rushed into his arms, crying. Harry shook hands with young Jack Lewis.

"You look a bit dirtier than when I last saw you," Harry said.

Jack Lewis nodded. "We've been in a couple of shows."

"Is that what you call them, shows?" Harry asked.

"You have to call them something," young Jack Lewis answered. His face was suddenly grinning.

He's only eighteen, Harry thought, only eighteen. "Come on inside, we've got our own mess, a couple of rooms borrowed off the officers."

They went into the half-ruined Hôtel de Ville. It had once been a splendid Victorian building, but now they could see the sky through part of the roof. It was said to be safe, or as safe as anywhere could be unless a Big Bertha shell had their number on it. Big Bertha could fire twenty-two miles. They were well within range of other artillery. They had grown used to it.

"Aren't you going to congratulate your brother on his cap-

377

taincy?" asked young Jack Lewis. Mud had dried on his uniform, which looked as if it had been slept in a hundred times, which it probably had by now.

Harry laughed, fumbling for the bottles of vin rouge they had been given by the departing officers. It was not very good, but it was all there was. The whiskey had run out. "They say this stuff rots your boots." Harry poured them all large measures. "We've been promised hot food in hay boxes, when it comes." He raised his glass formally. "Congratulations, Adam. And good luck." He then pretended his drink had gone down the wrong way and collapsed into a mock coughing fit. This cheered everybody up, and they were even more cheered by the arrival of the promised hot food in the metal hay boxes. The meal was tinned stew, and they ate it with appetite, by the light of candles. The windows of the room were permanently blacked out by beams nailed across them. The room contained a few iron army cots with doubtful-looking blankets and palliasses thrown across them. Since the night was warm, they had no need of a fire, so they sat and ignored the low rumbling of the guns and talked of the London shows. All the officers they met asked them about the shows—what was still running? Was *Chu-Chin-Chow* still on? Was *Maid of the Mountains* still at Daly's? The rough red wine was potent, and Clara sat in her battered chair, young Jack Lewis's greatcoat around her shoulders, and thought: we might be on the moon, it's all so unreal.

"Anyway, I'll book you in at all the shows," she said, "I'll see you get seats. I'll chase everybody at every box office for you."

"Thanks." Young Jack Lewis smiled. It was a tired smile. "I'll look forward to that."

Suddenly she knew he did not feel he would ever see them, and her heart froze, for him, for Adam, for all the men out here, in this awful place. She glanced across at Harry and Adam, who were deep in conversation about the Alhambra. "I hope Marta can keep it going," Adam was saying. "Do you think you could go up and see her, give her some confidence? I don't know what she will do if I . . . if anything happens to me. . . ." Clara waited for Harry to protest that nothing would, but he did not. "She might close it, I could not blame her but—"

"We'll go up soon as we can, you can rely on it," said Harry gently. "Drink up, old mate, and don't worry your head about the Alhambra."

"No." Adam looked down into his wine. "I suppose it does seem rather petty, out here."

"Not petty," Harry answered. "Bloody stupid, more like."

A battalion runner came into the room after knocking respectfully, with a message for Captain Abbott. He seemed to be astonished to see Clara in such a place and hardly took his eyes off her except to salute Adam and say, "Colonel's compliments, sir, and can you come back to BHQ for briefing, sir? No need for Mr. Lewis to return, the colonel said, sir. Just briefing for company commanders only, sir." He looked at Clara, who covered up her ankles with young Jack Lewis's greatcoat. "I have a car outside, sir."

Adam stood up wearily, braced his shoulders. He put out his cigarette, pocketed his silver cigarette case. Plainly nobody smoked a pipe out here.

"Sorry to end the party. I must get back, you heard the message." He nodded to Lewis. "You stay here, old son. Come along later."

Young Jack Lewis nodded. He looked suddenly young again and very frightened and terrified of showing it, Clara thought. Her eyes went to Adam's, but he was pulling on his greatcoat (they take them everywhere, she thought, they must sleep in them), and his face was composed. He had to think of his men now, and that plainly made things easier for him. She kissed him, and he said, lightly, "No need for good-byes, I may well be back. Depends what it's all about."

Harry pulled on his ulster. "Any chance of coming with you? I mean, just to have a look round, up nearer things."

"Harry," Clara interrupted, "you've been up there—"

"It isn't the line," Adam said. "We're only two miles farther up. I daresay I could risk it. If the colonel says no, I'll send you straight back." Harry grinned at Clara, and she thought: you great fool, but her heart went out to him. She knew that the more he talked to men who had seen action, the better he could play to them. He would never be somebody who went onstage to make them forget. It was his strength and, as far as most bookers and managers and people who ran the business were concerned, his weakness.

When they had gone, young Jack Lewis said shyly, "Adam did awfully well in the last show. He's up for a Military Cross."

Oh, God, Clara thought, don't let him be too brave. Yet she

was proud. "Is that why he's been promoted so soon?"

"P-partly." Young Jack Lewis seemed to have almost lost his stutter in France. "We had a lot of—"

"Casualties?"

"People posted to other units."

"Casualties."

"We did lose a l-lot of people, yes."

"Oh, my God!"

"Don't tell Adam I s-said anything. I promised I wouldn't."

"It's all right. Harry and I have been out here once before. We have a good idea how things really are."

Young Jack Lewis puffed deeply on his gasper. He had plainly learned how to smoke. "Should all be over soon. The Yanks are making the difference."

Clara put her hand on his. "Oh, you poor boys. It's awful."

Young Jack Lewis blinked. "It's not what I expected. Not what they said at school. It's just like . . . a butcher's shop . . . and we're the m-meat, that's all."

"You'll come through, both of you, I know you will."

Young Jack Lewis shook his golden hair. It looked dull now, as if it hadn't been washed for weeks. "No. Adam might. N-not me."

Clara was shocked to tears. "Don't say that, please."

He looked at her. "All right, I won't say that."

"Did you lose my photograph?" she asked.

He fumbled in his tunic pocket. "There." The photograph was thumbed and creased. "I've shown it to rather a lot of people, but it's always been next to my heart. Most people I show it to think you're my girl, and I don't t-tell them otherwise." He put the photograph away. "Sent up my s-stock no end in the battalion, until they found out you are Adam's sister. S-sent his stock up then, probably why they made him captain."

"Is he a good captain?" Clara felt a great undertow of pity for the boy, and the power of it unnerved her. Better to get onto safer topics.

"Bravest officer in the battalion. Even the colonel says so."

"Oh, I don't like that."

"No." Young Jack Lewis blinked. "I'm j-just happy to get through these shows. Just so long as I don't let anybody d-down, myself or anybody else, you see?"

380

"Is it so bad?"

As soon as she said it, she knew she should not have. The tears came suddenly into his eyes, and he blurted out, "It's terrible, Clara. It's awful, and I know it'll go on till I die. People don't last out here, there's no chance of it—" He stopped. "What am I saying!" He fumbled a grubby khaki handkerchief from his trouser pocket and blew his nose. "You said you'd sing 'The Garden of Your Heart' for me, and you never did."

Clara said quickly, "I didn't see you in the audience, so I couldn't."

"Well, I'm an audience now."

"I hardly know the words."

Young Jack Lewis poured himself a large measure of the rough wine. "Just hum it then. Anything will do."

Clara sang very softly, her voice hardly carrying above the rumble of the guns:

> If I could plant a tiny seed of love
> In the garden of your heart. . . .
> Would it grow to be a great big bloom one day?
> Or would it die and simply fade away?

Somewhere out of the darkness a voice called, "Lovely," and one or two soldiers applauded.

Young Jack Lewis looked at her as if mesmerized.

Clara put her hand out and drew him toward her. He tried to pull away, but she held him firmly to her. He said, "I shouldn't, your husband—"

"Shush. Just stay there."

He sat with his head against her breasts for almost an hour, not talking, his eyes closed. At some time she could not be sure when, for all this was as unreal as the moonscape around them, she opened her dress and allowed him to kiss her breasts, and later she comforted him completely, feeling nothing at all except a deep pity. Then she closed her eyes and slept, and when she opened them, he was gone and it was day again.

Much later Harry Viner came back, looking very tired. "They're going into the line again. I gave them a bit of a giggle, told a few gags." He looked at her hopelessly. "I did all I could, Clara."

Clara nodded. "Yes. I know."

The telegram from the War Office came a week later. They were back in London, playing the Bedford, Camden Town. Clara was dry-eyed, but Harry cried, harsh, masculine tears. "They both went in the same attack, young Lewis as well. Christ, what a bleedin' horrible waste." Clara said nothing, and Harry asked, "Did you expect this?"

"Yes. Didn't you?"

"Yes. No. I suppose so." He sat down. "I don't think I can go on and be funny tonight, Clara."

"Yes, you can. We both can. No point in not, it won't bring them back, will it?"

Harry Viner looked at his wife, surprised. "We could beg off, get replacements?"

"No. Let's just forget about them, if we can, and play to the ones out there. They'll be going to France soon enough."

Harry nodded. "It'll cost me a pint of blood to do it, but if you insist."

She insisted. And they did it.

The War ended as suddenly as it had begun.

They were in London when it happened, and Harry stood at the window of their suite in the Cadogan Hotel and looked down at the crowded street and the sound of cheering. "The whole town's gone mad, but I don't feel like celebrating, do you?"

They worked, top-of-the-bill, through the first months of the Peace. Clara had a letter from John Hyatt, postmarked New York City. John was out of the army and back at work again, he wrote. His family was well. He was working on a stage musical with his partner, Jimmy Cowley, and they were doing well enough. Show biz had changed with the War; he had come back home to find himself out of fashion. It was all ragtime and jazz now—the new black music from the South, he expected they'd get it in Europe soon. Nobody wanted ballads just at the moment, except what remained of the vaudeville audiences. A lot of vaudeville houses were doing poor business; many were closing. Everybody was going wild about these silent movies. Nothing in them for a songwriter, not yet anyway. He could not see a lot of future in silent movies. Vaudeville had recovered from bad times before and no doubt would again. He hoped to see them both soon, one side of the

Atlantic or the other. He had left a loose-leaf letter for Clara to read to herself, and it simply said:

It was nice to see you in Richmond Park at the concert, even if only for a few hours. Best love, John.

She put the letter away, at the back of the press-clipping book. John Hyatt had sounded content, from his letter.

If he was, Clara thought, then that was as it should be. At least he was still alive. That, in the summer of 1919, was something.

Clara and Harry worked London during that summer. In September they went North to see Marta. She was brave, dressed in black; there were only two servants in the vast house and, to Clara's shock, a "For Sale" notice in the garden. "Is it really for sale?" she asked her sister-in-law.

"I can't keep a place this size for just one small girl and myself, can I? Besides, the rates and heating are terribly expensive. It will just have to go, Clara. I'll be lucky if I can find a War profiteer to buy it."

Clara looked around the drawing room, the room Papa had died in. It looked the same, only shabbier. Everything did, in the whole country. Nothing had been replaced for four years. Adam's portrait, in his uniform, was draped in black crepe. She shuddered and looked away. "I know," Marta said, "but it's there, it's like selling the house and probably selling the Alhambra, it's a fact of life, it has to be faced."

Both Clara and Harry were still.

Harry said, "He wouldn't have liked you to do that, sell the Alhambra, Marta."

Marta shook her head. "I have to do the best for his child and for myself. I have kept the Alhambra going with the aid of a manager. I think there's no real chance of my going on doing it. People are going to these picture houses nowadays. . . ."

"They'll never come to anything!" Harry interrupted.

"My information is they're full every night. One has just opened, opposite to the Alhambra. Now the War is over they're getting the American films. Charlie Chaplin, he's the comic our audiences are queueing to see, across the street."

"I know the films are getting a following," Harry protested.

"Some managers are running mixed bill, cine-variety—"

"We tried that," Marta said wearily. "Our regular vaudeville people stayed away, and the ones who like these things didn't come because we weren't showing a full bill of film."

"What they can see in it, I don't know," Harry said harshly. "It's just knockabout comedy; it's nothing they can't see on the stage, and they can't *hear* a blessed thing." He shook his head. "They're just following a fad; the War's over, and they want something different."

"The empty seats aren't a fad, Harry; they're a fact." Marta poured tea; she was the grand lady still, Clara thought, admiring her really. She supposed that part of the house and some of the contents were, morally, hers, but in law everything belonged to the widow.

Marta might have read her thoughts. "Before I sell, come and take what you like, Clara."

"If I took it," Clara asked, "where would I put it? Artistes don't have homes. They just float around, like gypsies." She went into Papa's library, nevertheless, and took his Japanese snuffbox. It was small enough to carry anywhere with her. She took Adam's small silver cigarette case. It was old and battered and was the one she had seen him use in France. Presumably it had been returned. She wondered if Marta would let her have it and then thought what the hell, she has the house and the Alhambra and what money there *is*, and she put it in her handbag along with Papa's snuffbox.

When she went back into the drawing room, Harry was sitting leaning forward urgently, talking to Marta, whose lips were pursed in disapproval. "Why not do a Christmas Panto?" Harry was asking. "A good panto will bring people back to the Alhambra. You could run it for six weeks and show a profit and be into the New Year in style. If you sell, all you'll have is one big fat check, but if you keep the Alhambra open, you'll have an income for years."

"Putting on a Christmas Panto would take money I do not have. I will not have any money at all until I sell this house. Adam left me very little, and most of it is gone, on the Alhambra."

"Supposing," Harry looked at Marta, but Clara knew he was talking to her, "supposing we found the money, Clara and me, to put on a big Christmas Armistice Show?" He stood up and walked over to Clara. "If it clicked, we'd work till March. What do you say?"

Clara felt chilled. "How much money would it take?"

Harry did not look at her. "About six hundred pounds, all told. Yes, I reckon we could do it on six hundred pounds."

Six hundred pounds was exactly the sum they had managed to save. Despite their great success, money still went out very fast.

Marta looked doubtful. "I don't know, Harry."

Harry said, to her, but to Clara as well, "Once it's been a success, I'll come into management with you, we'll do other things, we'll run a proper variety hall, I don't know, we'll have to see, but what can you lose, letting us try, we're not asking you to invest a penny, and you could be on a winner, Marta."

Clara said nothing. She waited. The six hundred was their insurance against bad times: broken dates, spells "out," illness, the state of the nation, the state of the business. It was their catchnet. No, she thought, we can't do it, Harry, we really can't, even for the Alhambra, even for Papa and Adam or for anybody, we can't please see that, my dear, dear love.

Marta turned to Clara. "You heard all that, Clara, what do you say?"

There was a silence in the room, save for Papa's old brass-faced grandmother clock ticking away, as it always had. Presumably that would go, too. It would all go. There was no reason why the Alhambra should go as well.

"I think Harry's right. Let us try."

Marta looked at her a long moment, then nodded. "As you wish. All I can say is good luck!"

The Alhambra was packed.

Outside, flyposters told the populace, "The Nite of Nites, at the Alhambra. Viner and Viner and a Host of Talent. Seats in all parts at Popular Prices."

Harry looked through the peephole. He turned to Clara. "It's full. It's packed. There isn't a seat in the house. It's all been worth it, love!" He embraced her. "Every bloody awful moment of it."

It had been bloody, he thought; booking acts was not the same as *being* an act. It took patience and a hard heart, and Harry did not have a hard heart. He paid too much, and he knew it, but he did not mind. Harry knew the artistes he wanted, and he had mostly got them.

They were to begin with a chorus of *Giggles and Girls.*

385

Standing in the wings, ready to go on, Harry said, "No. It's wrong."

"What is?"

"Dancing and flags and singing to open the show."

"Harry, it's what we rehearsed!"

"It doesn't have to change anything. I'll walk on and do a few minutes cold."

"To *open* the show? Harry—"

Harry beckoned to the stage manager. "Tell the musical director there's a new first act. Tell him no music."

"No music," asked the stage manager. "Are you sure?"

"No music," Harry said. "People don't believe in flags and flag-waving anymore, they've had a bellyful. . . . Get that message to the musical director, right?"

The stage manager nodded and went.

Harry pulled his uniform cap around his head, picked his tunic open, let his trousers down a hitch, undid a bootlace. Clara watched in silence as he broke a cigarette in half and stuck it droopingly in his mouth. "I need a beer bottle and my kit bag." She found them. "Tell the electrician, nothing on me but a single spot, nothing, you understand?"

"Yes," Clara said. I hope this is right, it has to be, she thought.

"No music." The stage manager was back. "The musical director is—"

"Never mind the musical director. One spot. On me. From the top. Curtain up, slow. Now!"

The stagehands looked at one another. The curtain went up, very, very slowly.

Harry Viner walked out onto the stage of the Alhambra Music Hall, where he had "died" all those years before, where Clara Abbott had rescued him with her call from the gallery.

He felt almost as terrified but not quite. Perhaps he was just older.

The spot held him as he weaved his way from the backdrop curtain up the empty stage, as if drunk, the cigarette unlit, the bottle of beer sticking out of his pocket, the rough khaki tunic unbuttoned. The house buzzed and then was silent. Harry stopped only when he reached the footlights. He waved at them blearily, staring at the silent black beast he could not see, that he loved and hated in turn, sometimes at the same time. He hoped there were a lot of ex-soldiers in the audience; there surely had to be.

He tried to light his cigarette and failed. Three times.

The audience did not laugh. It waited.

Harry slowly unbuttoned his uniform.

He leaned forward.

"I'm *Out,*" he whispered, a man who imparts a great secret, a never-to-be-expected wonder, a miracle.

Silence. Then a sudden gust of laughter.

The soldiers know what I mean, he thought. They're *Out,* too, and they know it's a miracle.

Harry could do no wrong after that.

He gave them his comic soldier, demobbed into a cold bleak Peace. "No jobs for soldier boys, they've got lassies working now, they tell me. Well, I've nothing against the women, you know," said Harry, "outside o' working hours."

More laughs.

He did his frankfurter sketch, substituting with a sausage. It brought the house down.

Finally, he took Clara's hand and said, "Thank you with all my heart, you good and generous people. I met my wife in this theater. I'm going to ask her to sing the song she has made famous."

Clara, to loud applause—for was she not one of the Great Beauties now, known to every man and woman in the street?—sang:

> A soldier came out of the army today,
> He winked at me in the street and did say,
> 'Are you going my way, miss?'
> He was ever so manly. . . .
> Naughty but Nice, Naughty but Nice,
> Never Been Kissed in the Same Place Twice!

Almost an hour late the curtain came down, and Harry and Clara went around into the main foyer in their stage clothes and shook hands with people as they left. They seemed older than the audiences Harry remembered in the past, but he supposed everybody was getting older. When the Alhambra was empty, he stood and watched the cleaning ladies at work. Then he went cheerfully backstage to the office.

"What a night!" he said.

Marta was sitting there, to his surprise. With her was a man in a dark overcoat and pince-nez. She introduced him. "This is Mr. Austin of Hammersly and Austin. He's my lawyer."

"Is he here," Harry asked, "to make my will or his?"

"He's here," Marta said, wearily, "because he has a definite offer for this theater. I'm refusing it. Anyway, for now. We have good bookings. We can soldier on. Papa and Adam would have wanted that."

Clara and Harry both kissed her. Mr. Austin of Hammersly and Austin looked disapproving. Harry said, "Marta, we'll stay as long as you need us."

An hour later they were in the street, elated, arms around each other. "Did I tell you," Clara asked, "that I love you and that you are the best comic in the world?"

"I like the second part," said Harry. "And you can sing a bit yourself, darlin'!"

They stood together in the dark street and looked at the large, shuttered Alhambra, quiet now everybody had gone home. From across the street came the noise of the picture palace, which played on late, illegally, so popular was it. The manager stood outside in evening jacket and dickey front. "I hear you're closing, Harry," he called. Harry recognized him as the former assistant manager at the Alhambra, Mr. Sykes. He said, "Oh, it's you?"

"Got to earn a crust, Harry," said Mr. Sykes, apologetic. "You did well tonight, I hear."

"Booked up for three weeks already," Harry said.

"It's this place," opined Mr. Sykes. "Packed every night, Harry. It'll blot vaudeville and music hall out. Blot 'em out."

"What!" Harry laughed. "Blot out Sandow, lifting a horse? Blot out Blondin walking Niagara? Blot out Leotard, the Daring Young Man on the Flying Trapeze—dead at twenty-eight, famous? Blot out Marie Lloyd, sitting amongst her cabbages and peas? Blot out Dan Leno? Blot out Bill Fields and Fanny Brice and Pat Rooney and Eve Tanguay? Blot out Sparrow, the fruit nut?"

"Who?" asked Mr. Sykes.

"Nothing," said Harry Viner, who was ever so slightly tipsy by now, as he considered he had every right to be. "Nothing will ever blot them out, Mr. Sykes; they'll stay in the memory, Mr. Sykes, for ever and ever, amen."

Clara took his arm, and they walked slowly along the dark

streets toward their digs. "The idea," said Clara, "what nonsense," hugging his arms, very tired and very, very happy.

Still laughing, they walked past the Alhambra and out of the street, the tinny piano music of the cheap picture palace fading behind them, into the small, anonymous night noises of the city.